EIGHTH HOUSE
Jason Blacker

Also by Jason Blacker

A Lady Marmalade Mystery
Beggar's Pardon
Sins of the Father
Gandhi's Sorrow
Phantoms of the Pharaoh
The Baron at Bishops Avenue
The Priest at Puddle's End
The Golf, Cheese and Chess Society
Politics and Poison at Princes Gardens
Lady Marmalade Cozy Murder Mysteries: Box Set (Books 1 - 3)
Four Red Diamonds (A Lady Marmalade Mystery 4 Pack)
Heartless
Loose Lips
Misery's Company
Poisoned Heart

An Anthony Carrick Mystery
Fourth Wall
Fifth Estate
Sixth Sense
Seventh Son
Eighth House
Brotherly Love
Anthony Carrick Hardboiled Murder Mysteries: Box Set (Books 1 - 3)

First Feature
Money Ain't Nothing
All In
Four Ways to Midnight
Second Fiddle
Third Base
Washed Up
Anthony Carrick Hardboiled Murder Mysteries: Box Set (Books 4 - 6)

Carbon Heart Silicon Soul
Jupiter: Book 1
Juno: Book 2
Juventas: Book 3
Bellona: Book 4
Mars: Book 5

Head Case Trilogy
Head Rush

TaXI Adventure
Ta.X.I. to Angola

Standalone
Can You Please Be Quiet
Dust on His Soul
Flowers For The Journey
Forever Famine
Livid Blue

My Son And I
Ruffled Feathers
Running Red River
When There Was One
Red Reign
The Enigma Evolution
Small Boy
Carbon Heart Silicon Soul: Books 1 - 3 (Jupiter, Juno, and Juventas)
Carbon Heart Silicon Soul: Books 4 - 5
Lady Marmalade Cozy Murder Mysteries: Box Set (Books 4 - 6)

Watch for more at JasonBlacker.com.

Table of Contents

For my wife and son, with love, always.

Birthday Week

October in The Big Orange can be just as hot as July. Sometimes hotter if you're enduring a heatwave. But not this October. This October was seasonal. That's what the weather man kept saying on TV. Expect a seasonal fall. A seasonal October in LA is mid to high seventies.

I don't know why the tourists don't come out in October. October is a nice month in LA. Sometimes the skies are clearer and the smog clears out and you can't taste it anymore. This was one of those Octobers.

The kind of October where the sky is softer. More fragile. Thinner. Hard to put your finger on it. But you know what I'm talking about if you've seen it. The blue is paler. More like a proper sky blue and not the deeper, darker cobalt it usually is.

This is what I was thinking about as I sat on M's deck in Hidden Hills looking out over other expensive houses at an ocean that was far away and bleeding into the sky. I had a coffee and my mind was on cigarettes. It had been a while since I'd had a smoke, and mornings like this still didn't seem complete without one. So I sipped on my creamy and sweet coffee while M was in the kitchen making brunch. She didn't want any help. Didn't need it either.

So here I was sitting on a deck in an expensive part of town feeling like I was sticking out like a sore thumb. It's quiet here out in Hidden Hills. Almost feels like you're not really part of The Big Orange. You're in a small alien cove observing LA. You're not part of it. Well, maybe you are, but you're part of the problem. This is hermetically sealed LA.

Less than a third of Angelenos are white. Out here it's almost ninety percent. But it's expensive to live in some parts of LA, Hidden Hills being one of them. There are a lot of guards to pay for, for one thing. And who does their own lawns now anyway? Not anyone up in these hills and dales.

It was my birthday last week. M had wanted to get me a Tesla like hers. I demurred. I get it's a great car. But I live in an apartment in Santa Monica and a Tesla would be stripped down to nothing but its nuts in the time it would take to have a nightcap.

I'm all for electric vehicles. The sooner we have them the better off we'll be. I read someplace that the smog in LA is robbing us of something like three years of life. Fossil fuels have helped build civilization. But just like a toddler learning to ride a bike you've gotta get off the training wheels. Oil is a training wheel. But electric vehicles aren't ubiquitous and they're not cheap enough for the average Joe. I like to think of myself as an average Joe.

None of the neighbors were out. The ambient noise was the dullest of hums. Almost sounded like the ocean far off. The thrum of waves crashing distantly against sandy shores. But it was just the cacophony of a baker's dozen million souls rubbing up against one another.

And that's what I like about my LA. I like being in the thick of it. Sure, Hidden Hills had seen a murder in its time. Back in ninety-five, when I was a newly minted murder detective I caught a case up in these hills. A studio executive had been murdered by his wife's lover. It had been a conspiracy between the wife and the lover.

Speaking of murder. JR hadn't sent me a case recently. It had been a couple of months and I know there'd been murders in LA over that time. LA has as many murders, roughly, as there are business days in the year. Two hundred and sixty days in a year without counting weekends. Almost the exact same as the number of homicides last year.

I could use a distraction like a murder. The money would help too. Twenty seventeen had been a great year for income. I made almost eighty grand that year. Last year I didn't even make fifty and this year will be more of the same. And here's the thing. I think M was looking to tie the knot soon. But I couldn't do it, not without a steadier income. Just wouldn't be right to her.

And yeah I get it. She owns a third of Stratham Surgical Services which makes her, on paper, a billionaire. She doesn't give a fallen leaf for what I make. Doesn't need to. But a man's got his pride.

I thought I caught a whiff of bacon, but I knew that couldn't be coming from inside M's house. She doesn't eat bacon. Doesn't eat animals at all. Out of respect I don't when I'm with her either. She'd probably found some fancy new fake bacon. I'd come to enjoy the fake meats she'd found. They'd gotten better, she'd said, in the past ten years especially. I took the last sip of my coffee and put it down on the table.

The sun was starting to peek around the corner of the house. It was creeping up on me on the deck. Soon it'd be hot and we'd have to put the umbrella up for shade. I looked out across the bald heads of the houses. Their pates the wide gamut of shit browns and blacks. Smog lay across the valley like a gray-brown specter. I wondered who was getting murdered in this city today.

Morbid, yeah, but that's why I do this. If we can catch these assholes and put them behind bars then maybe they'll be less inclined to commit atrocious acts in the future.

Sometimes I can get why someone murders someone else. Most times though, I don't. It's usually over the smallest thing. A guy gets jealous over a girl. A son argues with his father. Stupid shit like that. But like I said, murder is a business and I'm not talking about organized crime. I'm just talking your regular murders. It's a business I'd sooner see go bankrupt. But so long as we live amongst assholes, assholery is gonna happen.

I heard the sliding door open behind me. I turned to look at M. She came over to me and bent down and kissed me. I smiled at her.

"Brunch is only a few minutes more," she said, picking up my empty cup. "Would you like more coffee?"

"Please, M," I said. "You're a doll. You need a hand?"

She smiled at me and touched my nose.

"No, I just want you and I to have a lazy, cozy day. Besides it's your birthday," she said.

"It was my birthday," I said, "on Wednesday. Now it's Sunday the thirteenth. Long past my birthday."

"It's still your birthday week."

And with that she turned and walked back into the house before I could offer any redress.

It hadn't been a good year for art sales. Not out east at The Bauhaus and not here at the Triangle Gallery. You'd think a fella that was showing on both coasts would be doing alright by his art. You'd be wrong. I was on the farm team. The bench of the farm team. I might have my art up at these fancy galleries but that didn't mean folks were there looking for an Anthony Carrick original.

But time was a river that wound through many vistas and lands. Things can change if you hold on. More than that, the arts have to be a passion. Few will earn enough to make a living from it, so you might as well enjoy it.

Dish for Gods

I got up off my lazy ass and walked back into the house when M started bringing the food out. I helped her with cutlery and condiments. We sat down to feast. And a feast it was. There was bacon, sausages, scrambled tofu, toast and slices of fresh tomato. All the meat was fake but tasty. I put margarine on my toast, bacon on the margarine and scrambled tofu on the bacon. Topped it off with a little steak sauce and my day was starting off on the right footing.

We tucked in without speaking for the first few minutes. I was on my third coffee. My bladder was in troubled waters.

"This is just terrific, M," I said through a mouthful of food.

"Glad you like it. You've got to keep your strength up," she said, smiling at me.

We dug in more and kept busy with our thoughts. A neighbor drove by and we waved courteously at her. M knew a lot of her neighbors. Hidden Hills likes to think of itself as a city. I don't. But this "city" had around five hundred families living within its borders. A lot of them are celebrities and sports stars.

"I think it's going to be a hot one today," I said, nodding south towards the ocean.

"Just heard the weather report while I was cooking. It's going to be a nice week weather-wise," she said. "Warm and with clear skies."

I nodded.

"Don't forget," said Emily, "we're heading over to Mom and Dad's for dinner tonight."

I hadn't forgotten. They lived literally next door and her brother on the other side. M's house was in the middle.

"Sounds good," I said.

We finished our food in silence and then I turned my chair slightly to look out towards the ocean.

"You're awfully quiet," said M, looking intently at me. "Penny for your thoughts."

I smiled at her.

"Yeah, sorry. I was just deep in thought when we started eating. Went down a bit of a rabbit hole."

"About what?"

I shrugged.

"A bunch of things. Our country being run by a narcissistic lunatic for one thing. Race relations in this county as another thing. You'd think that in the twenty-first century we'd have figured it out by now. How to get along, that is."

M nodded and listened, watching.

"Then I got to thinking about the last few years. Twenty seventeen I almost made six figures. Not all of it from my art, but a good half of it to two-thirds. Never made six figures in my life. Wouldn't mind knowing what that feels like."

I grinned at her. She smiled politely.

"Last year I didn't even make fifty grand. This year more of the same. Probably a little less unless I have a couple of quick sales before the end of the year and a consult or two with the boys in blue."

"More than that," said M. "I think you could use a case, am I wrong?"

I shook my head.

"No, you're not wrong. It's complicated. I'd sooner see the murder business bankrupt, and yet I'm pulled in with the puzzle of it."

"That's because you're good at it," she said. "And you have this thirst for justice. It's one of the things I love about you."

"It is a little macabre though. Always fishing out in the murky waters of humanity. Picking through the garbage and detritus of human lives wasted. It's pointless and futile. Like a hamster on the wheel. You just keep spinning round and round not getting anywhere. And nothing changes."

"But the lives you touch are changed. The murders you help solve give some solace and comfort to the victim's loved ones. It's important work, Anthony. Can you imagine the alternative?"

"And what's that?" I asked.

"Nobody caring. Murderers getting away with it. We'd have anarchy in the streets," said M, inflecting her voice for the last bit to sound like a news announcer.

I nodded absentmindedly. We went back to sitting in silence. M got up and started to take the plates in. I helped her. We came back outside with fresh coffee for her and more of the same for me. She brought my mug out on account that I took a detour to help out my drowning bladder. The sun was lapping at our feet on the deck. The bit of it was warm through my socks.

"What time is dinner at Han and V's?" I asked.

Han was M's father's name. It was a nickname he used which he liked. After Han Solo, I suppose, though the nickname was short for Hanford. I called M's mother V. That was short for Vail.

"Six thirty, the usual," said Emily, looking out into the distance.

We didn't speak for a few minutes more.

"When do you see Lloyd again?" asked Emily.

I looked over at her.

"This week. Tomorrow actually, now that I think about it. Not sure how much longer I'll need him. Why do you ask?"

Emily leaned in towards me and put her arms on the table. She smiled and looked down for a moment, gathering her thoughts to speak. I could see we were going to have a conversation.

"I think you should make use of his help," she said. "He's good, isn't he?"

I nodded. I wasn't about to steer this jalopy.

"I like him just fine."

"Just fine?"

"I like him a lot. He's a good guy. What's this really about, M?"

She looked into her coffee mug. I'd heard that reading tea leaves is easier than reading coffee grounds. She looked back up at me.

"You had a bad dream last night," she said. "You woke me up with a start. You yelled out 'So-yi'."

I nodded somberly. So-yi's death still bugged me. It was the main reason for seeing Dr. Lloyd Ainley.

"Do you remember what it was about?"

I shook my head. I didn't actually, which was a nice change. Usually those nightmares woke me up each time they visited. But it had been some months since I'd remembered a dream with her in it.

"It was probably the same dream I have all the time. The one that wakes me up," I said.

"About her death?" asked Emily, tentatively.

I nodded.

"Will you ever tell me what happened back then, out in New York?" she asked.

I had given her the summary. That So-yi had been murdered while trying to help me on a case. That she was a fine detective with the NYPD, but M got no further details.

"No," I said.

M looked up at me and frowned.

"Look," I said. "I've seen some horrible, fucked up shit in my life, that was the worst. Maybe because it involved me personally. But you don't want to know, M. Nothing good will come from knowing. I still suffer these nightmares..."

"It's PTSD, Anthony, it's very serious, but it's treatable. That's why I'm asking about Dr. Ainley."

"I'm seeing him tomorrow," I said.

"I know that, but I don't think you should be thinking about leaving his care right now. Did you take your medicine?"

Sometimes M called cannabis my "medicine". I shook my head.

"No, I didn't bring it out here with me last night," I said.

"I'll get some and keep it here for you. It helps, right?"

I nodded.

"I sleep like a baby with it," I said. "I'm sorry I startled you with my dream talk."

"That doesn't bother me, Anthony. I'm just worried about you, that's all. I've seen what PTSD can do to people, soldiers mostly. I don't want anything to happen to you like that."

"It won't."

"You say that like it's a fact, but how can you be sure? How can I be sure when you won't talk to me about it?"

"You have to trust me, M. I have you, I have Aibhilin. I'm not about to feed myself a lead pebble."

M stared at me for a while.

"What happened to those men that murdered So-yi?" she asked.

"They got what they deserved. Justice was meted out," I said. "You know that."

"They were also found murdered, Anthony. What kind of justice is that?"

"The best kind," I said, grinning at her.

"Don't make light of that, Anthony. Were you involved?"

"Listen, M, I love that you're worried about me. But I'm not going to talk about what happened out in The Big Apple. I'm okay with how justice was delivered. That's all I'm going to say about it."

M nodded and leaned back in her chair.

"What kind of oil do you take for helping you sleep?" she asked after a while.

"High THC oil. They say the indica strain is best, but I seem to be able to sleep just fine on any kind of high THC oil."

"I'll get some," said M, not really acting like she was talking to me. She folded her arms across her chest and sat back in her chair. We sat in silence for a while.

"I'm going to have to check on Pirate this afternoon. Top him up with food and give him fresh water."

All I got was a nod. We sat and drank our coffees.

"You know you can talk to me about anything," said M at long last.

I nodded.

"I know."

"I've seen death, Anthony. Up close in all its grotesqueness."

I nodded again.

"I am the coroner of this city."

More nodding. I was beginning to feel like a bobblehead being taken for a ride in the back of M's car.

"All I'm saying is that you can tell me what happened in New York. I won't judge you and I won't blab to the cops."

I looked over at her.

"You know what happened in New York. I solved a couple of cases, one of which happened to be So-yi's case, the detective who was helping me. She was murdered by some bad hombres and those bad hombres were murdered in return. I mean what do you expect when you live by the sword?" I said. "You die by the sword."

In the corner of my eye, as I sipped my coffee and gazed towards a hazy ocean, I could see M ruminate on her big finale.

"Did you do it, Anthony?"

"Do what?" I asked, acting dumb.

"Kill those bad hombres, as you like to put it."

"Listen, M. I don't know why this is so important. There were a lot of people involved. I know what happened and I'm okay with the outcome. But what that case showed me is that there are a lot more moving parts out there controlled by a conspiracy of dunces."

"Don't you mean A Confederacy of Dunces?"

"No, that's a novel. Maybe dunces is the wrong word, these people are quite smart. All I'm saying is that there are some really powerful people plotting and planning to rule us all, it would seem, and so I wouldn't worry about the death of a couple of dirtbags."

M didn't say anything.

"They were carved as a dish fit for the gods," I said, grinning at her, trying to bring her around.

She looked up at me with an arched eyebrow.

"A dish fit for the gods. What a bizarre way to put it," she said.

"Let's kill him boldly, but not wrathfully. Let's carve him as a dish fit for the gods. Not hew him as a carcass fit for hounds. And let our hearts, as subtle masters do, stir up their servants to an act of rage, and after seem to chide 'em."

That made M frown.

"It's Shakespeare," I said, "from Julius Caesar."

"Random is what that is," said M.

"It's a play about murder, jealousy and revenge," I said. "Not random at all to what we've been talking about."

I grinned at her, picked up my coffee cup, walked around to her side of the table and kissed her on the forehead.

"Want more coffee?" I asked.

She shook her head. I went inside to put my mug away and to visit the latrine. Coffee was using my bladder as a punching bag.

Dead Wood

I got back to my place a little after one. Pirate was happy to see me. He was right at the door almost tripping me up as I walked into my apartment. I closed the door behind me and squatted down and petted him for a while. Then I went into the kitchen with him following me like a chaperone. The cat had eaten about half his dry food. I picked it up and put it on the counter.

I opened up a fresh can of wet food and that got him meowing in agreement. I put a dollop in a fresh bowl and put it down for him. He went at it like a hungry lion. I left his dry food on the counter. Dry after wet was a vomit if you made me bet. Pirate had fooled me just one too many times with that trick. Playing it up like he was a starving waif of a cat that needed double feedings. Those big sad-looking eyes. Well, one of them at least. He's missing the other one. Nope, too many times I'd given him a little dry after wet. Not happening anymore.

I took a look into the fridge for something for myself. I found a couple of beers so I grabbed one and popped off its cap. I didn't bother pouring it into a glass. I took it into the living room and plopped on the couch. I turned on the boob tube and surfed channels until I got bored and left it on some baseball.

With that and with a half-drunk beer on the coffee table I promptly zonked out. I dreamed of So-yi getting murdered again. You know how it went down. I was tied up and beaten while those two assholes had their way with her before murdering her. I was trying to help when one of them started zapping me with what looked like a cattle prod. Only they never had cattle prods.

But they kept doing it. They pushed the prod at me for a while as it buzzed and then took it away. It was very rhythmical. Buzz and a poke then pulling it away. Buzz and a poke and then pulling it away.

I woke up to find my phone vibrating in my pocket. I fished it out and looked at the number. It was Captain John Roberts. I answered it.

"If you're gonna keep a guy on the line so long you should get yourself a music service so I have something to listen to other than ringing on the other side," said Roberts.

"Or, maybe I was deciding if I wanted to speak to you. See how long you'd let it ring before giving up," I said.

"Or, maybe the old man was napping on the couch."

"You got eyes in my apartment?" I asked.

"I've got eyes into your very soul, Sid."

I laughed.

"Got good news for me?"

"If by a murder we'd like you to consult on then, yeah, Christmas came early this year."

"Tell me more," I said, my interest peaking.

"We've got a dead woman up near the Calabasas Landfill."

"Ok," I said. "I'll meet you there."

"It's a bit awkward to get to," said Roberts. "There's a small valley of burnt up trees north of the landfill just at the south edge of the Cheeseboro and Palo Comado Canyon. Best bet is to take Lost Hills Road all the way until it takes a sharp right at the north side of the landfill. About three hundred feet a service road scissors back heading west, that's where we are. You know what, I'll just mark it on Google Maps and send you the location."

"Anything else you want to tell me about this dead woman?" I asked.

"Not at the moment," said Roberts. "She's young, maybe mid-twenties and attractive."

"Ok, I'm on my way. Send that location."

"Will do."

We hung up and I put my phone back in my pocket. I noticed half my beer hadn't been drunk. I finished that up thinking about a dead woman lying in a valley of dead, burnt trees.

Why was she put out there, I wondered. By the way Roberts described it, it looked like it was pretty out of the way. My first thoughts were thinking that maybe the killer, or whoever dropped the body off, and that might not have been the killer, had wanted to ditch her at the landfill.

But that's not a good idea. A landfill is a terrible place to try and lose a body. There's too much man and machinery around. Even if you could place a body in a landfill without being noticed, the machinery and the men working the landfill would soon uncover it. Landfills require a lot of maintenance.

Maybe he'd figured it out as soon as he got to the landfill and therefore had to come up with a plan B on the move. And nine times out of ten, it was going to be a guy who did something like this. I was pretty sure about that.

I grabbed Pirate's bowl from the counter and put it back down for him to nosh on. I took care of his business and scratched him behind the ears for a couple of minutes before I left.

By the time I got into my car and started towards the valley of dead dolls it was a little before two. I decided to take the PCH up to Malibu Canyon Road which becomes Los Virgenes. I left the virgins for Lost Hills Road which took me into the landfill.

PCH was not the quickest, but it was sure the prettiest and I wanted a view that would put me in a good frame of mind. My earlier conversation with M was still on my mind.

The traffic was steady going. It was a Sunday afternoon after all. Took me around forty-five minutes to make it up there. On Las Virgenes I wasn't sure if it was an omen or just coincidental, but it got me thinking about the young dead woman in a crop of dead trees.

The coroner would tell us if she was a virgin or if she'd recently had sex. I was betting that she wasn't a virgin. A dead woman dropped off like this, out of sight, most likely murdered, was probably not a virgin. Eight times out of ten, maybe more, maybe less, a murdered woman was also the victim of a sexual assault.

As I drove up the dirt road towards the distant police cars and coroner's van I thought about what I had before even having gotten to the scene.

I had an attractive young dead woman. Most likely murdered, and if she was murdered there was a good chance she had been the victim of a sexual assault as well. Other than that, the rest of the pieces would come in time.

I pulled up at the back of the line of vehicles and got out. It was a warm day and the sky was unburdened with clouds.

Jane Doe

The coroner was not going to be Emily. I knew that for a fact, and it wasn't because I saw who the coroner was on the scene. It was because I had just left M at her home in Hidden Hills. Today was her day off.

I made my way towards the police tape where a young officer stood sentry. I hadn't seen him before.

"Anthony Carrick," I said. "Captain Roberts invited me up."

I was expecting him to lift the yellow tape and let me through. But he wanted a little more conversation.

"Yes, sir. Can I see some ID?" he asked.

He had taken his small notebook out, looked at it and nodded. That meant my name must have been in there but he wanted to verify me. I couldn't blame him. I fished my driver's license out of my wallet and showed it to him. He nodded and I put it back.

"Thank you, Mr. Carrick. Would you like an escort?"

"No," I said, and I dipped under the yellow tape as he held it up for me.

I walked the remainder of the way down the dirt path, slowly. I was looking for evidence. Whoever dropped her off must have driven here somehow. Maybe a car, a truck, a van. Could be pretty much anything.

At the start of the path there were multiple tire tracks and shoe imprints all over the place. Halfway down the path they started to thin out so that by the time I got towards the end the shoe prints were few and there only appeared to be one set of tire tracks. They were widish. That probably meant we were dealing with a full-sized sedan, a truck or a van. Might not help us very much.

I noticed the Beast and Sonny before I saw JR. The Beast is Detective Gregory Beeves and Sonny was Detective James Forrest. Both were homicide detectives and both were around five eight, five nine. They were also both black. That was about all they had in common. Well that, and working together.

Sonny was slender where Beast was stocky. Sonny was, well, sunny in disposition whereas Beast was more sober. But they made a hell of a team.

"Well, if it ain't Sonny and Cher," I said, grinning at the two of them.

"AC," said Beast as we shook hands. Same with Sonny.

"We got this," said Sonny.

"Not according to JR you don't," I said, grinning.

Sonny laughed out loud. Roberts was further up in the thicket of trees, leaning down with the coroner. The coroner I could now tell was Dr. Jabez Deerstalker. The only Native American coroner in the coroner's office, and one of Emily's best. If there was one thing to nitpick with Jabez, it was that he lacked a sense of humor.

"JR's in deep conversation with Jabez," I said, nodding towards the copse of trees where they were located. I could see portions of a cloth over a body.

"Yeah, it's Sunday. Took Jabez and his boys a little longer to get here. They only arrived a little before you. Maybe five minutes ago," said Sonny.

"What have we got?" I asked.

"A dead female in her mid-twenties," said Beast.

"A murdered female you mean?" I asked.

Beast shrugged.

"Hard to tell at this stage. Probably. Go have a look for yourself. No obvious signs of trauma."

I nodded. That was interesting. Homicide always investigated suspicious deaths even if they turned out to be natural. But most times detectives have a leg up from the start. Most times, it's pretty obvious if a person was murdered or not, just from looking at the body.

"What are your first thoughts?" I asked, thinking I was likely not going to get much out of them.

"Dead female in her mid-twenties," repeated Sonny.

I nodded.

"Thank you, detectives Laurel and Hardy," I said.

Sonny laughed.

"Seriously, Anthony. There's not much to go on right off the bat. Go have a look. Like Greg said, there's not much there yet. Best we have is some tire tracks. Looks like the person who dropped her off wiped away their footprints."

I nodded some more.

"I'm going to call it a murder," I said. "We've got a dead body dropped off in a pretty isolated place. Driven here somehow and we think the person who dropped her off cleaned up their shoe prints. That sounds sketchy to me. We've probably at least got an accomplice to the murder if not the murderer himself."

"Two thoughts," said Beast. "We don't know she was murdered yet and we don't know if the driver who brought her here was male."

"You're fun at funerals," I said, and turned away from them and headed up towards the good doctor and Captain Roberts.

I stepped on a twig and it cracked under foot. Roberts craned his neck to look around. He saw me and stood up. Deerstalker did the same.

"Come here often?" asked Roberts, grinning at me.

"Only when I'm dropping off the trash, which it looks like our perp mistook a young woman for," I said.

I nodded at Deerstalker, he nodded back. We didn't shake hands. I was not gloved up and he and Roberts were.

"Your two comedians down the hill didn't have much to offer," I said, jerking my thumb behind me. Roberts followed my thumb and nodded.

"You know how the Beast is. He takes this seriously. Doesn't speak out of turn."

I nodded. I looked behind the two of them at the shrouded body.

"Can I take a look?" I asked, thrusting my chin towards the body.

"Yeah, come have a look," said Roberts.

He and Deerstalker took a couple steps back towards the body. Roberts fished into his trouser pockets and pulled out a pair of latex gloves. He handed them to me and I put them on.

"You take the sheet by the feet and I'll take it by the head. We'll pull it off of her nice and easy," said Roberts.

We leaned down and did that, carefully laying the cloth next to her with the side that was touching her now facing towards the sky.

"Was she moved or was this how she was found?" I asked.

"Nobody's moved her as best we can tell," said Roberts.

I was looking at a brunette who was lying supine. Her eyes were closed and her hands had been interlocked and placed over her stomach. Her legs were straight. She wore a merlot colored satin dress that didn't look like evening wear as much as lingerie, though it came down to just below her knees. Her ankles were crossed and her hair had been placed on her left and over her shoulder. Her head was placed on a pillow or ladder of sticks.

I scanned over her body. Her arms were bare and her lower legs including her feet. The only thing she wore was the dress which had two thin straps over her shoulders. She wore no jewelry on her hands or face. No earrings, though both ears were pierced. She was dolled up as if she had been out for the evening.

She didn't look like a prostitute. She appeared well fed and healthy. If she was a walker of the night she was likely a discreet and highly paid one.

Cops and Trees

I stood back up and looked around. Then I turned around and looked back at Deerstalker.

"Any marks on the body that would indicate how she died?"

"No obvious signs of trauma so I can't determine cause of death. I can tell you when she died, approximately. Somewhere between two and four in the morning. I can narrow that down once we've done the autopsy."

I nodded at him. I looked over at Roberts.

"Any scars, tattoos, birthmarks? I didn't see any."

She looked like a doll in many ways. Her skin was unblemished, except for the signs of death. Other than that she showed no moles, birthmarks or anything of that nature that stood out.

"Nothing that would help identify her," said Roberts. "We haven't moved her and we're disinclined to take off her dress here. Jabez will let Cardigan know when she's on the slab. He'll take those pictures and those notes before the autopsy. Sometime this afternoon."

Deerstalker nodded.

"I'd like to be there to see for myself," I said.

"I'll call you before I autopsy her," said Deerstalker.

I nodded and looked at Roberts.

"Where is Cardigan?" I asked.

"He went off somewhere in that direction," said Roberts.

"Looking for truffles, I imagine."

I looked in the direction that Roberts was pointing which was straight ahead of him but I didn't see Cardigan.

"Can we take the body, John?" asked Deerstalker.

Roberts nodded. Deerstalker looked behind me at his men who had been slowly inching their way up towards us since I had arrived.

"Let's you and me give them some room to work," said Roberts.

We took a few steps back from where we were.

"I should probably make sure we have enough booties for you," said Roberts, though he wasn't wearing any himself.

Beeves and Forrest joined us. They weren't wearing crime scene booties either.

"Sonny told me any footprints or shoe impressions had been wiped away," I said.

"Looks like it," said Roberts. "Still, CoD is up my ass about proper crime scene preservation. We're gonna have to start wearing gloves and boots at all crime scenes when we're called out, regardless of evidentiary state."

"Lucky to be you," I said.

"I'm just spreading that luck around."

CoD was the Chief of Detectives. Otherwise known as Roberts' boot to the neck. But that was being unkind to Luca Abt who was the current CoD. He was a good cop. A guy I'd trust to do the right thing, but he was a stickler for process and procedure.

I didn't care about crime scene booties one way or the other. I wasn't so sure it was for evidentiary preservation as much as it was to prevent the many clods traipsing around crime scenes and thus bringing evidentiary chain of custody under question. For that reason alone it was probably a good idea.

We watched the coroner's lads put Jane Doe in a body bag and zip her up. They were careful. Everything went into that bag with her. They were wearing booties and gloves and the sheet that had been covering her went in with her.

They picked her up and carried her down the slight slope towards more leveled ground where their gurney was waiting. They put her on the gurney and rolled that towards the back of the van where she was slid in. They closed the doors behind her.

I looked around at the crime scene. There was nothing of note that had been left behind other than the pillow of twigs. Beeves motioned to one of the Field Investigation Unit guys to come over.

"Grab those twigs over there. Her head was lying on them," he said.

FIU did so. That was about the only other bit of evidence I could see that had been left after she had been taken.

We all walked back up to the spot and took a closer look. Nothing was there except the faint impressions of her body on the sandy soil. Lots of footprints of course, but those were ours.

"Odd place to put her," I said. "You'd think he would have carried her deeper into this copse of trees. Would have taken a little longer to find her."

"Maybe they got spooked. Maybe she was too heavy," offered Beeves.

"I'm not sure about that," I said. "She died between two and four. I'm probably going to say closer to two. You've got to allow for time to get out here from wherever she was."

"If she was in the Mulholland area, that's not too far away," said Roberts.

"Mulholland is close. Hell, she could have been driven out from Hollywood Hills in less than forty minutes at four in the morning," offered Forrest.

"Malibu's less than thirty minutes away," said Beeves.

Roberts nodded.

"But you look at the way she was dressed. She's an attractive woman, well put together. Probably not a street hooker. I'm thinking she likely came from a nicer part of town."

"I agree," I said.

"That's what we're saying, Captain," said Beeves. "There are a lot of nice areas within about forty-five minutes of here."

We nodded at each other. Feeling like we were getting somewhere when we were in fact standing still.

"Like I was saying," I said. "Why place her here? One hundred yards, hell, even fifty yards further into this copse and she'd become much harder to see. Especially if you covered her up with twigs and sand and some of these dead leaves."

"Probably got spooked, like I was saying," said Beeves, again.

I grinned at him.

"Or he's a weakling and can't pick up a one hundred pound woman. Like you were also saying," I said.

"I'd probably put her at one ten to one twenty," said Beeves, splitting hairs with me.

"Ok, kids," said Roberts. "Let's not get into a pissing contest."

"I'm just not sure he got spooked or he's a weakling. The tire tracks came to within, what, fifteen or twenty yards of where she was found?" I asked.

"Something like that, FIU could tell for sure," said Roberts.

"Right, so he got his vehicle pretty close to the drop off area, and we're probably talking sometime between four and five-thirty," I said.

"Why those hours?" asked Forrest.

"They're quiet and it's before this place opens," I said.

"Except it's Sunday. The landfill isn't open today," said Forrest.

I nodded.

"Right, forgot about that. Still, you'd probably want to move the body under cover of darkness. And seeing as how it's closed today, how would he have gotten spooked?"

"Could have been a mountain lion or something that scared him off," said Beeves.

"Could be," agreed Roberts. "What are you getting at, Sid?"

"That body was immaculate. She looked almost like a doll. No hair out of place. Her makeup still on as if she was just about to go out. The guy took care to remove all jewelry, and I'm assuming we have no ID or no way of identifying her at the moment..."

Roberts nodded.

"Maybe her death was accidental, but there sure was a lot of care put into disposing of the body. Why make it so hard to identify her if you leave her so close to this path here?" I said, pointing at the dirt road where all our cars were.

"You raise some interesting questions, AC," said Forrest, "but I'd like answers to the more fundamental questions, like who is she and what time was her death? Also, how did she die?"

I nodded.

"Yeah, but those are the easy questions. We'll have those questions answered by the end of the day. Maybe two days at the most. But this scene here, this is what intrigues me. She's a beautiful woman who was almost dropped off at a dump like garbage. Yet he must have had second thoughts. He placed her nicely down here, stripped away most identifying factors of himself and her, and laid her head to rest on carefully placed twigs. Looks like remorse to me."

"Well, a landfill is a busy place," said Roberts. "Not on a day like today, but come tomorrow and she would have been found quite quickly."

"Yeah, and here we are. We've found her already and it's not yet tomorrow. Speaking of which, who found her?"

"Security when he was doing his rounds," said Beeves.

I nodded.

"So we have security, and yet the guy still brings her in here. Was he seen?"

Roberts shook his head.

"No, he got in someplace where there aren't any cameras and the security guard said he didn't see anyone enter or exit," said Roberts.

"And even though this isn't open on Sundays still looks like a bunch of people are here working," I said.

"You probably met the security guy when you first arrived," said Roberts.

I shook my head.

"The security arm was up and I just drove on through. Maybe he was on his rounds again."

I noticed Mike Cardigan out of the corner of my eye. He was wearing crime scene coveralls, booties and gloves as well as a white paper face mask that was around his chin and not around his face. He walked towards us.

"CoD is gonna love you guys," he said, grinning at the four of us.

"Only if he finds out," said Robert. "You wouldn't snitch on your brothers, would you?"

Cardigan was still grinning.

"Nah, you know me, Captain, I just like to have fun with it."

"Did you find anything interesting?" I asked, changing the subject.

"I did, I found some wonderfully yummy chanterelles up there," said Cardigan, pointing behind him. "Not too far, incidentally, from some wonderfully formed death caps."

"Are you talking about mushrooms?" asked Roberts.

"Why yes, Captain, yes I am," said a grinning Cardigan.

"Not that I want to speak for Sid here, but I think he was asking about the crime scene," said Roberts.

"Ah, yes, the crime scene. No, I didn't find anything related to the crime scene. Took some shots of the tire tracks, the area around here. But as is plainly obvious to anyone with eyes, this is probably not where she was murdered, or where she died. I guess we have yet to determine cause of death. Whoever brought her here took precautions."

"You're feeling your oats this afternoon," I said.

"Been here a couple of hours already and it's supposed to be my day off."

"Welcome to the LAPD, where you too can work twenty-four seven," I said.

That got a chuckle from Cardigan.

"What time did the call come in?" I asked.

"Twelve thirty-two this afternoon," said Beeves, not looking at his notebook.

"From the security guy?" I asked.

Beeves nodded.

"Said he likes to take a walk up towards these hills here on his lunch break," said Beeves, pointing to the hill just above us which had not been burned recently. "Apparently saw her just as he was starting out on his lunch break."

"Well, I think that about wraps it up here," said Roberts. "Beeves and Forrest see if you can't get a copy of any footage from say last night through to this afternoon around noon. I saw a camera up by the guard station when you drive in."

Beeves and Forrest nodded.

"You'll get a call from the coroner before he autopsies, Sid, and I'm going back home to my wife and kids," said Roberts.

"I want to speak with the guy who found her," I said. "And the foreman if he's here."

"Follow me down and I'll introduce you to the security guy on my way out," said Roberts.

I nodded.

"See you two at the coroner's later," I said.

Forrest and Beeves nodded at me and walked off towards their cars. Roberts and I followed them. I got into my car and followed Roberts out.

Out and About

There's really only one way into and out of Calabasas Landfill and that's up through Lost Hills Road. On the east side of Lost Hills Road, where it turns west is the security box with the barrier arm that was up when I drove through it. As we got down there, it was still up. I started to wonder if that was a permanent feature of the landfill. Not that it would prevent the unauthorized from getting in. You could always go around on the left side in the exit lane to get in. More than that, on the right was a big parking lot and facility building that you could just drive around. Security was not of high importance here, clearly.

The guard was in his box. This place was quiet. There was some heavy machinery up on the top of the landfill, moving soil and trash around. The security guard was speaking with someone in a car. He was explaining to them that the landfill wasn't open. The car drove around his box and left.

Roberts and I walked up to the box. It was large enough that the three of us could fit inside without being elbows to ribs. Roberts asked him if we could enter. He said yeah.

"I'm Captain Roberts of homicide. This is my associate Anthony Carrick," he said.

Roberts showed him his badge. The security guy nodded.

"I was talking to a couple of your guys earlier," he said, grinning at us.

"Detectives Beeves and Forrest, probably," said Roberts.

"Yeah, that's them. I'm Arshile Gorky," he said, shaking our hands vigorously like he was trying to get coins to shake loose from our pockets. "Friends call me Ash."

"For obvious reasons," I said.

"Well, yeah, I suppose so," he replied, his enthusiasm for us deflating a little.

"I understand you called it in. The dead body," said Roberts.

"Yessir. Horrible thing to have happened to such a beautiful young woman."

I looked around the small space. There was a computer and monitor at his desk. Half the computer monitor was taken up with two video feeds from two cameras. The one camera was pointed towards those arriving at the landfill, the other was pointed to those coming from the landfill. The other half of the computer screen was a game of solitaire that Arshile was playing.

There was an ashtray with six dead cigarettes in it, all unfiltered. Next to that was a pack of bubblegum-flavored bubblegum. Arshile was standing up, he was around average height. A little taller than me, a little shorter than Roberts. Cinched tight by a belt was a stomach that had eaten about fifty pounds more BBQ than he needed to have eaten over the years. On the belt was a canister of pepper spray and a collapsible baton. There was also a pair of handcuffs.

Arshile had black curly hair that was salted with gray. Same with his stubble, and across his upper lip he wore a seventies porn star's mustache that looked like it had been put on too loosely.

"When did you put in that call?" asked Roberts.

Arshile looked up at the corner of his security box. I followed his gaze. A spider was busy working on a web in that corner. Arshile didn't seem to notice.

"Must have been around twelve or twelve thirty," he said.

"Is that a usual time for heading out on your rounds?" asked Roberts.

"Well, not specifically. They want us doing rounds about every ninety minutes. I was supposed to come off shift at noon but Brad, he's supposed to relieve me, called in sick. So I'm doing some extra time."

"What is your shift supposed to be?" I asked.

"I work a two week rotation. Friday, Saturday, Sunday in the first week from midnight to noon. Thursday, Friday, Saturday, Sunday for the second week from midnight to noon."

"And this week?" I asked.

"This is the first week of the two week rotation. The short week," he said.

"You like your job?" I asked.

He tossed his head from side to side like he was quickly trying to get water out of his ears.

"It's a living," he said.

"How long have you been doing it?"

"Ten years. Been with Calabasas for three."

"What do they pay you?" I asked.

"Shit," he said, grinning. "I'm at the top of the scale. Fifteen bucks an hour."

I nodded.

"Not a king's ransom," I said, commiserating with him.

"Not a pauper's ransom neither," he said. "What do you guys make?"

I looked at Roberts.

"What are they paying freshmen now? About thirty bucks an hour to start?"

Roberts nodded.

"Rookies, I think you mean," he said.

I grinned at him then turned back towards Arshile.

"You thinking of applying?" I asked.

He tried to get more water out of his ears.

"I'd like to, but I'm not gonna lie. I had a couple of juvie beefs that might hold me up."

"Like what?" asked Roberts.

"Grand theft, GTA. But like I said that was a long time ago."

Roberts nodded.

"Yeah, that'll prevent you from getting on."

"I figured. But I've changed my ways. I really like being on the right side of the law now."

"So, at around twelve or twelve thirty you found out that you were doing extra hours and so you decided to do your rounds at that time," said Roberts.

"Well, not exactly."

"What do you mean?"

"My supervisor had called and left a message on this phone here," he said, pointing to a landline on the corner of his desk. "But that was at around eleven this morning. I try to do my last rounds by around eleven so whoever's here at noon to relieve me can take a half hour or so to do their paperwork and get ready for their shift before they've gotta go out on their first rounds."

"But management would probably prefer that they go out after they've been here for ninety minutes, right?" I asked.

"Well, actually they prefer to see the timesheet filled in every ninety minutes regardless of when you got on shift."

"You were doing Brad a solid then," said Roberts.

"We try to help each other out."

"You were out doing rounds at eleven but you didn't see anything then. Correct?" asked Roberts.

Arshile nodded his head. He reached out just to the side of me and picked up a clipboard hanging by the side of the door. He looked at it and then turned it towards us.

"These are the times I went out on my rounds," he said.

Roberts took the clipboard and we looked at it. There were several sheets of paper on it. The top one was dated Sunday the thirteenth of October. There were just three columns vertical and perhaps twenty or more rows horizontally. The first column was narrow and was named "Time" at the top. The second column was named "Initials" and it too was narrow. The only initials on this page in this column was "AG". The last column was the widest and it was named "Notes". Most of the rows in that column had "N/A".

The second from last "Notes" row had Arshile's scribble that I deciphered as, "Dead female body northwest edge of landfill." The time he had started on his rounds for that row was at twelve nineteen. He had last been out on his rounds at two forty-seven this afternoon. Before that, they were within about a fifteen minute window of a two hour time frame from the last time he left for his rounds.

I noticed that but I figured it was because the ninety minute window probably started when he got back from his previous round not from when he started that round. But I asked anyway.

"Every time you head out seems to be around two hours or so from the previous time you went out on your rounds."

Arshile nodded.

"Yeah, but it'll take me around a half hour or so to do the checks on each of the rounds. The ninety minutes starts when I get back."

Roberts was still looking at the clipboard.

"I see you went out at around twelve when you found the dead woman. Before that you went out at just before ten thirty, then around eight fifteen and just after six. That's three other outings when the sun was up and you saw nothing until the last round when you went out at twelve nineteen."

"Well, to be honest with you, Captain," said Arshile, "it's still pretty dark at six, six fifteen in the mornings. But you're right about the eight and ten check, it's light then, but I'll be honest with you, I didn't get up into the northwest corner of the landfill until my twelve o'clock check."

"Why's that?" asked Roberts.

"We only have to do a thorough check of the landfill once a shift. It usually takes an hour to an hour and a half. Most of the rounds we do are closer. We're checking the buildings and the equipment pretty much. That's all in this lower half of the landfill where we are."

"So why did you only do your big check at noon?" asked Roberts.

"Well, like you said, I like to do the complete check of the landfill during daylight and I'll be honest with you, I was dragging this morning."

"Except you were supposed to get off at noon, so you said. Which means you wouldn't have done your complete check if Brad hadn't called in sick."

Arshile nodded. His mouth was upturned slightly.

"You're right, I almost fucked up. Like I said, I was dragging this past shift. Just felt down a quart."

Roberts nodded slowly. I decided to change tack a bit.

"Those cameras work, I see. Do you save the video?"

"Yeah, the cameras work, but it's only the two of them. They're automatically deleted after forty-eight hours."

"That's not a long time," said Roberts.

"Well, Captain, nothing much happens around here usually. In my three years working here, this is the first time we've had a homicide."

"How do you know it's a homicide?" asked Roberts.

That question unsteadied Arshile for a moment.

"Well, I don't. But why else is homicide out here?"

"Homicide attends all suspicious deaths. Some turn out to be accidental. A good chunk are suicides," I said.

Arshile nodded.

"I'd bet it was a murder," said Arshile.

"How's that?" asked Roberts.

Arshile shrugged.

"You saw her. A beautiful woman like that, dressed fancy in a sexy way, placed out here at the dump. Why would anyone do that if it wasn't suspicious?" he asked.

"Did you see any trauma to the body?" asked Roberts.

"I don't understand, Captain," said Arshile.

"Any violence. Did you see any signs of violence on the body?" asked Roberts.

"Well, no. But I've seen plenty of murder mysteries on TV. There's lots of ways to kill a body. Maybe poison. Maybe suffocation."

"I wouldn't trust the accuracy of murders you see on television," I said.

"Did you know the woman?" asked Roberts.

Arshile shook his head.

"Take another look," said Roberts, fishing his phone out of his pocket and finding a picture of Jane Doe and showing it to Arshile.

Arshile looked at it for a time, all the while shaking his head, slowly.

"No, I've never seen her. Do I look like a guy who would get to hang out with a woman like that?"

"I try not to make assumptions that way," said Roberts.

"It's kinda sounding like you're treating me like a suspect," said Arshile.

"It's just routine," said Roberts. "You're the last person that saw her, so we just want to rule you out."

"Maybe I need a lawyer," said Arshile.

"You have been watching too much television," I said. "We're just asking questions. You'll want a lawyer if we charge you with something, which we haven't yet, right?"

Arshile nodded.

"Anything else you forgot to put in your statement?" asked Roberts.

Arshile thought for a while and then slowly shook his head.

"No, I think it's all in there."

"If you think of anything else, let us know," said Roberts, giving Arshile one of his cards.

Arshile took it and raised it towards the ceiling.

"I sure will, Captain."

"I'd like to get a copy of that video from both cameras," said Roberts. "Can you do that for me?"

"I sure can, but I don't have any USB sticks."

"I've got one in my car."

Roberts left.

"It was Detective Carrick, right?" Arshile asked me.

I shook my head.

"No, just plain old Mr. Carrick. Anthony's fine. I consult with the LAPD on some of their murder investigations."

"I bet you've seen some shit, then," said Arshile.

I nodded.

"You must have seen some weird shit here, no?" I asked.

Arshile shrugged.

"Not really. The smell's not great when you get closer to the fresh stuff. I mean it's a dump. There's not much here worth rifling through or stealing. Most people only come here if they need to unload their junk. Worst I've seen is a homeless guy who decided to pitch his tent not far from where that woman's body was. Had to get him hauled out of here a few times with your guys' help. That's about it."

"When was that?"

"Ah, probably over a year ago now. Spring or summer of last year I want to say."

I nodded, and Roberts came back into the small office. He handed Arshile a small USB stick. Arshile looked at it.

"This is only sixteen gigabytes," he said.

"Yes, it is," said Roberts.

"How much video do you want on it?" Arshile asked.

"From midnight until noon," said Roberts.

Arshile sat down at his desk and looked at the USB stick he was holding in both his hands.

"That's twelve hours. You'd probably need at least two of these."

"How many hours can I fit on that?" asked Roberts.

"Four, maybe five hours."

Roberts looked at me.

"Shit," he said, and then he walked back out.

"What's that about?" Arshile asked.

"He's probably getting another stick. We figure Jane Doe was probably murdered between two and four. That means we probably want the video from at least two this morning."

Arshile nodded.

"Is that arm bar usually up?" I asked, pointing at the bar just behind us and outside his door.

Arshile nodded.

"Yeah, though usually I'll keep it down from midnight to six. But as you can see, it's easy to bypass it if you're really interested in getting into the dump. But why would you?"

Roberts walked back in with another USB stick which he handed to Arshile.

"See how much you can put on these two starting from two this morning," said Roberts.

Arshile nodded. He plugged in the first stick and started tapping away at his computer.

"It'll probably take several minutes," he said.

Roberts nodded. He jerked his head in the direction of the door.

"We'll just be outside. Holler when it's done," said Roberts.

And with that, we both walked outside and stood by our cars. We were out of earshot from Arshile.

1984

"What do you think of him?" Roberts asked me, leaning against the car.

"Got an unusual name. Russian, maybe?"

I had my hands thrust into my trouser pockets.

"Hard to say at this time. We don't know much about him. I knew of an Arshile Gorky, the painter, who was Armenian American. Hanged himself at the age of forty-four back in the mid-forties I think. Good painter. I'd own some of his stuff if I could afford it."

Roberts shrugged.

"You know the most arcane things sometimes."

I shrugged.

"That's from art history back when I was at art college. Most of the other pearls of wisdom I throw before you, you swine, I get from reading books. You should try it sometime," I said, grinning.

Roberts laughed out loud.

"Did you guys run him yet?" I asked.

Roberts nodded.

"Nothing more than he told us about. That theft beef and that GTA. Both when he was seventeen. Nothing else."

"That's a long time ago. I put him, what, probably in his mid-thirties?"

Roberts nodded.

"Almost twenty years ago and nothing since. If you're asking if I think he's good for this, far from it. Only the biggest idiot would shit where he works."

Roberts nodded and looked around.

"Still, there's something about him that just rubs me the wrong way."

"It'll come to light if it's important," I said. "By the way, what did his statement say?"

"Nothing unusual, but he's not eloquent or loquacious."

I laughed.

"Fancy way of saying he kept it brief."

Roberts grinned.

"These are some of the things I've picked up from you over the years. But, yeah, his statement was short and just kept to the facts."

"Which is usually what we like," I said.

Roberts nodded and folded his arms over his chest.

"You're right. But it was unemotional, nothing that we didn't know from looking at the scene. His statement described how he was doing his rounds when her red dress..."

"More like wine, burgundy or deep purple," I said.

"I think you called it merlot," said Roberts, grinning at me. "In any event, this is what he said. He called it a 'red' dress. He went to investigate and then describes what he found. Jane Doe, dead on her back lying on a nest of twigs..."

"Only her head was on twigs, and more like a pillow than a nest," I said.

"I'm telling you what was in his statement."

I nodded.

"He said she was lying on a nest of twigs and she was lying stomach up."

"Stomach up?" I asked.

Roberts nodded.

"That's what I mean, a little weird. Unemotional, and he describes her instead of lying supine, or face up, as stomach up."

I shrugged.

"Some people have a different vocabulary," I offered.

"Sure. Then he ends with saying he called the police but that he didn't touch the body. But for a guy who just found a dead body, he doesn't seem all that fazed. Most Joe Public always comes across a little wobbly after seeing a dead body, especially if it's their first."

"True, but so far there aren't any signs of violence. She looked really good for being dead. Maybe that's why."

Roberts nodded his head, bouncing it from side to side.

"Captain," came Arshile's voice from the security office. He was standing in the doorway holding the USB sticks towards us.

We walked over to him.

"Finished?" asked Roberts.

"Yes, sir. Seems like we got it all on there on these two sticks. Two a.m. to noon today. I guess they're not as high quality as I figured they were."

"What do you mean by that?" I asked.

"Well, I figured somewhere around four to five gigabytes per hour if it was 1080p. Seeing as how it got pretty much all of it on here, the quality's probably only 720p."

"And what does that mean?" asked Roberts.

"Means it'll look good on the monitor but if your guy's captured on it, you're not going to get great results blowing it up, it'll get pixelated, or blurry."

Roberts nodded.

"720p you said," I said.

Arshile nodded.

"Must be," he said.

"But on those windows on your monitor it says 1080p," I said.

Roberts looked at me. Then he walked back into the security office forcing Arshile backwards.

"Yeah, you're right, it must downsample when I saved it to these sticks."

I pointed to the description overlaid on the current live video feed we saw on Arshile's monitor. In the upper right corner in white writing bordered in black on both video feeds was some details. The first line had the date and time. The second line had the camera name. "Camera 1" and "Camera 2". The third line had the video quality. "1080p x 30fps" it said.

"Like my partner said, it suggests this is at 1080p and 30fps. I'm assuming that last bit is frames per second," said Roberts.

Arshile nodded. He sat back down at his desk and looked at the live feed.

"That's right. I don't know what to tell you, Captain, I saved it at standard quality which should have captured it just as it is. I'm just assuming that it downsampled, I don't know for sure."

"Ok, just redo it so that I can see for my own edification," said Roberts.

"I don't understand," said Arshile.

"I want to watch you do it again to satisfy my own curiosity," said Roberts.

"Yes, sir," said Arshile.

Roberts handed him the two sticks back. Arshile took them and put one on his desk by the side of his keyboard. He put the other USB stick into his computer tower which was on his desk against the far wall not far from his monitor.

We watched him open up the software application which was called "V.I.S.O.R.". V.I.S.O.R., I saw as the application opened, stood for "Video Identifying Security Operator's Recordings".

This time we watched Arshile manually adjust the settings to save the video to the stick.

"You see, Captain, standard quality is 1080p at 30 frames per second," said Arshile, showing us on the application's window. When he chose "Standard Quality" the application showed "Quality: 1080p" and "Frame Rate: 30fps".

"Just do it manually," said Roberts, pointing at the application window.

Arshile nodded. He chose manual from the drop down menu. And from the "Quality" dropdown menu he chose "1080p". He could choose from "1080p", "720p" or "480p". From the "Frame Rate" drop down he chose "30fps". He had a choice between that and "15fps" or "7.5fps". Then he chose the date and time stamps for the video he wanted to save. He chose the destination which was Roberts' USB stick and he saved it.

About three or so minutes later, it requested another USB stick. Arshile took out the first one and put in the second one. About another two minutes later he was done. He handed both sticks to Roberts.

"Was that both cameras?" I asked.

Arshile shook his head.

"No, you have to do one at a time. I can do the rear facing camera but I'll need another couple sticks."

Roberts grumbled something then left the security office again. He came back in not too long after he had left. He was carrying another two USB sticks which he handed to Arshile.

"Do the same with these but for the rear facing camera."

Arshile nodded and got to work.

"How many of those do you keep in your car?" I asked him.

"Half a dozen. I got them on sale. Now I'll have to get more. I've only got two left."

"Yeah, but how often do you need to use one of these?"

"Welcome to nineteen eighty-four, Sid," said Roberts. "This is homicide and everybody seems to have a security camera now. It's extremely helpful. I have all my guys keeping USB sticks in their grab bags. At least weekly we're using them."

"We live in a surveillance state. Is that what you're saying?" I asked.

"Look around you, Sid. Cameras are everywhere. If it isn't a fixed video camera it's the smartphone in your pocket. And a lot of companies are friendly with LEOs. My favorite is Ding Dong."

"Ding Dong?"

"Yeah, they make doorbells and other home security accessories that record live or on a motion sensor. Ding Dong's biggest selling feature to the customer is that they'll store the video feed for free the first year. After that the cost is small apparently. But what it means is that I can just write them a request, give them a case number and they'll release any video they have. The customer none the wiser."

Roberts was grinning at me.

"Seriously?"

Roberts nodded.

"Ain't life grand," he said.

"And how often do you make these sorts of requests?" I asked.

"If a murder's in a neighborhood and not in a business park or something, then every time. You'll be surprised how often we'll get something from them."

"Interesting. Helpful to LEO, but man, that rubs me the wrong way. I see that conflicting with the first and fourth amendments at the very least."

Roberts shrugged.

"Hasn't been tested yet in higher courts," he said.

"Still, you're just writing a Dear John letter and getting all this surveillance footage?"

"Yup."

"I'd probably get a warrant if it was me," I said.

"Yeah, but most times we don't know what we need or what we've got on any of that footage until we get it."

"I think you're playing with fire, JR," I said.

"Uh, I'm finished," said Arshile.

He handed Roberts the other two USB sticks. Looked like he wanted to say something. His mouth opened partly, but then he thought better of it.

"You Armenian?" I asked.

"No, sir. I was born here in LA. My parents are Ukrainian. My mother loved the painter, Arshile Gorky, and when she married my father and took his last name I was given the painter's first name because my father already had the last name. Not the best name for a kid as you figured out. We're not related to the painter if you're wondering."

I nodded at him. Then I looked over at Roberts.

Roberts nodded and looked at me.

"Let's see what Trees and Forest have for us," said Roberts.

We left Arshile to his little cage.

Y2K Decay

"Trees and Forest?" I asked.

"Beeves and Forrest," said Roberts. "It's like rhyming Cockney slang. Like if we were talking about Aibhilin I might ask you how's your bricks and mortar."

"Bricks and mortar, that's Aibhilin?" I asked.

Roberts shook his head.

"No, it's rhyming slang. Bricks and mortar refers to daughter. See how it rhymes."

I nodded.

"So we've just come back from talking to Arshile about the brown bread."

I frowned.

"Brown bread, dead. We were just talking to him about Jane Doe, our dead woman."

"Ok, I think I'm getting it."

"And we were just up in the northwest corner of the landfill with a butcher's hook," said Roberts, grinning at me.

"I don't get that," I said, shaking my head.

"Butcher's hook, taking a look."

I nodded.

"This copper I was talking to at a convention recently was from The Met, otherwise known as Scotland Yard..."

"I know what The Met is," I said.

"Right, and he started sharing all of this with me. Telling me how police work is mostly all about plates of meat."

I frowned and shook my head.

"Plates of meat, feet. Police work is a lot of walking around on your feet."

I nodded.

"Well, this ain't Cockney and I prefer chewing through my shoe leather over plates of meat."

"Cockney isn't a place specifically though it generally refers to London now," said Roberts.

"Great, can we generally refer to the English language from here on out?" I asked, grinning at him.

We walked across the road towards the main building which is where we assumed Beeves and Forrest would be. Inside we encountered a long counter and behind that were some desks and chairs and beyond that a couple of offices.

A young woman got up from behind one of those desks and walked over to us. Roberts showed her his badge.

"I'm looking for my two detectives," he said. "Are they here?"

"They're in the back," she said, pointing to our left with her right hand. "I'll buzz you in."

We walked to the end of the counter and heard the door unlock. Roberts opened it and we walked on in. This part was a large warehouse. I wanted to say that it looked about half the size of a football field. There was a lot of space.

At the far end were Beeves and Forrest talking with a guy in a visibility vest and a hardhat. There were several small pieces of equipment down at that end and a couple of other guys working around them. There was a small bobcat not being used, a guy in a forklift driving it around and moving pallets of things around.

On our side of the warehouse were several appliances in reasonable shape considering we were at the dump. There were also a couple of large boxes filled with miscellaneous items, mostly in good shape. I saw kids' toys, teddy bears and things like that. Amongst all of this were some couches and chairs in reasonable shape.

We walked on down towards Beeves and Forrest. The guy they were talking with was stocky, of average height, and had a five o'clock shadow. His hair under the hardhat was brown. He was also wearing safety glasses. We got there just as Beeves and Forrest were wrapping up their conversation with him.

"Thank you, Steve," said Beeves.

Steve walked away from them as we approached. To our right a large rollup warehouse door was open, letting in the warm breeze from outside. Hanging from the tall ceilings were large fans that revolved about once every second. I couldn't feel the air they were supposedly circulating.

"Captain, and Mr. Cool," said Forrest.

"Found out anything helpful, Sonny?" asked Roberts.

"Not much," said Forrest, looking at his notes. "That was Steve Snyder we were talking to. He's the foreman here and he got in around eight this morning but he didn't see anything. He's been working in here all day. First he heard about Jane Doe was when Arshile came and informed him."

"When was that?"

"He said around twelve thirty, one o'clock. He asked Arshile if he'd called the police and Arshile said yes. It must have been shortly after we were called. So probably closer to one."

"And did he go out to take a look?"

Forrest shook his head.

"Nope. Said he's been in here all day. He said he knew better than to go walking around a crime scene. Said he learned that from TV," said Forrest, grinning. "But he told Arshile to go and wait close by Jane Doe until we got here. So that's helpful."

"Who arrived on scene first?" I asked.

"Matt Stone," said Beeves.

"I didn't see him around," I said.

"He's on patrol. His sergeant got here shortly after him and took over."

"Who's his sergeant?"

"Pedro Noyce," said Beeves. "When we got here we relieved him by which time FIU was on scene too."

I nodded.

"Stone's an eager beaver," I said. "I think he'll make a good detective someday."

"Needs to put in his time first," said Roberts.

"He's got three years on, or thereabouts. I was in homicide in my third year on the job," I said.

"Yeah, but you're a special snowflake, Sid. They haven't done that since," said Roberts. "Now you need five years patrol minimum."

"They weren't that picky back then," said Beast, grinning at me.

"And they say you have no sense of humor," I replied.

"You're not old enough to remember how it was back in the day when The Clash was on patrol."

"I've heard about that," said Beast. "Johnny Rotten and Sid Vicious, those were your nicknames given by a couple of punks. But riddle me this, Johnny Rotten and Sid Vicious aka John Lydon and John Ritchie were actually with the Sex Pistols. So how do you get The Clash out of that?"

"Well, Joker, which band's name do you think fits a couple of beat cops better. The Sex Pistols or The Clash. We were known to clash with the bad hombres back in the day and I guess that's how the guys saw us."

"Riddle me this was the Riddler's line, not Joker's," said Beeves.

"I know that too. Unlike my thumb sucking colleague," I said. "I'm old enough to remember watching Batman reruns on the TV where you had to get up to change the channel."

"My hat's off to you, gramps," said Beast, grinning.

"Ok, kids. What else did Steve give you?" asked Roberts.

"Not much," said Sonny, looking at his notes. "Like I said, he waited here. Another reason he gave was that he didn't want to get involved in it."

"In what?" asked Roberts.

"Didn't want the hassle of having to be called to court as a witness," said Sonny.

"Smart man," I said.

"What about the other guys?" asked Roberts.

"He said we can talk to them but he doubts anybody else saw anything. When Arshile came and told him about Jane Doe, he told Arshile not to mention it to anyone else."

"That sounds sinister," said Roberts.

"No, Captain, I don't think it was. He said he's got a skeleton crew today and he needed all hands on deck. Couldn't afford to have his guys out there being lookie-loos."

"Speak to all of them anyway," said Roberts.

"Will do," said Sonny.

"Anything else? Did you show him a picture of her?" asked Roberts.

"No and yes. We showed him a picture. He didn't recognize the body and he didn't have any other insight to offer."

"Actually," said Beeves, "he did say that he'd only ever once known of a body being discarded here at the landfill since he's been here."

"And how long is that?" asked Roberts.

"Said he got hired on here the year the dump opened which was ninety-one."

"Twenty-eight years he's been working here," said Roberts.

"Got hired right after high school he said," added Sonny.

"That puts him around mid to late forties. Our age," I said. "Seems about right."

Roberts nodded.

"What case was that?" asked Roberts.

"It was something similar as he recalled. Didn't remember the name of the deceased, but said a female was found half-naked but she was dumped close to where this body was found. Said it was New Year's Day in two thousand. He was working then and he was the one who found the body."

"Anything else?" asked Roberts.

"No, Captain. That was pretty much it."

Roberts nodded his head slowly for a while. Then he put his hand in his pocket and fished out the four USB sticks and handed them to Beeves.

"Talk to everyone else who was here today, then I want you to review these sticks. We got Arshile to load both cameras onto them and they should have all the footage from two a.m. last night up until noon today. Pay special attention to the first few hours and see if we can't find a van or car or something that looks like it doesn't belong."

"Got it, Captain, what are you gonna do?"

"I'm going back home to spend the rest of my Sunday afternoon with my wife and kids."

"Ah, the privilege of rank," said Sonny.

"And you, Mr. Cool?" asked Sonny.

"I'm going home to spend the rest of my Sunday with Mr. Walker and Mrs. Ryder."

Sonny frowned.

"Booze and baseball," said Roberts.

"Ah, right. Johnny Walker and Rebecca Ryder, the sports announcer," said Sonny.

"One other thing," said Roberts, looking at Beeves and Forrest. "See what you can find out about that homicide from Y2K."

Beeves and Forrest nodded.

And with that, Roberts and I turned around and started to walk out of the building.

"I remember a Jane Doe from New Year's Day in two thousand, it wasn't our case as I recall and we weren't asked to help on it. I remember it going cold. Ring a bell for you?" I asked.

"Vaguely," said Roberts. "I knew it couldn't have been ours, we cleared all our homicides when we were working together back in the day."

"Two thirty-one for two thirty-one, partner," I said.

Identity Crisis

I went home and put on my painting apron. It looked like a Jackson Pollock only it wasn't worth near a fraction of one of his paintings. I was working on a current piece. I had titled it "America: The Grave". It was an abstract piece exploring the dire situation that I thought America found itself in currently. Not grave as in a place to bury dead people but grave as in a serious predicament.

The political situation and the social situation we found ourselves in was top of my mind for my country I loved. From where I was standing, we had a racist buffoon in office who was only agitating other racists and frightened people to become their lesser selves.

At this stage it was only a rough sketch, I was barely into the first fifth of the painting. Just as I was getting into my groove after about a half hour of painting my phone rang. I put down my palette and brush and picked up the phone. I knew who it was because I'd received calls from this number often enough that I'd labeled it "Coroner". Usually that "Coroner" was M, but today it had to be Deerstalker.

"Carrick," I said.

"Anthony, it's Dr. Deerstalker. I'm ready to start the autopsy in about a half hour if you want to take a look at the body. There is a scar that you might be interested in seeing. No other identifying marks on the body."

"Thanks, Jabez, I'll be right there."

I took off my apron and placed it over a wooden chair I kept near the easel for this purpose. I went into the kitchen and added more dry food to Pirate's bowl. He didn't move from his perch on a tall cat tree in the kitchen that looked out onto the street. There was a tall tree just outside the window that often held choir practice for a large number of birds. Occasionally we'd even get blessed with a songbird now and then. I'd seen the song sparrow, Bewick's wren, goldfinches, the oak titmouse and northern mockingbirds.

We didn't get them often, but I'd seen them now and then. Probably helps that I live on the third floor in apartment 333, which, incidentally, made no sense. There were maybe ten to twelve apartments on the third floor, nowhere near thirty-three of them. But that was the Vista Al Mar for you. You've met my neighbor, Martha Muniz. Sweet old woman who'll keep an eye on Aibhilin now and then. Well, her apartment is 312.

Most apartments and houses I've seen have odd and even numbers on opposite sides of the road or hallway. But that's the charm of Vista Al Mar apartments. Looked like a blind kid on too much sugar was sent running down the hallway with a bunch of numbers and randomly put them on doors.

Even the name of this place, Vista Al Mar is quaint. Most of you know that it's Spanish for sea view. No apartment in this place has a sea view. I don't even know if any of the apartments here had a sea view when the place was first built back in twenty-eight. It's in the Art Deco style, which is an abbreviation of the original French, "arts décoratifs", which as you can imagine is decorative arts.

The building has recently been painted a salmon color. If that salmon was conflicted about its identity and couldn't tell if pink was for boys or girls. Art Deco is a pastiche of different influences. Vista Al Mar has the predominant blocky influence of Cubism mixed in with a bit of Fauvism as I have been told that the original paint was even pinker than we have now. On top of that there's almost a hint of the gothic around the windows and the main entrance where the break with straight and angular lines comes undone. It's a building with an identity crisis and I guess that's why it appealed to me.

Not that I have an identity crisis. This building just seems like a mutt. With the same happy-go-lucky temperament, but if you look too closely you see bits and pieces that just don't seem right on an Art Deco building.

But I wasn't here from that obsequious architecture rag "Architectural Angst" which was all about poking fun at these old Art Deco buildings. At least it seemed like they picked on Art Deco primarily. And Vista Al Mar had made it into the magazine some years ago when it was in even worse shape with paint peeling and the homeless urinating on its keystones.

I grabbed my hat and left the apartment. I got into my LeSabre which was now coming on twenty years old. What's nice about brown as a color for a car is that you hardly notice the rust. I took the I-10 east which had me overshoot the Los Angeles County Department of Medical Examiners and double back on Daly Street for just a couple of minutes. I was there in under twenty-five minutes.

I showed my driver's license at the front desk and after a brief phone call I was let in. Security asked if I knew where I was going and I gave him an affirmative. I'd spent many a day and some nights here with M helping her out on a case.

The ME's office has over two hundred employees. I don't know how many of them are medical examiners. Probably not enough according to M. There are bodies on backlog because they're understaffed.

But that wasn't what was on top of mind as I made my way to the autopsy room where Deerstalker was going to be conducting an autopsy. What was top of mind was trying to figure out what this scar was all about. And what caused it. Was it a sport accident or just a childhood mark of memory?

Scars are like that. They're like carved blazes on the trail of life. I have a handful of scars all over my body. I remember the event that caused each one. There's this scar across my big knuckle of the middle finger on my right hand. I got that one from punching my father in the mouth while he was on one of his benders and berating my mother and me until I couldn't take it anymore when he started slapping my mother around.

It was the first time I'd knocked anyone out. My father used to be a semi-pro fighter. But he was a brawler, he didn't have soft hands but he could take a punch. And that's how he fought, he'd sometimes win by taking more punishment than his opponent. Needless to say, he wasn't ever good enough to make a living out of it.

If I was feeling charitable I might say that my father was a raging alcoholic because he probably had CTE, which is chronic traumatic encephalopathy. I didn't figure that out myself. M suggested it based on what she's learned about my father. And yeah, that might have been much of his problem. But he was also just an asshole. Plain and simple.

Then there's this scar across the left eyebrow. Hard to see, but that I got from a fight in the ring when I was thinking about turning pro and fighting guys heavier than me to improve. Fight was stopped and I lost on account I was bleeding like a broken sewer.

There are others here and there. The most recent is probably the scar in my lower belly I got up in New York when I was shot. That one I only think about when it hurts. Thankfully it doesn't hurt often. But what happened in New York. That whole situation I think about often.

As I walked down the hallway I thought about what Deerstalker said. He said there's a scar I should take a look at but not many other distinguishing marks. That's unusual. Boys are criss crossed with scars if they've had any sort of long leash during childhood. Even girls though. Not that I've done an official study of it but I had to figure most girls would have a few distinguishing marks even if they weren't scars. Many have tattoos now.

Body Ablaze

I entered the main autopsy room. There were two bodies in here. Another coroner, Dr. Jack Wagner was just finishing up in one corner of the room and putting the body away in the cooler. He came up to us as I was walking up to the table with Jane Doe on it.

"This yours, Anthony?" asked Wagner.

"Yeah, it's unusual. No distinguishing marks on the body other than what Jabez was going to show me."

Wagner looked over the body. Only her face was uncovered by a white cloth that was draped over the rest of her body.

"I see what you mean. The face is unblemished. I can't see even a freckle or a mole," said Wagner. "What happened?"

Deerstalker remained mute.

"She was dumped at the dump. Calabasas landfill. Dressed in what looked like a negligee. No jewelry and no identification," I said. "Don't know the cause of death yet either."

I looked at Jabez, he gave me a slight shake of the head.

"No violence seems to have been committed upon the body," I said.

Wagner nodded.

"You ready?" asked Deerstalker.

I nodded.

"Like Jack was saying, this is an exceptionally unmarked body. Hardly any freckles and no moles."

"How old would you put her at?" I asked as Deerstalker started to pull the cloth off her body, showing exceptionally perky breasts that were clearly enhanced.

"I'd put her in her early to mid-twenties," said Deerstalker.

Her body was smooth and although the color was an off-white, the color of death, it was as unblemished as Deerstalker had said. I could see no marks on her upper body. Her areola and nipple were smooth, small and pink. She almost looked as if she had been sculpted from marble.

"I've never seen a woman so unblemished," I said.

"Neither have I," said Wagner. "The physique is remarkably unblemished."

"It is very unusual in my experience as well," said Deerstalker.

Jane Doe was untanned.

"An advertisement for the benefits of sunscreen," I said.

Wagner smiled. Deerstalker had pulled the cloth down over her ankles. She was as naked as a penitent's soul. Except for her head where you'd expect her hair and her eyebrows, she was otherwise hairless. And she was otherwise unblemished except for a small scar that Deerstalker did not have to point out. It was to the right and slightly lower than her left hip bone and closer to the inguinal ligament than her midline. Most underwear would probably have covered it.

It was raised and looked glossy if not waxy. Hard to tell if it was recent or some years old on account that the body was waxen and mostly white. I almost put my finger out to touch it, but then realized that this was a dead body and I should be a little more respectful.

The scar was about an inch and a half to two inches long and made up of three Chinese characters. At least they looked Chinese to me. The scar was made up of these characters each about the size of my thumbnail. I got out my phone and took several pictures.

"I don't suppose either of you have any idea what this means?" I asked.

Deerstalker shook his head. Wagner who was on the other side of the table leaned over to look more closely.

"No, I don't," said Wagner. "Looks Chinese though, doesn't it?"

Deerstalker and I nodded. I'd seen Chinese characters get popular as tattoos in some quarters over the past decade or two. But scarification had never really caught on in a big way. Maybe that's because life gives you plenty of scars.

"Does that scar look new to you or would she have had it a while?" I asked.

Deerstalker looked at it. He walked around to Jane Doe's left side where I was. Wagner was on the opposite side. Then he took a gloved finger and gently rubbed it as if he might understand them as braille. He slowly shook his head.

"It's well healed. Other than it being at least six months to a year old, I can't give you an answer beyond that. Certainly not within the last six months."

I nodded and looked over the body once again, up and down. She was remarkably unblemished for an adult body. The odd freckle or small, flat mole but nothing really of note other than the scar. Her fingertips were a little stained with black grease.

"FIU has taken the prints," I said.

Deerstalker nodded.

"Yeah, they finished up just a little before you got here," said Deerstalker. "Prints and dental they took. No word yet, but maybe we'll get lucky. You'll likely hear from them tomorrow or early in the week."

I straightened up and nodded. Wagner bade us both farewell and left the room. He wished me luck on the case too.

"Nothing else you can or want to add to what I already don't know?" I asked.

Deerstalker smiled at me and shook his head.

"I don't know much more than you at the moment," said Deerstalker.

"Any first guesses as to cause of death? Suffocation or strangulation maybe?" I asked, looking down at the body and realizing that strangulation was probably off the table as there weren't any marks indicative of that type of death around her neck.

"I'm fairly certain it's not strangulation," said Deerstalker, leaning over her head and feeling around her windpipe and neck. "No strangulation marks as you can see and no obvious trauma to the neck, larynx or trachea."

I nodded. Deerstalker opened up each eye and looked at it as he shined a flashlight into each pupil.

"No petechial hemorrhaging either, so it's unlikely to have been suffocation," Deerstalker added.

"So she wasn't strangled or suffocated to death then," I said.

"I didn't say that, Anthony. Don't put words in my mouth. It's quite unlikely to have been strangulation and also possibly not suffocation. I'll need to take a closer look. This is what autopsies are for."

"If she wasn't strangled or suffocated, and let's just play Devil's advocate for a minute, then what are the possibilities?" I asked.

Deerstalker wasn't up for a game of what-ifs. So I continued.

"Could she have suffered violence that hasn't left a mark?"

"Possibly. I've seen cases of non-stroke brain hemorrhage as a cause of death due to a blow to the head that left no obvious surface trauma without closer inspection. But that's rare."

I nodded.

"If I was a betting man, I'm going to go out on a limb and say she was poisoned somehow."

"Probably a safe bet. Just from the quick visual I've done, I think there's a good chance that was her mechanism of death. Toxicology will help."

I nodded.

"Who'd want to poison such a beautiful woman?" I asked to nobody in particular.

"That's your job," said Deerstalker. "I just figure out the mechanism of death. You've got to figure out the reason."

I nodded at him and patted him on the shoulder.

"Do you know at this stage if she's had any intercourse, or worse, has she been raped?"

"I don't know that yet, but that will be part of my discovery," said Deerstalker.

"Please give me a call once you've found anything out," I said.

"Will do," said Deerstalker.

A Love Supreme

I left him with a dead Jane Doe and walked back out to my car. I got in and then got back out. It was a hotbox inside. I then got back in again, opened the windows and then started the air conditioning. Then I got back out and thought of cigarettes.

I needed to do some thinking and cigarettes had helped turn the gears. Instead, I reached inside the car again and took my kombolói off my rearview mirror and started to turn the beads in my left hand. That got me thinking that I was seeing Dr. Ainley tomorrow morning. I wasn't sure what time. I pushed that thought aside and started thinking about Jane Doe instead.

All I had was a dead woman on a cold steel slab. A beautiful woman in her early to mid-twenties. I kept harping on her looks because the case was bizarre. No obvious trauma and she was laid carefully at the dump but without any way of helping us identify her.

A casual observer might suggest that perhaps she was the victim of an accidental poisoning. And that might explain it. But I didn't like it. Her placement as she was found was too careful. Somebody freaking out about her accidental poisoning would dump and run. They wouldn't carefully place her head on a pillow of twigs and remove all her jewelry, and I'd bet Franklins against Washingtons she was wearing jewelry. Especially on the evening she died which was likely Saturday night or early Sunday morning. For one thing both ears were pierced.

A rational person would have called the police if my Jane Doe had accidentally been poisoned. No, this was more sinister. Could she have been doing drugs and overdosed? Yeah, I could see that. But the way she was placed out of the way and left to the wild animals suggests something more was going on.

And that got me thinking. She'd been left out on the northwest side of the landfill for at least eight or more hours. It was surprising that no coyotes or mountain lions had found her. A lucky break I guess.

I turned my thoughts to the naked Jane Doe I'd just seen. She didn't look like a woman who'd had children. At least not obviously so by the look of her smooth and firm stomach. And surely she would have fielded many offers for marriage.

Maybe she was married. After all, her jewelry was gone and having stayed out of the sun I couldn't tell if there had been a wedding band on her finger. But wouldn't somebody be missing her already? I took my phone out of my pocket and looked at the time. It was nearing six and the sun was doing the limbo on the western horizon.

I might have been expecting loved ones to be worried too soon. If she'd been out with friends on Saturday evening perhaps her partner or her lover or her parents had figured she'd stayed over night. If she was being missed then the calls would likely be coming in tomorrow about her whereabouts. I put that thought aside. If she was being missed this case would go down a lot easier and quicker.

But if she wasn't. Then that got me to thinking about her figure and her doll-like porcelain skin. Her augmented breasts. Granted, this is LA and a lot of women do enhancements for all sorts of reasons. But this woman was young and dead and I suspected foul play.

That got me to thinking she might be a hooker. Probably a well-priced hooker and not a street walker. That could be a line of inquiry. Without further identification I'd start calling on the escort agencies in town come tomorrow. See if they recognized her.

I took my phone out again and called dispatch. I had a special number for them. It was easier that way to have my identification verified. The line rang longer than I thought it should. Then I was put on hold. That had seldom happened.

After hearing how I could call nine one one if this was an emergency and other information about how to report different, minor crimes a bunch of times the call was answered.

"Mr. Carrick," said the voice on the other end.

"How come I'm always lucky enough to get you, V?" I asked.

Vail Bowdey was the one dispatcher that it seemed I always got on the horn when I called in. She reminded me of my mother. But not physically. Vail was a large woman probably carrying an extra four stones she didn't need to. Stones in the archaic system of British weights and measures is roughly fourteen pounds a piece. You do the math.

My mother is slim and probably forty or so years older than Vail. No, Vail reminds me of my mother because she has a young son who is around twelve or so, the same age I was when my mother brought me out here from Stillwater, Oklahoma. Vail also recently left an abusive husband a couple of years back and is making a new life for her and her son. That's where she reminds me of my mother.

"You're just lucky, I guess," she said, laughing on the other end.

"You must be busy so I'll keep this short," I said.

"Yeah, sorry about the wait, when it rains it pours as they say."

"I understand. Don't sweat it. I was wondering if Detectives Vick Lowe or Mike O'Toole were working today?"

"Give me a minute to check, okay?"

"Sure thing."

Vick "the brick" Lowe and Mike "limey" O'Toole were two vice detectives I'd known back in the day. Mike is Irish, but that's the way nicknames go. I was hoping they might have some insight on the scar I had just seen on Jane Doe. If she was a hooker they might have some knowledge about it. Vail was back on the line moments later.

"Hi, Anthony?"

"Here."

"Thanks for waiting. Detectives Lowe and O'Toole aren't working today. They are in tomorrow if you want to try and reach them then?"

"Thanks, Vail. Real quick, how's Connor?"

"He's doing great, thanks for asking Anthony. He often asks about you. He came third at the US Junior Chess Championship over the summer. He got a prize of three grand."

"Wow, that's terrific," I said. "Just terrific. And didn't he win the state junior championship just this year too?"

"You remembered. Yeah, he won, and that came with a five thousand dollar prize for first place."

"Of course I remembered," I said. "Connor's a good lad. He'll soon be supporting you in a lifestyle you're not yet accustomed to."

Vail laughed.

"Well, there's more money out there for good chess players than I imagined. Magnus Carlsen earned over six hundred thousand last year for winning the 2018 World Chess Championship. Plus there are endorsements that make that much or more, or so I've heard."

"That's something else. Amazing what people can make a good living at nowadays," I said.

"I know, right. Right now though, Connor is focusing on making enough money over the next few years to pay for college. But I think if he keeps up his good performance he'll probably get a scholarship to UCLA."

"You must be very proud. How old is he now?"

"I am. He turned fifteen just a week ago."

"I still remember him much younger. What day did he celebrate?"

"His birthday's on the ninth."

"Ninth of October?"

"That's right."

"I knew there was a reason I liked him so much. That's my birthdate too."

"Connor will be ecstatic to hear that," said Vail.

"I'll let you go. Wish him the best from me. I hope to come and watch him at a tournament sometime."

"He'd really like that, Anthony. Have a good day."

"Bye, Vail."

I hung up and looked at my phone. There wasn't much to see, but I was thinking about Connor and me.

He reminded me a lot of myself. At least a few years ago when I had first come to know him. He's a quiet introverted boy who enjoys chess. Believe it or not, I was a quiet introverted young boy who loved art when I was his age. Only my father wasn't going to have a "pansy" for a son so he taught me to box on top of beating me up to keep me strong.

In a way it worked. Not that there was ever a risk of me becoming homosexual, but my father was frightened like that. He grew up in a different time. That's charitable. But he was also just an asshole. His lack of success in the ring was at our expense. He was nothing but a washed up alcoholic bully. But I did learn to fight and my introversion was put to bed with my bruises every night.

Enough about me. Maybe I'll talk to Lloyd Ainley about it tomorrow. See if he can offer any great insight. I got back into my car and turned on KJAZZ. The car was cool. Too cold, so I turned down the air conditioning. A Love Supreme accompanied me home.

I got home just after part four, "Psalm" had started. I was in church. This is one of the best jazz albums of all time. You can't just leave in the middle of it. So I stayed in my car and listened to the last five minutes until it ended. I had forgotten about the case. I had forgotten about the misdeeds and misgivings of my fellow man. I had been wrapped up in a love, supreme.

Happy Little Trees

Monday morning I was up just after eight a.m. It wasn't so much the brightening day that was creeping into my room that woke me up. I woke up because I had a dead arm. Pirate had decided that he wanted to sleep on it. That had caused the nerves to get pinched. I had to use my other arm to pull my dead arm out from under him.

I held my arm loosely across my stomach as I lay on my back putting faces on my popcorn ceiling and waited for the frustrating pins and needles. Pirate stood up and arched his back. Then he looked at me in the eye with his one good eye. He was not happy. He licked his lips, walked over my lower stomach which reminded me that I needed to get to the can, and then jumped off the bed. I heard his feet make a soft thump on the carpet.

My brain was piggy in the middle between my arm and my bladder. My bladder won and I got up out of bed with my left arm still tingling and made it to the can. A few minutes later I was starting to feel like I belonged in the land of the living. I went into the kitchen and started making coffee. Pirate was sitting, staring at me by his empty bowl. I opened a fresh can of wet food and gave him a good dollop.

I put the can into the fridge and looked around in it for a minute. I had eggs and bacon and sausages, but I didn't feel like something that rich. The coffee had started brewing and the smell put a smile on my face. The day didn't start properly until you'd had your coffee. I took out a loaf of whole grain bread, the butter and the blackberry jam. I had decided on something simple. Toast and jam.

By the time the toast had been toasted to within an inch of its life the coffee was ready. I spread the butter and jam on the toast's dark brown, almost black face. I poured a cup of coffee and walked into the living room where I sat down on the couch and put my toast on the seat next to me. The coffee was put on a coaster on the coffee table. I picked up the remote and channel surfed for a while until I came up on some sports.

The Rugby World Cup was going on and I caught a game. It must have been a replay but I watched it anyway. It was the USA versus Tonga. After around eighty minutes of play Tonga walked away the winner with thirty-one points to our nineteen.

I hadn't really watched a lot of rugby but I caught on pretty quick. The idea of it is to get the ellipsoidal ball across the far end of the field. Right under the H goalposts if possible. The ball has to touch the ground on that end. This is similar to football. Instead of a touchdown it's called a "try". The name makes sense, because these men are really trying to get the ball down to that end.

A try will get you five points. A successful try will also let you kick the ball through the goalposts but above the horizontal bar for another two points. The kicker is placed in line with where the ball was touched down during the try. So touching the ball down just behind the goalposts gives the kicker the best chance to earn those two points. A penalty or drop goal is worth three points.

The idea, obviously, is to score tries and get those kicks converted for seven points total. This is done by passing the ball from player to player as you run down your opponent's half of the field. The ball cannot be thrown forward. Only laterally or backwards.

If it seems complicated it's not. Simpler rules than football and, accepting the hate for this, a more enjoyable game. Far less stoppages and more time on the clock for play. They also seem to be taking brain injury more seriously. Hits anywhere around the neck or head will get you booted off the field with either a yellow or red card. I made a note to try and pick up a couple more games if I had the chance.

I looked at my phone as it vibrated. The time was just after ten. I had to try and get ahold of Lowe and O'Toole and I also wanted to find out what was on the video footage from the landfill. And if the stars were truly aligned I wanted to know who our Jane Doe was.

But none of that seemed interesting to my phone. My phone was telling me that I was seeing Dr. Lloyd Ainley at eleven. I must be his last appointment of the morning. I had plenty of time to get there. In fact, I had almost a half hour before I had to get going so I put on my painting apron and went to my easel.

Golf was on the TV but I didn't fancy something like that. I channel surfed and came upon Bob Ross' The Joy of Painting. I let that play for a bit while I painted. Grinning at his "happy little trees". I wasn't painting happy little trees. Mine was a little more abstract and a little more political than Bob's landscapes.

But Bob was good company. I got why he was so popular. We painted together. Bob chatting over my shoulder until it was time for me to put down the paint and palette. I was probably a few weeks away from finishing my painting while Bob was almost finished with his by the time I turned off the TV.

I put some dry food down for Pirate and grabbed my fedora as I walked out of the apartment, locking it behind me.

Dr. Ainley's place is only about a twenty minute drive from where I live. And on a mid-morning Monday a twenty minute drive in LA is pleasant. It was smooth driving without the usual cadre of assholes you'll find on most streets driving in LA.

I arrived at his office feeling in good spirits and wondering why I even needed to see him. I had slept well. Primarily thanks to the THC, and I hadn't been woken up from my New York nightmares as I'd come to call them.

In fact, waking up from my nightmares was becoming less common, and I was grateful for that. During a full week I was only woken from a night of sleep by So-yi's screams two or, at most, three times. That was a win.

I got out of my car at five minutes to eleven and walked into his office located amongst a gaggle of other offices in a nice part of town. Not far from Beverly Hills. Well, actually, that's a bit of a fib. It's strictly in Beverly Hills, only not in the residential part.

Gone Surfing

Aire was the first to greet me. That's Lloyd's wife. She's a breath of fresh air. A warm, bubbly hippie who always seems thrilled that you've come for a visit.

As usual, I was the only one in the waiting room. In the building where his office is located you won't find Dr. Ainley's name on the business list in the lobby. And that's not because his business has some cute name like "Psych U Out" or "Shrunken Heads". No, the reason you won't find Dr. Ainley listed on the building directory is because of the work he does. He's the epitome of discretion.

His office is number three oh one. The third floor, and all that's on the door is the number three zero one as part of the numbering scheme of the office complex generally. Next to the door is a small doorbell. You push it and hear nothing. But shortly afterwards a shadow comes over the peephole and then the door is opened by the vivacious Aire.

You're in a waiting room that's large enough to seat a handful of people, except there's only one couch and one recliner. Besides, who wants to be waiting their turn amongst a murder of mental cases? I don't.

Aire had offered me a coffee, a cappuccino or a latte. She'd just bought a new espresso maker that she loved. Her enthusiasm was contagious so I accepted a cappuccino. She disappeared around the corner when she left her desk. I got up and went to the short side of the counter surrounding her desk. I peeked at her computer terminal and noticed it was locked. I was happy about that.

I went and sat back down. I picked up an issue of The Economist from a couple of weeks ago. The main story was about AI taking over Wall Street. I wasn't much interested in either Wall Street or robots. I flipped through the pages mostly just keeping my idle hands away from devil's work until Aire came back out from the kitchenette, at least that's where I imagined she was, with my cappuccino.

"Here you go," she said.

I took the mug from her and gave it a sniff. I'd asked for two sugars. I put it to my mouth and took a taste of the creamy, sweet foam and coffee. It was one of the finest cappuccinos I'd had. Mind you, that's not saying a lot. The number of times I'd had cappuccinos or any other fancy coffees in my life I could probably count on one hand.

"Where's yours?" I asked.

"Honestly, Anthony, I've already had two this morning. I'm now just sipping water. Is it good?" she asked.

"Best cappuccino I ever had."

She laughed and nodded.

"And I don't say that to just any old cappuccino."

She laughed again and walked back to her desk behind the counter. I was sitting against the wall facing her. The door I had walked through was to my left. The door I would walk through next was to my right and perpendicular to the door I had previously entered. This door leads to a short hallway and then to another door where Lloyd's office is. This way, the previous patient can leave discreetly without having to see who's coming into the batter's box next.

I could hear muffled voices coming from behind door number two. They were soft enough that not only couldn't I hear what was said, I couldn't really make out if they were male voices or mixed. Though I knew one of them had to be Lloyd's.

I was expecting to see Lloyd come through door number two moments after his previous patient had left through door number three. That didn't happen. I heard the voices stop. I heard door number three close gently and then nothing. I stared at door number two as if I were Superman with my X-ray vision. I wasn't, on both counts.

A clock just behind Aire was showing a couple of minutes past eleven. She noticed my gaze.

"I hope you'll forgive Lloyd, Anthony, he's running a little late this morning. Shouldn't be long now."

I nodded and concentrated on my cappuccino. I stared at the coffee table in front of me. There were other magazines on it which didn't really call out to me. I saw a men's fitness magazine, a few women's magazines.

The Economist, like I'd said. There was also a National Geographic and a running magazine. Maybe others. Some were a couple or three deep and I didn't go fishing through them.

Classical music was playing from somewhere behind Aire's counter. I recalled seeing a small radio on her desk. These are the things a bored man sipping on a cappuccino thinks about.

My monkey mind then moved onto the surfboard which was in the corner. If you've kept up with me you'll know that Lloyd Ainley was a semi-pro surfer back in the eighties and nineties. It was one of his old surfboards. He has a theme going on in the waiting area that is surf and ocean related. The colors are beach colors. Blues and yellows. It really creates quite a tranquil environment.

I was looking at his surfboard, which wasn't there before, and wondering what it must feel like to stand proud on something like that with a wave driving you towards the beach like a fleet of stallions, when door number two opened and I looked over to see a smiling Lloyd.

I got up and walked over to him, carrying my cappuccino. We shook hands.

"Sorry to keep you, Anthony, I hate to be tardy like this," he said.

I looked over to my left at the clock above Aire's desk and it had barely gone four minutes past eleven.

"Not a problem, doc," I said.

"Please come on through. I see you're trying Aire's world famous cappuccino, can I get you anything else?"

"I'll take a viable suspect on a case I'm working if you've got one, otherwise I'm fine, thanks," I said.

Lloyd grinned and waved me through.

Devil's Advocate

I was only about a third through my cappuccino, but it had lowered the cappuccino enough in the mug that I wasn't worried about spilling it. I followed Lloyd down the hallway towards his door.

"My patients have needed a little more of my time today so I'm off to a late start. I should be able to catch up by taking a shorter lunch."

"I'd hate to do that to you, doc. I could always come back next week," I said, grinning at the back of his head as he opened the door and we walked into his office.

He offered me the couch or the big armchair. I took the big arm chair like I had done most times I'd been here.

"That's quite alright, Anthony. I've got you now and I'm going to hold onto you for the next hour. I think we're making progress."

I nodded, but inside I wasn't quite as optimistic as he was. How do you make progress over death? Something so final. There are no take backs, no mulligans, no walks. It's a strike and you're out. I sipped on my cappuccino and then sat down.

"Your waiting room is a little different. The surfboard I hadn't noticed before and the Buddha's portrait or picture is gone."

"You've got a good eye," he said. "I can see why you're an excellent detective. About once a month we tweak the waiting area. Aire likes to do it and keep it fresh for our patients."

I nodded and sipped my cappuccino.

"That surfboard in the waiting area is actually one of the first surfboards I used around thirty years ago or so. If you know anything about surfing tech, you can tell by looking at it."

"Is the manufacturer still in business?" I asked.

Lloyd nodded.

"Yeah, they're called Whet Saddles. They're still in business and I still use them. I was sponsored by them early on. And by sponsored I mean they gave me a new surfboard each year. I like them mostly because they stick to their cooking. A lot of the big companies are into clothing, wetsuits and all sorts of accessories. Whet Saddles only makes surfboards and associated accessories."

I nodded.

"I was wondering what it must be like to ride on top of waves like an ocean cowboy," I said.

"It's exhilarating. It's why I still do it. Mind you, at the current rate we're polluting our waters it'll soon become hazardous."

"That's a real problem?"

"You have no idea. But we're not here to talk about surfing and pollution. Tell me about how you're doing. How are your nightmares lately?"

"They're the same when I have them. But I don't have them every night like I used to. I only have it once or twice a week now. Thanks pretty much to cannabis to be honest. I sleep really good on it."

"I'm glad to hear it. How much are you taking now?"

"I'm up to ten milligrams of THC. I'm not keen on going higher than that, pun intended, because that amount still makes me feel it. Hard to describe. A little wooly headed and a little distracted, but it does make me feel drowsy when I'm getting ready to go to bed."

"And you take it around an hour or two before bed?"

I nodded and sipped more cappuccino.

"And the CBD. You still taking that during the day?"

"Yeah, same amount. I don't feel any different on that one to be honest."

"The effects are subtle. As you know, CBD doesn't make you high, but it should help you relax and help with the PTSD."

"Could we not call it that? I'm pretty sure I don't have PTSD," I said.

"And I'm pretty sure that you do, Anthony. That's my diagnosis. You're hyper-vigilant, you're having nightmares about So-yi's murder and you're prone to anger very quickly."

"Listen," I said, getting a little testy. "There are plenty of reasons to get angry. Our country's circling the drain and we've got assholes killing good people on a daily basis. My job's no cakewalk and I'm no different from my father."

Lloyd listened and nodded.

"What would you like to call it?" he asked.

"I don't know. I had a traumatic event. I was almost murdered and I saw a fine officer get raped and murdered in front of me."

"Ok, let's call it the event," he said.

"I call it NYN, like the number nine, but it stands for my New York nightmare."

Lloyd nodded thoughtfully.

"Fair enough, we'll call it NYN or refer to it as your New York nightmare. Tell me about your father."

"God dammit, now you sound just like a psychoanalyst. My father was a raging alcoholic. You know this."

"Yes, but I don't know how that made you feel," said Lloyd, talking as quietly and comfortably as a priest taking confession.

"Jesus, Lloyd. How do you think it made me feel? I was a boy who had to learn to box when I had no interest in violence. In fact, I was a young shy boy. But I'll tell you one thing, I'm grateful to that old bastard for forcing me to learn how to fight. I found out I was pretty good at it."

Lloyd nodded and kept soft eyes on me. He didn't rise to my anger and he gave me space to dissipate the heat in the room.

"Would you be willing to share with me what's bothering you this morning, Anthony?"

I drank down the last of my cappuccino and put the empty mug on the long coffee table to my left. I took a deep breath.

"We've found another dead body," I said.

"That's not unusual for you," he said. "What makes this one particularly upsetting?"

"She's a young, attractive woman whose name we don't know and who was discarded at the dump. Only she didn't seem abused. Let me show you something," I said, as I took my phone out of my pocket.

I unlocked it and searched for the images of her scar. I held my phone out towards Lloyd.

"What do you make of this?" I asked.

He took my phone and looked at it. Then he zoomed in with finger and thumb and shook his head.

"Looks like Chinese characters," he said.

I nodded.

"We have no idea who she is and how she died. It upsets me because I'm sick and fucking tired of women and children getting abused and murdered. Makes me worried about Aibhilin."

Lloyd had kind eyes. He was in the right line of work. He was the eye when the storm was all around him. I could use some of his equanimity. Why didn't he just prescribe some of that?

"Perhaps it goes deeper than that, Anthony," he said. "Maybe it brings up old feelings from childhood."

"Like what," I snapped, not meaning to. I just hated being a pinned butterfly under a microscope.

"Well, we've talked a bit about your father. How he abused both you and your mother. Would you consider that maybe this case, the one you've just described, brings back those memories of troubled times in Oklahoma?"

I could have used something to do with my hands. Maybe I should bring in my kombolói next time. A squeeze ball would be helpful right now. Even another coffee to hold in my hands. Instead I started tapping my fingers on the armchair's armrest.

"I don't know about that, doc. I've seen plenty of female victims in my time. Probably more than fifty percent of the homicide victims I've investigated are women. I just hate assholes, and murderers are assholes."

Lloyd listened and nodded.

"To play Devil's advocate," said Lloyd, "this latest case is hot on the heels of So-yi's death. The two, in combination, could be making it much more difficult for you to assess the emotional toll it's taking."

"I don't think so, doc. I'm a few murders away from So-yi and New York. I've had a couple of female victims since then. Two just recently."

"Are you talking about the fortune teller case."

I nodded.

"Were the female victims in that case attractive?"

"I'm sure some men might have found them attractive. They weren't my type. In any event, what's their attractiveness got to do with my feelings about the case? I take offense at that, doc."

Lloyd shook his head.

"No, Anthony, you're misunderstanding me. You have mentioned how attractive So-yi was, and now you've also mentioned how attractive this latest victim is..."

"I'll stop you right there, doc. This victim's attractiveness is a clue in the case, nothing more."

"Still, she's attractive and so was So-yi. Furthermore, I got the impression that So-yi liked you, that there could have been something there under different circumstances and perhaps at a different time. You're an attractive man and you have a charm. I'm only suggesting that perhaps this victim is bringing up some of those conflicted feelings you had for So-yi."

I took a deep breath. I didn't like these sessions. The only reason I was going was because the hour with Lloyd was less unpleasant than having to argue with M over not going.

"Maybe," I said at last. "Maybe I'm also just tired from all the bullshit people are up to every day."

"Tell me about that."

"Nothing to tell, doc. It's the daily grind. Last year I thought I was on to greener pastures. I sold eighteen paintings. I made a little over eighty grand for the year. Most I'd ever made in my life. This year, I've sold only six paintings and I'll be lucky to see thirty grand unless my pal throws me a couple more homicides. That's what I'm tired of, doc. I'm sick and tired of having to look at dead bodies to earn my living."

"Being an artist isn't easy," he said.

Physical Conversations

" What's wrong with trying to make a living as a painter?" I asked him.

"There's nothing wrong with it, Anthony, but I imagine it's a long, hard road without any guarantees."

I didn't say anything to that.

"Was your father supportive of your art?" asked Lloyd.

"I'm sure you can figure out the answer to that."

"I'd like to hear it from you."

"No, he was not supportive. In fact, he was antagonistic towards it. Saw nothing redeeming in it. Thought that all artists, at least the men, were queer or pansies."

"Are those the words he used?"

"He liked the word pansy. He used that a lot to refer to me. When he was particularly upset he liked to call me a faggot. When he was angry at both my mother and me he'd tell her she was too soft, that she was raising a cock-sucking faggot. I could go on."

"Please do."

"He'd goad me with these stupid rhymes. And it always got me riled up."

"What sort of rhymes?" asked Lloyd.

"Tiny Tony is a phony. Tiny Tony wants to buy a pony. Tiny Tony is lonely. Stupid shit like that."

"And that's probably why you don't like being called Tony," he said.

"You think."

We took a moment to lengthen the emotional space between us. I wasn't finding these conversations therapeutic at all. If anything, they just dredged up the past and made me angry.

"You're not a particularly short man, Anthony. How tall are you?"

I gave him a look.

"Five nine, five ten, depending on who's asking," I said.

"The truth's asking," said Lloyd.

"Closer to five nine then. Haven't measured myself in a while. Last time I was officially measured was at the police academy. They put me down at five nine and one third."

"That's right around average," said Lloyd.

"How tall are you?"

"Around the same height you are. I usually say five ten, but last I was actually measured I was at five nine and three quarters."

"Why does it even matter?" I asked. "Nothing I can do about it."

"I'm just trying to figure out why your father was calling you Tiny Tony. Were you small as a boy?"

"I was a late bloomer. But listen, doc, it's not the words he used, it was the incessant badgering that wore me down. The constant bitching, the mercurial personality."

"Do you think you have a problem managing your anger?"

I looked at him and he held my gaze while I thought about how to answer that loaded question.

"No," I said. "I've never hit a woman, and I've never laid a hand on Aibhilin."

"That's not what I was asking," said Lloyd.

Lloyd was the kind of guy who asked questions that I would have punched him in the face for if he was anyone else. But he had a way of asking questions that didn't indicate malice. He was calm, and his eyes shone kindness. There appeared no malevolence to any of this. In fact, if anything, there was a sincerity to his willingness and eagerness to help. I took a deep breath.

"No, I don't think I have a problem with anger," I said.

"What about your police jacket? If I was to look at that, would there be any complaints about your conduct?"

I wasn't sure what his angle was. Being a cop ain't an easy job. You're dealing mostly with assholes every day.

"You'd find a few," I said.

"How many is a few?" he asked.

I looked at him. Lloyd was a smart man and he had a way of digging through the shit to get to the diamonds.

"I stopped counting at thirteen," I said.

"How many, Anthony?"

We stared at each other for a while, like two Billy Goats Gruff trying to figure out if we were gonna butt heads or not.

"Seventeen," I said.

"You have to agree that is a lot, don't you think?"

"No, not particularly. I was on the job for ten years. I must have been on at least two or three cases a shift. Let's call it two. Let's also say there were two hundred and fifty shifts a year. Five hundred cases a year and I was on for ten years, that's five thousand different interactions. Most interactions are with more than one person. We're looking at a fraction of a percent of them when some whiny, sniveling bastard gets upset because they got what was coming for them."

"I've talked with many police officers, Anthony, and many of them went their whole career without having a single conduct complaint."

"Easy to do if you're riding desk all day," I said.

"They weren't. What about your friend John Roberts?"

"What about him?"

"How many complaints does he have on his jacket?"

I shrugged.

"How many from the last time you knew?"

"Three," I said, tiring of this conversation.

"And did he earn those when you two worked together or before?"

"You can probably guess the answer, doc. Ok, I get it, I'm a little handsy sometimes but I can tell you this. None of those assholes who I had physical conversations with didn't deserve it."

"I'm not here to judge you, Anthony, I'm here to try and help you. I'm not saying anger is always bad, but it is more often than not an unhelpful emotion most of the time."

I didn't say anything.

"Over the next week, or before I see you next, I'd just ask that you think about how often you're getting angry during the day and write down what it was that got you angry."

"I'll do my best. But what I will tell you, doc, is that cannabis seems to chill me out more."

"It does have that effect on most people," said Lloyd. "You're happy with the amount you're getting and the dosage?"

I nodded.

"Yeah, I'm not looking to get stoned out of my mind, doc. I'm just looking at getting a good night's rest. It seems to help with that most nights."

"It's okay to increase it a milligram or two if you need it. I'd prefer to see you sleeping good at least six nights out of seven."

"And I'd prefer a stiff drink and a naked woman. But we don't always get what we want."

"Perhaps next time we can talk about that."

"I can talk about that all day," I said.

"I meant your preference for flippant remarks when we're trying to get somewhere."

"The journey is the destination, doc. We're all trying to get somewhere when all we're doing is heading for the same destination... endsville."

Lloyd looked at me for a moment with a slight smile on his face.

"There it is. I don't know if that's wisdom or flippancy," said Lloyd. "I'll believe it's wisdom."

I nodded.

"It is indeed."

"We're making good progress, Anthony. Believe it or not, that chip on your shoulder is visibly shrinking."

I nodded. I figured we were getting to the end of the session. Soon, I'd be a free man.

"I'll book you in next week at the same time," said Lloyd, standing up out of his chair. I joined him.

"Let's say two weeks if that's alright. I've got Aibhilin next week and I'd like to focus on her."

"Two weeks it is then," said Lloyd, leading me down the hallway to the exit.

Just as we got to the last door I turned towards him.

"How are things out in Texas?" I asked.

Lloyd shrugged.

"You think you know people sometimes, and then they go and lose their minds. Phil is in jail now, but Shak's devastated. He had to buy Phil out of the business, but more than that, he's pretty upset with what Phil's done. Shak's actually thinking about selling to Surf Mart and moving out here."

"It'll be nice to have him out here. I like him," I said.

"That whole grift that Phil was trying to pull, that didn't bother you?"

"A lot of things bother me, doc. Spicy food that upsets my stomach, toilet paper that's under and not over, toothbrushes that haven't been rinsed properly, jackasses that don't signal, hipsters growing shitty beards..."

"I get it," said Lloyd, smiling.

"But no, what Phil did doesn't bother me. People will do the weirdest things when they're under pressure, financial pressure especially. At least we got to the bottom of it and he wasn't dead."

Lloyd nodded.

"Yeah, still, it bothers me. You think you know someone and then something like this happens."

"We're all just trains on a track," I said, "and sometimes the track breaks."

Lloyd nodded, we shook hands and I left.

Limewater

Igot out to my car and admired it amongst the BMWs, Porsches, Mercedes and other luxury vehicles. It was another warm day so I opened the car, turned it on and put on the A/C. Then I got back out again and looked at my phone. I didn't have any messages. I called dispatch and waited until I got through. It didn't take as long this time. But it wasn't Vail. I asked about Detectives Lowe and O'Toole. I was put on hold for a minute and when dispatch got back on the phone she told me they were at a dive bar in Echo Park by the name of Limewater.

Echo Park is a confusing place. Maybe it's only confusing to me. It's a place that got gentrified and has improved a lot since the movie studios left in the early part of the last century. You've got your gang injunctions which keep the local hooligans mostly out of the area. But I can't help feeling that the place is just looking for the authorities to turn their backs so that it can become the cesspool it was once renowned to be.

It was also part of Edendale. Such a charming name, no wonder they dropped that moniker when the studios left. There's really nothing Edenic about it. Well, perhaps for the lake. That's nice. But I wasn't here for a boat ride or a stroll in the park.

Speaking of movie studios. Edendale, which included Echo Park back in the first part of the twentieth century, was located in the area and it's home to the many silent movies produced during that time. Charlie Chaplin's first movie was shot in the area and it was home to the Keystone Kops. Maybe that last part, the Keystone Kops part, is why it lost its shine. When the Kops left the lawless man entered.

More likely, the thin veneer of tinsel town lost its shine like much of Hollywood when you look behind the curtain and the fresh paint.

Speaking of fresh paint. I hadn't been to Limewater in many years. But as I pulled up in front of it I noticed the fresh paint. Soft lime greens and yellows on the outside. The 'e' in lime is stylized like a wedge of lime.

Limewater is on Sunset Boulevard. Depending on who's doing the telling, Sunset Boulevard either starts or ends in Echo Park. I'd say it starts there and passes along the gates of Hell Air, aka Bel Air, before vomiting all our hopes and dreams into the Pacific Ocean like a waiter-come-actor on a two-day bender.

I got out of my car and looked around. It was around noon thirty and Sunset Boulevard was busy. The sky was blue and the breeze was warm and the air carried the smell of hot dogs from a vendor not fifty yards from where I was.

I walked into the bar. It was dimly lit but the air was clean and the decor had been refreshed. It wasn't trying to be upscale but it was cleaner than I remember it. I saw Lowe and O'Toole in a booth in the far corner. They were facing me and Lowe nodded. There was someone else with them in the booth. All I could see was the back of his head. Dark hair in a buzz cut, close enough that I could see a couple of nicks and scars on the back of his head.

The place was mostly empty as I walked over towards them. I stood at the end of their table and looked at the guy they were speaking with. He only glanced at me. He was a latino with unremarkable features. A face you wouldn't look at twice. It wasn't ugly and it wasn't handsome. It also didn't have any obvious features that stuck out like a sore thumb.

The guy shuffled to the end of the seat and got out of the booth. He was a couple of inches shorter than me and walked out without saying anything to anybody. I sat down and tried to find an unwarmed part of the cushion to sit on.

"Who was that?"

"A banger turned informant. We're working on a case that could be huge. Russian mafia bringing in Eastern European women as prostitutes. Dude thinks he knows something about that. Time will tell," said O'Toole.

A waitress came by having noticed fresh meat in the seat.

"Can I get you a drink, handsome?" she asked me.

She looked like a Petty Girl. A pinup by artist George Petty. She had a figure, she was blonde, and she was pretty in a Marilyn Monroe sort of way. Her lipstick was a bright cherry red and her eyelashes were long and black. She had a fake mole right where Marilyn also had a fake mole. Above her left lip almost at the crease across from her nose. The clincher, if you needed any more evidence that our waitress was going after Monroe's look, her embroidered name tag on her shirt, just above ample bosoms you could ski down for miles, was also Marilyn.

"I'll take an Irish whiskey," I said.

Marilyn had a pencil stuck behind her ear which she didn't take out to write with.

"We don't have Irish whiskey, hun," she said. "I can get you a nice bourbon if you like."

"Got any Scotch whisky?" I asked.

"Afraid not, hun, just a couple of bourbons."

O'Toole had a smirk on his face that I ignored.

"Ok, give me three fingers of your Goldilocks bourbon," I said.

"Never heard of that bourbon," she said. "I can tell you what we've got..."

"I meant don't give me your cheapest bourbon and don't give me your most expensive. Something nice and tasty at the middle price point."

Marilyn nodded.

"I see. How about some Buffalo Trace, that's popular and I'm told it goes down easy?"

"Just what a thirsty man needs," I said.

She smiled at me and walked away. I watched her rear for a moment as she sashayed away. Her firm, round ass reminded me of two puppies fighting with a chew toy under a sheet.

O'Toole was snickering. I turned back to look at him.

"Are you always this difficult to take out on a date?" he asked.

"Not if you're buying, Limey," I said.

That shut him up. Lowe started to snicker. O'Toole, who was around my age, was a good cop. He was also mostly likable in small doses. But he was a racist and a homophobe and I could never figure out why.

"You're one of very few people who can get away with that, AC," said Lowe.

"What?" I said, feigning ignorance. "We're just having a conversation here."

Back in the day, O'Toole and I had gotten into a donnybrook. He'd been pushing my buttons and being disrespectful to some witnesses who happened to be both gay and black. Lloyd thinks I've got an anger management problem, O'Toole will put up his dukes if you looked at him sideways. That's what he did, we got into it and I knocked him out cold. Since then we've been more or less friends.

Marilyn came back to our table with my Buffalo Trace in a proper whiskey tumbler. I put my three fingers next to the glass and it was pretty much bang on. I took a sip. It was warm and smooth with a hint of caramel. I liked it.

"Anything else for you gents?" asked Marilyn.

O'Toole and Lowe shook their heads. She turned to me.

"You look like a man with a good appetite, can I tempt you with anything?"

O'Toole smirked again, a smile creased the corner of my mouth.

"Something funny?" she asked, seemingly getting just a little flustered.

"No, sweetheart. It's just that you're an attractive woman and a question like that from an attractive woman like yourself, well, it gets a man to thinking about things other than food."

"Maybe that was the point," she said, and I'm pretty sure she winked at me.

I grinned but I didn't say anything. That wasn't a road I wanted to go down and try to back out of later.

"Would you like a menu, hun?"

I was hungry but I didn't feel like having to choose something to eat.

"I tell you what. Ask your chef to give me what you'd feed your loved one. Something meaty."

"Red meat?" she asked.

I nodded. She left and turned her head back after she'd left and caught me having a look.

"Aren't you married by now?" asked O'Toole.

I shook my head.

"Heard she was turning you into a vegan," said O'Toole, trying to rile me up.

The thing with O'Toole is, he's like a fifth grader in an adult's body. What he thinks will piss you off doesn't and what he doesn't think will piss you off does.

"I eat vegan when I'm with her. Probably don't eat meat more than a handful of times a week," I said. "You should try it. Would probably turn you into a man."

"Eating leaves and flowers. Do I look like I need to lose more weight?"

O'Toole and Lowe were opposites. O'Toole had a hair-trigger temper where Lowe had the patience of a Hindu sage. O'Toole was skinny and short where Lowe was stocky and tall.

"You look like you need to lose some prejudice," I said, sipping on the bourbon that was going down as smooth as the curves on our waitress. "You should open your mind a bit, Limey, and try on something new. It might suit you."

"I've tried new things before. I don't like them," he said.

Sometimes there's no talking to O'Toole. I've given up trying to get him to change his prejudices. Hasn't worked. But, he's careful around me.

Scars in Bars

I sipped my bourbon. I liked it. Never heard of nor tasted Buffalo Trace but it was something to keep in mind in a pinch. O'Toole and Lowe were drinking something rust colored in tall plastic glasses. I was going to guess iced tea. I decided to ask.

"That's either regular iced tea you're drinking or Long Island iced teas," I said. "Which is it?"

"Regular unsweetened iced tea," said Lowe.

"That's about as unappealing a drink as you can get. Might as well have asked for a cup from the chef's rinse sink," I said.

"Coming from a man with such refined tastes he puts his nose up at bourbon. The All-American classic whiskey," said O'Toole.

"Irish whiskeys are the best and they were the first," I said.

Lowe shrugged.

"I don't know much about whiskey, except I know I don't like it," he said.

"You're probably one of those douchebags..." said O'Toole.

I looked up at him sternly.

"What did you just call me?"

O'Toole grinned.

"A smart mouth will get a smart smack," I said.

"Let me rephrase the question, your honor," said O'Toole. "You're probably one of those guys that has a hierarchy of drinks. Am I right?"

"You mean my preference for what I'll drink?" I asked.

O'Toole nodded.

"Exactly."

I nodded.

"Yeah, I have a hierarchy. Irish whiskey above all else. Failing that I'll take a Scotch. Never thought about bourbon before, probably because I never had a good one. But this here Buffalo Trace will make me think about that. Guess I'd put bourbon after Scotch. None of the above available then I'll move to brandy. No brandy, vodka. No vodka, tequila. No tequila and I'm probably not sticking around. In a real pinch I'll drink the adult fizzy pop they call beer which is just pop that thinks it's visited the edgy part of town. If I'm absolutely desperate and there's no beer I'll take a red wine. After that, it's coffee if no adult beverages are around. That's the list of a refined palate," I said.

O'Toole snickered.

"We've got a real sommelier here," he said.

What I heard sounded more like so-molly-her.

"It's pronounced so-mo-yay," I said. "And the word you're actually looking for is douchebag. Douchebag works in that context."

"What about white wine?" asked O'Toole.

"I'd sooner drink my own chilled piss," I said.

Lowe let out a big belly laugh which got O'Toole chuckling along.

"Other than you're both on duty, why aren't you having a proper beverage?" I asked.

"We don't drink," said O'Toole. "You know that."

"Yes, yes I do," I said, remembering. "Just as well. You'd probably be a demon on gin and juice."

O'Toole just grinned more. I sipped more of my bourbon. It was going down easy, in spite of the company I was keeping.

Lowe looked at me with his arms folded across his chest. Other than his half drunk iced tea there was nothing else in front of him on the table we were sitting at. I figured they must have eaten. It was lunchtime after all. There just wasn't any evidence of it.

"I'm sure you're not here to discuss your social drinking hierarchy with us, Anthony," said Lowe. "What can we help you with?"

I looked up at him and put my whiskey glass down on the table in front of me. I was halfway to finishing it.

"I caught another murder. Not sure if you heard of it," I said.

Lowe and O'Toole both shook their heads.

"A young woman was found dead at the dump. She looked like she was out for a fancy night on the town. Probably Saturday night. Might have been a high class hooker. She was found in a wine colored negligee.

Nothing else on. Don't know if she'd had sex but we'll find out. No indication of how she died, nothing on her other than the negligee. And I mean nothing, no jewelry, earrings, anything. She's attractive and probably early to mid-twenties. No cause of death at the moment either, but that's coming. I wanted to show you a scar she's got..."

Marilyn came up to our table carrying a plate with my food. She placed it in front of me. It was a steak with peppercorn sauce, home cut unpeeled fries and string beans.

"Every man I've liked has enjoyed the peppercorn steak. And you look like a man I'd like."

I nodded and grinned at her.

"I know you're a woman I'd like. And the way to a man's heart is through his stomach. Thanks, Marilyn."

"My pleasure, hun. Let me know if you'd like anything else."

"I'll take a water too."

I cut into the steak as Marilyn left, turning to see if I was looking at her. I wasn't. The steak was more interesting at this point. It was slightly charred and crisp on the outside but soft, tender and quite pink in the middle. The sauce was fiery for a peppercorn sauce but the flavor and texture were near perfect. I was impressed by what used to be a dive bar not some years back. They'd clearly improved their game.

I smacked a bottle of ketchup on the rear to pour some ketchup onto the side of my plate and I put a couple of home cut potatoes on a fork and dipped them in the ketchup. After that I tried the string beans. No ketchup. Then I went back for another slice of the steak and I was starting to feel like a man amongst the living.

"No rush, Anthony, take your time," said O'Toole.

I put my fork and knife down and wiped my mouth. I fished my phone out of my pocket and went looking for the photos I'd just taken of the Jane Doe. It wasn't hard, they were the last photos I'd taken with my phone.

"This peppercorn steak is good," I said. "You should try it next time."

"I just might," said Lowe. "We had the wings. They were good but that's not a meal."

I passed my phone over to Lowe.

"This pic was taken on her lower left inguinal area," I said.

"Inguinal?" asked O'Toole.

"The crease where her leg meets her body. Also known as the groin," offered Lowe.

"Yeah," I said, leaning back in the booth and pointing to my groin not far from my hip. "Just here is where it is."

Lowe nodded and looked from me to the picture.

"Looks like three Chinese characters," I said, "and my Chinese is not all that good."

Lowe handed the phone to O'Toole. O'Toole took some time to look at it and then shook his head. Lowe shrugged.

"Looks like Greek to me," said O'Toole.

"Looks more like Chinese to me," I said.

"Never seen something like that on a body. Never seen something like that anywhere," said Lowe.

I nodded, gritting my teeth.

"One of the employees at Calabasas landfill said he remembered something similar on New Year's Day in two thousand. A female body dumped at the landfill but he didn't remember the details. We're looking into that case as well, see if it'll give us something to go on."

Marilyn came back with my water. I grinned at her and she gave me a wink. She left again but this time she didn't glance back to see if I was taking a look. I was. I went back to my steak.

"Got any pictures of her?" asked O'Toole.

"Swipe left, there's a pic of her face there."

O'Toole swiped a couple of times until he found what he was looking for. He nodded.

"That's an attractive face for a corpse," he said. "Doesn't look familiar though."

He passed the phone back to Lowe who looked at the dead woman's face for a bit before he too, shook his head.

"Yeah, definitely attractive. Doesn't have the look of a street walker. She looks, I dunno, healthy, normal," said Lowe.

I nodded. Lowe passed me the phone. I took it and put it on the table in front of me, face down. Marilyn was making her way back again.

"How is the steak, hun?" she asked.

"As perfect as a full moon lighting a romantic beach on Valentine's Day," I said, grinning at her. O'Toole was smirking too.

"You're not only handsome, but you're a poet too. That is a rare treat," she said.

I didn't say anything.

"Just let me know if you need anything else," she said.

I smiled and nodded and she walked away. I put another mouthful of food in my mouth.

"Can't say I've ever seen anything like that on any of our hookers, Limey?" said Lowe.

"Yeah, Vic's right. Haven't seen anything like that. Kids nowadays though, you've heard about this next level tattoo thing which is basically just getting scars. They call it scarification or something. It's like branding on people, I guess. This is probably exactly that. You'll find out the Chinese means unicorns, rainbows and love or some other kind of bullshit. Probably got nothing to do with nothing," said O'Toole.

"Yeah, I've heard of scarification or this branding thing. You might be onto something there. Still, I need to find out what it means so we can rule it out."

"When did you land the body?" asked Lowe.

"Yesterday afternoon," I said, chewing a mouthful of food. "I got there around three. The call came in about twelve thirty."

"Dental records should come in today. If not, maybe there's a hit on her fingerprints," said Lowe.

"Haven't gotten any messages yet," I said.

"You know how it goes. The ME is constantly understaffed and overworked. You should know," said Lowe.

"Oh, I know."

I went back to finishing my steak and potatoes and green beans. I just needed to be patient, I said to myself. Jane Doe's real name would come to light. If not today then certainly by tomorrow. In the meantime I'd send the Chinese character scar to my guy in the FBI.

SAC

The Brick and Limey left while I was paying my bill. Marilyn had given me her number on the back of the receipt. I went up to the bar and thanked the bartender for his good pour on the bourbon. Marilyn joined us to take my money. I thanked her and turned to leave.

"Call me," she said, smiling at me.

I turned around and tipped my hat at her and left. Outside was warm. I got into my car and turned it on and put on the A/C. It was too hot inside to stay in the car. So I got out again. This was becoming a routine.

I stepped onto the sidewalk while my car started to cool and took out my phone. The hotdog vendor had a customer. I could still smell the hotdogs. I scrolled through my contacts until I came to S. I was looking for SAC. I dialed the number. It rang through.

"Nishio," said the voice on the other line.

"Tai, it's Anthony Carrick," I said.

"Mr. Cool, long time since I heard from you," he said.

He wasn't wrong. It had probably been over a year since we'd spoken. Taiju Nishio was a Special Agent-in-Charge (SAC) for the FBI. I'd worked with him on a case way back when I was just a detective one on homicide and he was a newly minted special agent. He'd done well in his career in the FBI and was now the SAC out of the Birmingham, Alabama field office. He'd been promoted from an assistant SAC out of the Charlotte, North Carolina office. He'd wanted to stay there, but their SAC wasn't going anywhere.

Back in the day a homicide case I had been working on was related to a terrorist ring Tai was working on as one of his first cases. Your first case can often set the trajectory for your career. That first case went well for the both of us. It eventually propelled Tai to SAC. Only the third American of Asian descent to manage that title.

"What can I help you with, Anthony?" he asked.

Over the years we'd kept in contact intermittently. He scratched my back and I scratched his.

"I've got a Jane Doe whose name we haven't determined yet. The only remarkable mark on her is a scar made up of three Chinese characters. I asked my guys in vice about it but it doesn't look familiar to them. Could you take a look at it?"

"Sure thing, send it to me. Listen, I can't talk long, we're about to breach a homegrown terrorist cell here, but I wanted to ask you about New York."

New York was becoming a nightmare. Not only when I was asleep but now in my waking world.

"What about New York?" I asked.

"Those two men who murdered Detective Park have now been found," he said.

"Good news, maybe there'll be some justice for her now."

Nishio chuckled in the background.

"What's so funny?" I asked.

"They're dead, Anthony, and something tells me you knew that."

"I didn't," I said. "I left the rotten apple shortly after Detective Park's funeral. Where were they found?"

"On a garbage barge," he said.

"How did they die?"

"They were shot in the head, execution style," he said.

I shrugged, Tai couldn't see that so I added to the conversation.

"Clearly their bosses must have been unhappy with them, after all, I'm still out here walking around when they thought they'd killed me."

"So you're saying they were murdered by their boss?"

"Why not?" I said. "These were well-trained men who knew what they were doing and didn't mind the wet work."

"Wet work, huh?"

I didn't say anything.

"Are you using that term casually or specifically?" he asked.

"Not sure what you're getting at. These men were well trained and working for an organization called Red Blade which, as far as I can tell, is part of Muspell Logistics which is a holding company for all sorts of front companies. I'm telling you, this is a well-run organization. They probably don't tolerate failure well."

"You think they might be Russian?" asked Tai.

I shrugged again.

"Dunno. Probably not. I figure they're international, wouldn't be surprised if they started out homegrown. Why are you asking about the Russians?"

"Wet work is a calque of the Russian mokroye delo," he said. "Translated that means 'wet business'."

"I wouldn't put any stock in it," I said. "I got a call from a guy from somewhere, though he sounded American, who called himself Albert Camus. Said those two assholes were working for him. Said he'd taken care of the problem."

"So how did you become a target?" asked Tai.

"I was out there helping out on a murder case. A journalist was meeting with this young guy who showed him a secret weapon in development. Really high tech stuff. Problem was, nobody was taking this young guy seriously on account of his mental health problems..."

"What sort of problems?"

"He was being treated for schizophrenia but he was very tech savvy. He was working for a company called Pipe Dreams. Probably can't be found anymore so I wouldn't go looking, but they're developing high tech weaponry. I had the blueprints..."

"Where are they?" Tai asked.

"They were on a flash drive that I wiped."

"You sure about that?"

"There might be another copy available someplace safe hooked up to a dead man's switch in the event that anything happens to me."

"Now you're sounding paranoid."

"This goes deep, Tai. I'm telling you, these assholes are well funded. You ever heard of the Bilderberg Group."

"Yeah, of course. They meet annually to promote free market capitalism."

I chuckled.

"What's so funny, Anthony? It's all above the level. Mostly politicians, business leaders and other leaders of science and industry."

"And they sit around a campfire singing Kumbaya My Lord and roast marshmallows. I don't think so."

"What do you know, Anthony?" Tai asked.

"Nothing but speculation. But my gut feeling is that the Bilderberg Group as viewed from the public is actually what you say it is. But what's behind the front-facing group is perhaps a little more aggressive."

"Tell me more."

"Here's the thing. I think there's a well-funded group within, or perhaps two factions fighting for the same but different outcomes."

"Which is?"

"World dominance."

Now it was Tai's turn to chuckle.

"You're sounding a bit paranoid now yourself," he said.

"I'm just telling you my gut feeling from having worked that case. I think there are puppet masters behind the curtain with their own agendas. Now whether that's conspiracy or capitalism I don't know. But having been on that case, Tai, I am now more open-minded about that possibility."

"Ok, Anthony," he said. "Just a head's up that the FBI is looking into it. These two guys were ex-marine and they're not the first to wind up with lead in their brains."

"I see."

"Gotta go, send me that image and I'll see what I can find out."

"Thanks, Tai. See you around."

We hung up and I leaned against my car with the warm air sniffing around like a lost puppy. Much like the FBI now, it seemed.

As I remembered it, Hans Marais was going to take care of the bodies. Maybe not as well as I thought he was going to. Still, I wasn't worried. The gun was untraceable and So-yi's place was sanitized thoroughly. Nobody could tell anyone died in there.

I went to my photos app and looked for a high quality photo of Jane Doe's scar. I zoomed in and when I was happy that it would give Tai a good view I wrote up a quick email and attached the image. I sent it off.

I put my phone back into my pocket and got into my car. I wasn't worried about New York. I was worried about figuring out who this Jane Doe was. I sat in the car for a minute and looked at the clock on the dash. It was just after one. I thought about heading back home or maybe to the beach. It was a warm day and quiet for a Monday. Strolling on the beach can get the rusted gears in the brain moving.

But every minute I wasn't working on this case had me worried. I didn't want to sit around and wait for something to happen. I decided to call JR, see if he had something. Surely the fingerprints or dental records would have come in by now or would be in any minute.

I fished out my phone and dialed Roberts.

"How's Nancy?" he answered.

"Dead," I said.

"And you killed her."

"Well, that was not really proven in court," I said, in all seriousness.

And it hadn't been. I really hadn't looked into it much. I'd never before been into punk and the real Sid Vicious and his winning life hadn't really interested me.

"What can I do for you, Ant-Man?" he asked, and I could hear the smirk behind his voice.

"Really, now you're going to use Ant-Man as my moniker?" I asked.

"Hey, you make it difficult. Tony's off the table, Ant just seems stupid. Nothing else much can be done with Anthony. Maybe An, or Thony. Ah, that gives me an idea, how about Thorny, that suits."

"It suits you," I said. "As a thorn in my side."

"What's up?"

"Jane Doe. I'd like to get a name so we can move on figuring out what happened to her. Do you have one for me?"

"No. Dental records have come back negative for LA and the state. Beast is now asking about the fingerprints, problem is, they're a little backed up. Promised we'd get something by the end of the day."

"That's unhelpful."

"Not really. Don't know if you had a look at her teeth..."

"I didn't."

"Well, they were perfect and brilliantly white. She's had good dental care in her life..."

"So she's definitely seen a dentist and yet there are no dental records in California for her. She could possibly be an out of towner," I said.

"Exactly. Sometimes the lack of information is in itself informative."

"Those dental records came back quick. We used to have to wait days for it, sometimes weeks."

"Yeah, well, that's AI for you now. It'll flag a small handful of potential matches and then the forensic odontologist determines which match is the one. Takes, as you can imagine, days and weeks off the work."

"Yeah, but how accurate is it?"

"Ninety-nine point nine nine percent accurate. That's more accurate than most trained odontologists, Anthony."

"What about a national dental records repository. I know we didn't have anything like that back in the day. But what about now. Like fingerprints."

"Afraid not, California only got a statewide repository a few years ago as AI came along and made it easier to manage. The feds haven't done anything like that."

"No surprise," I said.

"But seeing as how itchy you are to help out. Why don't you come down to the station and keep Sonny company as we look through the many hours of tape. That's going to take some time."

I didn't say anything for a minute. I was thinking about it. I didn't really want to sit in a police station for an hour or two and watch nothing happen at the dump. But the alternative wasn't much better.

"You don't care for my gracious offer," said Roberts.

"No, I like it. I'll swing on by. The usual puzzle palace?"

"Yeah."

El Camino Real

Roberts mostly worked out of the North Hollywood Station on Burbank Boulevard. That's called the usual. Sometimes he'll be out of Hollywood Station on North Wilcox. Neither were too far from where I lived in Santa Monica, but both were a bit closer to where I was in Echo Park. Hollywood Station being the closer of the two. Roberts just preferred North Hollywood Station to Hollywood Station because it had better facilities and there was always an office available with a couple of computer terminals for visiting 'dignitaries' as Roberts had kiddingly called himself at one time.

I knew my way there, but this being LA, you're advised to use AI mapping software to avoid the yahoos getting into fender benders and backing up traffic all over the place.

I turned down the AC because I was getting too cold and opened up my maps app. It had me on the one oh one as being the fastest route. Under fifteen minutes. I put it in my phone holder attached to a vent and plugged it into the cigarette lighter and started off. The one oh one is also known as El Camino Real, The Royal Road or The King's Highway. At least for the six hundred or so mile portion that connects the twenty-one Spanish missions in California.

If you know anything about our history with the Native Americans then something like the missions shouldn't be celebrated. So I call it the one oh one.

The one oh one dumped me out onto Burbank and just off of that was the station. There was ample parking. I pulled my jalopy into the first stall I saw and got out of the car. I walked into the station and greeted the desk sergeant.

"You know where you're going?" he asked.

I nodded and he buzzed me in. In the far corner of the building someplace were where a couple of offices often lay empty. That's likely where I'd find JR and Sonny.

Sgt. Hanford Timbal, the desk sergeant, is a weaselly looking man with pinched features. By that I mean that he looks like someone with very big hands took his face at birth while it was still wet clay and pinched it towards the front like a snout and left it that way.

But looks can be deceiving. Timbal is an average-looking man, if you can get past his pinched features, of average height. He's friendly and very congenial and looks more like a sniveling accountant than a policeman. But I've seen him involved in skirmishes more than once and he's a man I'd have on my side in a fight, that's for sure.

I walked down a hallway and then another one, peeking into the open doorways looking for Johnny Rotten and Sonny. I found them at the second to last office at the end just before the hallway ended. It was a decent sized office and there was room for the three of us in there quite comfortably.

They were both sitting down and looking at a monitor. I was perpendicular to the monitor and couldn't see anything. Roberts looked up at me and nodded.

"Good timing, we've just started. Pull up a chair."

I rolled over a small bar stool on wheels with a cushioned round seat that was in the corner. There was a bigger chair available but I didn't feel like pushing it around. I sat down and looked at what they were looking at. The video was timestamped at just after three in the morning when I started looking at it. It also had a little "6X" in the top corner opposite from the timestamp information on the original. It looked like it was being viewed at about six times the normal speed.

"This is going to take a while," said Sonny. "About three hours for both cameras."

"Judging from the timestamp it looks like you only started about ten to fifteen minutes ago," I replied.

Sonny nodded, keeping his eye on the monitor.

"I don't think it'll take us three hours to find what we need," I said.

"Depends what there is to be seen," said Sonny.

"Well, no," I said. "We've got the video from two a.m. until noon, right?"

Roberts nodded.

"That's three hours to view the tape on both cameras at six times normal speed. But I doubt that body was dumped anytime during daylight hours. I figure we'll find something by six a.m. latest."

"Right," said Sonny. "Hadn't thought about that, just doing the math on the amount of tape."

"I have come bearing gifts of good news and myrrh," I said, grinning.

Roberts smiled. We watched the monitor in silence. Nothing was happening. I mean, literally nothing. We were coming up on four that morning when we saw Arshile enter the frame of the front-facing camera. Sonny slowed it down to normal speed. It appeared Arshile was just having a smoke. He moved across the camera's view and then disappeared off to the right. He was gone for a few minutes and when he came back the only thing missing was the cigarette in his mouth.

"Maybe he just went out to have a smoke and take a piss," said Sonny.

"Something like that," said Roberts.

We watched in silence again for a few more minutes. Sonny had sped the video track up to six times again.

"You were going to figure out what that scar near her groin meant," said Roberts. "Any luck?"

I shook my head.

"Remember Limewater?" I asked Roberts.

He nodded.

"Yeah, that dive bar we visited a few times back in the day breaking up fights and arresting assholes. Down in Echo Park, right?"

I nodded.

"Yeah, it's trying to gentrify itself like the rest of Echo Park. I wouldn't call it upscale but it's a place you could take Jenn to and she wouldn't feel bad about it."

"Interesting," said Roberts, nodding noncommittally. "But probably not happening. Echo Park and I have too much history."

"The whole place just seems unsteady, like a bum that's showered and changed at his local Y before heading out for another bender."

Roberts frowned.

"What the fuck are you talking about?" he asked.

"Echo Park and it's gentrification. Doesn't seem reliable," I said.

Roberts nodded.

"Right, but I thought we were talking about Jane Doe's scar," he said.

"We are. Limewater is where I met Limey and Brick."

Roberts nodded.

"And what did they have to say about it? Have they seen something like it before?" Roberts asked.

I shook my head.

"No, they couldn't help. I called my guy in the FBI," I said.

"Tai?"

"Yeah, he said he'll look into it and get back to me. I texted the image to him."

We were both watching the monitor.

"He also mentioned New York to me," I said.

"Yeah, I'm sorry about that, Sid, that turned into a real cluster fuck."

I shrugged.

"We couldn't have known. But he said the bodies of those two assholes who murdered So-yi had been found on a garbage barge and now the FBI's looking into that."

"Why would they care? There wasn't terrorism associated with them, right?"

I shrugged.

"Who knows, there's a lot that's going on there that we don't know about. I told you about Albert Camus who called me, right?"

Roberts nodded.

"The philosopher?" asked Sonny. "Isn't he dead?"

"Yeah, the guy was using it as a pseudonym, clearly. The French philosopher's been dead since nineteen sixty."

Sonny nodded.

"He told me they'd take care of the justice. He practically apologized about those two plumbers," I said, putting "plumbers" in air quotes. "Anyway, I got the sense that this was bigger and deeper than just a couple of yahoos."

"I remember," said Roberts.

"Well, maybe the FBI's got some information on this group," I said.

"What were they called?" asked Roberts.

I shrugged.

"They worked out of a plumbing outfit called Pipe Dreams, but clearly that was a front. The larger organization seemed to be called Muspell Logistics, but I've got a feeling that's a holding company for these so-called legitimate businesses. Hans, from Assegai told me he'd worked with those two assholes in South America when they were working for an outfit called Red Blade. That outfit I'm pretty sure is legitimate. Anyway, it's not my problem now. I'll let the FBI handle it."

Roberts nodded. He was looking at me.

"You must be pleased that those assholes got their just desserts," he said.

"It is gratifying," I replied.

"But I have a suspicion that you already knew that justice had been served."

"First I'm hearing about it," I said.

"Right," said Roberts, grinning at me.

We both looked back at the monitor. Nothing was happening. I looked up at the top right and the time was five fifteen. I didn't think we'd been talking for more than a handful of minutes.

"Can you just stop it for a minute?" I asked.

Sonny paused the video.

"Do you notice the time, it's reading five seventeen. The last time I recall seeing the time was around four twenty or thereabouts. Did we miss anything, because I don't think we were talking for all that long."

Sonny looked at the time.

"I don't think so. I've been looking at it pretty much the whole time."

I looked at Roberts.

"Can't say I was paying close attention while we were talking," he said.

"Would you mind going back to, say, four twenty, just for my own edification?"

"Sure," said Sonny, and he started to wind it back at ten times. This caused the video to skip back in chunks. He was able to stop it at four thirteen.

"That's great, Sonny, thanks."

He started again playing it forward at six times the speed. I wasn't looking at the video so much as the time in the corner of the screen. The video was pretty much a still image. The only indication that time was moving was a tree branch with leaves that was in the upper right corner that you could see moving now and then with the wind.

At four thirty seven the time jumped ahead to five oh three.

"Stop," I said. "Did you see that?"

"See what?" asked Sonny.

They were so focused on the video that they weren't paying attention to the time.

"Go back to four thirty-five slowly."

Sonny started rolling back the time at two times the speed. He got to four thirty-five and stopped.

"Ok, now go forward at just regular speed and watch what happens at four thirty-seven."

Sonny hit play. The two minutes went by excruciatingly slowly.

"Watch the time stamp," I said, leaning in and pointing at the read out in the upper right of the monitor.

At four thirty-seven the time suddenly jumped to five oh three.

"Son of a gun," exclaimed Sonny.

He reversed the tape again and played it forward a few more times.

"I can't tell by the video image that anything changes," he said. "You have to look at the time."

I nodded.

"Exactly, nothing much happening on the video feed. A slight disturbance in the tree leaves on that branch there if you look carefully, but that could be explained away by a wind gust," I said.

"Well done, Sid," said Roberts.

We went back and forth over the time from around four thirty-six to around five oh five and nothing came into the video view.

"That's probably the time that whoever it was, came by to dump off Jane Doe," I said.

Roberts nodded.

"Now we know the time, let's take a look at the rear camera," Roberts said.

Missing Minutes

S onny opened up the other file from the desktop. He had saved all four flash drives to the desktop before I had made it to the Station. It started at two a.m. just like the other camera and Sonny scrubbed ahead to around four in the morning according to the time stamp. Then he fast forwarded it around six times again and stopped it just after four thirty-five. From there we watched it play at normal speed and just after four thirty-seven and some seconds the timestamp jumped ahead to five oh three.

The rear camera was just as difficult to see the break in time as no movement was happening in the frame unless you looked very closely and carefully at the trees on the left side of this frame.

We looked closely at the minute or two on each side of the break in time, hoping to grab a glimpse of tail lights or headlights on either camera. It was a hail Mary to no avail. Whoever had deleted that portion of the video had been very careful to delete any indication that a vehicle was arriving or leaving.

"Well, at least we know around what time the body was dropped at the dump," said Roberts.

"Yeah, that's helpful and it makes sense. It's pretty quiet around that time. But it's not all that helpful," I said. "No vehicle description let alone a license plate, and still no name for our Jane Doe."

"If it was all handed to us on a platter, Anthony, there wouldn't be much crime to be solved," said Roberts. "Besides, we have a lead."

I nodded.

"Arshile," said Sonny.

Roberts nodded.

"Yeah," said Roberts, turning to me. "I want you and Beast, when he gets here, to go and speak with Arshile again. I'd bet he took care of the deletion, and even if he didn't, he knows more than he's telling us."

I nodded.

"What about me?" asked Sonny.

"I want you to finish reviewing the whole video feed both back and front cameras from start to finish."

Sonny nodded with an upturned mouth. He wasn't hiding his displeasure.

"And to make it even more interesting, Sonny, I want you to start from the beginning and make careful note of anything anomalous on the video feed. Any person or vehicle or anything of note that comes into view, jot down the time and a brief note about it."

"Great. This is what I live for," said Sonny.

"I know it's not glamorous but it's necessary," said Roberts.

As he and Sonny were bickering back and forth, Beast entered the room and our focus changed to him. Beast was grinning.

"I come bearing gifts," he said, and in his hand he was carrying a piece of paper. He gave it to Roberts, who then gave it to me.

"We have found out who our Jane Doe is," he said. "Suzanne Valadon."

I looked at the sheet. It was a booking sheet that had a black and white image of her face. She was attractive and she was our Jane Doe. It had her fingerprints and other details. Her date of birth was the twenty-seventh of June nineteen ninety-six which made her twenty-three. There was an address in Provo, Utah and her parents were Christopher and Anissa Valadon. Suzanne was five feet five inches tall and weighed one hundred and ten pounds.

I took out my phone and took a picture of the sheet for reference. Then I handed it back to Beast.

"The fingerprints came through," said Roberts.

Beast nodded.

"Yeah, she and a couple of friends were pulled over in twenty fifteen for joy riding and DUI. They were apparently smoking a joint at the time. They were lucky not to have been given any time, but the judge fined them a thousand bucks each and they had to do a hundred hours community service."

Roberts nodded.

"Good work. Our plans have now changed. I want you and Sonny to go and visit Arshile. and Sid, see if you can't get in touch with the parents and find out how she came to be in LA when she's from Utah."

"That's fucking great, so I've gotta do the death notice," I said.

"Well, yeah. You've always been good at that sort of thing. You have a soft way about you that the grieved seem to respond to."

"Doesn't mean I like it," I said.

Roberts ignored me.

"What did you guys find?" asked Beast.

"There's about thirty minutes of footage missing from both front and rear cameras that we got from Arshile. From around four thirty to five or so. I've got a feeling Arshile deleted those portions before we got there, and if that's the case, he knows more than he's letting on. Sonny will fill you in."

Sonny nodded, grinning.

"This is not a bye," said Roberts. "This just means you'll need to review the tapes thoroughly when you get back. And Beast can help you. One of you do the front, and one do the rear. Won't take so long then."

"You and Carrick saw Gorky. Where is he today? Work or home?" asked Beast.

"He's not at work. The rest I'll leave up to you two fine detectives to figure out," said Roberts. "Let's get to it."

Provo to Palm Springs

I waited until Beast and Sonny had left to seek out Gorky. Then I turned to Roberts.

"Want to give me your credentials so I can find out where the Valadons are in Provo, if they're even still there."

"No, but I'll sign in and you can drive," said Roberts.

And that's what he did. He signed into his LAPD account and then offered me the seat while he stood behind me and observed. Was a time when he wasn't always hovering over me like a dad. But that was a time when we worked together and I was still seen favorably within the LAPD. Those days were over.

I was lucky in that the names, Christopher and Anissa Valadon were unusual enough that I thought there wouldn't be that many hits on the database for those names. Still, I chose just Utah for my first go around.

I typed in Christopher Valadon and got three hits. One was a man in his fifties that could have been the right age to be Suzanne's father. However, he was married to a Rebecca. Neither of the other two in Utah seemed related to her either. The second was in his seventies and the other one was from Salt Lake City and he was twenty-five.

Next I chose the whole of the continental USA and searched for Christopher Valadon. That time I got over two dozen hits. I briefly looked through them but figured it was too time consuming. I tried the mother's name. I figured an Anissa Valadon was a rarer combination than a Christopher Valadon and I was right. I only got five hits.

I looked through the names. Two were in the eastern states and neither were married to a Christopher. One of them was in her early thirties which was too young to have a twenty-three year old daughter. The other was the right age but out of Connecticut and married to a Kimberly Paylor.

A third Anissa Valadon was in Wyoming and she was a widowed, eighty-three year old woman. A fourth was from Minnesota and in her late twenties which couldn't have been Suzanne's mother and she was also single. The fifth Anissa Valadon seemed to be the correct one. She was married to a Christopher Valadon. She was née Mills and she was forty-three. Her husband, Christopher, was forty-five. They were the right age to have a daughter aged twenty-three although it meant they were young when they started.

Still, they were the only match that seemed like the next of kin. They were however, now living in Palm Springs. In a way I understood that. If they'd known their daughter had left for Los Angeles then moving out to Palm Springs made sense. But then the question was, why Palm Springs and not Los Angeles? That was a good question, Anthony, and one you could ask them in person.

"That looks like the right people," said Roberts, following me along my searching.

I nodded. I wrote down their address and telephone numbers on a pad of paper, tore it off and put it in my pocket.

"The thing is, if you know your daughter has moved out to LA, why not come out to LA? Why move to Palm Springs?"

"Because it's better," said Roberts.

"Depends what you're looking for. If you're looking for smaller, then yeah, it's better. If you're looking for culture then, no, it's not."

"Maybe they're retired and just wanted to be closer to their daughter. She is an adult, Sid, it's not like they're seeking out their troubled teenager."

"That's the thing, maybe she was a troubled teenager."

"This is why we do what we do, Sid, to find answers to these questions."

"And if they're retired, they're young to be retiring. They're a little younger than us," I said.

Roberts shrugged.

"Well, if you're moving to Palm Springs, you've obviously got some resources, unless you're working there. It's not a cheap place to live, Sid."

I nodded and stood up.

"I guess I will find out. Thanks for this. I'm really looking forward to telling another set of parents that their daughter is dead."

Roberts grinned.

"It's the nature of the beast," he said. "Besides, you do have a way with the grieved."

"So does Sonny," I said.

"Not the same way you do. Listen, Sid, it's really not punishment, but I think you're the best one for it. More than that, I trust you in sussing out the situation at home to see if there's anything the parents might know that they might not want to share, if you know what I mean."

I nodded. I did.

"Alright, I'll head out. I'm probably looking at a good hour and a half, two hour drive. Might as well get going now."

"Godspeed, Anthony," said Roberts, grinning.

"You're an ass," I said, grinning back.

I left the station and got into my car. I typed the address into my maps app and started off. I wasn't sure what I was going to say to them. And if they were decent folk they'd probably want to come back into LA to see for themselves that their daughter was dead. At least that's what I would want to do. As a bonus, maybe they'd know something about the scar.

The Interstate 210 was the route taking me out of LA, and my maps app was telling me I had almost two hours to go. I didn't mind driving on the main highways. Not when they were smooth sailing, and they were at this time. It was just after two thirty in the afternoon and the sky was blue and I was feeling pretty good for a man sent to tell parents their daughter was dead.

I started listening to KJAZZ but quickly thought better of it. I wasn't sure how reception would be along my route. Instead I pushed play on my CD player for some lucky surprise. I couldn't remember what CD I had in there. I grinned, hoping for the best. Alternatively it would have been back to KJAZZ.

I recognized the song immediately from its energetic piano plonking along with an urgency. It was Blue Rondo à la Turk, the opening track to one of the best jazz albums of all time. It was Time Out by the Dave Brubeck Quartet. It was only around forty minutes long, but those forty minutes moved your soul.

I'd worry about what I was going to listen to for the remaining hour and a bit after I'd been to church and finished listening to the sermon according to Dave. I relaxed and put a feather on the pedal as fancier cars than I was driving sped by. The music was putting me in exactly the kind of mood I needed in order to feel good about what I was up to.

And why shouldn't I feel good about it? The message was about the ugliness of humanity, but Roberts was right. I was probably the right person to deliver it. I had received commendations more than once for how I had interacted and aided grieved loved ones while on the job. I was feeling pretty good for a man with a depressing mission.

Jim Beam

Arshile Gorky lived in an apartment complex called The Blue Moon. It was located close to the Calabasas dump in a mixed neighborhood called Canoga Park. It looked like something out of the fifties or sixties. A place for young singles or young families just getting their start in life. This was just a stepping stone on their journey towards the upper class and becoming captains of industry and Hollywood stars. How dreams are shattered.

That's the impression you got walking up to the white and blue building that had not lived up to that promise. The lawn out front was patchy and the paint on the building was showing its age. Bits of it were peeling and some of it was cracked.

But none of this was of much note to Beast and Sonny as they parked their car and walked up the front path to the main door. It was a three story building and Gorky lived in three oh five. Beast pushed the button to call three oh five. It didn't take long before it was answered.

"Hello," came the reply.

"Detectives Beeves and Forrest, LAPD Homicide. We'd like to speak with Mr. Arshile Gorky," said Beast.

"Yes, detectives. Please come on in. I'm on the third floor."

Beast nodded. The main door buzzed open and Beeves and Forrest walked into the main lobby. From there they opened up a second set of doors and entered a hallway.

"Which side do you think he's on?" asked Sonny.

"Your guess is as good as mine," said Beast.

"When in doubt turn right," said Sonny, grinning.

Beeves shrugged and they turned right down the hallway and walked to the end where they found the stairs through a closed door. They walked up all three flights and just as they came out onto the third floor, three oh five was on their right. Forrest grinned.

"When in doubt, turn right," repeated Beeves. "Worked this time."

"Works more times than it doesn't," said Forrest.

Forrest knocked on the door and very shortly after it was opened by Gorky. Gorky was in baggy gray sweatpants, a pair of white socks and a white t-shirt with a neon art deco print of a palm tree with a pink sunset behind it. Looked right out of the eighties.

"Please come in," said Gorky, smiling all the time at the two officers. His left hand was outstretched towards the interior of his apartment. His breath sent rumors of liquor, perhaps whiskey.

Beeves and Forrest walked in. It was a short hallway with a kitchen on the left and storage on the right. Beyond that was a living area that had both a couch and armchair and a small dining table with four chairs around it. The dining area was first, the couch was towards the wall and a bank of windows which looked out onto a balcony which overlooked the car pad behind the apartment. The balcony was accessed through a door to the right, close to the wall. The same wall that the TV was up against. The couch and armchair were up against the opposite wall.

The TV was on a TV stand that contained a DVD player on a shelf underneath along with a cable box and a couple of small speakers. Next to the TV was a small side table with a couple of bottles of liquor on it and a few cloudy glasses.

Gorky led the detectives into the living area and pointed at the couch.

"Please have a seat on the couch," he said.

Beeves and Forrest went and sat down on an old gray couch and practically sank to the floor. The springs were shot and the couch was stained. Beeves didn't lean back on account of what he considered was filth. He leaned forward on his knees. As uncomfortable as Forrest who was resting against the back of the couch.

The apartment smelled of old stale smoke with a hint of fried bacon underneath it. Gorky went to the armchair which was on the closer side to the apartment door than the balcony. He picked up a glass tumbler that had about a quarter of an inch of tea colored liquor in it.

"It's five o'clock somewhere," he said, grinning. "I don't suppose I can interest yous in a splash of warmth."

Beeves and Forrest both shook their heads.

"Water?" he asked. "I could probably brew some coffee too."

"Good as we are," said Beeves, stiff as a board on the couch.

Gorky went over to the side table and opened up a bottle of Jim Beam Devil's Cut with a label that said as much upon what looked like a wooden background. Forrest noticed there was only about a quarter of the liquor left in the bottle. He also noticed that after Gorky had put in three ice cubes that were held in an ice bucket on that same side table, that he drowned them in the liquor.

Gorky returned to the arm chair and sat down on it. He raised his glass to Beeves and Forrest. Forrest noticed it was just after three and already Gorky had a slight slur.

"So what can I do yous for?" he asked, picking up a packet of Lucky Strike cigarettes, taking one out and sticking it into his mouth. He raised his free hand after putting the packet of cigarettes back on a round table to the left of him. "Wait, let me guess. Yous found out her name," he said, grinning.

He reached out for a Zippo lighter he had on that same table. It had barbed wire as a motif. He used it to light his cigarette. He put it back down.

"Shit, sorry, man," said Gorky. "Can I offer any of yous a smoke?" He picked up the packet of cigarettes and offered them to Beeves and Forrest. They turned him down.

Forrest was trying to figure out the use of "yous" by Gorky. He hadn't spoken like that yesterday when they had briefly interviewed him. He figured it must be the alcohol talking.

Gorky took a long drag on his cigarette and blew out a stream of bluish gray smoke as he tried to also add smoke rings to it.

"We are here to talk to you about our Jane Doe," said Forrest.

Gorky nodded, took a sip of his whiskey and looked at Forrest.

"You got her name?" he asked.

Forrest nodded.

"Suzanne Valadon. Does that ring a bell?" he asked.

Gorky looked up towards the ceiling. A ceiling with a couple of old, dry stains on it and a film of yellow nicotine.

"Can't say's I know anybody by that name," he said.

"You remember who dropped her off at the dump?" asked Beeves, who wasn't interested in beating around the bush. The sooner he was out of this cesspool of an apartment the better.

Gorky looked at him and frowned. Then he looked at his brown liquor which was resting in his hand and upon his thigh. He swirled it around a bit and then decided to take another sip.

"I used to buy the White Label bourbon," he said, nodding his head towards the almost empty bottle on the side table that he had forgotten to screw the cap back on to. "It's about seven, eight bucks cheaper than this here Devil's Cut. But, boy howdy, do those extra bucks make a difference to the taste. That's not to say the White Label ain't bad. I'm just saying for a few bucks more it's a lot tastier. Well worth the extra cheddar if you can spring for it. It all has to do with the extra care and aging it gets. And you'd expect that from a company like JBs, the oldest distillery in America. Founded in..."

"I can see you know a lot about whiskey," interrupted Forrest, "but I'm more interested in what you know about who dropped off Ms. Valadon early on Sunday morning."

Gorky looked at the glass he held in his hand resting the bottom of it on his thigh. He slowly shook his head while taking a drag on his cigarette. He looked up at Beeves and Forrest.

"I didn't see anything. He must have come by when I was on my security walk," he said. "Like I told the other two, I have to do my security checks every ninety minutes. He coulda just been waiting until he seen me leave the box."

"So you're saying you didn't see anybody slip by you who might have been driving a vehicle that could carry a body without anyone seeing?" asked Forrest.

"No, sir. It's like I said. I didn't see nothing."

"You know it's a crime to lie to the police during an investigation. That's called obstruction and can get you into jail."

Gorky nodded and took another sip of his whiskey.

"So I'm going to give you one last chance to come clean," said Forrest. "Who got by you and why did you let them?"

Gorky was looking at the glass that he kept resting on his thigh. The tumbler was starting to sweat, much like how Gorky was feeling. He took another long pull on his cigarette and blew it out towards the ceiling, gazing at the stains and the faces he could see in the popcorn. Then he shrugged.

"I dunno what to tell yous. I didn't see nothing."

"If you didn't see nothing," said Beeves, starting to get frustrated, "that means you saw something. What was it?"

"Man, why the two of yous hassling me? I didn't do nothing," said Gorky.

"I've had enough of this shit," said Beeves.

Forrest put his hand up to calm his colleague.

"Ok," said Forrest. "I'll toss you an easy one. Why is there around a half hour missing from the tapes you gave the other officers? And the same time is missing from both the front and rear cameras."

Gorky didn't say anything, he took a sip of his drink. It was going down quick and easy.

"Maybe it was a glitch. That sometimes happens."

Beeves stood up.

"Arshile Gorky, I'm arresting you for obstruction of justice. We're going down to the station where you can answer our questions."

Beeves started to walk towards him. Forrest had also gotten up from the couch by this time.

Coming Clean

" Ok, ok, man. I'll tell yous what happened."

He took another drag on his cigarette.

"I'm waiting," said Beeves.

"Ok, man. Geez. This guy drove up in a van. He almost caught me napping. I told him the dump was closed, that it wouldn't open until eight. He told me it couldn't wait. His boss had told him to get rid of a small TV that evening. Said he'd lose his job if he couldn't get rid of it. I told him I was sorry, but the dump was closed."

Gorky looked down at his drink and decided to take another sip.

"Then what happened?" asked Forrest.

Gorky didn't look at him.

"He pointed a gun at me and said we could do this the easy way or the hard way. He also took an envelope out of his jacket pocket and held it with his other hand. He waved the gun at me and said this is the hard way. Fifteen slugs with your name on it. Then he waved the envelope at me and said this is the easy way. One hundred Benjamins with your name on them. No questions asked, no answers given. So what'll it be?"

Gorky took his last pull on his cigarette and squashed it out on an ashtray that contained its fallen comrades. He blew smoke out from his mouth and nostrils and continued talking.

"What would you do? I took the money. I don't get paid enough to be a hero at my job," he said.

"So you didn't even wonder why a guy was determined to drop off a TV in the middle of the night either by force or by blackmail?" asked Beeves.

"Yeah, of course I wondered about that, but like I said, I wasn't about to be a hero."

"What happened next?" asked Forrest. He and Beeves were still standing.

"I took the envelope and he drove past me. Twenty minutes or so later he came back. He got out of the van and came into my booth, still waving that gun in my face."

"What kind of gun was it?" asked Beeves.

"I dunno. A handgun, big and black."

"Carry on," said Forrest.

"Well, he told me to erase the footage from the cameras. And he watched me while I did it to make sure I did it properly. Then he got back into the van and left."

"That means that it should have caught the back end of him when he left, but it didn't," said Beeves. "Why not?"

"He looked at his watch and he told me to make sure it only started to record again at five oh three. He left at five and the recording only started again at five oh three like he'd told me."

"Why didn't you just start it again as soon as he left so that it would capture something?" asked Forrest.

"I had set it up to erase from the time he said until five oh three. You can do that with the software, set it up so it doesn't record until a certain time."

"What time did he want you to start the erasure?" asked Forrest.

"Four thirty-seven. That was just before he came up round the corner towards me."

"What did this guy look like?" asked Beeves.

"Hard to say. I think he was wearing a disguise," said Gorky.

"Do your best to describe him," said Beeves.

"He was about my height..."

"How tall is that?"

"Five ten, five eleven," said Gorky. "He wore a black turtleneck and black pants with black boots and black gloves. He had black curly hair and a black beard. He wore black shades. That should have been my first clue something was strange. Though his eyes were blue. At one point he rubbed his eyes and the sunglasses lifted up enough for me to see his eyes. Average looking other than that."

"What makes you think he was wearing a disguise?" asked Forrest.

"His beard and hair were perfect. More than that, they seemed blacker than what you'd expect. And his eyebrows weren't as black as his hair or beard. And have yous ever met someone with blue eyes with black hair, black as coal, unless they've dyed it? Even just with the sunglasses it'd be tough to identify him."

Beeves and Forrest didn't say anything to that.

"Did he have any scars, missing fingers, tattoos, et cetera?" asked Forrest.

Gorky shook his head and drank down the last of his whiskey. For a man who seemed to have tied one on his speech wasn't as slurred as you'd expect.

"Well, there was one thing. His nose was thick and a little skew like he'd had it broken before. Then there was his ears. They looked all messed up like he was a wrestler or something. Maybe MMA." Gorky shrugged.

"That's helpful," said Forrest, trying to encourage Gorky to give them whatever he remembered. "Now tell me what sort of vehicle he was in when he arrived."

"It was a white Ford Transit van. The smaller one. Though yous could fit a few bodies in the back if you wanted."

"Tell me the license plate number on it," said Beeves.

"I didn't see the license plate number."

"What do you mean, you saw the van coming and leaving. Did it have plates on it or not?"

"Yes, it had plates, but they'd been covered up with duct tape."

Gorky was feeling uncomfortable with Beeves and Forrest hovering over him like helicopter parents.

"Was the van just plain white or was it a business van. Did it have any writing or logos on it?"

Gorky nodded.

"Yeah, the van belonged to a company called 'Lemonade Laundry'. There was a tagline too. I remember on account of how it made no sense to me."

"And what was that?" asked Forrest.

"Easy squeezy lemon cleany," he said.

"What colors? Were there any logos?" asked Forrest.

Gorky shook his head.

"No. The whole thing was just in this green and yellow, like a lemon yellow. The o in the lemonade was a whole lemon. That was all."

"Was the decal or writing on this van curved or stylized or was it just all written straight horizontally?" asked Forrest.

"All straight. The 'Lemonade Laundry' was in bigger writing and the tagline was underneath it. The o in the lemon of the tagline was also a lemon."

"Was it also colored yellow like a lemon?" asked Forrest.

Gorky nodded. Beeves and Forrest had their little notebooks out and they were taking notes. Forrest showed Gorky his notebook.

"Did it look something like that?"

Gorky looked at the logo that Forrest had tried to create from what he'd heard.

"Yeah, about like that but the letters were thicker and had, I dunno, like little hooks on them or something."

"Draw the first word, 'Lemonade' to give me an idea," said Forrest.

Gorky took the notebook and started writing on it.

"I'm not a good drawer, but this is kinda what I meant."

He handed the notebook back to Forrest. Beeves leaned in to have a look. The L was capitalized, the rest of the letters in the word were in lowercase. All the letters appeared to be serif fonts with a serif wedge at the end of the lower bar of the capitalized L. The way Gorky had drawn the letters looked very much like your garden variety serif font. A Times New Roman or Baskerville font type. It wasn't much to go on but it was something.

"So you took a ten grand bribe to let a guy drop a dead body at your dump," said Beeves, with bile in his throat.

Gorky shook his head.

"Look, I swear. I didn't know he was gonna leave a body behind. All he said..."

"Was he wanted to dump a TV and you believed him," added Beeves.

"No, it wasn't like that at all. I mean, I didn't believe he wanted to dump a TV, but I never, in a million years, thought it was a body. Sometimes folks come and they want to drop off some chemicals or other hazardous waste like that and they'll give me a couple hundred bucks. That's all I thought he was up to."

Gorky's eyes were getting wet. Maybe he did have a conscience after all.

"You're telling me that a guy waves a gun in your face and tells you this money or your life and you think he's just dropping off some chemicals or paints?" asked Beeves. Beeves was not hiding his displeasure with Gorky.

Gorky nodded, his eyes still wet.

"Yeah, that's exactly what I thought. I've never met a murderer before, okay."

"Really, Mr. Gorky?" said Forrest. "A guy hands you ten grand or threatens to kill you and you think he's the same as the other jokers handing you two hundred bucks on the DL to look the other way. Have any of them ever threatened you with a handgun?"

Gorky shook his head.

"When you put it like that, maybe I should've thought something more was going on. But man, yous gotta understand, I was scared and I didn't really want to think about it. I never had a gun shoved in my face before."

Beeves and Gorky looked at each other.

"You know we can charge you with being an accessory to murder after the fact," said Forrest.

Gorky didn't look at them. They still hovered over him and he felt uncomfortable. He reached for another cigarette instead and lit it.

"I'm telling yous. I swear to God I didn't know nobody had been killed," he said.

"Somebody," said Forrest.

"Huh," said Gorky.

"You didn't know that somebody had been killed, not nobody."

Gorky didn't say anything to that.

"What happened to the money?" asked Beeves.

"I kept it. After I found the body like I told yous, I knew what had happened."

"And what was that?" asked Beeves.

"That the guy who had threatened me with the gun must have murdered the girl and dumped her where I found her."

"And you didn't want to tell us that at the time," said Beeves.

"I was scared. I didn't know what to do. I'm sorry. You gotta understand, I don't make a lot of money. I'm barely keeping my head above water and my mother's sick. Her medicine costs a thousand bucks a month and all she has is her pension. I know I done a bad thing, but yous gotta believe me I had no idea that anybody had been murdered."

Neither Beeves nor Forrest were feeling sympathetic.

"Go get the money," said Beeves.

Gorky got up and squeezed his way past the armchair and Beeves. Beeves followed him into his bedroom where Gorky took an envelope out from his sock drawer and put it into a plastic bag Beeves was holding out. Then they went back out to the main area and Gorky stood with the two men.

"We're going to take this downtown and see if we can't get it fingerprinted."

"I told yous he was wearing gloves," said Gorky.

"Yeah, but did you see him put the money in the envelope?" asked Forrest.

"And then we're going to have a talk with our Captain and see what we're going to charge you with."

"Shit, man."

"But you've been forthright now and if you continue to be helpful, I'm sure we can sway our Captain for something light. That means you've gotta keep helping us when we need it and you've gotta stay close so we can find you easy. Understand?" asked Forrest.

Gorky nodded.

"We'll show ourselves out," said Forrest, and they left the apartment.

The Long Life

Palm Springs is a desert. It's a dry place that wouldn't be livable without a lot of help from human engineering. And it's come a long way from the early part of last century. It's an idyllic place for a lot of retirees, both straight and gay. Lots of golf, if that's how you like to savage the environment and waste water.

It's an opulent place and decadent. A mostly bucolic escape for the idle rich where the hoi polloi were carefully kept in their place. I didn't like it.

I came in on State Route 111 and jogged off onto Indian Canyon Drive before finding my way onto south second street, more formally known as South Calle El Segundo. That's where the Valadons lived. At least that's the best knowledge I had. I was looking for a complex of two story apartments that called themselves La Larga Vida. I imagined they knew it meant the long life. Perhaps that was optimism or wishful thinking.

The apartment complex wasn't hard to find. They were brown and enclosed by a metal fence. There was visitor parking on the northwest side of the apartment complex. I found a spot and parked my car.

I stepped out and it was hot. My maps app had indicated the temperature to be ninety-two, and it felt like it. I put on my fedora and walked towards a metal gate sandwiched between two adobe styled buttresses. The gate and fence that carried on from the two adobe pillars were only about four feet tall. I could have easily hopped the fence. But I wasn't here to interrogate suspects, I was here to try and soften the news that their daughter had died.

On the left pillar of the gate was a large silver metallic box that had a keypad on it and a display. You could use the keypad like a telephone keypad to search by name or you could just put in the apartment number. Press one to search by name, press two to enter the apartment number. I knew the apartment number so I punched in two, one three three.

I assumed that meant they were on the first of the two floors, but I didn't give it much weight. Assuming often makes an ass out of me. And going by my own Vista Al Mar, apartment one three three might even be a non-existent place.

While I waited, I pulled out my phone and looked at the time. It was just after quarter to five. If they were working they might have finished and could be home by now. I waited for what seemed like an hour. Then I punched the numbers again. This got someone's attention. It was a female's voice.

"Hello," she said.

"Yeah, my name's Anthony Carrick with the LAPD. I'm looking for Christopher or Anissa Valadon."

"What's this about?"

"I'd prefer to speak to them in person," I said.

"How do I know you're really a cop?"

"You don't," I said, looking at the metal box I was speaking at. It didn't look like it had a camera on it, so I couldn't show her my badge I probably shouldn't have kept when I left, though it's come in very handy from time to time.

Silence.

"I tell you what, why don't you call Captain John Roberts from homicide and ask him if I'm with him. You can look up the number online. That's probably best if you don't believe me."

I knew I shouldn't have mentioned homicide as soon as it came out of my yap trap.

"Homicide?" said the voice on the other line. "Is this about my daughter?"

The voice lost its confidence on that last portion of that sentence.

"Like I said, ma'am, I need to speak with Christopher or Anissa Valadon personally."

Some more silence. I was starting to think I'd arrived at a silent retreat.

"Ok, come on in. Follow the path to the end. We're the block of apartments looking out over the pool."

That wasn't helpful. Four blocks of apartments were overlooking the pool. The gate buzzed and I let myself in. I figured she'd meant the block of apartments furthest away from me. I started heading for them. The path happened to travel straight, to the side of the first block of apartments, along the front of the left block and then I arrived at the block facing me. I started traveling down the front of this block of apartments, looking at the numbers.

Three quarters of the way down a door opened up on the main floor and a woman with brown hair peeked out from behind it. I walked towards her. It was apartment one three three. I put my best hail-fellow-well-met smile on my mug.

"Anissa Valadon?" I asked.

She nodded her head. She was around five feet five inches tall and probably weighed just a little less than me. She was plump with short cropped brown hair. She wore very little makeup but she wasn't much to look at. She was in a long dress with a blouse over top. She looked more matronly than motherly and she looked to be in her fifties rather than her early forties.

"Can I see your ID," she said.

"Sure thing," I said, fishing into my front pocket where I had put my badge that, yet again, was becoming helpful. I showed it to her. Most people nodded and you put the badge away again. Not Anissa. She took a close look at it and read my name and my rank. After several seconds, she looked at me and I put my badge away.

"You don't have jurisdiction out here, Detective Carrick," she said.

"No, ma'am, and you're not in trouble. Please call me Anthony," I said. "May I come inside?"

She nodded and opened the door wider. I walked in past her.

"Please call me An, or Ani," she said.

I smiled and nodded. I waited for her to close the door and invite me in further. On the left was a closet and what I presumed was storage, on the right was an open kitchen with an island that was perpendicular to me. In the kitchen was a man who also looked like he was in his fifties. He had thin gray hair parted on the left. He was in jeans and a checkered short-sleeved shirt. He was gaunt and he had a couple days growth of stubble on his face. His eyes looked tired and worn out.

An old nursery rhyme came to mind as I looked at the two of them. Jack Sprat could eat no fat, his wife could eat no lean. This man came over towards me, leaving the bags of groceries he was unpacking on the kitchen island. He held out his hand. I took it. It was warm and strong as iron.

"Christopher Valadon," he said. "Call me Chris." He had maybe a half inch to an inch in height on me.

"Anthony Carrick," I said, "from the LAPD."

He was unmoved.

"Let me unpack these groceries really quick," he said. "There's stuff that needs to be in the freezer. Can I get you some tea or coffee?"

"I'd love a coffee. Two sugars and cream if you've got it."

Christopher nodded and Anissa showed me into the living room where I sat down at a small dining room table with four chairs around it. It took up a portion of the large space. Beyond that was the usual stuff you'd find in a living room. A couch, two armchairs, a large, low rectangular coffee table that had this morning's paper on it as well as a copy of the Book of Mormon and a couple of remotes for the TV hanging on the wall above a small open cabinet containing a cable box and DVD player.

"Let me get you your coffee," said Anissa, and she disappeared back into the kitchen.

I was sitting with my back towards the kitchen and the hallway. I didn't like it. I got up and sat on the opposite side. Not long after, Anissa and Chris came out of the kitchen. Chris was carrying two mugs, he placed one in front of me. It was a plain white mug, nothing fancy. The same as theirs. They sat down. Chris opposite me and Anissa to my left. We were all drinking coffee. Mormons don't usually drink coffee or tea or alcohol. But I'd worked with enough Mormons at the LAPD that I knew not all were as strict following the advice from the Doctrine and Covenants. And in my experience, it appeared that the D&C was more like suggestion rather than prescription. But I was not a Mormon and didn't know much about it to tell if the D&C was prescription or suggestion.

I knew one Mormon cop who drank close to a half gallon of cola each shift. Health wise he'd probably have been better with tea or coffee.

The living room was simple but comfortable. It fit in well with the apartments which also appeared simple and comfortable. For Palm Springs

I was probably in the cheap seats and the Valadon's living setup gave no pretense otherwise.

The furniture appeared comfortable, sturdy and yet not fancy. Nothing was fancy in the Valadon's home. The TV, although being a flatscreen, appeared to be at least five years old. Looking at the two of them even their clothes looked simple, well worn without being tatty and plain. The folks appeared humble or at the very least lacking ostentation. Anissa was looking at me nervously. Any moment she was about to erupt with questions, I was certain of it.

"Is this about Suzy?" she asked.

"Yes, ma'am, I'm afraid it is."

About the best way to give notice of the death of a loved one is to not beat about the bush. Come out with it quickly, softly but truthfully. Then give the bereaved time to digest the information and seek further clarification. That's what I did.

"Your daughter, Suzanne Valadon, was found deceased in Los Angeles," I said. "I am very sorry."

And that was all I said. I had pitched the grenade and now waited for the explosion and how that would go. There was silence for a while. This is not uncommon. I looked from the two of them down to my coffee. Then I took a sip. I had found the one place where the Valadons didn't appear to scrimp and save. The coffee was some of the best coffee I had drunk in living memory. I nursed my cup. I had a lot of questions for them, but now was not my time. They needed time to sit with what I had given.

"Are you sure? Are you sure it's her?" asked Anissa.

"Yes, ma'am. We're quite sure. We matched the fingerprints to an incident in Provo some years ago. Twenty fifteen, I believe it was. Joy riding and drug intoxication due to marijuana. I also have a photograph if you would like to see. But please, I must warn you that it is a morgue photograph and you might not want to see it."

I looked at Christopher, he nodded grimly, which I took to mean that he knew of the Provo incident.

Shadow of Death

66 Yea, though I walk through the valley of the shadow of death, I will fear no evil; For You are with me; Your rod and Your staff, they comfort me," said Anissa.

"Psalms, chapter twenty-three, verse four," said Christopher.

I nodded. Anissa was staring at the wall opposite her. She had her hands around her mug of coffee. There was more silence. It felt like an ocean of silence that could swallow us up and drown us. I kept to my own counsel. Anissa turned to me.

"Can I see the photograph?" she asked. Her eyes were moist but her voice did not crack.

Christopher put his arm on her forearm.

"Are you sure?" he asked his wife. She nodded her head.

"Was it..." and he stumbled on the words coming up and out of him. "It wasn't a violent death, was it?"

He was a man on the verge of overwhelming grief.

"No, sir, there were no signs of violence on your daughter's body. We are still trying to determine the cause of her death."

"Can I see the picture of my baby?" said Anissa, getting strident.

I fished out my phone, opened the app and tapped on the image of her face. I handed the phone to Anissa. She took it and she stared at it for a long time. Then she gave my phone to her husband and the grief shook her and she started to sob. Christopher looked at the photograph. He nodded and slid the phone back towards me.

"Excuse me," he said, and he got up from the table and went into the kitchen where he took down a box of tissues from on top of the fridge and brought it back to the table. He took one for himself and blotted at his eyes. Anissa took a couple. She still shook with the emotional turmoil. I waited.

When you've done this as many times as I have, the large stretches of silence are no longer deafening. Nor are they unexpected or awkward. I just sat and waited. I drank more coffee.

"What happened to her? Where was she found?" asked Christopher, stepping in with questions when his wife was clearly unable to.

"There is a landfill in the northwest part of Los Angeles in an area called Calabasas. She was found, clothed, but without any makeup or jewelry, at the north end of this landfill. As for what happened to her, we are trying to understand that, and when you're ready, I have some questions that could help me understand what happened to her."

"A dump!" sobbed Anissa. "They put her at the dump like garbage!"

She was overcome with her grief.

"We feel that she was placed there with care," I said. Not that it was helpful, but maybe it might be, just a little bit.

Christopher dabbed at his eyes some more. He looked at me through pools of sorrow.

"Was she..." And he choked on the words again. I gave him time.

"Was she... you know, was she... raped?"

He looked down.

"I'm afraid we haven't determined that yet," I said.

"What do you know?" asked Anissa. "You don't know what happened to her, you don't know if she was raped. What do you know?"

I let her express her anger and grief. After some time when I thought she was finished I responded.

"We do know that she died during the early morning hours of Sunday. Her body was found at around noon by security at the landfill doing their rounds. Within the next couple of days we will have a lot of your questions answered."

Anissa took another couple of tissues. She blew her nose, got up from the table and went into the kitchen where she threw out her tissues, put some cookies on a plate and brought them back. Simple chocolate chip cookies. This might seem unusual, but folks handle grief in their own way.

I remember one of my earliest death notices, the wife of the deceased cooked a five course meal and made me wait and eat with her. It was good food which she hardly touched. Grief was a beast of its own. A monster really, and each person's grief was their own unique monster.

"Please have a cookie," said Anissa.

I obliged. Nobody else did. But you don't want to complicate things further. It was the same with that five course meal I told you about earlier. I ate it all.

"What was she dressed in?" asked Anissa, slowly gaining composure.

"She was found in a wine-colored negligee," I said. "Did she own something like that, that you know of?"

Christopher shook his head, but he wasn't likely to know. I looked at Anissa. She slowly shook her head.

"We're Mormon, Mr. Carrick," she said, "and we have sacred undergarments that we wear. Though Suzy didn't."

"And what do those look like, for young women?" I asked.

"They're similar for men and women. White, two-piece garments. The lower garment is pants, for men and women and ends just above the knee and the upper garment has short sleeves like a t-shirt, though Suzy didn't want to partake in the endowment ceremony and our bishop agreed," said Christopher.

"What's the endowment ceremony?" I asked.

"It's to prepare Mormons for the afterlife, but part of the ceremony is that you receive these temple garments," said Christopher. "But Suzy wasn't a great Mormon."

"She was a difficult child then," I said.

Christopher nodded.

"She had always been strong-willed and stubborn. But she was a kind and gentle girl."

I looked at Anissa. She had nothing to offer.

"Were there other incidents like the one in Provo four years ago?" I asked.

Christopher shrugged. He looked over at his wife.

"Not that we're aware, but it wouldn't surprise me, Mr. Carrick. We never allowed any drugs or things of that nature in our home but Suzy had a lot of non-Mormon friends and she spent a lot of time with them."

"You're originally from Utah," I said. "What made you come out here to Palm Springs?"

"We came out here to look for Suzy," said Christopher.

"Did you have reason to believe she was in Palm Springs?" I asked.

Christopher shook his head.

"We heard she had moved out to Los Angeles. She wanted to be an actress," he said.

"So why Palm Springs?"

Christopher looked over at his wife again, but she had nothing she wanted to offer up.

"I don't like big cities, Mr. Carrick. We moved out to Los Angeles in twenty sixteen and lived in Echo Park for about six months. I didn't like it. Big cities are full of worshippers of materialism. We moved out here shortly afterwards and I've spent most of almost every weekend I get off in Los Angeles looking for her."

I nodded and sipped my coffee. I was running out.

"Did you have any idea where she was in Los Angeles, any clues?"

Christopher shook his head.

"We reached out to her best friend just before we left Provo, but all she knew was that Suzy had left for Los Angeles. Jocelyn said Suzy was going to contact her once she had settled down, but she never did."

"Jocelyn was Suzy's friend?" I asked.

"She was Suzy's best friend, but she's no good for her," said Anissa.

"Jocelyn Mudge was Suzy's best friend as Ani said. I last spoke with her just a couple of months ago, but she said she still hadn't heard from Suzy," said Christopher.

"I'd like her details. It's a lead that I'd like to follow up on," I said.

"I'm not sure what you'll get out of her. I've kept in touch and she says she hasn't heard anything. I believe her, unfortunately," said Christopher.

"Nevertheless, it's a lead I'd like to follow up on. I've been known to be quite persuasive at times."

Christopher nodded. He put his hands in his trouser pockets but didn't find what he wanted. He got up from the table and went into the kitchen where he found his phone on the island. He came back to the table carrying it in his hand.

"I've found her phone number when you're ready," he said.

I opened up my phone and nodded at him.

"Jocelyn Mudge at eight oh one, five five five, four three nine five," he said.

I typed it into my phone.

"Mudge is spelled as it sounds?" I asked.

Christopher nodded.

"M-U-D-G-E," he said.

I nodded.

"When did she leave for Los Angeles?" I asked.

"About a year after that police incident in twenty fifteen she left," said Christopher.

"Twenty-eighth of June in sixteen. That's when she left," said Anissa.

"Day after her twentieth birthday," I said.

Anissa's eyes were still wet. She nodded.

"Did she give you any indication that she was leaving? How was her twentieth birthday party?"

Anissa shook her head.

"She mostly celebrated her birthday with her friends. She had become more distant, especially in the year since she had been arrested by the police. Chris was adamant that she have a birthday dinner with us, and then she left shortly thereafter. We never saw her again."

Anissa started to sob quietly.

"Was she angry leading up to her leaving? Was the birthday party happy?" I asked.

"I wouldn't say she was angry, but she had been dissatisfied with her life for a while. She had become increasingly moody. When we did get into arguments, it was always about the strictness of her upbringing. She was a free spirit searching with an unquenchable thirst," said Christopher.

"What do you mean by that?"

"She never seemed satisfied with her life. At least not for the past few years. Since she became a teenager really. I'd say thirteen or fourteen, she was always looking for something. Something to fill a hole she had for some reason. I can't say I understand it, Detective, I've always been happy with the teachings of Christ and I have found solace in our scriptures. Suzy seemed to have an itch she just couldn't scratch."

"And that evening of her birthday. She gave no indication that anything was wrong?" I asked.

Christopher shook his head.

"No, in fact it was one of the few times she seemed happy," he said. "That was unusual, but perhaps not that unusual. She did enjoy her birthdays generally. But in hindsight I wonder if I had misread anything that night."

Anissa was dabbing at her eyes.

"Your wife said that you never saw her again, but you knew she was heading to LA. How did you know about that?"

"She had spoken on occasion about becoming an actress. I wasn't all that supportive. Well, we weren't. We've heard stories of young women being manipulated by men who promise acting opportunities and it usually becomes something ugly."

"Like what?" I asked, knowing full well what he meant.

"I don't know if it's true, but I've heard they get put into prostitution. It's also not an easy way to find work, I'm sure. I'm sure there are a lot of young people hoping to strike it rich and become the next Julia Roberts, but I can't imagine it's that easy. We also received a letter from her later that week."

"Can I see it?"

Christopher nodded and got up from the table.

Invisible Weight of Grief

While Christopher went for the letter, Anissa said nothing to me. I took another cookie and dipped it into my lukewarm coffee. I ate that to give me something to do. And then I finished my coffee and wasn't offered another one. I didn't mind. By the time all of that was done, Christopher was back.

He handed me an envelope that had been carefully opened along the top. I looked at the front of it for a while. Then I turned it over and looked at the back. There was nothing on the back. It was a plain white envelope you could find pretty much anywhere.

The front was addressed to Mr. and Mrs. Valadon at the address I was currently at. The markings over the postage stamp indicated that the letter had been mailed in Provo, which meant she must have written it and mailed it before she left.

I opened up the letter and read it. It was one page and a quick read. It said that she was heading to Los Angeles to become an actress. She was thankful for everything her parents had done for her but that she had to follow her dreams. She said she would make them proud of her and that she would write monthly at the very least. She signed off with "much love" and "Suzy" was the last word on that letter. This letter wasn't all that helpful.

"This letter was mailed the day after her birthday," I said. "It was sent from somewhere in Provo, probably as she was leaving."

Christopher nodded. I placed the letter on the table and took a photograph of it with my phone. I did the same with the front and back of the envelope. Then I carefully put the letter back into the envelope and slid it back over to Christopher. He didn't touch it.

"Do you recall when you received the letter?" I asked, looking at my phone and going to my calendar and going back to twenty sixteen. "I see that the twenty-eighth of June was a Tuesday."

"We received it on that Friday, the first of July," said Anissa. "We had already called the police by that time. I had told Chris to call them the next morning when Suzy hadn't come back home. He waited until that evening, and only after having called her friend Jocelyn who had said she had left that morning from her place."

"So you knew she was staying overnight at her friend's place on the night of her birthday?" I asked.

Anissa nodded.

"We had long before then given up trying to argue with her. Jocelyn seemed nice enough until she got Suzy involved in that incident the year before. But Suzy was stubborn and willful. We had tried giving her curfews and taking away her overnight privileges but it didn't work. Later we heard from the police that Jocelyn knew that Suzy was planning on heading out to Los Angeles. But by then she was probably already there. We probably got that news the same morning that the letter came in the afternoon's mail," said Anissa.

"I'm sure you showed the police a copy of the letter," I said.

Anissa nodded.

"Didn't do much good. They didn't seem particularly interested in it. In fact, they didn't much care about Suzy having left. They told us that she was an adult and that unless we had legitimate reason to be concerned for her safety or that we thought she had been abducted against her will, there was not much they could do."

Anissa fell silent. And it was true. Suzy was a twenty-year-old woman. She might not be of legal age to drink but she was legal enough to live on her own and make her own life choices.

"What did she take with her when she left here to spend the night with her friends on her twentieth birthday?" I asked.

"Just a small backpack and her handbag," said Christopher, looking at his wife.

She didn't add anything to his response.

"And how much clothing do you think she could keep in her backpack?" I asked.

Christopher shrugged.

"Perhaps a couple of pairs of pants and the same for tops if you're also putting in some toiletries and under clothing. The next day, when we got concerned that she hadn't come home, we noticed that her toiletries were gone."

"What sort of items? Makeup, lipstick as well?"

Christopher shook his head.

"No, just the basic things like toothpaste, toothbrush, a hairbrush. That sort of thing," he said.

"She also took floss and lip balm, a simple cross necklace she had. She was also wearing a gold necklace that Chris and I had bought her for her sixteenth birthday along with matching earrings," said Anissa.

"And what did these look like?" I asked. I was taking notes in my notebook.

"Gold colored. They were eighteen karat gold and the earrings hooked into your ears and dangled little hearts from them. The necklace was a simple gold chain with a slightly larger heart on it. The heart was inscribed on the back, 'Love, Mom and Dad,'" said Anissa.

"Have you heard from her since she left these past three years?" I asked.

Anissa nodded.

"We received three letters from her. The first one was about a month later and was filled with enthusiasm still. The second one was about three months after that and was less enthusiastic. She complained about how hard it was trying to make it as an actress. She said it seemed like everyone was an actor in Los Angeles. But she was working at a diner and still trying to get auditions and pursue her dream."

"Could I see these?" I asked.

Anissa nodded and got up from the table.

"The third letter came about six months after the first and was more mixed," said Christopher. "She had lost her job on the one hand but had met a guy who she seemed excited about who could get her introductions to the right people, but it also ended less hopefully. She said if she hadn't made anything of herself within a few months she'd be coming home. There was almost a bit of desperation in her tone."

Christopher looked over my shoulder. His sad, wet eyes looking for the memories of his happier daughter. Anissa came back into the room and handed me three envelopes. They were just as carefully opened as the first.

I took my time and read through all of them. They were easy reads, less than a page each. And on each of the three envelopes there was no return address. The first two had been mailed from Echo Park, going by the zip code. The third had been mailed from Beverly Hills.

The letters were just as Anissa and Christopher had indicated. The third, and last one was perhaps the most forlorn. There was an indication that she would be coming home shortly if acting didn't work out. It felt like a last ditch attempt to make something of herself.

She briefly spoke about this man she had met who had connections to get her started. I didn't like the sounds of it, and especially with the hindsight that I was dealing with a deceased young woman. Most likely murdered. She gave no information about him other than referring to him as the man who could get her started. But there was more desperation in the tone of the letter than hope.

I took photographs of all letters with the envelopes and slid them back towards Anissa. She picked them up, neatened them and put them back down close to her.

Red Diamonds, No Ace

" None of the envelopes have return addresses," I said. "The last one sent was postmarked the first of May." I looked at my calendar again. "That was a Monday and around ten months after she left."

There was no question in what I'd said and nobody offered any information.

"I'm assuming you haven't been able to get a hold of her at all?" I asked.

Christopher shook his head.

"How would we, Detective Carrick?" said Anissa. "We don't know where she is."

"I noticed the first two were mailed from Echo Park. Is that why you chose to move there at first?"

Christopher nodded.

"We only got out here about eighteen months ago. After that last letter when we hadn't heard from her again for a while we decided to try and find her. We arrived in California at the end of February last year. We lived in Echo Park at first, but then we realized that the last envelope was mailed from Beverly Hills but we can't afford to live there, Detective, so we moved out to Palm Springs where we both found work…"

"What do you do?"

"I'm the Head Groundskeeper and An is the Assistant Manager at the pro shop," said Christopher.

"This is at a golf course here?" I asked.

Christopher nodded.

"Red Diamond Cliffs Golf Course," he said.

"Did you inquire around the acting schools in LA?" I asked.

Anissa nodded.

"Yes, but they were very unhelpful," she said. "None of them were willing to give the names of their students. A few would acknowledge if they had a student by the name of Suzy Valadon, but none of them had heard of her."

This case was frustrating me. I was getting nowhere. I had no leads and I had nothing I could come up with to explain what had happened to Suzanne Valadon. I needed answers like the Catholic Church needed forgiveness. And unlike them I wasn't getting any.

"Did Suzanne have any tattoos, birthmarks or scars that you knew about?" I asked. I was making another Hail Mary.

"No, she was a perfect baby. She had no marks, no freckles really. I was always so envious of how perfect her skin was," said Anissa.

"I'd like to show you something," I said, opening up my phone and finding the picture of her scar I had taken earlier. "Have you seen this before?"

I showed it to Anissa, she took my phone and looked at it for a while, slowly shaking her head. Then she passed it to Christopher who also looked at it for a while before shaking his head and returning the phone to me.

"Is that her?" asked Anissa.

I nodded.

"It appears to be some sort of scar or branding and best I can tell it seems to be three Chinese characters. You're certain you've never seen it?"

They shook their heads.

"Where is it located?" asked Anissa.

"Just around her inguinal crease," I said.

They both looked at me as if I had spoken Swahili.

"That's the groin area. It's placed towards her midline just inward from the crease your thigh makes with your lower body. Left side."

"Why would she do that to herself?" asked Anissa of no one in particular.

"I'm assuming she didn't know Chinese?" I asked.

Christopher shook his head.

"She had tried taking Spanish at school, but she wasn't very good at languages," said Christopher. "She wasn't really the best student, and it wasn't for lack of trying. She averaged a C."

I had nothing for the Valadons and it appeared they had nothing left for me. I almost asked about seeing their daughter's room but stopped myself in time. This wasn't where Suzanne had grown up.

"Is there anything else that you can share with me that might help? Anything at all. Ex-boyfriends, friends, anything at all."

I felt like I was at church. Right in the front row with my rosary and the only prayer I remembered was Hail Mary. But where was this grace I needed?

Anissa and Christopher looked at each other.

"Jocelyn was her closest friend. Another one who was often with them was Rebecca... Rebecca...," Anissa looked at Christopher. Christopher shrugged.

"I don't remember her last name," he said.

"Jocelyn would know," said Anissa. "But I'm not sure you'll find them particularly helpful. Christopher tried speaking with them a few months after Suzy had left but they didn't seem to have any more information than what we had."

Anissa looked back at Christopher. He nodded.

"I reached out to Jocelyn's parents. They invited me over and we spoke with Jocelyn together. Like Anissa said, Jocelyn didn't know anything that we didn't. She only knew it sooner than we did," he said.

"What do you mean by that?" I asked.

"Well, Jocelyn knew that Suzy was planning on moving out to Los Angeles well before we did. Other than that, she had only received one letter from Suzy, and that was about six weeks or two months after Suzy had left. That was the last Jocelyn had heard from her."

"Do you know what that letter said?"

Christopher nodded.

"Yes, Jocelyn's parents, Mark and Mary, made her get the letter so that I could read it. It was similar to our letter only the tone was warmer, more friendly, as you might expect for a letter written to a friend. But there were no details. She was in the first month or so of moving to the big city and she was full of wonder and excitement still. She was very cagey though, never gave any indication of where she was or who she might have met. It was mailed from Echo Park, though. I remember that."

"Same zip code as your first two letters," I said.

"I believe so. I didn't keep the information. But I did take down the zip code at the time and verified it later on the internet and that's when I learned it was the Echo Park zip code. If I remember correctly, I think Echo Park has only one zip code."

I didn't know about that so I took his word for it. We didn't speak for a while. I was busy ruminating thoughts, trying to turn them into leads without getting anywhere.

"I'm sorry we haven't been more helpful, Detective," said Christopher. "We've tried our best, but we just didn't know where our daughter was."

Christopher choked on those last few words. His wife handed him a tissue and put her hand on his. He dabbed at his eyes and gave her a sweet smile. Now it was only the two of them. Or so I thought.

"Do you have any other children?" I asked.

Anissa turned to me and nodded.

"Gavin is studying economics at Utah State," she said. "He's in his third year."

"So he's younger than Suzanne," I said.

Anissa nodded.

"Two years younger."

"Do you still have Jocelyn's phone number?" I asked.

Anissa nodded.

"I've kept it. We haven't spoken to her since we sat down with her and her parents but her parents have been very kind during this time. But that's not to say they've kept in touch. Not that we've made it easy. Only our closest friends know we're out here."

Anissa fiddled away at her phone and then gave me Jocelyn's number.

"Like I said, we haven't remained in contact. But that was the last good number I had for her."

"Can I get your numbers for further follow up if needed?"

Anissa nodded and gave me both her and her husband's telephone numbers. I looked at my notebook. I had taken a few notes since I had arrived. Not a lot mind you on account of how little any of us knew about what had happened to Suzanne Valadon. I closed up my notebook and put it on top of my phone. I had exhausted all questions I thought might be helpful.

"I believe that's all I have for you at the moment. Is there anything else that you can remember that you might think is important?"

I looked at Christopher and then to Anissa. They were quiet for a moment. Then Anissa shook her head. I looked at Christopher again.

"She was a good girl, Detective Carrick, she really was. She might have been lost but that doesn't mean anyone had the right to hurt her," he said. "Please bring her justice. Bring us justice."

He held onto those words to the very end when a tear rolled down his cheek. I felt terrible for them. Not the least of which was because I had no goddamn leads to go on. Like a priest looking for confessions at a nunnery, I had nothing.

"I will do my best," I said. "I will leave no stone unturned to bring to justice whoever did this to your daughter."

My first mentor, Detective Armando Ferrari, no relation to the car company, taught me the value of honesty and honor. One of my first cases as a newly minted homicide detective back in the day was a horrible rape and murder. The parents were shattered. They were literally shells of themselves. Their daughter had been valedictorian, worked to help her family and to get into university. She was an All-State swimmer before that was all taken from her brutally.

They had asked me the same thing. They had asked me to get justice for their daughter. I had sworn to them that I would. Arman took me aside and told me never to lie to a victim or their loved ones ever again.

"The only people we lie to, Tony," he said, "are the assholes we're going to put away."

He was the only one who's ever been able to call me Tony for any length of time. He was more of a father figure to me than my own father.

Anyway, long story short, we found the asshole who did it. A weasel of a man, not some big monster I was expecting. I got to him first and I was hellbent on beating him to a pulp and well on my way when Arman pulled me off. Arman was a short, stocky man, but like a bulldog, there was nobody he would cower from.

He protected me from IA fallout on that occasion. The rapist filed a complaint and IA looked into it. Arman said he never saw anything, that the guy must have done that to himself before we had got to him. Our stories were straight and the complaint went unfounded. Arman also told me that was my one and only mulligan. From then on, I played it mostly straight with him.

He was only partnered with me for three years, but those were the most educational and informative three years on or off the job. I started thinking I should talk to him. We had kept in touch and he had a way of making me see things differently.

I got up and started to put my notebook and phone away. While I had been reminiscing neither Anissa nor Christopher had added anything else.

"I want to see my daughter, Detective," said Anissa.

I nodded.

"I'm sure we can arrange that," I said.

"Now, Detective. I can't wait not knowing. I need to know with my flesh and blood. I need to look at my daughter's face. I can't rest until I've seen her and said goodbye."

I nodded at her and sat back down.

Death is Silent

" I need to make a phone call to the Medical Examiner's office to see if we can get it setup. Give me a minute," I said.

I took out my phone and dialed a number I had called on many occasions. Mostly used to speak to M. I pulled my phone from my ear and looked at the time. Then I put my phone back on my ear and waited for someone to pick up. It was five thirty, give or take some change. Closing time. However, the ME always had someone available until eight or nine who had access to the coolers. Occasionally later.

"Hello," came the voice. It was Deerstalker.

"Jabez," I said, recognizing the voice.

"If this is about Valadon, we don't have the tox screen in yet."

"It is but not about toxicology," I said.

"How can I help then?"

"Her parents want to see her tonight. We're just leaving Palm Springs and should make it back by eight. Will there be somebody there to help with the viewing?"

"This is highly unusual, Anthony. You know we don't usually allow public access here."

"I know. I'll vouch for them and they won't be out of my sight. You can call Emily if you'd like. I'm sure she'd authorize it," I said.

I was using M as the Chief Medical Examiner. It was cheap but I was in no mood to argue.

"Okay, give me a second and let me see who's working late."

I waited on the other end. Anissa and Christopher stared at me. Jabez might be all business and seriousness, but when it came to helping out he had a big heart. Especially true when it was the grieved he was dealing with. I'd also never seen him act with indignity towards the bodies he autopsied. He was very respectful of the victims and other deceased that landed on his slab. Unlike another coroner who had been sacked many years ago for acting unprofessionally.

"We've got a resident here helping out with paperwork. Let me tell her that you'll be around. Hold on a minute."

I held on and waited for another couple of minutes.

"All set, Anthony. Dr. Fahdah Sarraf will be here and she's expecting you. She goes by Fay."

"Thank you, Jabez."

We hung up and I looked over at Anissa and Christopher and nodded at them.

"There will be someone there to help us," I said.

"Thank you. I won't be able to rest until I've seen her with my own eyes," said Anissa. "I hope you understand."

"I do."

"Could you give me a few minutes to get ready?" she asked.

I nodded. Christopher didn't say anything. Anissa got up from the table and left.

"I hope this is not inconvenient for you, Detective?" he asked.

"Not at all. If it will help I'm all in. And please, call me Anthony."

Christopher nodded and gave me a small smile. I had long ago given up on trying to dissuade grieving loved ones from viewing their deceased loved one. And that wasn't just for especially violent cases. But ninety-nine times out of a hundred, loved ones, and especially parents, want to see their child one last time. I get it. I'd probably want the same if it was me. The word of a stranger often doesn't feel like reality. Only seeing the body brings that sense of finality. However, ninety nine percent of the grieved saw their loved ones after the coroner had released the body to the undertaker.

"Have you done this often?" asked Christopher.

I nodded somberly.

"Many times."

"Doesn't it affect you?" he asked. "Having to do this. Does it get easier?"

"The answer to the first question is yes, the answer to the second is no. It has never gotten easier and it does affect me. But I burn that anger and sadness as fuel to use in bringing justice to bear. I have found that being stoic is of better help to the bereaved."

Christopher nodded slowly and smiled sadly.

"Do you have any children, Anthony?"

"I have a daughter. She's twelve years old."

More slow nodding and sad smiles.

"Keep her safe," he said. "Don't let her out of your sight."

His plea was earnest, as you'd expect from a man who had lost his daughter.

"I will," I said.

The rest of the time we sat in silence. It wasn't long, perhaps a couple more minutes. Then Anissa came back in. She had freshened up, brushed her hair and put on a bit of makeup. We got up, I put on my jacket and fedora. Christopher and Anissa grabbed jackets from the closet by the door.

"I'm assuming you'll want to drive yourselves?"

Christopher nodded. He had grabbed his car keys from the kitchen counter.

"Stay close to me so that I can lead. We're in no rush and we'll get there safe and sound."

They nodded and we left the apartment. They had asked where I had parked. I told them. They said they'd come around to that side. I waited in my car and waved at them as I saw them approach. The gate slid open and they got in behind me and we started off on the roughly two hour journey.

It was fairly uneventful. The first half hour or so we were having a staring contest with the sun as it slowly set on the western horizon. But shortly after six it had dipped behind hills and trees and the going was much smoother. It was during that time that a call came in from Tai. I considered picking my phone up and talking to him. But the sun was in my eyes and the traffic was heavier than I was expecting so I let it go to voicemail. My car's not fancy enough to have bluetooth.

We got to the Medical Examiner's offices a little before seven thirty. Traffic had opened up once the sun had gone down. I got out of my car and stretched my legs. I went over to the Valadon's plain, white Corolla and opened the door for Anissa.

They both got out and I had a few words with them.

"We'll need to sign in and show ID to security. He'll then ring up Dr. Fahdah Sarraf, or Fay, and she'll come and get us. Usually a couple of security guards will be with us during the viewing, though they'll be discreet. Take as long as you need."

I looked at both of them searchingly.

"Why security guards?" asked Anissa.

"There have been incidents previously where the bereaved have acted out of character," I said, charitably.

Anissa nodded.

"Whenever you're ready, let me know and we'll head on in."

Christopher inhaled the air and then turned around and took in the neighborhood. There wasn't much to take in, it's a busy commercial area where the ME's offices are, but perhaps he was giving himself the courage he needed. After a time he nodded and looked at his wife. Then she nodded and I walked them into the main foyer. Gerald was behind the security desk.

"Good evening, Anthony, good to see you again," he said.

I nodded.

"I have Mr. and Mrs. Valadon with me. Dr. Sarraf is expecting us."

"Yes, she is. If I could get you to sign in while I let her know you're here."

I nodded. I added my name and signature to the book. Then I moved aside to let Christopher and Anissa add their names and signatures. Christopher offered his driver's license to Gerald but Gerald cupped the phone and shook his head.

"You're with Mr. Carrick, he's vouched for you."

Then he turned back to the phone and told the person on the other end that we were here. He hung up and turned to me.

"She'll be right out. Please have a seat if you'd like. And, Anthony," he said.

I nodded at him.

"Would you like my company or can you handle this on your own?"

"I'll be alright. The less spectators in the stands the better."

Gerald nodded. I thanked him and turned towards Anissa and Christopher.

"Please have a seat if you'd like. It won't be long now."

"I'd prefer to stand," said Christopher. Anissa nodded in agreement.

"Gerald and I go a long way back," I said. "Even still, some of the security guys can be sticklers for the rules. Gerald has a big heart."

"He seems nice," said Anissa.

And moments after that the door to our side opened up and Dr. Sarraf came out and introduced herself to us. She was wearing a white overcoat over dark blue slacks and a lighter blue flower-patterned blouse. She had long, straight black hair and she wore glasses. She was an attractive woman and she wore just a modest amount of makeup. Her accent was American.

"Mr. Carrick," she said, holding out her hand.

I shook it. It was warm and firm.

"Please call me Anthony, Dr. Sarraf," I said.

"Fay, Anthony," she said.

I nodded.

"This is Anissa Valadon and her husband Christopher Valadon."

Fay took Anissa's hand, shook it carefully with her other hand over top.

"I am so sorry for your loss," she said. "I'm Fay."

And I thought Anissa would burst into tears. She shook Christopher's hand more formally but also offered her deepest sympathy. She was a warm and compassionate woman. M had chosen well. Well, she had long ago told me that kindness was the most important skill she looked for in her staff. Fay was proof positive of that.

"Are you ready?" she asked the Valadons.

They nodded. I stretched my hand towards the door and they followed Fay through it as I brought up the rear. We walked in silence for what felt like eons, down a couple of hallways and taking a couple of turns until we came to one of the main autopsy rooms. It was not the same room that I was in when I viewed Suzanne's body.

Inside the room was sparse. There was a body draped in a white cloth somewhat in the middle of the room on a metal gurney. The lights were soft and warm and not terribly bright. They gave the room a warmer, friendlier ambiance. I thought that was a nice touch. The room I had been in earlier was just bright, cold white lights. This was a much better setup for the bereaved. The counters on the edges and the tool trolleys were all carefully put away and cleaned up. No tools of the coroner's trade were visible. Fay had taken the time to create the right environment and I would sing her praises to M when next I saw her.

We walked towards the body and Fay went to the opposite side, Suzanne's left side, and stood with her hands clasped in front of her by Suzanne's shoulder. The body was not yet visible.

We waited until all of us were standing next to the covered body. Well, I wasn't. I stood just to the side and behind Christopher who was standing next to his wife. She was standing opposite the body from Fay. Fay looked at Anissa and Christopher. They were staring at the undefined body under the cloth. Then they looked up at her.

"Are you ready?" asked Fay, softly.

Waxing Brazilian

And I noticed that there was a tool tray on a trolley just a few inches from the table that Suzanne Valadon was on. On that tray was a box of tissues. Fay took opposite sides of the cloth on opposite sides of Suzanne's head and pulled back the sheet and laid it carefully across her upper shoulders.

This was not a funeral parlor and hence there was no mortician to put makeup on Suzanne's face. We were left with the blunt mask of death. Some thought that people who were dead looked peaceful. Perhaps that was true for grandpa who died in his sleep in his rocking chair enjoying The Price is Right. But there was nothing natural about Suzanne's death and I couldn't help but think that the face looked waxy, almost fake as if someone had spilled soured milk all over her face. She was the color of cold, grayish-white marble.

Anissa nodded and then started sobbing. Fay picked up the box of tissues and offered them to her. Anissa took a couple. Christopher kept staring at his daughter's face as a tear rolled down his cheek and his lips turned tight as if they were nothing more than a bloodless gash in his face. After a time he too nodded. Fay pulled the sheet back over Suzanne's face.

"Can I see her scar?" asked Anissa, composing herself.

Fay nodded.

"It's easier to see from this side," she said.

Anissa walked around her daughter's head, putting her hand on the covered forehead for a moment. Her eyes were wet and glassy and red. She stood to Fay's right as Fay had moved down towards the lower half of Suzanne's body. Fay looked at Anissa and she nodded to her.

Fay carefully pulled a portion of the cloth by Suzanne's left hip up and onto the body, being careful to preserve Suzanne's dignity. Nevertheless, the scar was close enough to the pubic area that a portion of that was visible. Anissa looked at the scar made up of three Chinese characters.

"What does it mean?" she asked.

"I don't know," said Fay.

So Anissa looked at me. Christopher was still standing slightly in front and to my left, unmoving, as if Medusa had turned him to stone.

"I have my contact at the FBI looking into it," I said. "None of our members in vice have seen anything like it."

I bit my tongue. I'd given too much away again. If she had heard me talking about vice there'd be more questions about why we thought their daughter was a prostitute. And I didn't know that for certain. I hadn't heard back yet from Deerstalker on whether she had had consensual sex. But Anissa had more pressing concerns and emotional turmoil swirling in her mind that she didn't notice or didn't think more carefully about what I had said.

Anissa looked back down at her daughter's body.

"Did you shave her?" she asked, looking at her daughter's groin. Even though Fay had been discreet, she had to uncover enough of the pubic and groin area that you would expect to see pubic hair there.

Fay shook her head.

"No, we have not shaved any of her hair anywhere," said Fay. "She must have had a Brazilian at some point before."

Anissa tenderly rubbed her fingers across the scar as if she were blind and trying to read braille. After a moment she was done and Fay pulled the sheet back over the area. Suzanne was once again fully shrouded. The strongest smell in the room was a faint mixture of bleach and other clinical cleaning chemicals.

I looked over at Anissa.

"I'll walk you out," I said.

Anissa nodded. Christopher had grown roots, had not said anything and was still staring from my side of the table at where his daughter's scar was. Anissa came round and put her hand through his arm and led him away from the table. I walked them out of the building and back to their car. Christopher never said anything and Anissa led him to the passenger side. I closed the door on Christopher and walked Anissa round to the other side. I held open the driver's side door and after she had gotten in I leaned in.

"I hate to ask you this, but you seemed surprised that your daughter had no pubic hair. Is there a reason you wouldn't have expected her to have had a Brazilian?" I asked.

Anissa looked at me for a moment before speaking. Then she shrugged.

"I don't know, Detective, to be honest with you. It just seemed strange. Obviously I haven't seen my daughter naked since she was a child, but she had no boyfriend that I was aware of and that's not something a lot of women of our faith do to themselves."

I nodded and hung on her door for a moment wondering if there was anything else. Anissa looked at the steering wheel, put the key into the ignition and started it up. Then she looked over at her husband with a sad smile. He stared out the window, unmoving.

"Drive carefully," I said. "I'll text you my number, and if you need anything at all, please call me."

Anissa turned to look at me.

"We need justice, Detective. Nothing more and nothing less."

She grabbed the door handle and I let go of her door. She closed it. I watched them drive off and when I could no longer see them I took out my phone and texted her my number.

"AC - 310-555-2640"

As I started walking back towards my car I had a thought. I veered off back towards the building and reentered it. Gerald was there. He looked up and smiled.

"Forget something?" he asked.

I shook my head.

"I have a question for Fay," I said.

"Head on through. She should be putting the body back in the cooler. The main autopsy room. You know where that is?"

I nodded and walked towards the locked door that gave me access to the main building. Gerald buzzed me through and I walked these empty corridors filled with the ghosts of the deceased. The lights were low and intermittent on account it was now after hours. But it gave the place a more spectral feel. The main autopsy room was where I had earlier seen the body with Jabez. And that's where I found Fay. She was just closing the door on

Suzanne under dimmed lights when I arrived. I knocked on the main door so as not to frighten Fay. She turned around and smiled at me.

"How did it go?" she asked.

I shrugged.

"Tough to lose a child," I said. "Christopher never said a word, and Anissa drove them home. Terrible thing they're dealing with."

What else can you say? Words are nothing more than the ghostly death of prior thoughts. You can't hang anything on them and they come up wanting in situations like this.

"It's a terrible business we're in," said Fay, smiling wistfully. "But I comfort myself with the knowledge that we're helping to bring justice and, if not justice, at least an understanding of how they died."

I nodded.

"Something that Anissa said got me thinking."

"What's that?" asked Fay.

"She asked if we had shaved her daughter and that got me thinking that the way she was found seemed like she might have been intimate recently, or perhaps that's how she made a living. As an escort or prostitute. My question is, had she had sex recently?"

"Good question. I haven't looked at the file, but I can do that for you if you'd like?"

I nodded. Fay went over to a sink along one of the walls and washed her hands.

"Come with me," she said, "and let's find out. How was she found?"

"She was found naked in a burgundy negligee, and when I say she was naked, she was wearing no jewelry or anything at all other than the negligee. That was on Sunday morning which means to me that she was probably out Saturday evening into early Sunday when she died. And the way she was left, carefully, undisturbed and dressed as she was makes me think she might have been intimate with someone. And probably someone who didn't love her much, if at all. Because if it was a boyfriend and she'd died of natural causes you'd think he'd have called the authorities. And all of this makes me think that she might have been a prostitute and perhaps a high paid one."

Fay nodded.

"That would make sense. Such a beautiful, young woman. A tragedy, really. But then isn't that our business, dealing in tragedies?"

I nodded, and followed Fay to the offices which were along the sides of the building where the windows were and the natural light could come in. Not that there was light to be had now, it was just around eight at night.

Fay walked into an unnamed office not especially close to M's. This office contained three desks with their fronts together in what would look like a T if the desks had been narrower. Now they were all put together. Two perpendicular to the entrance and the back one parallel. Fay walked to the right desk that faced the window. The blinds had been lowered.

"Pull a chair around," she said as she sat down.

I grabbed the chair from the opposite desk and pulled it around and sat at her left elbow as she logged in and started searching the files.

"You'll probably get the report tomorrow, maybe Wednesday by the latest depending on when we receive the report back from toxicology, and genetics."

"Genetics?" I asked.

Fay was staring at her screen and flipping and scrolling amongst a few documents at a rate that I couldn't keep up with.

"Yes, Jabez found three samples of semen. One sample was taken from her throat, another was taken from her vagina and the last was taken from her anus. Can't tell yet if it's the same donor or not, that's where the genetics report will come in. It'll also tell us if that person, or persons is in the sexual offender's database," said Fay.

I wasn't counting on that. Not that it couldn't be the case, but the way the body was left at the dump, with care, made me think that we were not likely dealing with a sexual predator.

"Three samples," I said. "So if I can get some clarity from you. Would I be right in thinking that she would have had oral sex as well as anal and vaginal intercourse then?"

Fay nodded, and turned to me.

"That's correct. Not sure how else she could get semen down her throat unless she was into kinky things."

I nodded.

"You never know," I said. "Anything else that catches your eye from the report?"

She grinned at me.

"Well, the report is not official yet and hasn't been fully written up so you should probably wait for the official report. But nothing remarkable caught my eye. As a young woman we wouldn't expect her to have much disease of the organs yet. No liver inflammation or atherosclerosis of note. All the organs looked to be healthy. And with no physical signs of violence she was either poisoned or..."

I waited, but Fay didn't finish her sentence.

"Or, what, Fay?"

She looked at me and smiled.

"Well, this is pure speculation on my part so pay no attention if it doesn't make sense. And it's certainly not official."

I nodded.

"We're just having a conversation, doc," I said, smiling back.

"I'm just guessing now, Anthony. But the way you describe how she was found just makes me think that she wasn't poisoned. Or at least not purposefully. Correct me if I'm wrong, but it sounds like she was placed at the dump with care and being dressed in a negligee as you said, just makes me think it was something else."

"Like what?" I asked, having a sense of where she was going, but wanting to hear it from her.

"This could be an accidental overdose," said Fay. "But we won't know until we get the toxicology report back."

I nodded. That had crossed my mind.

"Right, I had thought of that. But dumping her off like that suggests to me that we're still likely dealing with at least manslaughter."

Fay nodded.

"Absolutely. A crime was committed but I'm just not sure it was murder."

"Going back to the semen found, was there any suggestion she was raped?"

Fay shook her head.

"No, it doesn't appear like that. It appears the sex was consensual. Depending on what the genetic testing says, she might have been involved in an orgy. They have those sorts of things out in New York, and I'm sure they have them here as well."

I nodded. I had heard of things like that but I had no first hand knowledge of them. I preferred to steer clear of humanity's cesspool unless I was the one draining the swamp.

"Well, you've given me something to think about," I said, still a man with loose ends that didn't seem attached to anything.

"Perhaps vice could help you with these sex parties," she said.

I shook my head.

"I've talked to them before about that sort of thing. Problem is, most of these orgies take place in private homes amongst consenting adults and no crime is committed as much as I might find it distasteful. Nobody knows what the scar is about either."

I looked at Fay. She shrugged.

"Looks Chinese to me, which is to say I have no idea what it means."

I nodded. I sat and thought for a moment.

"I've taken enough of your time, Fay. Thank you for doing this."

I stood up.

"You're welcome, Anthony," she said. "I hope you find justice for her."

"If it was an accidental overdose that's not going to comfort her parents much. How do you get justice for a life that was never dealt aces, doc? And Suzanne's life appears to have had more than its fair share of troubles."

Fay didn't say anything to that and so I left her office and found my way back to the main entrance where I said farewell to Gerald for the second time this evening. There were only three cars in the parking lot and one of them was mine. I got in and started it up. I decided to head to a place where they knew my name and the thinking spirits and libations poured freely. I had two choices in that regard. Wot Ales Ye or Sonny McLean's. Wot Ales Ye was closer to home and I might be needing a lot of thinking juice this evening.

Ianfu

Thinking juice hadn't been a friend of mine the night before. I'll blame Caolán, the barkeep for my troubles. He had an unsteady pour which meant his two finger pours sometimes turned into three fingers. He also had been serving me a good Irish whiskey which kept tasting like more to me.

It was a little after nine when my eyes opened to a shattered sun that I thought would honestly make my eyes bleed. But worse than that was the headache.

It felt like I had two ice picks stuck in my brain. Both had pierced my eyes and where they met in the middle of my brain thunder rolled and lightning sparked. I felt like a hobbled up old man. I put my feet tenderly on the carpet and pushed myself into a seated position.

My tongue was sandpaper and my eyes felt like ground sand had been rubbed into them. I was not happy. More than that, I started to wonder if all this drinking was doing me any favors.

I got up and went into the bathroom. I rinsed my mouth and drank some water. I took a couple of headache pills and brushed my teeth. Then I got into the shower and steamed some life back into myself. I got out and dressed and went into the kitchen. Pirate's bowl of dry food was almost empty. I picked it up and put it on the counter. Thankfully, he wasn't much of a jumper.

I got out a new bowl for him and took some wet food out of the fridge and put a spoonful of that in his bowl. All the time he was weaving in and out of my legs like a drunkard. Like I might have been the night before. I placed the bowl down and he went to town, removing himself as a tripping hazard.

I put the can of his food back in the fridge and took a look at what else was in the fridge. Nothing inspired me. In fact, the thought of food started to make me feel queasy. I decided on coffee and figured I'd give myself time for any hunger to appear. While I was making coffee I downed a glass of water from a glass I had left on the counter. I had a vague recollection of having done the same last night when I got home. But much of last night was a blur.

I went into the living room and put on the TV to catch some sports highlights. Then I fished out my phone to look for messages. I had none. That was weird, because I remembered I had not taken a call from Tai on my way back from Palm Springs last night. I checked my call history and it told me I had checked my voicemail at around midnight last night.

I didn't remember what Tai had left on the voice message so I dialed in again. But the computer generated voice of my voicemail system told me I had no messages. I must have deleted it. I cursed. I checked my call history again hoping I hadn't drunk dialed him at midnight. I hadn't.

Still, I was in no state to talk with anyone yet. I needed some time to recover from the damage I had inflicted upon myself.

I absentmindedly watched sport highlights as I listened to my coffee machine making its last gasps as it finished up brewing. I was more interested in the big-bosomed sports announcer than in much of what the actual results were.

I put my hands into my head and rested my palms over my eyes. I had to start seriously considering quitting booze, or at least drastically cutting my intake. I was sure I had spent over a hundred bucks last night and probably drank a half bottle of whiskey. Easy. Minimum. And that didn't sound like something to brag about.

The coffee had stopped brewing so I got up from the couch and went into the kitchen to pour myself a large mug of the dark pick-me-up. I splashed cream and tossed sugar into it and gave it a good stir. I took the mug back to the couch with me and admired the sports announcer's assets and took a sip of the hot liquid. Like magic I started to slowly feel better. The aspirins or whatever pills I had taken earlier were also helping take the edge off my headache.

Still, I needed a few minutes more before I could decently interact with anyone. I lay back on the couch and stared at the boob tube. And that's what it literally was. She had some of the finest boobs I had seen in a long time. I rested the coffee mug on my knee, holding it carefully by the handle. I took my time to drink my coffee and to watch the announcer.

About twenty minutes later, during a commercial break, I went back into the kitchen to get a second mug. Now feeling like I belonged in the land of the living, I figured I could make that call to Tai. I also wanted to reach out to JR and find out how Sonny and Beast had gotten on with their chat yesterday with Arshile. I took a couple of sips of coffee and took my phone back out of my pocket. It was leaning towards ten. I dialed Tai first. A few rings later and he picked up.

"Tai, Carrick, how are you?"

"Anthony, I'm doing good thanks. Yesterday's breach went over without a hiccup. But that's not why you're calling."

"No, I got your message last night, but you didn't share any details," I said, not remembering and hoping he'd just left a message asking me to call him back. I was right.

"Yeah, I don't usually leave any messages pertaining to work. That stuff gets stored on servers we don't control and, despite what the carriers might tell you, it isn't automatically deleted after a few months or six months or whatever. We've recovered messages from over a year prior."

"Good tip," I said.

"Something to think about, but that's also not why you called me. I'll be honest with you Anthony, there's something bigger going on with your case."

"Uh huh," I said, taking a sip of coffee.

"Seriously, Anthony, I think you've opened up a Pandora's box of a case here."

"I'm all ears," I said.

"In the last fifty or so years, there have been four other cases of women found dead without apparent violence and with the exact same scar as your Jane Doe..."

"Suzanne Valadon," I said.

"What's that?"

"Suzanne Valadon is her name. I couldn't get back to you last night because I was with her parents. Suzanne Valadon is our deceased."

"Good to know, give me a second to write it down. Just like it sounds?"

"Yeah, listen, what do those Chinese characters mean before we get into more depth."

There was a bit of silence on the other end. Tai was probably making note of Suzanne's name for his records.

"Yeah, ok, so the scar. You're technically right in that they're Chinese characters but they're called kanji. They're the borrowed logographic Chinese characters that are used in the Japanese writing system. The three characters are a translation of the Japanese ianfu, which means comfort woman."

Comfort woman, I thought to myself. That seems like prostitution.

"That's basically a prostitute, right?" I asked.

"Well, yeah."

"And they were mostly used during the Second World War, right?"

"Also right," he said.

"We're over seventy years removed from that war and I don't believe comfort women are a thing anymore, am I right?"

"Well, technically yes, but it's become a more generalized phrase for prostitutes and is still in use by some for that purpose."

"Ok, I'm with you so far. I had thought she might have been a lady of the night, but the way she was dressed, the way she looked, healthy, I figured she might have been a highly paid escort or something like that. Are you now telling me we're looking at the Japanese yakuza or Chinese triads operating in LA?" I asked.

"Our best intelligence says not. We don't believe that these women are part of the yakuza or triads."

"Then why the scarification?" I asked.

"Probably as a mark of ownership to whichever group has turned these women into prostitutes."

"Can you send me what you've got on this?" I asked.

"Sorry, Anthony, you know I can't do that. But listen, there isn't much, and I'll tell you over the phone what we've got. Do you have time?"

"All the time in the world," I said. "But listen, you're Japanese, aren't you?"

"What are you implying?"

"Nothing, but this being kanji, that's Japanese right?"

"Ok, I get it. I'm Japanese like you're Irish," he said. "Do you speak Irish?"

"No," I said.

"There you go. I don't speak Japanese, well, not enough to get by on, and I certainly don't read it."

"Understood."

"Good, now let me tell you what I've got."

"I'm all ears."

Sugar and Spice

" Nineteen seventy-seven, a young woman was found on the outskirts of the Black Forest in Germany. This was near the town of Baden-Baden. She was twenty-one and dressed much like your victim. She was in intimate nightwear and nothing else was on her. No jewelry or makeup. In fact, it appeared that she had been scrubbed clean before being laid to rest."

"How was she found?"

"Lying on her back with her arms folded over her stomach wearing nothing but a white piece of lingerie. It was more like a nightgown but a sheer piece that was meant to be used as lingerie. Why do you ask?"

"Suzanne Valadon was lying on what appeared to be a pillow made of twigs. Anything like that?""

"No. Just as I described. The police officer who found her thought, at first, that she might have been sleeping before he realized that she wasn't."

"No violence on the body?" I asked.

"No, nothing," said Tai.

"How did she die?"

"I'm getting to that. It appeared that she had engaged in sexual activities. Semen was found vaginally and it didn't appear to be rape from the account at the time."

"What about anywhere else?"

"What do you mean?"

"Semen, was there any found in her throat or anus?"

"Not that it was disclosed on the report."

"And it appeared consensual?" I asked.

"That's right. What about your victim?"

"They collected three samples of semen. From the vagina, anus and throat. Don't know any details yet. Like if it was one subject or more," I said.

"I see."

173

"How did this woman die?"

"Overdose of drugs. Cannabis, cocaine and ketamine. The cocktail seemed to have stopped her heart."

"Was the killer ever apprehended?"

"No, and she was a young woman, like your victim, who had left home for the big city."

"What about the others?" I asked.

"The second and third victims were found in Russia. The first one was a woman of twenty-three found similarly dressed in a piece of lingerie. One piece of lingerie. This one was black and she was lying prone under a tree in a park in Moscow. This was in eighty-eight. Semen was found in her vagina and anus. Two different donors. There was also cannabis and ketamine found in her system but that's not how she died. Seems she died from asphyxiation. Likely sexual kink gone wrong."

"And no one was arrested for that either?" I asked.

"No, trails ran cold. Third victim was found in a wooded area just outside St. Petersburg in ninety-one. Pink one-piece lingerie this time. She was found lying on her back, hands by her side. No makeup or jewelry. Same with the other two victims. No signs of violence. She died from a drug overdose, mostly cocaine, and she appeared to have a weak heart which gave out from the high cocaine consumption. She also had cannabis and ketamine in her system. Two different semen samples were also taken from her from two different donors. Vaginal and anal."

"How old was she?"

"Nineteen."

"And the fourth victim?"

"She was found in your neck of the woods. At the same Calabasas landfill and similar location to where your last victim was found."

"What was her name so I can read the file?"

"I thought you might ask that. One second, let me check my notes."

I waited for a bit on the other end of a silent phone.

"Here it is. Grace Cossington Smith. Grace Smith was twenty-two years old and found dressed in a red teddy. What's a teddy?" asked Tai.

"Your wife could probably tell you," I said.

"That's not her thing."

"You didn't look at the pictures?"

"No, Anthony, I was doing this for your edification, not for my own."

I laughed on the other end.

"Far as I know, a teddy is like a one piece swimsuit, only you don't go swimming in it, if you know what I mean."

"Thanks. So yeah, she was found in a red teddy. Blood red, so the report said. Interestingly, she was the first victim with other marks on her body beyond this scar that you've found on yours."

"Yeah, what was that?"

"A large butterfly tattoo on her lower back. Very low down."

"That's all?"

"Yeah, when you take a look at the pictures you'll be able to see it. Apparently it's very well done, brightly colored."

"How did she die?"

"She had ketamine and cannabis in her system too. Though she died like the second victim. Asphyxiation."

"Two by asphyxiation and two by drug overdose," I said, mostly to myself.

"There was one other unusual aspect to this victim's death not found with the others."

"What's that?" I asked.

"The sex was rough. Semen found from one man in both vagina and anus. She was possibly raped, but that was inconclusive based on what her possible lifestyle was. If she wasn't a prostitute, and all these cases are being treated as though they were, which is reasonable, then it would look like rape. But you don't know. Some prostitutes have clients who like it rough."

"Why do we think they were all prostitutes?" I asked.

"Same reason you probably do. They had all had sex shortly before their deaths or murders. They were all young, attractive women, and the four I've just spoken about were all runaways before the age of eighteen. This last one for instance, Grace Smith, ran away from home at the age of sixteen from what was apparently an abusive family. She's from your neck of the woods. Oklahoma."

"Where?"

"Tulsa. Parents were royal assholes from all accounts when the local detective interviewed them. Not sad at all. In fact, get this, and this is a direct quote from the mother of Grace, 'she was an ill-tempered child and got what she went looking for.' Can you believe that?"

"Of course I can," I said. "And you do too if you've been on this job longer than five minutes."

"Yeah, you're right."

"And these other kids, they all came from dysfunctional families?" I asked.

"Yeah, appears so. At least from what can be read between the lines. How about your victim."

"Doesn't appear so. I was with the parents most of last night and they genuinely seemed torn up about it. In fact, they moved out from Utah to California to look for their daughter."

"That's tough, Anthony. Anything else you need?"

"What makes you guys think these are related? They're all over the globe except for your last one and mine."

"MO is very similar in all cases. Beautiful young women cut down in their prime all wearing some sort of lingerie and without any makeup, jewelry or anything else of that nature. Then they all have this scar that yours does and were all left lying as if someone had cared how they were left. Oh yeah, I forgot to tell you this, but this last one, Grace Smith, she was found pretty much how your Suzanne Valadon was found. Lying face up with her head on a pillow of twigs."

I thought about what he'd said for a minute on the one end of a mute phone. They were obviously related and yet I doubted we were looking at a serial killer. They were all over the world which would be extremely unusual for one killer.

The thing is though, they were all dressed similarly and stripped of any identifying items including jewelry. They were also all placed in similar locations in the sense that these locations were park-like. But I figured that must have to do with just getting rid of the bodies. But if you're trying to get rid of a body, the way they did it made me think they wanted the bodies to be found. Each and every one of these women had been left near population dense cities, or even within such cities.

And then there were the actual deaths. None of it looked like premeditated murder. More like sex or drugs gone wrong. I had a hunch we weren't looking at these women as being out for the night with one or even two johns. These women, if I was a betting man, were involved in an orgy or sex party that got out of hand.

"You know," I said. "I think these two case here in LA might have the same perp."

"Because of the twigs?"

"Yeah, they're the only two victims placed like that."

"I was thinking the same."

There was more silence over the phone.

"I also don't think these women are common hookers," said Tai. "I think we're dealing with a professional class of criminal or organization."

"What makes you say that?"

"All inquiries in all cases went cold. Not much evidence to pursue and because of that the trails went cold. Even the parents and friends of the victims didn't have much to add. In those four cases I told you about, the closest to the time of murder that a friend or loved one had come into contact with the victim was eighteen months. Police couldn't get anywhere with that."

"You're saying you have no idea who did this then?"

"Well, it doesn't look like any of them were victims of premeditated murder," said Tai.

"Yeah, but there's negligent homicide, manslaughter for sure. Crimes have been committed, Tai."

"I hear ya, Anthony. What I'm saying is that if you're asking me, I think we're likely dealing with an international prostitute ring."

Captain Obvious was using his superpowers again.

"One last thing before I let you go," I said.

"Sure, anything."

"Any connection you could see with my victim and the Calabasas victim from Y2K?"

"Not that I can think of. Nothing appears to connect them. They're from different cities, hell, different states. Both were brunette, young and by all accounts attractive. Incidentally, the two from Russia were blondes and the one found in Germany had black hair. It's a small thing, but perhaps worth mentioning. All these women were citizens of the countries they were found in. So we've got two Russians, two Americans and a German."

I nodded on the other end of the line without speaking. That nod drifted into silence.

"Anything else?" asked Tai, after several moments had passed.

"Uh, yeah, sorry, Tai. I'm just thinking about this case. I can't see any good leads at the moment."

"Yeah, this is a tough one. You've got four priors that were never closed, the batting average is not good. But if anyone can get anywhere, I'd put my money on you."

"Thanks," I said.

"Just wear out some shoe leather. I don't see how else to get anywhere."

"Thanks for your help, Tai. If there's anything else you can think of, please call."

"Will do."

We hung up and I finished the rest of my cold coffee. I was starting to get an appetite, but I wanted to first see what Roberts was up to. The only solid lead we had was Gorky. Maybe he'd seen something. No, he must have seen something or who erased portions of the video I'd seen yesterday? Food could wait, maybe good news was waiting for me with Roberts.

Everything's Not Nice

I looked at my phone and tapped on Johnny Rotten's details. I put the phone to my ear and waited. After three rings he picked up and answered.

"What's going on?" I asked.

"Nice to hear from you too," he said, with a smile thick as a booty behind the voice.

"Just got off the phone with the FBI," I said.

"Still no love, no sweet nothings whispered in my ear," he said.

"Well, how's this for a little sugar and spice and everything nice. The FBI is aware of four other victims like ours. I'll fill you in when I see you. By the way, in the meantime, why don't you find the file on that young victim from the Calabasas landfill from Y2K. Her name was Grace Cossington Smith."

"Now you're tickling my interest," said Roberts. "Actually, this is a good time. We're just up here at North Hollywood. Swing by, I want you to go back out with Beast and pick up Gorky."

"What's he done?"

"It's more like why didn't Beast and Sonny bring him in yesterday?"

"That's a question I don't have an answer for. What did they say?"

"They wanted to ask me first. But really, I think they didn't want the hassle of the paperwork."

I laughed.

"I know what that's like," I said. "I'll see you when I get there."

"Take your time, it's not like we're on a murder case or anything."

I said goodbye and hung up the phone. I looked at my coffee. The cream had sort of left a skin on top of it. It didn't look appealing, so I took the mug into the kitchen and emptied it into the sink. I put Pirate's bowl of dry food on his mat. He eats his food on a mat because he's like a toddler with the mess he makes. Bits of drying wet food were scattered about the mat like shrapnel from a small grenade that looked like it'd gone off in his bowl.

He nudged my calf and I reached down and petted his head as he purred. My headache was just about all gone but I wasn't feeling as good as I'd wanted to by now. And it wasn't the hangover. That was taking care of itself.

No, it was this case. Everywhere I looked I saw dead ends. Dead ends and details. We had all the details but everything pointed to dead ends. Her parents hadn't helped. Not that they hadn't tried. I now knew what the scar meant but that didn't lead me anywhere. If tox came back with cannabis, ketamine and coke in her system, that'd just prove she might be part of this global prostitute ring just like Tai thought.

And I'll be honest with you. The LAPD doesn't have the resources, and if I read the room accurately, nor the inclination to pursue an international prostitute ring. Especially if these women weren't intentionally murdered. But maybe I'm just an old, grumpy man shaking my fists at the sky.

I grabbed my jacket and donned my fedora and left Pirate to his bachelor pad with strict admonitions to behave himself. He actually meowed at me. And what I thought I heard was a big 'piss off'. Cats!

My thirty minute drive had me thinking a lot about this place. I needed a lead like a dying sinner man needed a confession. What I had was loose ends that tied me in knots.

Late Night Laundry

I found my way to the back corner of the North Hollywood station where Beast and JR were having a friendly argument. I only caught the tail end of it but it was about having left Gorky behind at his apartment. Roberts figured they'd have more influence if he'd been charged with impeding a police investigation or aiding and abetting a murder. But Beast was saying that they didn't know if it was murder yet.

"And it's probably not," I added as I walked in.

They both looked at me as if I'd just appeared out of thin air.

"What isn't what?" asked Roberts.

"Murder. Suzanne was probably not murdered," I said.

"Let's take a minute to get settled," said Roberts. "First, fill us in on what you found out from our friendly neighborhood FBI guy."

I pulled a chair from an empty desk and sat down. They were already seated.

"There's good news and then there's bad news," I said.

"Always the bad news first," said Roberts.

I nodded.

"Ok, this case of ours is likely part of an international criminal organization, and probably a prostitution ring."

"Why's that bad news?"

"Because the four other cases like this that the FBI is aware of have run cold. All leads led to nowhere."

"And the good news?"

"We now have two victims from LA and that might get us somewhere," I said, lying through my teeth. I wasn't really expecting anything from the Grace Smith case to help us. Not if we didn't get much from our current victim. But I was keeping an open mind.

"Sonny's just gathering that file on Smith," said Roberts. "We'll see if there's anything in there to help us. What did you learn?"

"We have four other victims with similarities to our victim. Two were found in Russia. The middle two, actually. Let me start from the beginning. All victims were citizens of the country they were found in. At least that means that we aren't looking at women who are being trafficked. That's something."

"Or maybe the four victims just happened to be citizens of the country they were found in but if this is international like you say it is, then there's a good potential they could be moving women around but none of our victims happened to be those," said Beast.

"Fair point," I said. "What we do have is that all victims were young, late teens to early twenties. Attractive and mostly unmarked except for the scars and how they'd been placed. That ties them all together. The first victim was found in seventy-seven on the outskirts of the Black Forest near Baden-Baden, Germany. She was twenty one years old. She was wearing a white one-piece item of lingerie, much like ours from what I was told. She had semen in her vagina but it was determined she was not raped. She died from an overdose and was found with cocaine, ketamine and cannabis in her system."

Nods all round.

"The second victim was a twenty three year old who was found in eighty eight under a tree in a park in Moscow..."

"That's ballsy," said Roberts.

"Didn't help us," I said. "All leads and details lead to dead ends. She was wearing a black one-piece and again, no makeup and no jewelry just like all of them. She was a blonde. The German had black hair. She had cannabis and ketamine in her system but she died of asphyxiation..."

"Or murder," offered Sonny.

"That's not what Tai seemed to think. Seemed like it was a sexual kink thing that got out of hand. She had semen in her vagina and anus from two different donors.

"The third victim was a blonde nineteen year old found in a wooded area near St. Petersburg. This was in ninety one. She was wearing a pink one-piece, no makeup, no obvious violence. Even the first one from Russia who died of asphyxiation, it was hard to tell it was that from just looking at her. This third victim had ketamine, cocaine and cannabis in her system too. Semen also from two donors. Found in her vagina and anus."

"And what do you know about the fourth victim? Grace Smith, right?" asked Beast.

I nodded.

"Yeah, Grace Smith. Twenty two, found at the landfill on New Year's day in two thousand. Only ketamine and cannabis in her system. She was also asphyxiated and again, Tai thinks it's sexual kink gone wrong. She was a brunette and wearing a one-piece, teddy they call it."

"And that's a what?" asked Roberts.

"It's like a one-piece bathing suit but not made for swimming if you know what I mean."

Roberts nodded.

"What do the Chinese characters mean?" asked Roberts.

"Right," I said, pulling out my notebook. "Ianfu. Basically means comfort woman. Like the Japanese used during World War Two. It's another word for prostitute. Not really used much nowadays but some corners still use it as slang for prostitutes."

"That sounds like a great lead. Did Tai have anything to say about a Chinese triad or Japanese yakuza connection?" asked Roberts.

"Funny you should say that. He did indeed," I said.

Roberts grinned. I was grinning at him.

"He said there is no connection that INTERPOL has found between these women and an Asian prostitution ring."

"What does he think the connection is?" asked Roberts, who was no longer smiling.

"He doesn't know, only he thinks it's a bigger organization or, and I'm putting words in his mouth, it's an organization that we're probably not familiar with and that has huge resources."

Roberts nodded thoughtfully for a moment.

"What are you thinking?" he asked me.

"Well, from what I've learned, I figure these women are probably high class prostitutes working for a global prostitution ring. With the same scars, and the same way they were discarded. They're all beautiful and young and found with semen I'd say that's clearly what we're looking at. But who?

I don't know that. I mean, how many sex parties or orgies are going on under our very noses in private homes here in LA and around the country? Probably more than we know of. Probably a lot more."

"We've gotta get into one of those parties then," said Roberts.

"I don't know how that's possible. Let's say this group has been going since the mid-seventies. Our first victim was found in seventy-seven. Over forty plus years they've only left four victims. Maybe there are more that we just don't know about. Four victims in that time and how many parties have they had? A couple a year, half a dozen? Who knows. But that's a lot of parties that have been kept under the radar. We don't know who they are, we don't know how to get involved even if we knew who they were, and with this kind of group, I'm sure they're very slow to admit any newcomers. But really, we have no idea who they are."

"You're not sounding optimistic," said Roberts.

"I'm not. How do you catch a ghost?" I asked.

"Captain," said Sonny.

We all turned to look at Sonny. On his screen was the Grace Smith file. This one had been digitized already which was a small mercy.

"I've got the Smith file here. Pretty slim. Not much to it. No leads really to pursue."

"Who was the lead?"

"Detective Ferrari. Armando Ferrari," said Sonny.

"Really?" asked Roberts.

"Yeah, why? Is that important?" asked Sonny.

"Detective Ferrari was one of the greatest detectives this force has ever had. He was also Carrick's mentor."

I nodded.

"You should go and speak to him. He's retired now, right?" asked Roberts.

I shrugged.

"Don't know. We haven't been in touch for, shit, it's gotta be coming on ten years or more," I said.

Roberts nodded.

"Well, see if you can't get a sit down with him and pick his brain about this case."

"Sure, I was thinking about that anyway. He's been on my mind lately. But if he was lead on this and it wasn't solved, then we're in for a tough slog."

"We'll worry about that once we've run out of leads. What does the jacket have?" asked Roberts.

"Not much. There weren't any witnesses. Guys at the landfill had nothing to offer..."

"We should talk to them again. Wasn't it the foreman who found her, didn't he tell you that?" asked Roberts.

Sonny nodded.

"Yeah, I'll talk to him again. Ferrari did the usual kicking over stones and rocks, but there really wasn't anything to go on. Her parents didn't seem especially unhappy about her death, but friends and neighbors said the family was troubled. They weren't surprised she left home when she was sixteen."

"Ferrari wouldn't have left a stone unturned," I said.

Sonny nodded.

"Yeah. His notes are thorough. He canvassed the neighborhood around the landfill going from house to house. Only one person had anything to offer. They saw a white van driving around early in the morning. Around three a.m. The van appeared to be a laundry van with the name..."

Sonny scrolled through his pages.

"Ten bucks says Lemonade Laundry," offered Beast.

Sonny nodded.

"Yeah, that's right," he said.

"How'd you know?" asked Roberts.

"That's what Gorky said the van he saw had on it. A smaller Ford Transit van with the logo of a laundry company on it. 'Lemonade Laundry', he said, with the tagline 'easy squeezy lemon cleany'. The 'o' in Lemonade was shaped like a lemon."

"What does this neighbor say about the van? Did he pick up on the logo?" asked Roberts.

"It isn't described in Ferrari's notes, other than the neighbor noticed the van was white and the company name written on it was 'Lemonade Laundry'. It's not described at all and there's no reference to a tagline. The neighbor was suffering from insomnia and was taking their dog for a walk. Traffic was very quiet, and so this van was noticeable and it turned left onto Lost Hills Road which leads to the landfill. Came off of Parkville Road."

"Any plate info?" asked Roberts.

Sonny shook his head.

"Neighbor didn't take note. He just thought it was odd that a laundry service van was out at that time of the morning and seemingly headed towards the landfill on New Year's day."

"What did Ferrari find out about this Lemonade Laundry company?" I asked.

"Well, that's where it gets interesting. There is no company in the whole of California with that name."

Just as I figured, I thought.

"Anything else of note?" asked Roberts.

Sonny shook his head.

"Nobody, not even her family, had heard from Grace for over eighteen months. The parents weren't all that put out. Police had known them from prior domestics and friends of Grace had spoken about abuse that she seemed to have suffered at home."

"What sort of abuse are we talking about?" asked Roberts.

"Friends didn't say. Said Grace never specifically talked about it, but comments she'd made to her friends seemed to indicate that her home life was not a happy one. She left school and her home when she was sixteen. Ferrari pressed one of the friends and she thought that Grace might have been sexually abused by her father."

"And we only ever attended on domestics?" asked Roberts.

"According to Ferrari there were over a dozen calls to the home for domestics. Last time we attended was in two thousand and seven and homicide was lead on the case," said Sonny.

"He killed his wife?" asked Roberts.

"Other way round, Captain," said Sonny. "The wife killed the husband. Slit his throat and stabbed him over twenty-one times with a filet knife."

"What about? She'd just had enough of the abuse?" asked Roberts.

"I'm quoting here. She said, 'I'd had enough of his bitching about my cooking.'"

Roberts shook his head.

"Jesus H. Christ," he said. "Ok, this is what we're gonna do. Carrick and Beeves, I want you two to go and pick up Gorky. Charge him with tampering with evidence, or even better, accessory to murder and bring him down to the station and toss him in a cell. Let him sweat it out and maybe we'll get more out of him. Forrest, I want you to see if that neighbor is still there and find out if anything else comes to mind. Then go and see the foreman at the landfill, he was the one who found Smith, right?"

Sonny nodded.

"Good. Then when you get back, take a look through the domestics on Smith's parents and see if anything stands out. Carrick, when you and Beeves are finished interrogating Gorky, reach out to Ferrari and see if there's anything else he remembers that isn't in the report."

Black Beard

Beeves and I hopped into an unmarked, gray late model Chevy Malibu. Beeves was driving and that was just fine with me. He knew where he was going. He'd visited Gorky just the day before.

"Where we headed?" I asked, trying to make conversation.

"The Blue Moon apartments in Canoga Park. Know it?"

I shook my head. Beeves was watching traffic.

"What did he say yesterday?" I asked, as Beeves drove west along the one oh one.

"Nothing at first until we started leaning on him. Then he came clean. Said a guy drove up in a white van and said he needed to drop off a TV and his boss would be pissed if he didn't. Gorky told him the dump was closed. Guy put a handgun in his face and had an envelope in the other hand. Said they could do this the easy way or the hard way. Gorky chose the easy way."

"Which was the envelope," I said. "How much?"

"Ten grand," said Beast.

"And where's that now?"

"Forensics, getting fingerprinted."

I nodded.

"What did this guy look like?"

"Gorky said he was in all black. Turtleneck, black pants, black boots, black sunglasses, black gloves, black beard and black curly hair. Oh yeah, the guy had very blue eyes."

"How'd he see that through the sunglasses?"

"He removed them at one point to scratch his face or rub his forehead. Gorky seemed to think the beard and hair might have been fake or dyed. Seemed to think it was unusually black and didn't quite match his eyebrows."

"Anything else?"

"Yeah, thought the guy might have been a wrestler or MMA. His nose was busted and his ears thick."

We drove on for a while through fairly steady traffic. Beeves was a cautious driver. A sober man without much of a sense of humor.

"What do you think about this case?" I asked.

Beeves shrugged, keeping both hands on the steering wheel. Ten to two just like they teach you. He didn't look at me. Eyes straight ahead. Occasionally he glanced at his rearview.

"I don't think Gorky's gonna know much more than he already told us. He got a ten grand payoff to let Mr. MMA drop something off at the dump. He was told it was a TV, but obviously he didn't believe that. He's taken a couple of hundred bucks here and there when folks want to drop off chemicals and hazardous waste. This time was ten grand. Said he didn't think it was a TV, but didn't think the guy was dropping off a body."

I nodded.

"I don't think he was told, nor was he going to ask what was being dropped off."

"He was told it was a TV."

"Yeah, but clearly you're not gonna give a guy ten grand just to let you drop off a TV after hours, and especially when the guy comes back and watches you erase the recording."

"Did we get how tall he is?"

"Around five ten, five eleven."

"He couldn't start recording as soon as the guy got back into his van?" I asked.

"Apparently, you can prevent the cameras from recording until a certain time, and that's what he made Gorky do."

"Smart," I said. "But this guy doesn't seem like the mastermind."

"I agree," said Beeves. "Probably just the hired hand who does the cleanup."

"Do you think there's anything else we can get out of him?" I asked.

"Who? Gorky?"

I nodded. Beeves still hadn't peeled his eyes from the road. Beeves shrugged.

"He seemed forthright," said Beeves, "but you never know how being charged with a felony can open you up a little more. We'll see. Once he's sweated in the room for a while he might remember something else."

I nodded.

"Here's hoping," I said. "We need a good lead on this case because everywhere I look I see us bumping up against dead ends."

Beeves didn't say anything for a while.

"Maybe your old mentor, Ferrari, might have something."

"Maybe," I said. "Ferrari was good. If he didn't find anything there probably wasn't anything to be found."

We drove the rest of the way in silence. I didn't like this case. We had a good idea who our victim was and her family. But that led nowhere. We had a description of a person involved who appeared to be wearing a disguise, driving a van for a company that probably didn't exist. Valadon wasn't murdered, which meant he probably wasn't the killer. Maybe he was just the driver and the dumper. Maybe he was these women's handler or maybe he just supplied the drugs. Maybe he was none of these things except the driver. Maybe he was all of them. Didn't matter. We didn't have any way of knowing who he was.

No plates, no honest description and if he was wearing gloves in the van, he was probably careful enough to wear gloves when putting the money together for Gorky. Or maybe that was someone else. I was thinking about all these sorts of angles when Beeves stopped the car right in front of The Blue Moon apartments. Nothing much to look at. Much like any other apartment complex in this part of town.

We got out of the car, and walked towards the main entrance.

"He's in three oh five," said Beeves. "Top floor on that side."

He was pointing to his right at the top.

"Front or back?"

"Backside, overlooks the parking lot for residents' cars."

Beeves pushed the button for three oh five. We waited for a while. Nothing happened. He pushed it again.

"He wasn't scheduled to be working today was he?" Beeves asked.

I shook my head.

"He works either Friday, Saturday, Sunday or Thursday, Friday, Saturday and Sunday. This week he starts on Thursday. He should be here," I said.

Beeves nodded at the intercom box and pushed the button again. We waited around half a minute.

"Maybe he's gone out," I offered, though my mind had gone to a darker place considering what we'd come out here to investigate. I watched Beeves push number one oh one. The name next to it was 'Manager'. That buzzer push got answered.

"Blue Moon Apartments," came a thick phlegmy voice that belonged to an old man.

"Detective Beeves and Carrick," said Beeves. "We need to speak with one of your residents."

"Who?"

"Arshile Gorky."

"Just a minute."

We waited around another thirty seconds. Outside it was warm for the middle of October. But not warm enough that I was sweating under my fedora and jacket. I was goldilocks. The sky was mostly blue with torn cotton swabs for clouds.

I watched an old man leaning on a cane make his way to the inside door. He opened it and shuffled past. He wore sweatpants, a white t-shirt that had a coffee stain on it under a beige robe. He came up to the outside entrance and looked at us through the door.

"I need to see ID," he said, coughing.

Beeves unhooked his badge from his belt and pressed it against the door's glass pane. The manager looked at it for a while, craning his head towards it. Reminded me of a turtle.

"That's your shield, I need to see ID."

Beeves took his ID out from a back pocket and flipped it open so the manager could see his ID. It had his photo on it, his name and signature. His badge number too. After a while he nodded and Beeves put his ID away. The manager opened up the door and we took it from him and walked in.

"Sorry 'bout that," he said. "Nowadays we get all sorts of scammers trying to harass our residents. I can't let anyone in without ID."

"I understand," said Beeves as we walked into the main lobby sandwiched between two doors.

"Weren't you the fella that was here yesterday with that other fella?" the manager asked.

"That's right," said Beeves. "That was my partner, Detective Forrest."

The manager nodded.

"What's your name?" asked Beeves.

"Clive, Clive Fossil," came the answer.

"Thank you, Clive," said Beeves. "Would you mind coming up with us? We'd like to check on Gorky."

"Well, I'm not sure I can let you in without a warrant or extreme circumstances," said Fossil.

Fossil was a good name for him. He looked old and worn out. He reeked of cigarette smoke. He wasn't fat but he wasn't slim. He was probably only in his sixties but he looked twenty years older.

"I fear these might be exigent circumstances," said Beeves. "Gorky's an important witness in a murder case we're investigating. We need to ask him some more questions, but more importantly, we want to check on his welfare now that he's not answering. He told us yesterday he'd be home all day."

Clive nodded.

"Ok, that's good enough for me. You know where he is. I'll get his key and meet you up there."

We nodded and exited the second door into the main hallway. I held it open for Fossil until he got through. Then I followed Beeves right.

Light of the Blue Moon

We made our way up the staircase. I figured we could wait for hours for the Fossil to make his way up here. But wasn't that life? You move someplace and then you wait for a while. Move. Then wait. And that's what we did. We moved up the stairs to the third floor and exited the stairwell to find Gorky's apartment on our right. The door was white and looked like it had received a number of coats of paint. Three oh five had been stenciled onto the door.

Beeves put his ear to the door, slowly and quietly. He held it there for several seconds. Then he knocked on the door. We waited. I was bladed towards the door on the right side by the doorframe. Beeves put his ear towards the door to listen again. I was concerned for him.

Once, when I was a junior street cop, we had gone on a call to check on the welfare of someone. My partner at the time was a grizzled veteran. Been on patrol all his twenty-odd years at that point. He told me to always knock on unknown doors from the side. Ideally by the door's frame which is thicker and will give you a little more protection.

And that's how we knocked. He on the far side of the door, me on the near side. He knocked. Nothing. He knocked again. No answer. He knocked a third time and announced that we were police and the bullets came flying through the door. We ducked and backed up. Squeezed into the door frames of his neighbors. Called backup and waited, our guns drawn and our breath heavy.

A short while after the bullets stopped flying a guy came out carrying a pistol. He looked left which is where I was but I got my rounds off before him. Ever since then, I've never knocked on a door facing it.

I gestured towards Beeves to give himself some room. Stand at the edge of the door. He did a half-hearted attempt and shuffled a couple of steps to his left. It was something. He knocked again. Loudest yet.

"Gorky! This is Detective Beeves with the LAPD. Open up!" yelled Beeves.

It was loud enough that the neighbors must have heard us. We stood and waited. Across from three oh five was three oh six. The door opened and I watched it carefully. A small, older woman in her seventies popped her head out.

"Are you the police?" she asked.

Beeves nodded and pointed to his badge on his belt. We moved towards her.

"Detective Beeves and Carrick," he said, nodding his head at me. "Have you seen Mr. Gorky leave the apartment this morning?"

She shook her head.

"I haven't seen him leave this morning, but he did get a delivery from UPS earlier," she said.

Beeves nodded.

"What time was that?"

"It was a little before nine, which is odd, because the UPS driver is usually only here between eleven and noon. He's pretty reliable that way. And he came at eleven forty-five. He just left about five or ten minutes ago."

"Maybe he was making two deliveries," said Beeves.

"He's never done that, detective," she said. "He's very reliable, he never makes two trips here, and the UPS man who was here to deliver to Arshile, well, he wasn't Colton."

She had a noticeable stoop in her carriage. Her hair was in curlers and had left auburn for the more frisky town of burgundy. She too, was dressed in a bathrobe. A white one with pink flowers on it.

"How do you know it wasn't Colton?" Beeves asked.

I glanced back at Gorky's door. Nothing was happening there even though I thought I heard something.

"Well," she said. "Colton is a big African American man and very friendly. This man was shorter and slimmer."

"My height or closer to his?" asked Beeves.

"Can you come and stand nearer the peephole?" she asked me.

I moved closer towards the door and she looked from me to the peephole and back. She nodded her head.

"Yes, he was close to your height," she said. "Maybe a little taller."

"How tall would Colton be?" asked Beeves.

I looked down the opposite end of the hallway, Mr. Wheezer and Mr. Shuffle was slowly making his way towards us. The old lady put her hand up on the door, about four or five inches higher than I was.

"He's about that tall," she said.

That put Colton somewhere between six one and six two if I was a guessing man.

"And Colton came by not long ago," said Beeves. "Did you ask him if he had been around earlier?"

"No, detective, because he didn't have a package for me today, but I saw him through here," she pointed at the peephole, "and I know Colton very well. I usually get a package from him once a week at least. The man who was here wasn't Colton."

"Did he have the uniform?"

She nodded.

"And he wore the hat they have too. Colton doesn't wear the hat, says he finds it too tight around his head."

"The UPS baseball cap?" asked Beeves.

She nodded.

"And this man, was he carrying packages?"

"Just the one, but instead of handing it over to Arshile he said something to him and then he went into the apartment. But only he came out about seven to ten minutes later."

"Did you hear anything? What he said? Or any sounds coming from the apartment?"

"No. My hearing isn't what it used to be," she said.

"This earlier UPS delivery man, was he white or black?" I asked, getting a piece of the conversation.

"White, and he had a black beard and he was wearing sunglasses," she said.

"Anything else?" asked Beeves.

The old lady thought for a while and then shook her head. Then she nodded her head.

"Well, now that I think about it. He left Arshile's apartment and he was still carrying the package he had come to deliver. Maybe it wasn't for Arshile."

I didn't like the sounds of that. I looked at Beeves and he gave me a small nod. Beeves reached into his back pocket and pulled out a business card. He handed it to her.

"If you remember anything else, please call," he said.

She looked at the card, gave Beeves a small smile.

"I will Detective Beeves," she said.

Then she closed the door and Fossil was almost upon us.

"What's her name?" asked Beeves, looking at Fossil.

"That's Mrs. Francis Fisher," he said. "Been here over ten years. A little longer than I've been here."

Beeves made a note in his notebook.

"Got the key?" he asked.

Fossil nodded and we moved over towards Gorky's door. I didn't have my gun handy. I'd left it in my apartment. Beeves was dressed to kill but he hadn't unholstered his gun. I wasn't especially worried. Fisher had seen the first UPS driver leave. It took some agonizing extra seconds for Fossil to fumble with the key and get it into the lock. I noticed his hands trembled but he wasn't scared.

Blood Money

After what seemed like two sunrises and two sunsets, Fossil unlocked the door. Only it wasn't unlocked. But it took him that long to figure it all out. At this point, Beeves decided to unholster his weapon.

"Let me go first," he said, pushing his way past Fossil.

I followed Beeves and Fossil followed me inside. Everything looked fine at first. We entered into the short hallway and then past that and into the living room where we found Gorky. I was expecting blood and brains on the couch and the wall behind it. Pleasantly there wasn't any.

Gorky was sitting in the middle of the couch, his eyes open and watching a news channel on TV. But his eyes were dead and glassy. He was wearing a Hawaiian shirt and blue sweatpants. It was hard to see the bullet wound at first from all the color on his shirt. But there it was, a wine colored stain that had spread like a blooming flower.

"Call it in, I'm going to secure the apartment," said Beeves, and off he went with his gun leading him on.

I pulled out my phone and called nine one one. Told them what we had and to send the coroner. I hung up and wondered if it was M who was going to come on out or someone else. Heavy breathing and sighing took my attention away from that. I turned to see Fossil leaning heavily on a table. His face was ashen and he was making all sorts of odd sounds as if he were a fish just hoisted from water to land.

I walked up to him and grabbed a chair. I placed the chair in the narrow hallway and faced it towards the door. I grabbed Fossil by the arm and steered him to it. He sat down heavily and I told him to put his head between his legs.

I went back into the living room and gauged the scene. One bullet wound had likely torn up his heart. I imagined he died quickly. Gorky's hands were slack and by his sides, palms up. His gut looked like a beach ball stuffed under his shirt. His mouth was slack and hanging open. It wasn't the worst death I'd seen. Not by a long shot. Pun intended.

In fact, a long shot often makes you look worse. It takes a higher calibre round, often, and more velocity. Well, you can imagine what that does to a gelatinous body.

On Gorky's lap was a neat stack of one hundred dollar bills. Maybe about a half inch thick. I didn't touch anything. I didn't have gloves and I wasn't expecting to come across a murder.

I looked around the room. The TV was on all day news and the sound was modest. Everything else looked undisturbed. There was a recliner to Gorky's right. My left as I looked at him. A cigarette was in an ashtray on a small coffee table next to the recliner. It had burned itself out at around the halfway mark. Next to it was a lighter with barbed wire on it. A Zippo. That was placed on top of a pack of cigarettes.

Looked to me like he'd been sitting in the recliner before he got up to answer the door. Then I figured the guy told him to let him in because he was probably carrying his gun in the UPS package. They came into the living room and UPS got him to sit on the couch where he was given his delivery of lead from inside the box. The money might have been in there too, or maybe that was in his pocket.

From what I could see the place hadn't been torn apart. In fact, it didn't look disturbed at all. At least not the area I was in and looking at. Beeves came back and holstered his gun.

"Where's the manager?" he asked.

I nodded behind me. Beeves followed my gaze. Fossil still had his head between his legs.

"Anything interesting in the rest of the place?" I asked.

Beeves shook his head.

"No. Place looks undisturbed except by Gorky. Nothing looked tossed around. Nothing's broken. This is probably an assassination."

I nodded. We both looked at Gorky for a while.

"I was expecting blood and brains on the back of the wall there," said Beeves.

"Me too. I'm glad that's not the case."

Beeves nodded.

"Well camouflaged on the shirt he's wearing. Have you moved anything?"

I shook my head.

"Nothing. Haven't touched anything either."

"Good," said Beeves, nodding.

"You might remember me from LAPD homicide, starring as the winningest detective," I said.

Beeves offered me a small smile. He might have been on the floor rolling in laughter if he were more of a light-hearted fella. Getting a chuckle out of the man took a lifetime of dedication or so it seemed.

"You called it in?"

I nodded to that too.

"Give me a second," said Beeves.

He walked back to Fossil and started to talk to him. He was suggesting that Fossil didn't need to be here. I heard Fossil stand up and Beeves offering him a card for crisis counseling. Despite his somber personality, Beeves was a good cop and a kind man.

I went back to assessing the scene. We hadn't asked Mrs. Fisher if she had noticed the UPS guy wearing gloves or not. It probably didn't matter. If he was wearing gloves there'd be no fingerprints. If he hadn't been wearing gloves there'd probably not be any fingerprints. This was a hit job and probably carried out by a professional.

The way this case was going I had grave concerns about closing it. And that pissed me off. I hadn't yet managed to find a case I couldn't solve. Maybe this was going to turn into my Waterloo. I brushed that aside. This case had just begun. I needed to focus on the task at hand.

I looked around at the scene again. I found nothing new. Nothing looked disturbed. Looked like a professional hit. No violence, no struggle. No obvious evidence. I walked over to Gorky and leaned down to look at his hands. His fingernails really. I could see nothing that indicated he'd got a piece of his assailant under his fingernails. Of course, CID would check for that. But if this was the same organization that had dropped off Valadon after her OD, there probably wouldn't be any easy evidence to find. Maybe no evidence to find at all.

I heard the door close. Beeves walked back in and stood next to me. I had straightened up by that point. I closed my eyes and tried to remember what scents I had picked up when I had first entered the apartment.

I had smelled the residual scent of gunpowder. Now there was the lingering sickly sweet metallic smell of death. That mostly came from the blood. Beyond that was the stench of shit. If Gorky had been murdered around nine then his bowels had a long time to relax before rigor mortis. Shit, piss and blood. It was a cocktail with an ugly stench.

I'd gotten used to it but it's still never pleasant. I turned to look at Beeves.

"This is probably the same guy or group who had dropped off Valadon," I offered.

Beeves nodded. He kept staring at the body.

"Yesterday he told us about the guy who was driving a white van with that Lemonade Laundry logo. This sounds like the exact same guy. Black beard, dark sunglasses, around the right height as described by Fisher."

"Should've brought him in yesterday," I said, poking the bear a little.

Beeves didn't say anything. He kept looking at the body. The apartment door opened again. Beeves and I both looked in that direction. A couple of uniformed officers walked in. Young guys probably come to look at their first dead body. They walked right in and stared past us at the body. Beeves looked at them.

"What did you need, Stockton?" asked Beeves, looking at the young guy's name tag.

"Uh, nothing, detective," he said, seeing Beeves badge on his belt. "Uh, we just wanted to see if you need any help."

"Did dispatch indicate I need help?" he asked. His tone was getting testy.

"Um, no sir," said Stockton.

His partner's name tag read 'Barren'. The two of them were no longer so chipper.

"Did you forget about crime scene sanctity?" asked Beeves.

"No, sir."

"Then why the fuck are you walking around in my crime scene fucking up what little evidence there might be?"

Stockton swallowed.

"Get out, and don't let anyone in who isn't CID, from the coroner's officer or has a rank higher than mine. Got it?"

"Yes, sir."

And with that Stockton and Barren turned around and walked out with their tails between their legs.

"Fucking millennials," said Beeves, who was now talking to me but looking back at Gorky. "They think this shit is a video game. No wonder cases get tossed."

I nodded.

Used to drive me nuts when uniform wanted to come and do some rubbernecking at my crime scenes. But after you've seen a couple of dead bodies, more or less, you lose your appetite for seeking out more.

While we waited, I figured I'd get Beeves focused back on the scene.

"What do you make of the stack of cash on his lap?" I asked.

Beeves looked at it.

"How much do you think is there?"

I looked at the stack.

"Hundred dollar bills. I figure that'd be around ten grand."

Beeves nodded.

"I think you're right," he said. "If that's the case, that's the exact same amount he was given when the driver came to drop off Valadon."

"Maybe it was half up front, the other half upon assassination," I said.

Beeves looked at me. He was still in no mood to crack a smile.

"Didn't mention anything like that when we interviewed him," said Beeves. "Besides, what's a dead man gonna do with ten grand? More like a sick joke."

I didn't say anything. I didn't know why the killer would leave ten grand on the dead body like that. We'd just take it into evidence. What did it serve?

Beeves pulled out his phone and called Roberts. Roberts was already on his way. Less than five minutes away from what I could gather listening in. I went and took a look at the rest of the apartment.

Dirty Laundry

Gorky's apartment offered no insight as to what had happened earlier in the day. It was as you would expect for a bachelor pad for a guy in his mid to late thirties who likely hadn't seen the comforts of a woman for some time.

There was dirty laundry piled in one corner near the closet in his bedroom. His bed was unmade and slept on only one side. The near side to the door where a night table was. There was a small desk in the corner of the room with scraps of paper on it and men's magazines. It also had on it an old laptop. Probably older than five years judging by the thickness. But I could be wrong.

I took out my handkerchief and opened up the lid, careful not to leave any prints. It offered me a login screen. I thought about that for a moment, couldn't come up with a password for Gorky so I looked around on the desk for inspiration. Mostly bills and other opened mail. Some scraps of paper with numbers on it, both added up and subtracted. Initials next to the numbers. Maybe it was his budgeting.

I went back to the login screen and typed in 1-2-3-4-5-6 and hit enter. The laptop didn't like that one. Next I tried Q-W-E-R-T-Y. Didn't like that one either. Then I tried logmein, both lower caps, mixed caps and upper caps. Didn't like any of them either. I closed the lid with my handkerchief. TID could try and figure that out.

There were no drawers on the table and nothing else of interest to me. I looked in his closet which was open but didn't offer up any secrets. Clothes, baseball caps. Looked like Gorky might have been a Rams fan. That was pretty much the only NFL team's baseball caps he had. The rest were logos of one sort or another. Most of his clothes were casual. But he did have one dark grey suit in his closet. Weddings and funerals, I figured.

That was pretty much all there was to see in his bedroom. I opened up the drawer in his night stand before leaving. That wasn't very interesting either. A couple of knockoff watches. Loose coins and some small bills. A couple of pens and a pad of paper that didn't look used. Mints, a sleep mask and earplugs. I did notice there was no ashtray or cigarettes in his room. That was unusual for a smoker.

I walked into the bathroom after leaving his bedroom. The bathroom was as expected for a thirty-something bachelor. A damp towel hung carelessly on a rack. The damp bath mat crumpled by the bath. A bathtub that needed a clean a year ago. An old razor on the edge of the sink and a toothbrush in a chipped coffee mug that probably hadn't been replaced since his last dental visit. The chipped coffee mug was plain white with black writing on it that read, 'Coffee, because crack is bad for you'.

The toothpaste tube had been squeezed from the middle and was about half used. Splinters of stubble were all over the sink, so much so it looked like the sink needed a shave. The medicine cabinet was directly above the sink and its mirror was splattered with what looked like a petri dish of spit and dried up toothpaste.

I opened it with my handkerchief and realized I'd be burning my new white hanky as soon as I left this place. Inside were a couple of bottles of pills. One was insulin, the other was lisinopril. I took out my phone and tapped away at it. I learned that lisinopril was taken for high blood pressure and congestive heart failure. Gorky was young for either of those conditions, but judging by the shape he was in, I figured those meds fit.

A pack of unopened razor blades, deodorant, small box of band-aids, a bottle of unbranded aspirin and one of acetaminophen, Alka-Seltzer and a used tube of A535 rounded out the medicine cabinet's content. Underneath the sink was a single roll of toilet paper in a torn plastic bag that looked like it once held captive eleven of its neighbors.

From the look of things at this end of the apartment it looked like Gorky's assassin hadn't been anywhere in this place other than to carry out his business. I closed the medicine cabinet and walked back out into the main living room again where Beeves was still standing looking at Gorky. His left elbow resting on his right wrist and his left hand under his chin and across his face.

There was a knock at the door and Cardigan and friends walked into the scene. I nodded at Cardigan. He nodded back. Beeves still had his back towards him.

"You ready for us, Beast?" asked Cardigan.

"Yeah," said Beeves, talking to Gorky. "Do your thing."

Cardigan came in with his box of goodies followed by a couple of other guys.

"I'm going to give them room to work," I said. "I'll be outside."

I left Beeves staring at a dead man and made my way outside. It was nice to get away from the stench. I walked out into the hallway and down the flight of stairs and back outside. The day was warm but not hot. The sun was bright, but rheumy, or watery in appearance, as if the sky had been painted over with a thin film of vaseline.

I leaned against the hood of our car. A cigarette was what I needed, but I didn't have any. I folded my hands in front of me and tilted my fedora further down my forehead. I saw Roberts roll up in his car and park across the street from us. All we needed now was the coroner and we'd have a happy family reunion.

Roberts walked across the road and looked like a man troubled. He walked up to me and stood in front of me.

"He's dead, I assume?" he asked.

"Dead as a doornail, a dodo, dead and done. Nail in the coffin, dead as a dead end..."

"I get it. Goddammit, should have brought him in yesterday," said Roberts.

"That's what I said."

I grinned at Roberts. He was in no mood for grinning.

"So what are you doing out here?"

"Contemplating my navel, because there's fuck all to think about," I said.

"What do you mean?"

"There's nothing to fucking go on, John," I said. I usually only called him John when we weren't fooling around.

"Walk me through it," said Roberts.

"Neighborly lady across the hall said a UPS driver delivered a package for Gorky this morning around 9. Only he wasn't the regular UPS driver. This guy looks like our man in the laundry van. Sunglasses, black beard, et cetera. Was carrying a box and left with the same box."

Roberts nodded.

"An assassination," he said.

I nodded.

"Looks like he got inside. Forced Gorky onto the couch and shot him once in the heart. Then he left. Place looks undisturbed otherwise. Weirdly, ten grand was left in his lap."

That caught Roberts' interest. He looked at me.

"Ten grand exactly?" he asked.

I shrugged.

"I didn't count it. I guess it's around ten grand. Why?"

"I read the previous DB's case and ten grand was left with her too."

"You talking about Grace Smith from Y2K?"

Roberts nodded.

"That's interesting, but more importantly, there wasn't any ten grand left with Valadon, was there?"

Roberts was looking down with his fingers to his lips.

"Right?" I asked again.

He looked up at me. And nodded his head vigorously.

"Yeah, no, there wasn't any money found with her."

"So why you harping on this?"

He looked up at me again.

"Well, Gorky is connected to the driver who dropped off Valadon. Maybe the ten grand that Gorky got was supposed to be left with Valadon. If so, now we have something that connects them."

"We already have a connection. I told you about what Tai explained to me. We're dealing with an international criminal organization that's probably better funded than we are. An extra ten fucking grand is not the smoking gun."

I wasn't mad at him. I was mad at myself and this case. There was nothing to go on and it was pissing me off.

"Sorry, JR," I said. "It's this case. Everywhere we look there's nothing but dead ends."

Roberts nodded.

"Let's just work what's at hand," he said. "Maybe Ferrari will have something for you that'll help. And Forrest is following up that lead that remembered seeing the van. Maybe something will come of those things."

"Hail Mary after Hail Mary and I'm not even religious," I said.

I was in a foul mood. Nothing was likely to bring me off the edge.

"I know this might be hard for you to understand, but in the real world not every homicide or suspicious death is solved," said JR, putting his hand on my shoulder. "We can't all be golden boys. Maybe this one won't be solved today. But maybe next year, or the year after. Whoever these assholes are, Sid, they'll fuck up one too many times and when they do, we'll be there to pinch the bastards like we always do. But for now we follow the evidence."

What evidence, I thought to myself. I fished out my phone.

"Just give me a second," I said to Roberts.

I dialed SAC Tai. I wanted to ask him if money had been left with any of the other three girls.

"Yeah, Tai, Anthony Carrick. Good, thanks. Yeah, star witness has been murdered. Got a question for you. Ok, any money found with the other victims? Ten grand? Your best memory. I see. Not all the same. Uh huh. What happened to it? Ok. In every case? That's what you think? Ok, good. Yeah, thanks. If you can just confirm. Great. Bye."

I hung up the phone.

"What was that about?" asked Roberts.

"I was asking Tai if any of the other women had money left with them. He said they had, though he thinks the first two didn't have quite as much as ten grand. He's pretty sure the last two did have ten grand found with them. That would have been our Grace Smith and the Russian in ninety-one from St. Petersburg. All of that money eventually found its way to the families of the victim. Even with Grace Smith," I said.

"Really?"

I nodded.

"Yeah, I guess that would make sense. If we can't determine the money is from the proceeds of a crime, then I guess it could end up as part of the vic's belongings."

"Right, and Tai thinks it's death payment. To help with burial for the families."

Roberts looked at me steadily.

"So you might be right. The driver might have given the ten grand that was for Valadon to Gorky," said Roberts.

"See, that's what I don't get," I said.

"And what's that?"

"Our best guess, well, mine certainly, is that we're dealing with a well-funded international criminal organization that has sex parties. At least that's what I think is going on because none of the women have been purposefully murdered from what we can tell. And yet, here they are making rookie mistakes."

"Go on," said Roberts.

"I mean, come on," I said, gesticulating with my hands and I'm not usually much of a gesticulator. "There must be a dozen better ways to get rid of a body so that it's never found or takes a helluva long time to find. And ten grand as a death payment. Please, we're sorry your daughter accidentally died while getting fucked by rich, old, white men. Take ten grand and we'll call it even. Rookie mistakes, John, rookie bullshit."

"Maybe these bodies are placed where they are exactly so they'll be found, and that explains the money. If you don't want the body found then there's no need to put money with it."

"Yeah, but ten grand, John? Really, just ten grand? That's how they're saying they're sorry?"

"I don't think they're sorry, Sid, not one bit. I think this is just to cover funeral costs and a new dress or suit for the bereaved."

I looked at John. I wasn't sure if he was being funny or not. He wasn't.

"Ten grand is more like salt in the wound to me," I said.

Roberts shrugged.

"Maybe, maybe not. It would be enough to cover a simple funeral or a cremation. The Valadons for instance, they're not rich, right?"

"Working class," I said.

"So ten grand would go far with them. Maybe all these girls are from working class backgrounds. So maybe this still is a well-funded international criminal organization and none of this is accidental, except perhaps for the actual deaths."

"What about giving Gorky the money instead of leaving it with the body?" I suggested.

"That looks like an oversight, but maybe that was the driver's. If we don't get anywhere in a couple of days, we'll release a sketch of him to the public. This guy's the weak link, Anthony. If he's made one mistake, perhaps he's made more and that's the way we'll get to the top of this organization."

I nodded. Roberts patted me on the shoulder.

"Go reminisce with Ferrari. Maybe he'll inspire you in new directions."

And with that I watched Roberts disappear into the building. I pulled out my phone again and called dispatch to get a good number for Ferrari. Then I called him.

No Cow, No Dairy

Ferrari lives in Cerritos. Just a few blocks from where Roberts lives. He's never mentioned bumping into him so maybe he doesn't see him around. Maybe I'd ask Ferrari about that. Maybe they're just on bad terms. But that's hard to fathom as Ferrari was well liked by anyone who knew him. Some of it was his Columbo charm, some of it was his work ethic and the rest was the nature of the man. He was just likable. Hell, even his perps liked him.

You can be driving a Lambo or, hell, even a Ferrari and you're likely not getting from Canoga Park to Cerritos in under an hour. At least not during any regular sort of driving hours when most folks are using the asphalt.

I took the major routes as any sane person would. It's just faster that way. The one oh one to the four oh five to the one oh five which skipped me over top of Compton. What do you think of when you hear Compton? I think of N.W.A's 'Straight Outta Compton' and their track 'Fuck tha Police'.

Maybe you think about the Watts Riots from sixty-five. Watts being just north of the four oh five I was traveling on. Just north of Compton. Maybe you think of the ninety-two LA riots where the police beat Rodney King within an inch of his life. That didn't occur anywhere near Compton. Rodney King's ordeal started when CHP tried to pull him over in Lake View Terrace in the San Fernando Valley. That's far north from Compton. He was eventually stopped around Hansen Dam Park. Also far from Compton. Nevertheless, much of the rioting that ensued for the next six days occurred in South Central LA. Most of that does not include Compton though it borders it.

What am I trying to say? Not sure. Other than race relations are complicated. Not sure why. Maybe because we don't mix as well as we should with each other. There's an idiom, 'familiarity breeds contempt'. But I don't think that applies here. If you get to know people of a different race you're bound to learn things that help dispel your prejudices. More like familiarity breeds understanding. At least that's how I like to think of it.

But that's what I was thinking about. Compton, like most suburbs and bedroom communities in much of the larger cities, saw great growth just after the war. The fifties and early part of the sixties were great for these areas. For the whole country really. Nothing like a war and the death of tens of millions of people to spur on the engines of industry and create a rise in employment.

Then the Watts riots happened in the summer of sixty-five. Some other things happened in the summer of sixty-five too. Bob Dylan was booed for using an electric guitar at the Newport Folk Festival, shortly after he released 'Like a Rolling Stone'. LBJ signs into law the Voting Rights Act to end voting discrimination. That's worked like a charm! The Beatles are on Ed Sullivan. Sonny and Cher score a number one with 'I Got You Babe'. Yours truly was not born yet.

In other words, sixty-five, like pretty much every year before or since was a mixed bag. Overweighted by man's inhumanity towards himself.

I tossed aside those thoughts. Race relations wasn't about to be solved by reviewing some events from over fifty years ago. That required institutional, systemic and cultural change. Probably starts in the family. You sow suspicion about other people in the hearts of your children, you will reap a society on the cusp of all out race wars, which seems to be simmering currently, just under the surface under the current regime.

I spent the last five minutes of the journey to Cerritos trying to figure out where this case was going. But everywhere I looked, under each nook and cranny I came up with dead ends. I was worried. I wanted justice for these young women. More than that, it really scratched my craw to think that powerful men could get away with discarding young women like trash at a dump without recourse or consequence. That didn't sit well with me.

Yeah, the women weren't purposefully murdered, but they were not protected well enough. Now, I believe that prostitution should be legalized. The only reason it's not is because morally uptight and vocal constituents have an irrational fear of sex. And the only people getting hurt under the current illegal setup is prostitutes. Johns get fined and some of them might have to deal with divorces or other issues. But hookers are getting abused and murdered. Legalizing it would be safer both legally and physically. But that would require getting out from under the yoke of the nanny state. Made up of voters of a puritanical propensity.

I sighed, audibly, and that brought me out of my funk. I could only follow the leads, and the only lead I had in front of me was Ferrari, living in Cerritos, close to Roberts. Cerritos, you might know, means little hills. It used to be home to dairy farms. I might have mentioned that before. In the mid-fifties, dairy cows outnumbered residents here by twenty-nine to one. These little hills flowed with cream. Or so one can imagine.

There's an old country saying, or maybe there isn't. No cream without the cow. I'm not sure what that means, maybe that getting cream takes a lot of work and effort on the part of the farmer in caring for his cows for the little bit of cream that they produce. M would probably take issue with that.

Doesn't matter. I was just hoping that Ferrari might have some cream to share that would help me make better sense of this case. And failing that, maybe he had cream for coffee. And cream makes the bitterness of coffee easier to take. I had no fucking idea what I was rambling on about. I pulled up in front of Ferrari's place. I had visited him here a few times back in the day. That was a long time ago. Probably over twenty years now. I was much younger and Ferrari was a little older then than I am now.

The home was similar to all homes in the area. Off white painted outside with pitched roofs and a single attached garage in the front. If I remembered correctly it was a three bedroom ranch style home with a basement that was finished when I was last here.

I parked next to the curb and took a breath. I should have kept in touch with Ferrari better than I had. He was a good man and I'd heard that his wife had died in the last ten years or so. I hadn't reached out. I felt like a schmuck. Deservedly so. I grabbed a bottle of red wine I had picked up on the way here. It was a Vietti Barolo from twenty fourteen. The liquor store clerk said it was well respected. At a hundred and fifty bucks it better be. And at that price, the store clerk said I was practically stealing it. I felt like the one being robbed.

But with great mea culpa came great cost.

The Man from Turin

I got out of the car and put on my fedora. I looked at myself in the window of my car and adjusted my fedora a little more askew. I was nervous. I respected Ferrari. He had been the most important mentor I'd had on the force. Hell, probably the most important mentor I had in my whole life. He'd been more of a father figure than my father.

Grinning at myself in the window of my car, I figured that I was nervous because like a schmuck I hadn't reached out to him for over ten years. And that was because, if I was being really honest, I felt like I'd let him down. That's why I hadn't kept in touch.

I tapped the brim of my hat and walked up the concrete path to the main entrance of the house. I squashed the little white buzzer on a small black rectangle and waited. I didn't have to wait long. A short man with silvery gray hair, bushy and healthy, opened the door. He was just as I remembered him.

On his left wrist he had a watch. An understated Rolex. On his right wrist he had a chunky gold chain. On his left ring finger he had a simple gold wedding band. He was not remarried. At least not to the best of my knowledge. He wore a pale pink sweater over a collared shirt. The shirt was pale blue with darker blue circles on it. The cuffs were rolled overtop the sweater and clasped with cufflinks.

He wore beige, slim fitting slacks and brown Italian loafers on his feet without socks. Or maybe they were just ankle socks I couldn't see. He was a dashing and debonair figure.

"Mr. Cool, my favorite LAPD homicide detective," he said, coming forward and giving me a big bear hug. He held me close for several long seconds that might have felt uncomfortable for most but for me it was just the way Ferrari was.

He wore his heart on his sleeve. You knew where you stood with Ferrari, and I figured I still held some sway in his heart. I handed him the bottle of red wine when he released me. He took it and looked it over, holding it out with both hands and nodded.

"Twenty fourteen Vietti Barolo Rocche di Castiglione. The great fortress of Castiglione. Perhaps it will fortify our visit. Thank you, Anthony, this is a good wine, but more than that it is expensive!"

He took me around the shoulders and invited me inside his home. He took my jacket and my hat and placed them in the closet. I followed him into his kitchen. He handed me back the bottle of wine.

"Could you open that for me, a bottle opener's in the drawer over there," he said, pointing at it. "For tonight we dine on the blood of our enemies, and cheese. I have a nice Grana Padano which will go well with this. Let me cut some up."

I smiled at him.

"I don't know if you remember me telling you this, but I was born in Turin."

I had forgotten, but I played it as if I had remembered.

"Turin is in Piedmont, Italy, an area in northwestern Italy."

"I remember," I said, lying.

"Piedmont is also the region where that Barolo comes from that you gave me," he said. "Did you know that?"

I thought about lying again but decided against it. I didn't have the stomach for it. Not to my mentor.

"No, I have to admit I didn't remember that."

"You didn't remember I was born in Turin either, did you?"

I looked at him a little sheepishly.

"How could you tell?"

"We worked together for three years. You remember that part, right?"

His eyes twinkled, and his mouth creased into a smile. There was no malice in his tone.

"Of course I remember," I said.

"Well, I never had another mentee after you that lasted longer than three months. And after three others, I decided it wasn't worth my trouble."

"I'm sorry to hear that," I said. "I really enjoyed our time together."

That didn't get an answer. Ferrari had finished cutting up the cheese. I had poured the wine.

"Come, let us move to the dining table and enjoy our time together," he said.

He carried the cheese tray and I brought on through the bottle of wine and the two wine glasses. The table could extend to six but it was shortened at the moment to hold four. We took a corner of the table. Ferrari had his back to the window through which I could see his garden. He'd always had a green thumb and a special way with roses. The garden was overrun with roses. But in a decidedly organized fashion. There were roses from pretty much the entire spectrum of the rainbow.

I looked to actually see all the colors. There were white roses, pink roses, yellow roses, red roses and blue roses. The only colors I didn't see were green, orange and purple. Though some of the yellow roses were so vibrant that I wouldn't call you a bald-faced liar if you told me they were orange instead of yellow.

Ferrari raised his glass, I raised mine towards him.

"To long lost friends and reignited friendships," he said.

"I'll drink to that."

We clinked glasses and drank the wine. I'm not a big wine drinker, and certainly not a wine snob, but this Barolo was fine. Went down easy. I suppose that's to be expected from a hundred and fifty buck bottle.

"Where does the cheese come from?" I asked.

"The Grana Padano?"

I nodded.

"That's from northern Italy too, but more central. Made in the similar area to Parmesan, though that area is a little south of where you'll find most of the Grana Padano fromagers."

"You like your cheese," I said. "Well, your Italian cheeses anyway."

"I like most cheeses. But they're rich and as you get older a little goes a long way."

I smiled and nodded. Ferrari had left Italy when he was a young boy. Three, five years old, somewhere around there. Unlike me, he had lived in the country of his people's history. I hadn't. But he had gotten me into enjoying the finer things in life. Like Irish whiskey.

"You still enjoy Irish whiskey?" he asked, as if listening in on my thoughts.

I nodded.

"I was just thinking about that," I said. "How you helped me educate my palate."

Ferrari nodded.

"I do remember. You were curious about my knowledge of Italian food and cheese and wine especially. I helped you understand why I had come to favor Italian cheese, cuisine and wine over their French equivalents."

"And you swore it had nothing to do with your heritage," I said, smiling at him. Ferrari laughed.

"Yes, I remember that. It took you a while to believe me. Only when you had decided you preferred Irish whiskey to that Scottish swill that you came to understand and believe."

"Well, Scotch whisky is far from swill, but you're right. I remember over a weekend we tasted over a dozen bottles of whiskey..."

"Right. It was eighteen, I believe. Cost around five hundred bucks between the two of us for those bottles. Six bourbon, six Irish and six Scotch. Do you remember the outcome?"

I thought for a moment.

"Not specifically, but I do remember that I overwhelmingly preferred Irish whiskey to the other two," I said.

"I remember it being that six out of your top ten were Irish whiskeys, two were bourbon and two was Scotch."

"That's a good memory," I said.

Ferrari smiled.

"We were similar. Though my top ten, in addition to also containing all six Irish whiskeys in there, included three Scotch whiskies and one bourbon."

"Irish whiskey just tastes better," I said. "Smoother and cleaner. Scotch is too much burnt rubber and smoke for my liking, and shoe leather. Sometimes I think I'm drinking shoe leather when I drink Scotch. As for bourbon, similar to Scotch if I remember, but the burnt rubber and leather just brushed by the whiskey and wasn't involved in drowning it."

Ferrari laughed.

"You should have been a poet."

"I'm trying to be a painter and that's not worked out great just yet."

"Sometimes the world takes a long time to recognize our talents."

We sat in silence for a while, letting that simple but profound thought percolate.

"Your roses are doing well," I said, after a time, nodding outside just past the window.

"Southern California has an ideal climate for roses. One of the biggest problems for roses is fungal rot. Being dry keeps that problem to a minimum, same with rust. I haven't had a bad experience with that too often. Roses, Anthony, like most living things, just require care and attention. Like friendships, I suppose. Both bloom most fully when showered with care and attention."

I didn't know if that was a poke at me or just a general metaphor. I decided to clear the air in any event so we could get down to brass tacks. But Ferrari beat me to it.

"But you're not here to talk about roses or the past," he said. "Let's get to it."

"Actually, Armando, I do want to talk about the past. I wanted to say I was sorry that I haven't kept in touch all these years."

Ferrari smiled at me.

"I am too."

"It's been a long ten years," I said, taking a piece of cheese.

"What's been ten years?" he asked.

"Since we last saw each other."

"Try twenty-two years, Anthony,"

I frowned and thought about it. Ferrari was right. I hadn't met with him since at least before the Grace Smith case, which he was on and I wasn't. That was January first in two thousand. I recalled hearing that he was on it, but we had lost contact by then.

"Jesus, you're right," I said. "I feel like an uber schmuck now."

"I'm glad you're here now. But it pained me when we lost contact. Especially when Rose died."

I had heard about that too. She had gotten breast cancer when she was relatively young. Probably over ten years ago. She was around sixty, I'd guess. That's when Ferrari retired. I nodded somberly. The wine was no longer going down as smooth as it originally had.

"I'm especially sorry about that too. I've always been a bit of an asshole."

Ferrari shook his head gently and smiled at me.

"No, Anthony, that's not true. You're a good man who just had to fight his way out of a lot of bad times."

I don't remember speaking to Ferrari much about my childhood. It's not something I particularly like talking about to anyone.

"I don't remember us talking much about my background," I said.

"Didn't have to, Anthony, but what you did share gave me all the color I needed. In ninety-five your father died. We discussed that. You were adamant you weren't going to the funeral. I convinced you that you should. If not for him, for your mother and sister. Do you remember?"

I nodded. It came back to me as he started talking about it.

"My sister wasn't there," I said. "Haven't seen her since she left when I was eight. Haven't heard a word from her either."

"I remember," said Ferrari. "But your mother was there. And I'm sure it helped her."

I shrugged. She might not have gone if I hadn't taken care of the funeral arrangements. I'd always known my father as a washed-up alcoholic, semi-pro boxer, but by the time of the funeral he was a bum. Nobody was at his funeral except for me, my mother and the priest. I looked at Ferrari.

"What did I tell you about my father?" I asked, sipping on wine.

Playing Catch Up

" You know how it is, you spend long enough with an accused and you're bound to learn something. Not that that was how it was with you, of course. But we were together three years pretty much every day working together for ten hours a day. I'm sure you learned just as much about me and my family as I did yours."

That was true. I knew his wife was Rose. She was not Italian, she was American of Colombian parents, but she was quite pale. They had two kids together. Michael and Michelle. Last I heard, Michael was getting into technology and Michelle wanted to become a nurse.

"You were always a pretty private person, but three years is a long time to remain silent and we talked a lot about a lot of things. Not so much your childhood, but comments you made, how you reacted to certain victims, all of that gave me color into your early years."

"You were a good detective," I said. "The best I ever knew."

"Thank you, Anthony."

"I really am sorry I didn't reach out when I heard about Rose. I just didn't know how to. And as time goes by it just seemed to get harder and harder to reach out the more time put distance between us."

"I understand."

"How can I make it up to you?"

"There's nothing to make up. I know you're upset about it. I am too. Maybe we can move forward on a clean slate. I hope you'll visit more often moving forward. More wine?"

He was already pouring more in my glass. I didn't have the heart to tell him I didn't need any more. Probably because I wanted more. Need had nothing to do with it. He gave a generous pour, and between the two of us that was the end of a hundred and fifty dollar bottle of wine. He got up from the table.

"I'll get us some side plates so we can go sit down in the living room where it's more comfortable."

He disappeared behind me and reappeared after a short time with two side plates. He put several chunks of Grana Padano on my plate and on his. He offered me one and I took it.

"Let's move into the living room."

I followed him into the living room. There was a wood burning fireplace as a central feature and pictures of family on the mantle above the fireplace. The fireplace was not currently burning logs. Above that hovered a large flat panel TV. He offered me the choice of where to sit. I chose the couch. I put the wine and cheese plate on the glass coffee table which was partially covered with a white doily-type of table runner.

To the left of the fireplace, the wall was covered with photographs of family. The centerpiece was a large oval portrait in a rectangular frame of Armando and Rose. They were much younger in that portrait, perhaps a little older than I was now. Ferrari sat down in a large comfortable recliner to my left. His plate of cheese was on his lap and he took a chunk and put it in his mouth.

"The two of you look happy there," I said. "You must miss her?"

"That was our thirtieth wedding anniversary," he said. "I was fifty-six and Rose was fifty-four. It was the year before we found out she had breast cancer. I miss her everyday, Anthony. Every day."

"That's why you retired when you did, wasn't it?"

"That's right," said Ferrari. "That portrait of Rose and I," he said, pointing at it, "was taken in oh three. In oh four we found out Rose had cancer. The first few years looked promising but they were punishing on her. The chemo and the radiation, the surgery. She ended up having a double mastectomy. In oh seven, I retired when we learned that the cancer had spread to her liver. In oh nine she died."

I nodded and took a drink of wine. What do you say to a man who's lost his wife? I'm sorry? That hardly seems fitting. So I said nothing instead. I'd also been apologizing the whole time I'd been here it seemed.

"You're doing okay now?" I asked.

Ferrari had been looking at the portrait of his wife and him. She was a more attractive woman than he was a handsome man. He was nice-looking, charming even, but not particularly handsome. Looked very similar to Columbo, or rather, Peter Falk who played Columbo. Both nice-looking men but in my opinion not especially handsome. Ferrari had married up in life. At least as far as looks went.

"I am doing well, Anthony. It's been ten years, and time has a way of giving you space from the pain. Colleagues were also very helpful in the early months. Coming by to check on me. And I still keep in touch with some of the retired group. We have a bowling league and we meet at least once a month. That and my roses keep me pretty busy."

"What about your kids. Michael and Michelle, right?"

Ferrari took a sip of wine and nodded.

"Michelle moved out to your neck of the woods, Oklahoma."

"Whereabouts?"

"Lawton. She found work there after graduating with her nursing degree. She's since married and has two children. A boy and a girl. My granddaughter is sixteen and the boy is thirteen. I go out there at least once a year, usually around Christmas. Michael's in Silicon Valley with a tech company that provides some sort of AI database management solutions. I don't understand it very well, but he says the company he works for makes it easier to sift through lots of data quickly and accurately."

"What's it called?" I asked.

"HAIL. It started out as an acronym for Human Augmented Intelligent Logistics, but now the company just goes by HAIL. They seem to be doing well. He's now the Vice President of Interface Design. They're a big company. He's been with them for ten years, maybe longer. They're a fifty billion dollar company now."

I nodded and stuck some cheese in my mouth.

"I always thought Grana Padano was a harder, more crumbly cheese," I said. This version was only mildly grainy and quite creamy and mild in flavor.

"Depends on how long it's ripened for," he said. "This one is a young Grana Padano and hence not as dry and grainy. But how are you doing? Do you have someone special? You never had a problem with gaining the attention of the fairer sex."

I laughed at that.

"My burden," I said, though it was hardly a burden. "There is someone I'm seeing that I quite like."

Ferrari nodded.

"Who is that?"

"The Medical Examiner. I don't think she was the Medical Examiner by the time you retired, or at least certainly not the Chief Medical Examiner."

"What's her name?"

"Emily," I said. "Emily Stratham."

Ferrari shook his head slowly.

"Don't think I know her. But there's a Stratham family that owns a large surgical supply business based here in LA, I believe. I think it's called Stratham Surgical Services or something like that. Is she related?"

I grinned and nodded.

"The one and same. It's a privately held company owned by her, her father and her brother. The old man started it. It's very successful so I hear."

"Indeed it is. Probably over a billion in revenues annually I would imagine."

I nodded.

"How do you know about them?"

"I spent a lot of time in hospitals, clinics and with all sorts of specialists when Rose got sick. That company came up in research. They're regarded as one of the best suppliers of heart-related surgical supplies. Don't do a lot for cancer, but their scalpels are well thought of amongst the cancer surgeons we met with."

I nodded.

"It's going well, I assume?" he asked.

I shrugged.

"As well as can be expected. It's been a couple of years now and I get the sense that she wants to settle down."

"You sound unsure."

"Not about the relationship. Her family likes me. Her parents and her brother like me. I'm just not sure if I'm ready to settle down."

"Why's that? Does she want kids?"

"No. I'm just not sure I'm ready. I'd like to be in a better place financially. I had a good year a couple of years ago. Almost made a hundred grand for the first time in my life. This year I'll be lucky if I make half that much. My income is so variable and I'd like it to be more stable."

"Does it bother her? Has she said something that gives you pause?"

I shook my head.

"No, it's all me. I'd just feel better if I was more financially stable."

Ferrari looked at me.

"You've chosen a course that isn't likely to bring you that financial certainty, right? You're an artist which by itself is a hard row to hoe and on top of that your bread and butter is whatever the LAPD throws your way to help them with."

I sipped wine and chewed cheese.

"Maybe it would be good to settle down and not have to worry about money. Not that it's my business, but it might give Aibhilin some stability too. Do they get along well?"

I nodded.

"Like a house on fire. Sometimes they seem as thick as thieves. It's one of my greatest joys."

"But you're unsure," he said.

"Maybe it's my pigheadedness or old school thinking, but I'd prefer to be a little more stable. I mean what do I bring to a billionaire's table."

"Probably the same thing she brings to your table minus the financial rewards. And we aren't living in the fifties anymore, Anthony, in spite of what you think your fedora's telling you. This is a modern era and for a lot of young women I'm sure they're not focused on traditional roles. Certainly seems like she's very successful in her own right. And despite your protestations earlier, I don't really think you want a barefooted, pregnant woman in the kitchen while you go out and hunt and gather."

He was right about that so I didn't say anything to add to it. We sat in silence sipping wine and finishing the cheese.

Hair Trigger

After the silence stretched out awkwardly like a dog licking his balls for just a little too long, Ferrari broke it.

"I'm enjoying our reminiscing," he said, "but that's not why you're here, I think."

I nodded. I took the last sip of wine and put it down next to the plate that still carried a small chunk of cheese that I couldn't finish.

"You taught me everything I know about police work. About being a good cop and detective. But truthfully, Armando, I think the reason I lost touch was that I felt I could never live up to your standards or expectations. I've always had a hair trigger and that was something you didn't like about me."

Ferrari shook his head.

"Not quite true, Anthony. You were the best cop that I ever mentored. Like I said, I gave up after I'd tried it three more times after you. You had an exceptional talent for rooting out the truth, for getting suspects to talk and for seeing links the rest of us didn't. I mean, you're still the winningest detective the LAPD ever had. You never failed to lay charges in a case. Right?"

I nodded.

"The problem, as I saw it with you, was that you cared too much. Now that's not necessarily a bad thing, but your sense of right and wrong, your clear sense of justice meant that sometimes you chose to take matters into your own hands and I was worried that would get you into trouble."

"It's gotten me into plenty of trouble. I had a handful of complaints on my jacket before we were together and by the time I'd left I had seventeen complaints on my file. I never saw you get a complaint in the three years we were together," I said.

"I needed to set an exemplary example for you. I had three complaints on my jacket by then. By the time I retired I had seven."

I frowned at him. This was something I never knew.

"I didn't know that. Even JR only has three currently," I said.

"Who's JR?"

"That's John Roberts. Current captain of homicide. We worked together on the street before I got into homicide. He went into the Special Investigations Section before he bounced over to Homicide where we partnered again for a while."

"He must have a pretty good clearance rate, similar to you," said Ferrari.

"Similar. I got into homicide in ninety-five. Roberts joined in ninety-eight after two years in SIS."

Ferrari nodded thoughtfully for a while.

"My biggest concern with you, Anthony, was your temper. You had such a keen sense of justice that I had a feeling you'd want to take justice into your own hands and that's not our job," said Ferrari. "Our job is to arrest perps and bring them to stand trial with the DA. Ours is not to act as executioner and judge, and I worried that you would get yourself kicked off the force if you couldn't reel in your temper."

I nodded. He wasn't wrong.

"I knew your reputation before we worked together. Sid Vicious was your moniker you earned relatively early on in your career when you got handsy with a punk gang, right?"

I nodded.

"Frankly, you used excessive force then but you were lucky there were no cameras and that your partner, I think that was Roberts, wasn't it?" I nodded. "Yeah, and Roberts had your back."

"It might have been excessive force," I said. "But they were real assholes those punks. The guy I got particularly handsy with, as you say, was wanted for sexual assault, robbery and aggravated assault. He was a huge catch and he got what was coming."

"Except that the public has come to expect their police to not use excessive force like that. And now with smartphones and cameras everywhere, you're under the spotlight."

"I got out before that became a concern."

"I was just worried about where it might take you if you didn't try and curtail your enthusiasm. I mean, I know you grew up fighting and you probably came to enjoy it..."

I shook my head vigorously.

"I don't particularly enjoy it. Fighting in the ring is one thing. That's why they called me Smiling Irish. I enjoyed fighting in the ring. But on the streets, not so much. I was a quiet sensitive young boy who my alcoholic father didn't want to become a sissy because I was into drawing and painting and art generally. He thought that was pretentious and homosexual. He wasn't about to have a son grow up as a faggot so he turned me into the asshole I became. It became so that if there was going to be a fight I was gonna be all in."

"I understand that, but by the time we were working together you had long left your father and you were an adult. I was just trying to help you realize that you were your own man and you could make better decisions."

"I did my best with what I had been given," I said.

"I would have liked to see you stay on the job," he said. "You could have made chief if you'd have wanted to."

I shook my head.

"That was never going to be in the cards for me. Do I look like a politician? Besides, Burton is a corrupt asshole, I'm sure of it."

"The chief may be a shady character but you didn't need to antagonize him about it."

"The third time he pulled me off a case where I was following a hot lead I knew he was as corrupt as they come. All three of those cases were to do with senior politicians or business leaders and all three of those cases went nowhere after I was pulled off. That's not a coincidence, Armando."

Ferrari nodded his head slowly.

"You're probably right, but what good are you, now that you're on the outside?"

"And, what's more," I continued, "he's way too close to my ex's current husband. Have you seen the house that Burton lives in? That's a five million dollar house. How does the Chief of Police afford a five million dollar house on his salary of what, three hundred grand or thereabouts?"

"Something like that, but his wife works in finance," said Ferrari, "she probably out earns him."

"That's what they want you to think. I was looking into that, and she might work with a smaller investment bank but she's an administrative assistant not some big wig banker."

Ferrari didn't say anything for a bit.

"I didn't realize that," he said.

"That's the thing, I was getting too close to his corruption. Besides, does the fucking chief need to be earning that much as a civil servant?"

"I don't think it's excessive," said Ferrari, "when you compare it to what a recent graduate makes. They must be making fifty to sixty grand a year."

"I think recent graduates are making around seventy grand now."

"Well, there you go. The chief making five times what a recently hired officer is making doesn't seem excessive to me," said Ferrari.

"You could be right. But I think he's on the take. How can he afford a five million dollar house and that top of the line Tesla he likes driving around in?"

"Do you have any evidence?" asked Ferrari.

I shook my head.

"How do you get evidence on a guy like that? I don't have the time to tail him and he's surrounded by a cadre of security officers all who are also probably getting something on the side for turning a blind eye to his nefarious ways."

"That's probably why you got fired, Anthony. You can't go around making allegations about the chief being on the take and not have any evidence to back it up."

I nodded. He wasn't wrong. Me and my big mouth sometimes.

"You're right, but he's up to something. He's connected to some sort of bad shit and so is my ex-wife's current husband."

"How's he connected?"

"Not sure. But I've seen Artero, that's my ex's current husband, coming out of a meeting with the chief at headquarters, for fuck sakes."

I was getting riled up. Those two, Burton and Artero pushed my buttons.

"When was this?"

"Years ago. Shortly before I was forced to resign," I said.

"Maybe they know each other from before. What does Artero do?"

"He's in finances somehow. Don't know exactly what he does, but he probably moves money around different jurisdictions if I can read between the lines from what Racquel has told me."

"What's his business called?"

"LLC. Long, Ladron, Cooper. The initials are after the last names of the founders. Artero's last name being Ladron. I've never met Long or Cooper. And then there's the chief's wife working for that small investment bank called Plutus. That's it, just simple, plain old Plutus. Do you know what that means?"

"A surname?"

I shook my head.

"Plutus is the Greek god of wealth and maybe avarice. Definitely the Greek god of wealth. This is how open these assholes are about not giving a shit about the law."

"I think that's a bit of a reach, Anthony. Just because they name their bank after a Greek god doesn't necessarily mean they're trying to avoid the law."

"Their offices are incredibly difficult to get into. I couldn't manage it even in uniform. I had to follow one of their junior partners for a few nights on my own time to eventually get what I needed."

"What did you do?"

It almost felt like an accusation of some sort.

"Nothing, these assholes seem to think they're above the law. So I pinched him for breaking the law. I pulled him over after a heavy night of drinking for a DUI. More than that, there was a bag of cocaine on the lap of his passenger who was also a hooker."

"Did you take him downtown?"

"No, I leaned on him at the traffic stop. Gave him a sweet deal. Told the hooker to fuck off and then we had a heart to heart. That's when I learned that Phyllis, Burton's wife, was not actually a partner of the firm but more like a secretary. Though she was getting paid well, around a hundred grand, and that was back in two thousand or oh one, just before I was forced to resign."

"If what you're saying is true, how do you expect to get the evidence you need to lay charges?"

I shrugged and sighed.

"I don't know, Armando. I just don't know. My family's involved whether they know it or not, and I'm pretty sure Racquel doesn't know about it. Then there's Aibhilin. How would she do if I put her stepdad in jail? That would probably devastate her and she'd likely end up hating me for it. But all of that I could deal with if I had something solid to send to the DA. I don't. These people are really hard to pin down."

Ferrari looked at the portrait of his wife and then at the last sip of wine. He swallowed it down.

"You have my support, Anthony. You know that. I've always supported you, even when they forced you to resign, I had your back. That's probably why I never made captain."

I looked at him carefully.

"I wondered about that. Someone with your skill and clearance rate should have made commander at least. How come you never told me you went to bat for me? I never knew that and we'd probably not have lost touch all these years."

Ferrari shrugged and put his wine glass down. His cheese plate was empty on the table we were sharing.

"I didn't think I needed to. I thought you would have known as much from our three years working together. Sometimes, Anthony, if you'll forgive me for saying this, you tar everyone with the same brush. And not everyone is corrupt or corruptible as you might think."

"Fair point, but I didn't know which side you were on. I had few friends left towards the end and the deeper I dug the more it seemed like less and less of the force was trustworthy. If you'd only told me as much then as you have now. What I do remember is you trying to get me off my high horse."

"That's what happens when you get sucked into a conspiracy," said Ferrari. "Your whole world turns bleak and dark when it probably isn't."

I nodded.

"Anyway, that's history, though it continues to claw at me. It's a long term project. But I think it could possibly be connected to a case I had in New York a few years back."

"Tell me about that?" asked Ferrari.

Rotting Apples

" It was a weird and convoluted case," I said. "It started as a favor for Roberts. He had friends out in New Jersey whose son was killed by a hit and run."

"I don't follow the national crime trends, so I'm not aware of this case," said Ferrari.

"I don't expect you to be aware of it," I said. "It wouldn't have made national news. But it was interesting. Roberts had dated the sister of the woman who lost her son if I remember it correctly. Anyway, his name was Joseph Severn. I'll call him Joe. He was a reporter working for an internet rag and looking to get into the big leagues. He met with an unusual young man called Stanley Spencer. I'll call him Stan. They met at a dive biker bar which will become apparent shortly. Shortly after they left the bar Stan is run down by a truck and Joe, who goes to his aid, is shot in the back of the head."

"I thought you said he was killed by a hit and run?" asked Ferrari.

"Yeah, sorry about that, this was a few years ago now. Joe was murdered. They both were, but Joe was shot at point blank range. Anyway, it was a very weird case and I had a lot of help from a great detective out there, her name was..."

I took a moment to swallow the hot coal that was forming in my throat. My eyes got wet. Ferrari noticed. Concern drew worried lines all over his face.

"What happened?"

"Detective So-yi Park was raped and murdered right in front of me..." I took another breath.

"I'm sorry, Anthony. I can only imagine how that must be."

"They shot me twice in the stomach and roughed me up some. The only reason I survived is that So-yi had insisted I wear a vest. Only one of the bullets entered me. Still, I almost bled out and was saved by Roberts' friend and some South African military contractors."

I had lost my way. I had forgotten why I had started telling that story.

"What happened to those assholes?" asked Ferrari.

"They got what they had coming to them," I said.

"Did you... Never mind, I don't want to know," said Ferrari.

"They paid with their lives, Armando, that's all I'll say about that. Why was I talking about this case?"

"You said you thought it might be connected to the current case you're on."

"Yeah, right. Thanks. This reporter, Joe, met with Stan who showed him an advanced weapon that looked like an old school Nokia phone. It basically taps into all networks and has access to all sorts of information. It's also an EMP weapon and can disable humans within a certain distance. Nothing like you've seen currently. Probably stuff that will only come out into public knowledge in the decades to come."

Ferrari was listening intently.

"But more than that, this was being developed by a group with an unknown name but lots of business fronts. Those assassins who almost killed me and did kill So-yi, they were supposed to be plumbers from a plumbing outfit called Pipe Dreams. I ventured in there and as I tried to get into the back area of the offices I was zapped somehow and woke up lying on my ass and was told to get out.

"Long story short, there was a lot of weird stuff going on in that case. These weapons I've described and the weird Nokia lookalike phone that was next level advanced. The Bilderberg Group came up and other conspiracies."

"I thought the Bilderberg Group was a legitimate conference of American and European world leaders and businessmen," said Ferrari.

I nodded.

"Yeah, that's true, but behind the scenes, or in the shadows there appears to be an outfit of extremely well-heeled people who are working to make the world into their own image of what they want it to be and they'll do things to cause that to happen. Most of the wars for instance, since the Second World War especially, have apparently been started by these assholes who manipulate the world arena to cause these sorts of things to happen between governments and our elected or non-elected leaders."

"That does sound pretty conspiratorial," said Ferrari. "I don't think it would be that easy to keep a secret when more than a handful of people are involved."

"And that's what I thought too. But you only need a handful of people in the shadows to set up all these fake businesses to do their dirty work. There's no direct proof of any of this, but this case got me thinking that there was something going on behind the curtain of public life. Puppet masters, if you will."

"And how's that connected to the chief or your current case?" asked Ferrari.

"I don't know yet. But the chief seems untouchable so he could be protected by this group."

"You said there's no proof of this conspiracy. So how do you know for sure?"

"Well, I got an interesting phone call out of the blue after I had finished the case and made my way back here. The call came from a guy who called himself Albert Camus."

"The dead philosopher?" asked Ferrari.

I nodded.

"Clearly a pseudonym. How he got my phone number I don't remember and I don't think he told me. But he confirmed, verbally, much of what I've just told you. That there is a shadow group, or shadowy group that is working behind the scenes to create a united world, if I can put it that way."

"That sounds to me like classic Bilderberg conspiracy theory," said Ferrari.

"I know, and that's what makes this so awkward," I said. "And I'm not one for conspiracy theories. But be that as it may, this Camus fella told me as much so I believe it. I believe there are powerful people looking to mold the world in their own image. And that image is not far off from what conspiracy theorists believe. It would seem that there are shadowy players trying for a one world government. That's not a secret, one of the attendees said as much some years ago.

"And Camus hinted at the same. What was interesting to me, is the splinter within the shadow masters' group, if I can call it that. In a nutshell, it would seem that good and evil might be fighting behind the scenes to determine who comes up on top to develop this idea of a unified world. Or, maybe there's just one group with some corrupt powerful people involved that are doing nasty things. I don't know. But either way, I believe there are some shadow puppet masters working behind the scenes to create this vision of a unified world and they are powerful and mostly untouchable."

"I'm still not sure how this connects to the chief," said Ferrari.

"Well, that's my idea. I have no proof. But the way he lives, his expensive house and his fancy car. He doesn't earn enough to live that way honestly, so I think that he and his wife are probably pawns being used somehow. Probably moving money around and/or having access to the Chief of Police in LA conveniently means that some charges for some people are never laid. Look what happened to the three cases I was pulled from."

Ferrari nodded.

"How long have you been thinking about this?"

"Not long. I mean, when it comes to the chief, I've figured he was corrupt for some time but I didn't know how or why. Those pieces are starting to fall into place now that I've spoken with Camus and learned about this shadowy puppet masters' group."

Ferrari nodded and stood up. Our wine was finished.

"I'm getting some water, can I get you some?"

"Sure," I said.

He turned to leave and then paused and turned back to me.

"Just one more thing," he said, and I saw Columbo, but he wasn't holding a cigar nor wearing his raincoat. I cracked up into laughter.

"You've still got it," I said.

He grinned at me.

"Ice or no ice?" he asked.

"Ice," I said.

And with that he disappeared into the kitchen. I got up to stretch my legs. It was good to be with my friend and mentor. It seemed as if no time at all had gone by since we had last spoken.

I walked up to the wall of portraits and photographs. They were mostly of family. Both his daughter and son were represented many times. There were what I figured were their high school and university graduation photographs and a few of family vacations. One was definitely of the family at Disneyland.

But what caught my eye, which I had noticed briefly before, were two photographs. The one was a still image of Peter Falk as classic, early Columbo when Peter Falk must have been in his early to mid-forties and Columbo was at its height.

That photograph was signed and had an inscription. It read, "For my doppelgänger and a real LAPD detective. Best wishes, Peter Falk".

I looked at that photograph and then one of Ferrari's when he must have been around the same age. It was a family photo and the similarities between the two men were uncanny.

The other photograph that caught my eye was a photograph of Falk and Ferrari together. They were standing side by side and I noticed not only a similar height, with Falk perhaps a half inch or inch taller, but the resemblance was still uncanny. Even though the two men were likely around twenty years apart.

Ferrari came back into the room and saw me looking at the photographs. He walked up to me and handed me my drink. Ice water. I took a sip and it went down clean and crisp after the wine and cheese which had given me a small buzz by this point.

One of Five

" When was that taken?" I asked.

Ferrari took the photograph from the wall and looked at the back of the frame. Then he put it back.

"Two thousand and six in August. That would have probably been when he released his autobiography. Did you hear about it?"

I shook my head.

"It's called Just One More Thing. Very tongue in cheek. It was good as I recall. I used to have a copy, but I haven't seen it for a long time."

"The resemblance between the two of you is uncanny," I said.

Ferrari nodded.

"I know, I loved the show and when my colleagues on the job started calling me Columbo, I decided to go full Columbo."

We walked back to the comfy seats and sat down where we had last sat.

"Rumor has it that it was because of Columbo that you decided to become a cop," I said.

"When were you born, Anthony?"

"Nineteen seventy."

Ferrari nodded.

"Well, that means you were just a child when it came out. I was born in forty-seven. Other than a couple of pilots, Columbo came out from seventy-one to seventy-eight. I was twenty when I joined the force after a couple of years in the army and the jungles of Vietnam. I joined the LAPD in sixty seven, before Columbo was even a thing. Before the first pilot even, which came out in sixty-eight.

"I think the reason that rumor started was because I committed to taking on this personality on the job. Though when I came home I was just plain old Armando for my family and friends. But I enjoyed playing that character as a real life detective. I watched all the episodes and think I did a pretty good job. Though of course, I wasn't as rumpled as the character on television."

I nodded.

"You were like an upscale well-dressed version of the character," I said.

"I always liked to dress well," he said.

I nodded and sipped my water.

"How are you really doing, Anthony? How's Aibhilin?"

"Both of us are doing good. It's hard not having my baby doll with me all the time, and Racquel drives me up the walls sometimes, but I'm doing okay."

"I don't believe you," he said, softly with a warm smile filtering the words.

I grinned.

"You keep your cards close to your chest, but sometimes that's not helpful. I hope you're talking to someone about that New York incident. I did forty years on the force and never lost anyone right in front of me. I can only imagine. We lost guys of course, but never when I was personally there. It's not weakness to seek help, it takes strength and courage."

"Emily's making me see someone. He's good and slowly we're getting somewhere. Interestingly, he prescribed cannabis to me. Said he's seeing good results with it with veterans and others having trouble sleeping."

"I've heard it can be helpful for PTSD. Is it helping you?"

"When I remember to take it," I said. "It helps me sleep and keeps the nightmares at bay. I don't care for the buzz it gives me, at least not during the day when I'm working, though it doesn't seem to harm my painting, but for investigations I prefer to be sober. He's got me on CBD. Know what that is?"

Ferrari shook his head.

"It's one of the ingredients in cannabis, only it doesn't make you high. Still supposed to help with stress. I'll use that as an oil during the day. Again, when I remember."

"No shame in getting any help you can. I always preferred dealing with stoned suspects than drunk ones. They're way easier to deal with."

"My experience also."

Silence walked into the room and lounged about awkwardly like an uninvited guest.

"You still haven't told me about the case you're working on," said Ferrari.

"Right. It's interesting and there's a connection to you with it."

"Really? I am intrigued," he said.

"Do you recall a victim found at Calabasas landfill on January first two thousand? Her name was Grace Smith."

Armando nodded slowly.

"Yeah, I remember that case. Couldn't close it. Young woman, around early twenties, practically naked except for a piece of lingerie. One-piece red swimsuit thingy. I think they call it a teddy."

I nodded.

"Yeah, that's right."

"I remember her very well. For one thing, as I said, I couldn't close the case. For another, her full name was the same as an Australian painter. I always tried to see if any of the victims or perps had the same name as a famous or semi-famous artist. That was because of you. I remember when you used to point that out to me when we were on the job together."

"Point out what?"

"If the accused or the victim shared the same name as an artist. You remember that, don't you? Must have happened a few times we were together."

I nodded.

"Well, I kept doing it, because it was interesting and it reminded me of our time together. You could have won on Jeopardy if the theme had been all about artists."

"Well, art history was an important subject in art school. Plus knowing your artists gives you inspiration," I said.

"Well, now that I remember the case, how does New York fit into all of this?"

"I don't know for certain it does, it just seems to have ties in my mind."

"Tell me about it."

"Well, did you know that at the time she was one of four other victims who were found similarly around the world?"

"I did not know that," said Ferrari. "Are you sure? I reached out to the FBI and they didn't have anything to share."

"I'm sure. I spoke to my guy at the FBI..."

"You have a guy at the FBI?"

I nodded.

"Yeah, Taiju Nishio. He's the SAC out of the Birmingham, Alabama office."

Ferrari turned up his mouth and nodded.

"How did you make that contact?"

"He boxed for the FBI and won the light welterweight division at the ninety-seven police games."

"Right. The same games where you won, what was it, middleweight?"

I nodded.

"Yeah. We formed a friendship at that time and have kept in touch ever since. Back then he was just a special agent. But he's a good friend and ally to have."

"I can imagine. Because back then I also reached out to them, though I didn't have a 'guy' I could turn to, but they also made inquiries with INTERPOL apparently. Nothing came of it. But it was different back then. Digitization was just starting in earnest."

"And you probably got a lazy agent assigned to help you."

Ferrari bobbed his head back and forth.'

"Who knows. But Taiju found something?"

"Yeah. Let me tell you what I know. The first victim was a twenty-one-year-old woman found in seventy-seven at the outskirts of the Black Forest near Baden-Baden in Germany. She was wearing a white one-piece lingerie with no makeup or jewelry. Semen was found in her vagina but it was determined she wasn't raped. Died of a drug overdose apparently. Cannabis, cocaine and ketamine were found in her system."

"Grace Smith also had no jewelry or makeup," said Ferrari.

"I know. That's a common theme as you'll see. Second victim from eighty-eight. Twenty-three years old found under a tree in a park in Moscow. Black one-piece lingerie. Semen in vagina and anus from two different donors. Cannabis and ketamine in her system. Didn't seem to be raped but she died of asphyxiation."

"That's pretty much how Smith died if I remember correctly."

"You do remember correctly. Third victim found in ninety-one in a wooded area just outside St. Petersburg, Russia. Youngest victim at nineteen. Drug overdose with cocaine, ketamine and cannabis found in her system. Semen from two men. Found in vagina and anus. And that brings us to Grace Cossington Smith, same name as the Australian painter as you mentioned."

Ferrari nodded thoughtfully.

"Twenty-two-year-old. Cannabis and ketamine in her system. Asphyxiated and with one donor's semen in both vagina and anus. Appeared the sex was rough, though again, not determined to be rape. As you said, no jewelry or makeup. There is however one interesting connection between the two American victims. Your Grace Smith and my Suzanne Valadon, also found at the landfill."

"Yeah, and what's that?"

Laundered Bodies

" Do you remember your victim, Grace Smith, being laid upon a pillow of twigs?"

"Yeah, I do. That was something unusual about the case. Made me think that the perp felt guilty about what he'd done. There was no violence done to my victim other than the asphyxiation which the coroner thought had more to do with the sex than outright murder," said Ferrari.

"My victim doesn't appear to have been asphyxiated, though cause of death is unknown at this time, but she was found with her head lying upon a bed of small twigs. As you said, it was as if the guy who drove her and dumped her out at the landfill had remorse or, at the very least, cared for her."

"First of all you identified him as male. Secondly, you didn't identify him as a perp. But before we get to all of that, what makes you think all these cases are related? I understand that my victim and yours were found at the same landfill. That's a good start. Their heads were also laying upon some twigs and leaves, I like that as a connection too. But the rest of the victims, and the way they were dressed, I mean all that could just mean that the perps were trying to hide their tracks."

I nodded at Armando. He wasn't wrong.

"I haven't told you the best part," I said. "But you're right. A lot of similarities. They all were found without ID or makeup or jewelry or anything that could help identify them. Seems like the perps did their best to remove any evidence. But at the same time, they didn't try exceptionally hard."

"What do you mean?"

"All this care and attention to the exterior of the body. But each and every one of them was found with semen inside them. That's the most damning evidence. Especially for the last two. DNA is easy to get from semen now. I mean, what sort of evidence are they trying to remove from the exterior of the body that's so damning but leaving semen. You'd think if they were really trying that hard to eradicate evidence they'd have given these women enemas at the very least."

Ferrari nodded.

"Good point. You didn't mention semen being found on your victim."

"Yeah, right. There was. Semen was found in her throat, anus and vagina."

"That's the first where it's found in the throat," said Ferrari.

"Yeah, but that could just be that evidence collection is getting better nowadays," I said. "Doesn't necessarily mean that the others hadn't performed oral sex."

Ferrari nodded thoughtfully.

"All good points and I can see how they could be connected, but do you have anything a little stronger to suggest these victims might have been murdered, if that's even the case here, by the same perp?"

"Yes. There is one vital piece that ties them all together." I pulled out my phone and went to the image of Valadon's scar I had taken. I handed my phone to Ferrari. "Does this look familiar?"

"Yes, it does. That's the scar that Grace Smith had on her lower left abdomen, down by her groin," he said.

"Except this is not Grace Smith. This is the scar that was found on my victim, Suzanne Valadon. And also in the same place as the others. This scar is in the inguinal crease, just down by the groin on the left hand side, as each and everyone of the other four victims had. They all have this scar, Armando, in the same place. Of the five victims, only one of them has any other markings on their body, and that was Grace Smith with a large butterfly tattoo on her lower back."

"Yeah, I remember that, but I remember that scar even better as it was so unusual. Figured out it translated roughly to comfort woman or something like that. That gave us the evidence to believe she was a prostitute of some sort. We thought she was a prostitute for some sort of gang that was branding their women."

I nodded.

"But did you see it anywhere else?"

"No, that was the issue. No other prostitutes seemed to have that type of branding. It didn't help us get anywhere. My thinking started to drift away from common gangs to something more white collar. Something like sex parties. But of course, very few of those are we ever informed about."

"This is the evidence that ties all these victims together," I said. "I mean, what's the chance of this happening randomly in three different countries? And who even knows what these three kanji mean? I didn't."

"Neither did I. But one of our guys did. We had a Japanese American on the job who I knew quite well. He told me what it meant. I did some further research to see if I could get anywhere with that. These women were apparently either abducted from their homes which were under Japanese occupation at the time or they were lured in by lies and false promises."

I nodded. I knew all of that.

"Did you get anywhere with that line of inquiry?" I asked.

"No. The first line of inquiry was to see if this was attached to any Japanese yakuza or Chinese triad. Most of the big crime syndicates and gangs are involved in prostitution but it's usually all local. Very few are involved in international prostitution on account that these gangs are very protective of their local areas and any incursion that way will end up with fighting and prostitution is just not worth that sort of trouble. Now human trafficking is different but we couldn't find a connection there either."

"I came up empty too. Tai confirmed the lack of connection to any known international gangs. But like you said, international crime syndicates if they're in prostitution like to find their women locally, and most of them don't brand their women for obvious reasons, like bringing attention to themselves."

Ferrari nodded thoughtfully.

"We have two women from California. We have another two from Russia and one from Germany. All with the same scarring or branding. All young women under the age of twenty-five," said Ferrari. "They're all white, right?"

I nodded.

"They're all in good health, with no other body markings other than for Grace Smith. They don't have makeup or jewelry when they're found and they're left where they will be found, with care as to how they're left. Does that about sum it up?" asked Ferrari.

I nodded.

"Let me tell you how this victim turned up. We were notified by a security guard around noon thirty this past Sunday. Security guard's name is Arshile Gorky. I'll just refer to him as Gorky from now on. Said he was on his rounds he does every couple of hours or so. He works at the landfill. Said he found her when he was doing his rounds. He only checks the whole landfill every so often. Most of his rounds are closer to his security station where he checks the buildings and equipment.

"Gorky has a rap sheet for some youthful beefs, GTA and grand theft. We get the video footage from the cameras that face both incoming and outgoing traffic from his security box. We notice there's about a half hour of missing time. It's just erased. We figure that's likely when the perp was dropping off the body. Now the question is, where's Gorky at this time. I mean the landfill is not difficult to get into but you'd need to pass by those cameras, so it looks like Gorky knows more than he's letting on."

"Or he's involved," said Ferrari.

I nodded.

"He is, but not how you think. A couple of detectives went to lean on him a little harder when we found out there was missing video. Originally, Roberts and I had spoken to him and retrieved the footage. He came across very happy to help..."

"As they usually do," said Ferrari.

"Exactly. But this guy, you wouldn't have thought him good for it."

"Unless he's a Keyser Söze," offered Ferrari.

"Yeah, but that's a fictional story and he's no Keyser Söze, I'll bet my jalopy outside on it."

Ferrari grinned and nodded.

"I understand. But sometimes perps surprise you. Remember that sweet sixteen-year-old. In the drama club, A student, sweet as honey from a lilac valley and yet she was pimping out her seventeen and eighteen-year-old friends. A real sociopath."

"Yeah, I remember that case. She had murdered one of her friends because the girl wanted to get out. A true psycho. Still those are rare and if this Gorky was involved like that I'd have figured it out. But I know he's not as I'll get into in a minute."

"Ok, I'm all ears."

"Right, so our detectives visit him again and lean on him. He comes clean this time that, yeah, he let this guy through to drop off a TV. This guy, I'll call our perp, said his boss wanted him to get rid of the TV and when Gorky tells him that he can't let him through he gives Gorky an option. The easy way or the hard way. The hard way is at the end of a handgun. The easy way is with an envelope that contains ten grand."

"What was the perp driving?" asked Ferrari.

"This is another connection to your case. He's driving a Ford Transit cargo van. There's a logo on it that reads Lemonade Laundry with the tagline, easy squeezy lemon cleany."

Ferrari was nodding and shaking his head at the same time.

"I'll be damned. Same company as what one of the witnesses saw back on New Year's morning in two thousand."

"I know, we've got a detective following up with that witness if we can find him."

"And if he's alive. I'm not sure he'll remember much. He told me everything he knew."

"And what was that?"

"Not much. He was out taking his dog for a walk. He was a bit of an insomniac so he told me. He said he noticed this white van with that Lemonade Laundry logo on it, though he didn't recall the tagline. Said he saw it turn up one of the roads towards the landfill. Couldn't give a good description of the driver. The only reason he remembered the van was because it was quiet at that time of morning."

"What time was that?"

"I want to say three or four, somewhere around then. Very quiet traffic then so a laundry van would stick out. He didn't get a plate or anything. He did his best, but I got the sense that something was wrong with him."

"You thought he might have been involved?" I asked.

"Oh no, nothing like that. But his memory was unreliable. During the conversation there were a couple of things that gave me pause as to how reliable he would be in court. For example, I remember one thing, he offered me tea and then we sat down and talked. He offered me tea again and then went into the kitchen and brought out cookies. I never got tea. Stuff like that. Now that I think about it, he might have had early onset dementia."

"Was he old?"

"Well, older than you are now, younger than I am now. Probably in his early sixties back then. He might not be around any longer and if he is, I'm not sure how helpful he'd be. He didn't have anything of great note to share with me then. Of course I looked into that laundry company. Nothing by that name existed in California so that went nowhere."

"Sounds like you ended up in the same spot I am in now," I said.

"Sounds like it. Everything went cold."

"Was that the first case of yours that went unsolved?"

Ferrari shook his head.

"No, not all of us are wunderkinds. I'd already had a few before I mentored you. Had seven unsolveds by the time I retired, but that one was tough because of the young woman. She'd had a horrible childhood. You probably know all about that if you've seen the file."

I nodded.

"So what happened with this security guard? He got his ten grand, but he came clean when you visited him again. Anything helpful from that meeting?"

Six or Seven Figures

"Not especially," I said. "He was able to give a description, but I think the guy was wearing a disguise. The perp was wearing all black. Black beard, gloves, glasses, black hair and blue eyes. The perp went to scratch an itch by an eye or eyebrow and Gorky saw his eye color. Not much else to go on. Perp came back when he had dumped the body, which was unknown at that time, and then told Gorky exactly which times to erase and when to start re-recording again. All seamless."

"And no better description then?" asked Ferrari.

I shook my head.

"Average height, busted up nose and cauliflower ears meant Gorky thought he might have been a wrestler or mixed martial arts fighter. Thing is, Gorky had supplemented his income on occasion with people who'd slip him a hundred bucks or so to dump illegal stuff off at the dump. Usually paints or chemicals."

"What time was the perp at the landfill?"

"The missing time is from around four-thirty to five," I said.

"That's all you got from him?"

"Well, no. He gave the money back. Hadn't spent a dime. Probably figured since he'd found out that the perp had dropped off a body and not a TV that we were going to be investigating a murder and if he'd spent that money it would make him look more like an accessory."

Ferrari nodded.

"Did you bring him in and charge him?"

I shook my head.

"No, the detectives figured they'd gotten everything from him. They took the money into evidence and that's going to be fingerprinted, though I'm not putting much hope in that."

Ferrari nodded thoughtfully.

"You should have brought him down for questioning. Let him sweat in an interview room for a while. Threaten him with charges. You might get more out of him that way."

"Wasn't me who went to interview him," I said. "I went back out with one of the detectives who had originally interviewed him. When we arrived, he wasn't home. We convinced the apartment manager to let us in. We found him dead on his couch. Shot once in the chest at close range. Neighbor across the way, a sweet old lady, said that a UPS driver had arrived earlier that morning but that this UPS driver wasn't the usual delivery guy."

"How did she know?"

"She's a nosy neighbor and heard him banging on Gorky's door. Gorky lived across the hall from her. The usual UPS driver is taller and black. This guy was described just as Gorky had described the laundry van driver. Black beard, white, sunglasses etc. He went in with a package and came back out with the same package."

"Well, shit. That doesn't help. Maybe if he'd been brought in the first time you might have gotten something from him.

"I doubt it," I said. "These people look like they know what they're doing."

Ferrari nodded.

"You're probably right. It does look like it's the same people that dumped Grace Smith. I don't know what to say, Anthony. I was as thorough as I could be back then. In fact, I even solicited the help of a couple of young, eager rookies to canvass hookers, but none of them knew about prostitutes with those sorts of branding. No local hookers had seen any prostitute like that. We asked on the street and at the casinos. Nothing.

"As we've been talking I've been racking my brain for any lost morsel that might help. But I busted out on this one, Anthony. I came to the conclusion, similarly to you, that we were dealing with high class hookers. Or women that were used for private events. Home sex parties or orgies of some sort. It bothered me then, and it bothers me now that we couldn't put a finger on where or who these women worked for. Though at the time, I didn't know my case was associated with any others," said Ferrari.

"Did you look into escort agencies or the CIW?" I asked.

Ferrari nodded his head somberly.

"Both. None of the escort agencies knew about it or had seen such a brand on any of their women. The California Institution for Women let us interview a whole bunch of the inmates. None of them had seen or known a woman with such a scar or branding. We came up on dead ends just like you're bumping into."

I nodded and we sat silently for a moment while we digested the lack of clues.

"One thing I'm trying to figure out. Grace Smith was found with money on her. Ten grand, right?"

Ferrari nodded.

"Yeah, that's right."

"Well, Gorky was found with ten grand in his lap. At least that's how much I figured it was, about a half inch stack of one hundred dollar bills. A light brick of Benjamins. The lab will confirm. But interestingly, there was no money left with my victim, Suzanne Valadon. What happened to the money found on Smith?"

"It was taken into evidence. No fingerprints or anything like that were found, other than the victim's, so it was eventually returned to the victim's next of kin. In this case her parents, who didn't deserve it if you ask me."

"That's what I thought," I said. "Tai mentioned that the other three victims were also left with exactly ten grand with them. I'm trying to figure out why the perp would do that. The only reason I can come up with is blood money. Maybe it's guilt and so they left some money to make themselves feel better."

Ferrari nodded.

"That could be. We didn't know what you knew at the time so we thought it was her recent earnings. One angle we explored was that she was murdered in a botched robbery. But that quickly fell apart. First of all, the money wasn't taken and secondly the coroner seemed to think that Smith's asphyxiation wasn't intentional but rather sex play gone wrong."

"That's also what I heard about the other victim who died from asphyxiation in Moscow. Also looked like kinky sex gone bad."

We sat and ruminated on our thoughts for a while.

"I don't like it, Armando. I'm running out of leads to follow and the leads I've had keep leading me into dead ends."

"It's a tough case, Anthony. Sometimes we don't win them all."

"Yeah, I get that. But this one. It's like these perps think they have immunity from killing women for their sexual pleasure."

"But have they been murdered? Smith's case you could argue for manslaughter. But it sounds like all these women were perhaps not murdered so much as victims of negligence."

"We're splitting hairs. There was a lack of duty to care. Someone's plying these women with drugs and sometimes too much. That's at a minimum manslaughter. At most you could argue premeditated murder. And even if the asphyxiation is kinky sex gone bad, I'd still like to try these assholes for murder, Armando."

"What do you think the money is for?" asked Ferrari, changing directions.

"It's blood money, like I said earlier."

"For what? Ten grand. That's not a lot of money."

"That bugs me too. If this is an international sex ring of home parties or something it's gotta be well organized and funded. If they're sorry these young women died then ten grand is not much of an apology. Maybe it's a sick and twisted power play. Something like, look, we're sorry your daughter died in our custody while we were abusing her sexually, but listen, here's ten grand to make you feel better and maybe have a bit of a funeral on us. Fuck that, Armando. Fuck that."

I was getting upset.

"Do you have anywhere else to go?" asked Ferrari.

I didn't quite understand the question.

"You mean now, from here?"

"No, I meant with the case. Are there any other leads to follow?"

I shook my head wearily.

"No. Maybe something will turn up in Gorky's residence now that he's been murdered and we turn his place upside down. I'll find out the actual cause of death soon enough. But I doubt that will get us anywhere. We'll probably canvas the local escort agencies and hookers to see if they know anything but this case feels tight. It feels like whoever this is knows what they're doing. But there's a lot I don't like about it."

"Tell me about those things."

"Well, there's the money. If you're really sorry then surely you would have left at least six figures and I'd argue for seven..."

"That amount of money is hard to leave on a body," said Ferrari.

I nodded.

"Yeah, but the more I think about this case, the more I think these assholes could probably transfer that kind of money into someone's bank account without it being traced back."

"Possible, but that's speculation."

I didn't say anything to that.

"But the thing that bugs me the most about this is the way these women were left and the care taken to remove any identifying jewelry or ID from the bodies, and yet they're all full of semen. Semen makes for great DNA evidence. I don't understand that part."

"That is a head scratcher. Maybe none of these men are in any databases. If this organization is an organization of powerful men in places high up the food chain then, arguably, they won't have their DNA or fingerprints with any agency, I imagine."

"And if that's the case, why remove all identification and jewelry from these women?"

"I'd speculate that they do that to be thorough with the knowledge that law enforcement will be able to identify the victims in short order."

I sat and cogitated but my cognition wouldn't be agitated. I could come up with nothing. Ferrari was probably right, Forrest wouldn't likely get much out of Ferrari's witness from Y2k even if he was able to find him. That meant we were out of leads and running out of direction unless my mistress Fortuna blessed us with her favors. But she was a coy wench who didn't much care for me most of the time.

Ferrari looked over at me. His eyes were kind and soft. I looked back at him and shrugged.

"The first time I realized I couldn't close a case was very hard on me, Anthony. But I have no doubt you're doing the best you can."

"I haven't lost it yet," I said.

"What's your approach now?" he asked.

"After this I'll head back to the station and see if the detective who was looking for your old witness has anything from that. I'd also like to find out cause of death, though I probably know what that'll be."

"Which is?"

"Drug overdose. Didn't seem to be any sign of asphyxiation or strangulation from what I could tell and from what the coroner originally seemed to think. But that won't get me anywhere. Then we'll probably make some half-hearted attempts at talking to escort agencies and street walkers. That will come to naught because I've already spoken to vice and they've never seen anything like this."

Ferrari nodded.

"Eventually the case will run cold. But before that happens I'm going to reach out to Albert Camus and see if I can rattle his chain a little so that I get something."

"Just be careful with that, Anthony."

"Why?"

"Because these powerful people, if they help you once, they might think they have you at their service."

"I won't let him misinterpret that," I said.

"Good," said Ferrari. "It is better to keep the moral high ground than to be corrupted for a quick win."

There Was a Man

I left Ferrari's place in a mixed mood. It had been great to catch up with my mentor. But it had also not given me anything that I had come for. And that upset me in more ways than one. Most importantly, if Ferrari never got anywhere with the case, then my chances weren't looking great. Ferrari also didn't have anything to offer me, which didn't help.

It was a little after four-thirty when I left Ferrari's place with nothing much left to do. I had called Roberts but Forrest hadn't reported back from finding the laundry van witness. I told him I'd see him tomorrow. What I needed was two things. Something to eat and something to drink. I knew a place where they offered both items. Sonny McLean's. A simple Irish pub that offered good food and good drink. Better still, it was close to home so I could stumble there if I got soused. Now that wasn't my plan, but sometimes it takes a few sips of thinking juice to get my thinking straight and my mind bent.

Seemed to me that LA chips at your life in hourly increments. Most times it's hard to get between two places in LA in under an hour. And it took me just over an hour to get from Columbo's place, or rather, Ferrari's place in Cerritos to McLean's place in Santa Monica.

But that gave me a lot of time to think. And I came up with a game plan for tonight's thinking thoughtful thoughts thirstily through. And that was when I parked my car at home and decided to walk back to Sonny McLean's.

That was a good plan too as it gave me a chance to freshen up and grab a light jacket. Mid-October nights in LA can be cool. Pirate had also taken a dump and finished his food. That was another couple of chores I did before I left Vista Al Mar with a bounce in my step. Around ten minutes later I was at McLean's. It's a quaint Irish pub with dim lighting and lots of soccer paraphernalia on the wall. Especially from Manchester United and

261

Arsenal. But other teams were represented including some Irish clubs. The Shamrock Rovers was one team that caught my eye.

But over the years, baseball, football and basketball paraphernalia had started to carve out little places for themselves on the walls of Sonny McLean's.

I sidled up to the bar by a little after six. Perfect time for a meal and some whiskey. Sonny was bartending as he usually was. The place was about one quarter full and filling up. It could get slammed at times, but that was usually on the weekends and especially if there was a big game or a big fight on the TV. Tonight was quiet and probably wouldn't get more than about half full.

Sonny smiled at me and walked over. Instead of his usual uniform which consisted of a flannel shirt, Sonny was wearing a Limerick soccer jersey. Blue jersey with white trim around the collar and sleeves, with the castle as a badge. I pretended not to know what it was.

"I see you're sporting Argentina's colors tonight," I said. "Big game in South America?"

I grinned at him. He had a kitchen towel tossed over his right shoulder.

"You're a funny guy for a gumshoe," he said. "Don't know if Argentina has a game today. The only time I follow them is during the World Cup and it's not World Cup time. And the actual shirt I'm wearing is my home team's. Limerick F.C."

"The blue really matches your eyes," I said. "Have a date tonight?"

He grinned at me.

"My eyes are green."

"Well, those Irish eyes are smiling," I said.

"There was a PI I once knew, who didn't know his green from his blue. He came for the whiskey, when he was feeling frisky, but couldn't find anyone to screw."

"A bartender from McLeans, said he had fantastical dreams. He was out late at night, looking for a fight, but all he could do was to scream."

"That one'll cost you. What will you have?"

"Good cheap whiskey and something to drink," I said. "What do you recommend?"

"Good cheap whiskey is something to drink," he said. "You want something to eat too?"

He grinned at me.

"Yeah, that's what I said."

"If you're looking to impress the missus, you might like to tell her you had the wheatball sub. It's a meatball sub with spicy marinara sauce with a small side house salad. The meatballs, despite their weird name, are pretty tasty."

Seemed like everybody in LA was trying to feed me plants.

"Sounds delicious," I said sarcastically, "I'll give it a try."

Sonny nodded and ventured off. I stared at the coaster. It was for a local brewery. I had to try the fake meatball sub because when I brought M back here Sonny'd tell her he had offered it to me. At least this way I could say I tried but it wasn't very good. On the opposite side of the bar was a TV I could watch. Like all the TVs here it was tuned to sports if sports were playing. If not it was tuned to news. Currently the TV was showing a game of baseball. The Yankees were hosting the Astros. It was the third inning and the Astros had one on the board and the Yankees had two.

I kept my eye on the game for a few minutes until Sonny brought over my whiskey. I hadn't told him how much I wanted so he'd given me a generous two finger pour. It was a start. I sipped it. I liked it.

"Not too expensive, is it?" I asked.

Sonny shook his head.

"You're one of my stingiest customers, Anthony. Sometimes I swear you're Scottish."

I had to laugh.

"It's an eight dollar pour from West Cork. I don't think you've had them before. A group of childhood friends started the company as adults back in oh three. This is their blended whiskey from bourbon casks. Refined palates will taste citrus, honey, apple, and nutmeg. You'll probably taste shoe leather and cigarette smoke."

"No, that's not true. I taste apples and honey, if you've put out your cigarette butt in a rotting apple smeared with honey and stamped it out with your shoe. That's what I taste. My refined palate as you said."

Sonny nodded and grinned at me.

"In all seriousness, it's not a bad whiskey for a good price, right?"

I nodded.

"Not bad at all."

"It'll just be another ten or so minutes for the sub. Here," he said, picking up a small bowl from his side of the counter and putting it on my side of the counter. "Have some salted peanuts to make you more thirsty."

He went off again to make some drinks for one of his waitresses. It wasn't Aileen but someone new who I hadn't seen around here before. I looked at the peanuts and took a handful and ate them. That was a mistake. Made my whiskey taste like circus piss. And I wasn't even all that hungry yet.

I caught Sonny's attention and asked him for a water. He put one on another coaster for me and I took a few sips of that to cleanse the palate. Then my whiskey tasted better. Less than ten minutes later, Sonny was back with my meatball sub that had nothing to do with meat. He hovered over me as I took a few bites.

Now, I'm not a meatball sub kind of guy. The way I see it, putting meat between bread is a waste of two things. The meat and the bread. But this meatball sub was good. If you'd have told me this was a proper meatball sub I would've believed it. That's what I told Sonny. I picked away at the salad too. Sonny came and went as other customers and his waitresses needed drinks.

"What's on your mind, Anthony?" Sonny asked, after we'd chewed the fat for a while.

My food was gone. I'd almost finished it all, but it was a big sub and it came with a salad. I'm just saying. It was a lot of plants to eat. But genuinely, I liked it. I was also on my third whiskey at this point but you're not counting.

"Can't a guy just come to his favorite pub and have a drink with the barkeep?" I asked.

"A guy can, but you aren't that guy. Most times you're in here you're mulling over a case. Now I'm glad this is a place that helps with that. But I can also tell there's something on your mind. You've been coming here, what? Ten, fifteen years?"

I thought about that. I'd been coming here since I left the job. That's when I moved to Santa Monica and found my cheap apartment at the Vista Al Mar. That was over fifteen years ago. I nodded.

"Yeah, probably a little more than fifteen years."

"There you go. You're like a son to me, Anthony. There's only one other customer who's been coming here that long or longer. What I'm saying is, if you want to talk I'm listening."

"In the woods I found a Jane Doe, she was naked from her head to her toe. She had taken some hard drugs, given to her by thugs, and now I can't figure out her foe."

Sonny nodded thoughtfully.

"I heard about that. Is that the Jane Doe from the landfill?" asked Sonny. "It was on the news."

I nodded.

"Yeah. It's a tough case. Let me ask you something," I said.

"Anything."

I picked up my phone that was on the counter on my left side and I scrolled through the images to find one of just the scar. I showed it to him. He looked at it for a while, zoomed in, tilted his head this way and that before handing the phone back to me.

"Ever seen something like that?" I asked.

"Was this on Jane Doe's body?"

I nodded.

"Looks like Chinese writing to me," he said. "Never seen anything like this. Is this a branding or something?"

I nodded.

"Probably. Seems too neat to have been carved into her. It's not really Chinese," I said. "Japanese kanji I'm told."

"And what's that exactly?"

"As I understand it, it's the Chinese characters that have made it into the Japanese writing system. I assume if you've never seen anything like this before that you don't know what it means?"

Sonny nodded.

"Yeah, what does it mean?"

"Ianfu. Means comfort woman. I think Jane Doe was some sort of prostitute."

"Hmmm," said Sonny, with an upturned mouth as he nodded. "You might be looking at Asian prostitution rings then."

I shook my head.

"Doesn't look like it. I've spoken with Vice. They've never seen anything like this. Now keep this under your hat," I said.

Sonny nodded.

"The bartender's confessional is always sacrosanct," he said, and he wasn't even grinning as he said it.

"Four other dead women in two other countries were found with this same scar. None of those cases were closed with charges."

"So you're thinking an international crime syndicate of some sort."

I shrugged.

"I'm not even sure about that. I don't think this is a crime syndicate as much as a shadowy syndicate whose goal is world domination rather than criminal domination."

"That sounds a little bit like tinfoil hat thinking," said Sonny. "And I say that with all due respect."

"I know. It sounds crazy. But then, the things I've seen. This relates to more than one case I've worked on."

"If I'm reading between the lines properly, you're saying this case is not criminal in nature. Then why were these women murdered?" asked Sonny.

"That's the thing. We're not sure it's murder. We think their deaths are unintentional. Most are drug overdoses. But there's so much that bugs me about these cases and I just can't get a compass bearing on it."

"Perhaps the FBI or other federal agency can help?"

"They've helped as best they can."

I swallowed down the last of my whiskey. Sonny poured me another and put it in front of me.

"This one's on me," he said.

I nodded my appreciation.

"Maybe it's time to take your mind off the case and let it ruminate in the background," said Sonny. "How's Emily and Aibhilin?"

And that's how it went for the next little while. We engaged in small talk and shared a limerick or two. Then the pub started getting busier and Sonny was pulled away to attend to business.

I was left with my ruminating thoughts. And just like a cow, I chewed and chewed and tried to swallow them down. But they kept coming back up like bad acid reflux and every time I looked them over, nothing seemed to make sense and I had no more clarity than I had before.

After my fourth whiskey my head was starting to feel a little wooly and none of my thoughts made any sense. I spent that last hour sipping on water before I left for home a little after eleven. I was turning into a lightweight. But maybe that was the division I needed to fight in. This current case had me punching above my weight and it was showing.

Baked Beans and Bread

Wednesday morning I woke up pretty refreshed for a guy who'd drunk four whiskeys. But on the one hand that wasn't a lot. I could drink a half bottle of whiskey on a good night. And on the other hand I had sipped on water for the last hour or so I was at McLean's. And I'd had another glass of water when I got home before I crashed. I think I'd found the elixir to banish hangovers.

By the time eight o'clock rolled around I was in fine fettle and looking to close this case. Then I remembered that I had nothing to go on. I called up dispatch and found out that Roberts was at Hollywood Station.

I took care of Pirate and played with him for a handful of minutes. He likes chasing the feather I have on a stick sometimes. He's pretty spry for all he's been through. After a while he got tired of my dirty tricks and went into the kitchen and jumped on his cat tree to cackle at birds in a real tree outside the window.

He looked to me like a grumpy old man telling kids to get off his lawn. A crow flew by to see what the commotion was about and he landed on the outside window sill and started dancing up and down it as if to spite Pirate. He even tapped his beak against the window pane to piss Pirate off even more. Pirate swatted at the window but it was to no avail. Eventually the crow tired of pissing off the cat and flew off.

That's when I left and headed outside. I didn't get into my car right away. I figured I'd expense a breakfast on the taxpayer's dime. I crossed the street and went down a block. Not far from my favorite greasy spoon, Joe's Main Diner on Main Street, is a coffee shop with the very best New York style bagels.

It's called Baked Beans and Bread. Triple B to those of us in the know. It's a bad name for a coffee shop. Firstly, because coffee beans aren't baked they're roasted, and secondly, because Triple B doesn't sell bread. Lots of baked goods, but no bread. I had asked Sol Slonimsky about that. He's the owner of Triple B. He didn't have a better reason than he liked the sound of the alliteration.

Doesn't seem to have hampered business. On the weekends, Saturdays and Sundays, their bagels, especially, would be sold out by eleven, sometimes as early as ten. And they make dozens of several flavors everyday.

As I arrived a little before eight thirty, there was a lineup almost out the door. But most people were taking theirs to go. There was some seating available in the store. It was a busy place but the line moved quickly.

Sol was in the back baking more bagels. But the display case was full. The thing I liked about Triple B was that they made their own bagels and roasted their own coffee. They also used local businesses for their peanut butter and cream cheese. If you're ever in LA you've gotta look up Triple B. The best bagels and cream cheese you've ever had this side of New York and Philadelphia respectively.

I ordered an everything bagel with cream cheese and their dark roasted Ethiopian Sidamo. My favorite coffee beans. Some say you ruin Ethiopian Sidamo if you roast it beyond the second crack. To those I say, pish posh, you obviously haven't tasted Sol's dark roasted Ethiopian Sidamo. This is a great coffee from where coffee was born.

I sat at a counter that looked out onto the street. There was lots going on. A homeless guy who reminded me a little of Gristle sat outside with a blanket over his shoulders and a sign that read something, but it wasn't pointing at me so I couldn't tell what it said. He wasn't making a ton of money this morning.

Businessmen and women in suits rushed past, their self importance as apparent as if they were being pulled along by a tiger. Others, more casually dressed, flitted this way and that, stopping to look in on stores randomly. Either tourists or the landed gentry of the one percenters. Perhaps a combination of both.

I watched absentmindedly as the comings and goings of other lives filled my view for the briefest of moments before being swallowed up into their own lives. Most of the people, so it seemed to me, were, as Thoreau put it, living lives of quiet desperation.

It was apparent on their faces. The wrinkles creating maps of their struggles, the dour expressions read like open aired confessionals of all the dashed hopes and dreams like splintered shipwrecks upon the rocky cliffs of capitalism. I knew it all too well for I was one of the wounded. In fact, I was deep in a quicksand of despair with this Valadon case. But I decided not to depress myself any further than I had to by thinking about it. Perhaps Roberts had good news for me. Perhaps new clues had turned up.

So I packed away my thoughts about this case and focused on enjoying my bagel and coffee. I also watched those drift by outside on the current of self importance.

It seemed to me that there were only two groups of people who had what could be best described as a joie de vivre. Children and grandparents. Or folks who looked old enough to be grandparents.

Children up to around the age of eight or nine, from what I could determine from my sociological study from Triple B, appeared to have an almost unbounded joy and pep to their step. From around ten or eleven, you started to see that joy slip away like mercury being clenched in a fist. I put that down to the indoctrination of schooling to set us all up to be miserable adults in dead end jobs we hated.

The other group were those who looked to be in their mid to late sixties and older. They were the escapees both recent and past who had managed to free themselves from the clutches of dead end jobs and financial stress.

At least this was my café philosophy of the lives of those I saw rushing, swirling or even dawdling in front of me from my counter at the window. The middle fifty years, say from ten to sixty, seemed to be the hardest. Those were the years of clawing and fighting and struggling for the scraps to put on tables and the squirreling away of oil for the lamp to use during the dark nights of the soul and of old age infirmity.

But not to put too glum of an outlook on it all, perhaps this color was coming from my own dissatisfaction with the current case I was on. And that was true. Yet I had a nagging feeling that overall, my observance of the bulk of humanity, was that the bulk of our time was spent perhaps, in less than ideal worlds.

I checked in on myself to see where I stood. Self, I said, am I a man living a life of quiet desperation? And self said to me, Anthony, if you don't stop philosophizing and catastrophizing you'll drive us all to despair. All right, I said, just give me an answer. Anthony, I said to myself, you are not a man living a life of quiet desperation. And it was true. I worked when I wanted, and that was most often when I was asked to help Roberts on a case. And I painted what I wanted and sometimes they sold.

I wasn't a rich man by any stretch of the imagination, but what I was, was a man of options and a man of freedoms. And the freedom to choose how to live your life was perhaps the greatest freedom of them all. And I grinned at that. I was free to choose this day and what I did with it. And I would choose to pursue this case until I found some sort of resolution to it and if no resolution came I was still free not to be dragged down by it but to sit still and to know that at least I did my best. And if my best wasn't good enough then it didn't matter because it was all I had.

With that, I put my garbage in the composting bin on my way out and I dropped a Lincoln in the homeless man's cap that lay on the floor by his feet and by his sign.

The sign read: Dum vita est spes est.

"What does it mean?" I asked him, after I had put Lincoln to sleep in his cap.

He turned the cardboard sign around. On the other side was written: While life is, hope is.

I nodded and smiled at him.

"There is that," I said.

Coffee Klatch

Getting to Hollywood Station, on Wilcox, is one of those few trips in LA that doesn't take an hour. It only takes about half that long. On a good day you can get there in around thirty minutes. Today was a good day. The sun was shining and the sky was blue and the smog was low and parking was plenty. I found a space right outside on Wilcox Avenue.

I knew pretty much everyone who worked out of the Hollywood Division office as well as the North Hollywood Station on account of how often I was there helping Roberts on cases. In fact, the two Hollywood stations were the two that Roberts seemed to hang out the most at.

The front desk officer let me in and told me where Roberts was hanging out. I asked him how long Roberts had been in this morning. It was coming on nine-thirty when I asked. I was told that Roberts had made it in by eight.

JR had found a quiet office in the one corner of the station. Beeves and Forrest were inside with him. They were sipping on coffee when I walked in, and talking about something that I didn't catch on account they stopped talking and greeted me when I arrived.

"We were just going over next steps on the case," said Roberts as he sipped on his coffee. "There's a fresh pot in the kitchen if you want to grab some."

He raised his coffee cup as he said it. I shook my head.

"Just had some at Triple B," I said.

"And you've arrived empty handed, Anthony, are we no longer friends?" asked Roberts, grinning.

I nodded.

"Sorry about that, I should've got you something. But I was having an argument with myself and didn't think about it until I was almost here. What do we have so far? Did you find that witness from two thousand, Forrest?" I asked.

Forrest looked over at me and shook his head.

"I found him though. Went back to the address we had on file for him. House was bought about ten years ago, twenty-ten actually, from him and the couple who bought it are still living there. They had a next of kin contact that they gave on account that he was moved to a long term care facility at the time of the sale. He had dementia."

I nodded. Of course, I thought to myself, there'll be no lead that turns up worthwhile on this goddamn case. I sighed.

"I got a hold of the next of kin which turned out to be his daughter. He had ended up being put into the Piney Meadows facility but didn't last long. He died in twenty-fifteen. Daughter didn't have anything to offer about the case that she had learned from her father. She told me she had also been through all his things and she didn't find anything about her father being a witness to a van or to any police case for that matter."

I nodded.

"So it goes," I said.

"What's that supposed to mean?" asked Roberts.

"That this case is going nowhere, JR," I said. "Or are you holding out on me? This is one frustrating case."

"Tell us how you did with Ferrari," said Roberts.

"As well as Forrest did with the witness. But thankfully Ferrari is not dead. It was nice to catch up again. He was thorough with his investigation as we'd expect but he had nothing new to offer. He mentioned that at the time he thought the witness wouldn't be reliable. Is that in the report?"

I looked from Beeves to Forrest and back again. Forrest shook his head.

"No, the report mainly sticks to the facts without much speculation," said Forrest.

I nodded.

"Yeah, Ferrari thought the man might have shown early signs of memory loss or something. But what he did have to share wasn't exceptionally helpful, and as you know, Ferrari investigated Lemonade Laundry and came up with nothing in the whole state of California for a name like that."

"I made inquiries as well," said Forrest. "And there is still no company in the whole of the state of California with that name. Rather, there is no laundry company in the state called that. I did find a boutique advertising firm called Lemonade Laundry out of San Diego but there is no connection to our victim I could find. No Ford vans used by them either. The owner wrapped his electric SUV with the company's logo. The only similarity is that the logo also has a lemon made from the O in Lemonade."

"Go pay them a visit in any event. Just to confirm," said Roberts.

Forrest nodded.

"Ferrari said the guy had taken his dog out for a walk as he was an insomniac back then," I said.

Forrest nodded.

"That's in the report too."

"Interestingly, I asked him what happened to the money that was found on Grace Smith, Ferrari's victim. He said it was eventually returned to Smith's next of kin. I spoke with Tai from the FBI and he confirmed that all other cases were also found with ten grand either on or next to or underneath the body. All that money wasn't found to be associated with any criminal activity so it too went back to the next of kin."

"But no money was found with Valadon, right?" asked Roberts.

He looked around at all of us and we all shook our heads.

"I think that ten grand was the first ten grand given to Gorky. I think it was probably meant to be left with Valadon but the perp probably improvised. Did we get any hits on any of that money?"

Roberts shook his head.

"No. In fact, there were no prints on the money to speak of. It almost seems like the money was washed," said Roberts.

"So what's going to happen to it?" I asked.

"Well, the FBI's going over the serial numbers but this money also looks like it hasn't been involved in any crime other than the one Gorky is involved with. But because of that, it'll be kept."

"Right, but if it had been found with the body?" I asked.

"Then we'd probably give it to Valadon's next of kin," said Roberts.

"Exactly. I think this is blood money or guilt money for the next of kin," I said.

"Really, such a small amount?" asked Beeves.

I nodded.

"I know. It's an atrociously small amount. But all these women come from working class backgrounds. And the fuckers who did this probably know that and figured that ten grand was plenty for people like them to bury their loved ones."

"That still doesn't get us anywhere," said Roberts.

"Nothing gets us anywhere on this case," I said.

"We'll keep looking into any lead that presents itself," said Roberts.

"Have any of us looked into the rest of the landfill employees? Do background checks give us any cause for concern on any of them?" I asked.

Forrest shook his head.

"Checked everyone we've spoken to," he said. "Nobody has anything that would give us something to go on. Worst I saw was a DUI from ten years ago that the foreman was charged with. Other than that, the rest don't have any records."

"It would be nice to see if we can't take a look into their bank accounts just for certainty," I said.

"We were discussing that before you arrived," said Roberts. "Forrest is going to put together a warrant application for just that reason. Should be easy enough to get, now that we have two victims from that landfill."

I didn't really think anything would come of that, but at this stage, every stone had to be overturned.

Sandi

" Did we have any luck finding evidence of any kind at Gorky's place?" I asked, looking at Beeves.

Beeves shook his head. It looked almost unnatural as if his head were on a pole that was his spine and the head could only swivel.

"Nothing yet," he said. "They're not quite finished yet but they've searched high and low, dusted every nook and cranny of that place and there is nothing to indicate that anybody other than Gorky has ever been in that apartment."

I nodded and I was not surprised.

"The coroner did find something interesting," said Beeves.

"What's that?"

"He was shot through cardboard. A small piece of cardboard was found lodged in his wound, suggesting that he was shot through cardboard. When Anthony and I were there yesterday," said Beeves, looking at Roberts and Forrest now, "the neighbor saw someone, who was described similarly to the driver that Gorky let into the dump, enter into Gorky's apartment carrying a package. Looks like the gun might have been in that package which was likely just a cardboard box."

I nodded. That was not surprising. It was also good work. But it also wasn't a lead that we could follow anywhere.

"Just the one bullet?" I asked.

Beeves nodded. I looked over at JR.

"O Captain, my Captain, our fearful trip has barely begun."

Roberts grinned and nodded.

"What's so funny?" asked Beeves.

"The ship has weathered every rack, the prize we sought has not been won," said Forrest.

"WTF?" asked Beeves.

"The port is near, the bells I hear, the criminals are exulting," I said.

277

"While follow eyes the steady keel, the vessel grim and daring," said Roberts, still grinning.

"Oh, okay. It's gonna be like that. Is that some old-timey song or something?" asked Beeves.

"That is Walt Whitman's poem, O Captain! My Captain!" said Roberts. "You uncultured heathen."

Roberts was grinning at Beeves.

"My soul has grown deep like the rivers. I bathed in the Euphrates when dawns were young," said Beeves.

"Ok," I said. "It's like that. I know Langston Hughes, but do you know this? 'Twas brillig, and the slithy toves did gyre and gimble in the wabe. All mimsy were the borogoves, and the mome raths outgrabe."

Roberts laughed.

"You sound like you've just had a stroke," he said.

"Jabberwocky," said Forrest. "Lewis Carroll."

I nodded.

"That's a poem?" asked Beeves.

Forrest looked at him.

"A nonsense poem found in the sequel to Alice's Adventures in Wonderland," said Forrest.

"And that sequel was called?" I asked.

"Through the Looking-Glass, and What Alice Found There," said Forrest.

"If only we could find some evidence to get us somewhere," I said. "Speaking of which. Did the coroner come up with a cause of death for Valadon?"

Roberts nodded.

"Heart failure caused by an overdose of illicit drugs."

"Which drugs?"

"Cocaine, cannabis and ketamine," said Roberts.

"No asphyxiation then," I said, looking at Roberts.

"Nothing mentioned in the autopsy report. They did find semen in her anus, vagina and throat," said Roberts. "Two donors. One for the basement and one for the attic."

I nodded ruefully.

"Same donor for both anus and vagina is what you're saying."

Roberts nodded.

"And no matches on that?"

"Not yet, they've been sent to the lab but no word yet," said Roberts.

"Probably won't find a match," I said.

"Probably," agreed Roberts. "But no stone left unturned."

We all stood around nodding a bit. Roberts sipped his coffee and I rubbed my chin.

"Do we have anything else left to go on?" I asked.

Roberts looked at me and at Beeves and Forrest.

"Well, CID is still gathering evidence from Gorky's place. That's unlikely to bring us anything, but you never know. Forrest will go and visit Lemonade Laundry in San Diego just to get that off our list. Beeves will look through old cold cases where escorts or prostitutes were found murdered or overdosed."

"I will?" asked Beeves.

Roberts grinned and nodded at him.

"You will. We'll also canvas as many homes around the landfill as we can and we'll canvas hookers to see if they knew either of the two LA victims. Valadon and Smith. I'm all ears for other suggestions."

"What about getting a look at the other three files?" I said. "The two Russians and the German victim. Never know if Tai overlooked something. Couldn't hurt to put fresh eyes on that."

"I think that's a good job for you," said Roberts.

"Happy to, but Tai won't give the case files to me. You'll have to request them as a fellow LEO."

"Not a problem. Anything else?"

Everyone shook their heads. Roberts looked at me and put his hand on my shoulder. It must have been the sour look on my face.

"We can't win every case," he said. "Unless we get lucky, I'm not sure where else we can take this."

I nodded, pinching my mouth from one corner of my face to the other. I wasn't happy.

"You know I think this might be connected to that New York thing from a few years back," I said.

Roberts nodded.

"How so?"

"I don't know exactly. It just seems to me that we're dealing with well-connected people on an international stage."

"That's not much to go on," said Roberts.

"It's nothing to go on, but in fairness, that's more than we've got to go on right now."

"There's gotta be more than just a hunch, Sid," he said.

"It's something that Camus fella said to me. He said to me that he was taking a keener interest in his businesses now. He's well-connected, and if he's involved in some shady stuff like New York, then he might at the very least know about these prostitutes."

"Or, you got a prank caller."

I shook my head.

"No, it was legit. Him and his ilk are playing high stakes games the kinds of which we couldn't even get into the farm league of, even if we were millionaires. I'm going to reach out to him."

"He gave you his number?" asked Roberts.

I shook my head.

"He told me to call him back on the number he had called me from."

"I'm assuming you already tried calling that number back," said Roberts.

I nodded.

"I did. It goes straight to a voice message that says 'leave a message'. That's all."

"And you had it traced back to who?"

"Nobody. That's the thing. The number is untraceable. It jumps from state to state and even country to country. Each time you call it, it traces back to someplace different. No names, no company names either. These people are connected and savvy."

Roberts nodded thoughtfully for a moment.

"Can't hurt," he said. "Let's get back together next Wednesday and see what apples we've got from shaking these trees. That should give me time to get the reports from the FBI and hand them over to you for review. By then, Forrest should be back from Sandi and Beeves should have reviewed a bunch of files by then."

Three Before

There's one thing that can be said for Tai. He's thorough and he's diligent. What that means to me is that I got copies of the three reports by Friday. And that was translated copies from the original German and Russian. I spent the weekend reviewing them with M's help. Looking at them it was no surprise that the Russian cases weren't solved. There wasn't much to go on. Charitably, I wanted to put it down to different police investigation tactics and skills. But really, the Russians just didn't seem that eager to solve a case that included a victim who was probably a prostitute and came from a working class family.

The Russians conducted what I considered to be a routine and minimal investigation into both suspicious deaths. The coroner's reports in both instances were as thorough as ours at least considering the year they were performed.

The first Russian victim's name was Aleksandra Ekster. She was a twenty-three year old blonde woman found in a park in Moscow. Cause of her death was asphyxiation and she had both cannabis and ketamine in her system. Semen was found in vagina and anus and was determined to be from two different donors.

Aleksandra was survived by her parents who hadn't seen her in over five years. She had left home a little before her eighteenth birthday to travel to the big city. Her father was a mechanic who enjoyed his vodka. Reading between the lines it sounded more like he was an alcoholic. The mother worked at a bakery. Aleksandra also had two brothers. They were three and five years younger than her.

The youngest brother had received a letter from Aleksandra when she was twenty-one and he was sixteen. He had not shown the letter to his parents and by the time he was interviewed he was living on his own in Krasnoyarsk which was not far from where they had all grown up in Novosibirsk. I say not far even though Novosibirsk is just under four hundred miles from Krasnoyarsk. Still by Russian standards that didn't seem far at all. Novosibirsk to Moscow on the other hand, where Aleksandra's body was found is over seventeen hundred miles away.

The important thing was that this letter seemed to suggest that Ekster had found good-paying work. What sort of work was not identified in the letter but we've come to assume that was hooking kind of work. Still, the letter was upbeat and positive in tone. Aleksandra seemed to be happy. She said she worked with other great women and that her boss was generous. She didn't identify anyone by name and no company was identified either.

The focus of the letter was on letting Evgeni, that was her youngest brother's name, know that she was saving money to come for him within two years so that she could take him away from their horrible parents. The horribleness of their parents was not elucidated. Igor was her other brother but he was not mentioned in the letter Aleksandra sent to Evgeni.

I had a copy of the letter in both the original Russian and translated into English. It was a simple one page letter that had been mailed from Moscow. Aleksandra had therefore been in Moscow for at least two years before her death. That was the only letter that anyone in the family admitted to having from Aleksandra since she had left the family.

Her mother and father were not particularly perturbed by her death. In fact, her father was quoted as saying that she had always been a stubborn and reckless child. Igor was also quoted as suggesting that Aleksandra, or Aleks as they all referred to her as, was pigheaded and strong-willed and that she never listened to her parents. Aleksandra was the oldest of the three children. Igor, like his parents, did not seem much upset by Aleks' death.

Evgeni on the other hand was very distraught. When the police had found him at home he had already drunk a decent amount of vodka and was inconsolable for some time before trashing things in his apartment at which time the police had to arrest him and take him down to the station to finish the interview.

Evgeni was not quite twelve when his sister Aleks had left home, but he did suspect that his father had been sexually abusive towards her. The father was certainly physically abusive to both boys while the mother turned a blind eye.

Everything else in the case I already knew, but it was confirmation. Aleks was dressed in a black one-piece wearing no makeup or jewelry. With no identification on her and with Aleks not having a criminal record they had no way of identifying her. They reached out to the media and a few people came forward, those in Moscow who only knew her by her first name. A witness had said that Aleks had told her she had come from Novosibirsk. With that, the police put her picture in Novosibirsk's papers and that led to a positive identification.

Ten thousand Russian rubles were found attached to her wrist. It was made up of one hundred one hundred ruble notes. This money went to her father when the case was closed in the same year she was found.

The second Russian woman was a blonde nineteen-year-old found in a wooded area just outside St. Petersburg. Her name was Vera Mukhina. She also had semen in her vagina and anus from two different donors. She died of an overdose. In addition to ketamine and cannabis, cocaine was also found in her system. She had no makeup on and no jewelry when she was found. Ten thousand rubles was also attached to her wrist in one hundred ruble notes. Vera was wearing a pink one-piece.

By all accounts she came from a hard-working family. Her father drove a bus for the city of Kazan and her mother worked as a bank clerk for a bank in the city. They had five children of which Vera was the youngest.

When interviewed, the parents said that Vera had struggled with drugs and alcohol for a long time. Since she was twelve or thirteen. Siblings agreed with that assessment. After school, which she left when she was sixteen, she went to St. Petersburg. The parents only heard from her twice in those three years until she was found dead at the age of nineteen.

From all accounts she came from a decent family. There weren't a lot of resources available with such a large number of kids, but they had food and clothing. The two girls shared a room and the three boys shared a room. The parents weren't warm and exceptionally loving but it appeared that they were not abusive either.

That was all I could glean from the Russian cases. The authorities made some half-hearted attempts to interview some prostitutes, friends and family, but like all the cases so far, nobody had anything of value to add.

The same was to be said for the German woman. She was the first victim found that had the same branding or scar as the others. That was in nineteen seventy-seven on the outskirts of the Black Forest near Baden-Baden. A man, unrelated, walking his dog found her and called the authorities. Her name was Ursula Arnold and she was twenty-one. She was originally from Munich and she had one brother. The parents seemed loving and kind-hearted though the son had been sent to a psychiatric hospital when it was found he had been sexually abusing his younger sister. This had been apparently going on since she was twelve and the parents only found out by accident when the father came home one day early from work to find Ursula giving her brother oral sex on the couch in the living room. Vera was fourteen at the time.

Apparently, Ursula had not protested nor given any signs that she was being abused. The brother had said she enjoyed it. Naturally, nobody thought that was the case, but I had to wonder why she had not protested in those two years. One of the odd things about that whole debacle was the interview with Ursula shortly after her father had caught the two of them having sexual relations. Ursula didn't complain of any intimidation or violence on behalf of her brother. She also admitted to instigating it as often as he did.

Still, the authorities put that down to Stockholm syndrome, but I wasn't so sure. Ursula had become quite sexually promiscuous after her brother had been institutionalized. And at the age of sixteen she left home and from all accounts made her way to Baden-Baden.

Her father was a laborer for a construction company and her mother worked at a creche. I came to learn that a creche was sort of like a day care center. Ursula was found with ten thousand Deutsche Mark tied to her wrist. She was found wearing a white one-piece without makeup or jewelry. She had black hair and was found with ketamine, cocaine and cannabis in her system. Semen from one donor was found in her vagina.

Those were the three original cases. The best I got out of them was confirmation that both Smith and Valadon were related to the same group that had been responsible for their deaths. All three cases I had reviewed had photographs of the women.

None of the women looked as if they had been abused. Even the one from Moscow who had been asphyxiated, you couldn't really tell from the photographs. I figured that could have been attributed to kinky sex gone wrong. Still, it bugged me. If you were using women for sex orgies or sex parties or whatever the hell was going on when these women died, you had a duty to protect them. A duty of care like any reasonable human being.

I looked carefully at the scars of each woman. They were all identical, obviously, because they were all of the same three kanji. I thought it appeared to me that the two Russian women's branding was just slightly different from the German woman's. It seemed that the lines of the scars were ever so thinner in the Russians. I thought it might be due to different pressure or skin toughness or healing that created the difference.

That was one idea I had. The other was that I thought it might be due to a different branding iron. Perhaps by the late eighties these assholes had a need for a new branding iron. Or maybe each country these women were procured from used a different branding iron.

That was all well and good, I thought, but it still didn't get me anywhere. Friday night and all day Saturday I had been reviewing these cases only to find myself banging my head against brick walls. I had been bitching to M all night and all day about it.

I closed the files and looked at M who had taken to ignoring my intermittent bitching and was now watching a crime show on TV.

"There's nothing here," I said. "I mean, maybe small things, but nothing that'll get me anywhere."

"Maybe you should step away from it, darling," she said, getting up off the couch and coming over to the table I was at and kissing me on the forehead.

"You have no idea how goddamn frustrating this is," I said.

She looked at me thoughtfully for a while.

"Do you think it's because of this case specifically or because this case might be the first you don't end up solving?"

I shrugged.

"I don't know. I've never not solved a case before. But this one is frustrating as hell. Any clue, and most of them are just small little things, ends up going nowhere."

"Why don't you step away from it for a while," she said. "I have something for us."

I looked up at her and she grinned at me. She trundled off to the kitchen and a few minutes later she was back, carrying my vape.

"This is locked and loaded, pilgrim," she said to me, pointing the vape in my direction and putting on her best cowboy western accent. "You'd better come with me upstairs before things get out of hand. And no funny business."

"I'll be your huckleberry," I said, standing up from the table and putting my hands up as if in surrender.

She walked me upstairs to her bedroom where we vaped the cannabis and made love for what seemed like hours. The stars winked knowingly at us from outside in the dark blue heaven and after some time we collapsed exhausted, high and spent, having had the best sex in my life, and just as I was enjoying the remnants of that feeling, it was lights out. I slept like a baby and the ghost of So-yi did not wake me.

Mixed Messages

On Monday, Tuesday and Wednesday morning I tried not to worry about the Valadon case. That was easier said than done. The whole thing was bothering me and I couldn't put my finger on it. Sometimes I took things too personally. Maybe it was because I had a teenaged daughter. Aibhilin was showing the very beginning signs of becoming a woman, and that scared the hell out of me.

I saw my daughter with one foot straddled in childhood and the other stretching into adulthood. In half a dozen to ten years she would be the age of the women in this sex orgy case. That's what I'd come to call it. The best I could figure was that these women were prostitutes but not streetwalkers.

Maybe they weren't involved in sex orgies, but they were certainly having sex when they died, or they had had sex shortly before they died. Most of them had semen from more than one man. If that's not a sex orgy I'm not sure what is.

What was making it worse was the lack of clues to chase. It was slowly dawning on me that I might not break this case open. That was upsetting. More so because I was completing a portrait of Aibhilin that was a gift for her thirteenth birthday which was coming up in just a few months.

Every time I came to my easel and looked at Aibhilin's face I saw the five young women dead before their time. And it was hard to separate their faces from Aibhilin's. Perhaps that was what was making it so hard. Seeing my baby doll slowly leaving childhood and entering adulthood was scary enough. Knowing what dangers could await young women was even more distressing. And having to deal with that at the same time my daughter was growing up was just a slap in the face.

Add on top of that, I had this case where I was getting nowhere and I felt incompetent and powerless. If I couldn't seek justice for five young women did that mean that my own daughter's safety and innocence was at risk? That was what scared me the most.

And so I tried to spend time just on the painting. Trying to get lost in the colors and the lines and not so much the whole. It was the whole, the recognition of my daughter as I stepped away from the painting to view my work where my stomach started to get jittery.

I vaped cannabis and I painted. They seemed to help each other. The cannabis at least kept my anxious thoughts at bay and allowed me to see the art within the portrait.

And come Wednesday morning I didn't feel any better about the case. Primarily because I hadn't heard from anyone since the Friday before when I had met JR and picked up the files he'd received from Tai. No news in this case was not good news.

I put on my jacket and left my fedora at home. I left Pirate with enough food and I locked him behind in the apartment. I was starting to worry about everyone's safety. I got into my car and headed towards North Hollywood station.

Traffic was heavy but moving consistently. That gave me a chance to let my thoughts simmer as I headed towards the station. I arrived just after eight thirty. I figured JR would be there by eight along with Forrest and Beeves.

I was right. They were all waiting for me when I arrived, sipping coffee and eating pastries. JR had decided to help us carbo-load before we got into the details of the case. I took a chocolate eclair and a black coffee and added to it the ingredients that make coffee good. That's cream and sugar.

I had brought the copies of the three international files with me to give back to JR. I had taken the notes I needed which were minimal and infrequent. The files were not thick and there wasn't much of note in any of the cases. Not much that wasn't replicated in the other cases.

"Last man in, first man to spill the beans," said Roberts.

I took another bite of my eclair.

"I have nothing really to offer, other than this case is bugging me the more time I spend on it. Probably because it's reminding me that I have a daughter who'll become a woman in short order."

Roberts nodded.

"Melissa is the same age as Aibhilin," said Roberts. "This scares me too."

Forrest and Beeves nodded.

"My daughters are eight and six," said Forrest.

"Mine is five," said Beeves.

I nodded.

"I guess we all understand this in a personal way," I continued. "I looked at the files regarding the two Russian victims and the German victim. Not much to go on. Obviously, they all had challenging upbringings from working class families."

Roberts nodded and sipped on what looked like a fancy coffee.

"It looks to me that if you're looking for evidence on one of these cases you can look at any of them. They all have the same clues that go nowhere. One interesting item of note that's probably not helpful, is that it appears the Russian women were branded with a slightly different branding iron."

"How so?" asked Forrest.

"The lines on the characters of the scar seem a little thinner. I figure that's due to a different branding iron used. Maybe each continent uses their own instrument to brand these women."

"Maybe it's just the age of the scars," offered Beeves. "Maybe scars thicken over time."

I nodded at him and sipped my coffee.

"Yeah, I thought about that. But all the photographs in the case files were taken shortly after the women were found. And from my recollection, all of the women were found within twenty-four hours of their death. Additionally, they're all roughly the same age. The German woman, the first one found, was twenty-one. The two Russian women were twenty-three and nineteen respectively. Like I said, a minor detail I noticed but I can't figure out how it gets us anywhere."

"Still, good note, Anthony, you never know where it might get us in time," said Roberts.

"As for the rest, there really wasn't much of anything. Interviews went nowhere, like ours have. The families are all working class but nothing that ties them together. Some of the women, it appears, have been physically and/or sexually abused. But not all of them. Our Suzanne Valadon wasn't from all accounts. And the German woman had what seems like a consensual incestuous relationship with her brother. He was sent to a psychiatric hospital."

"What do you mean it was consensual?" asked Beeves.

"Exactly how it sounds. The father came home early one afternoon from work to find his daughter performing fellatio on his son. Through all the police interviewing, the daughter never once claimed she was abused or bullied into any of it. In fact, she admitted to instigating as often as her brother did. They chalked it down to Stockholm syndrome or something like that."

"I don't believe it," said Beeves. "The fact that she'd say something like that seems to indicate she was being manipulated at the very least."

I shrugged.

"I do believe it. The problem with what you just said, is the problem with culture to a large degree. Men can be all horn dogs but women can't. First of all, that's not equality amongst the sexes, that's misogyny. The only reason women aren't allowed to fully embrace their sexuality and instigate sexual relations with their loved one is because we want women to be as pure as the driven snow. As soon as we realize that women can enjoy sex just as much as men we might find we have better outcomes in certain cases."

"Well, that's certainly an interesting perspective to think about, Sid. Does it give you any direction to go on?" asked Roberts, cutting me off.

The thing is, neither Beeves nor me were all that argumentative.

"Not much of a direction. If they were all nymphomaniacs or women with large sexual appetites we might have something to go on. Maybe these women had been watched and studied carefully and chosen specifically for their sexual appetites. But like I said, culturally we won't allow ourselves to go there, so it never comes up in the files or investigation angles. Still, with the Valadon case, we didn't seem to get any indication that she had had sex previously or that she enjoyed it much. Yet, you know what they say about Catholic schoolgirls."

"What's that?" asked Beeves.

"That women who have grown up with repressed beliefs about sex or intimacy tend to be wilder in the bedroom. Could just be an urban legend. Can't say I dated many Catholic schoolgirls."

"You're thinking there's a chance that these women enjoyed sex quite robustly," said Roberts.

I shook my head.

"Not specifically. I'm saying it could have been a line of inquiry. Probably still wouldn't help us in any great way and that's why I never asked it of the Valadons. But yeah, I'm sure these women enjoyed sex. Now, whether they enjoyed sex with strange men is probably less likely and maybe that's why they were plied with drugs."

Roberts nodded.

"Was there anything else you were able to gather from the files?"

"Not specifically," I said. "But this has led me to a line of questions. What happens to these women if they get tired of their work? What happens when they age out, if they do?"

"If we knew the answers to those questions we'd probably know the answers to the important question of who's responsible for these deaths in the first place," said Forrest.

I nodded somberly for a while and ate the rest of my eclair.

"Beeves was just bringing me up to speed on what he found out from reviewing old cold cases with prostitutes as victims. Want to quickly go over it again?" asked Roberts, looking at Beeves.

Professional Union

"How about I start off with the bad news first," said Beeves.

We all nodded.

"The bad news, as I was telling Roberts and Forrest, is that there are thousands of cases out there involving prostitutes that have gone cold."

I furrowed my brow.

"Thousands," I said. "I find that hard to believe."

"This goes back to nineteen seventy," said Beeves. "There are a little over twenty-three hundred cases that have been digitized and hundreds more that still need to be digitized. I've only glanced at some of the paper cases. The digitized cases are easier to sort."

"I guess that's only dozens of cases a year that went unsolved. Jesus, that still seems like a lot."

"It's a dangerous profession, Anthony, and as you know, back in the day not all cops were as committed to solving all homicide cases with the same vigor," said Roberts.

"Which is an argument for legalizing the oldest profession in the world," I said.

Beeves and Forrest looked at me with worried brows. Roberts grinned. He knew my stand on most things.

"That way it's safer for the women because they're not trying to hide their work and it's safer all around from a health perspective."

"You might as well start advertising it on TV," said Beeves. "You're practically encouraging young girls to start hooking."

I shook my head.

"I don't think so..."

"Okay, okay. Let's get back on track," interjected Roberts. "Tell Anthony the good news."

"I'm all ears," I said.

"The good news is that from all the digitized files I searched through, the two thousand plus, there were very few cases where scars had been identified on the body of the victims. And those that did have scars, well none of them had scars that looked like Chinese characters, or, what did you say they were?"

"Kanji," I offered.

Beeves nodded.

"Right, no kanji. Then I looked at tattoos and some of those had Japanese or Chinese characters but I never came across a deceased with those three kanji in a row. The best I had were a couple of Chinese characters in a row. These tattoos were of things like 'love', or 'hope'. 'Power' or 'strength'. Nothing to suggest comfort woman or anything like that."

"If I'm hearing you correctly, then you're saying that you found nothing to follow, no clues to pursue and that's somehow good news?"

Roberts grinned, Beeves nodded.

"It's good news, because it means there aren't any further victims that we've been able to determine. This is not turning into a hooker's genocide."

I could see his point.

"Fuck, Rotten," I said. "Is there anything to pursue?"

Roberts shook his head.

"Forrest made some inquiries through Vice. We had some eager new recruits canvas hooker alley and other areas. We all took some time visiting escort agencies we knew the whereabouts of. Forrest went further than that and reached out to some young women on these escort sites for independent 'business' women."

"And that worked out really well, I'm sure," I said, sarcastically.

"Actually, no. Nobody I've reached out to or anybody else made inquiries of have seen this sort of scar on any of their colleagues."

I nodded.

"Now I'm beginning to feel like we're all getting cock blocked."

Roberts chuckled and shook his head.

"Sid, you always have the strangest ways of looking at things."

"I'll chalk that up in the compliment column," I said. "How many inquiries do you think were made by you and your team?"

I was looking at Forrest.

"We must have spoken with over a hundred women, pimps and Vice cops," he said.

"Being charitable then, I guess we can look at the bright side. Like Beeves said, at least this isn't an ongoing catastrophe, other than the dozens of these women who never get justice each year. Besides that, at least our victims seem to be limited and separate from most other common or garden prostitutes."

"To play devil's advocate," said Forrest, "we don't actually know these women are prostitutes."

"What the fuck," I said.

"Well, we don't have definitive proof."

"You mean like none of them are card carrying members of the Professional Union of Sisters Soliciting Ying-Yang," I said.

Roberts almost choked on his coffee.

"Goddammit, Anthony, you almost made me spit out my coffee."

"I don't get it," said Beeves.

"It's in the acronym," I said.

Slowly I watched the dawning realization cross Forrest's and Beeves' face until they started chuckling along.

"It's not just sisters that offer services for ying-yang, as you so eloquently put it," said Forrest.

"There's also the open coalition of Professionals Enticing Naughty Interest in Sausages," I offered. "Their requirements are less restrictive. Open to all sexes interested in servicing cock."

Roberts had to put his latte down he was laughing so hard. Even Beeves couldn't hold back a polite chuckle. Forrest laughed warmly and shook his head.

"I needed that, Anthony," said Roberts. "Nothing like a laugh to clear the air."

I finished my coffee and tossed the cup in the closest garbage bin. I wasn't as happy as they looked.

"I can't figure another angle on this," I said. "What can we agree on so far?"

"I think it's fair to say we're dealing with an international crime ring. That would be my opinion having reviewed all five cases," said Roberts, looking around.

"To play devil's advocate," said Beeves. "Could it not be a loose affiliation of criminal gangs using the same MO for their prostitutes?"

We all looked at each other. Roberts shrugged.

"I'm not sure about that," said Forrest. "First of all, I'd expect more than five victims. I consider five victims in a roughly forty-five year period to be pretty limited."

"I agree, I'm just trying to get us thinking differently," said Beeves.

"I like it," said Roberts. "We can't afford to get complacent. Here's another one. I don't think these women were murdered." He was looking at me.

I shrugged.

"You're probably not wrong, but I'd still like to see the perps swinging from trees," I said.

"They don't do that anymore," said Roberts.

"Okay then, what about off with their heads," I said.

"Can't do that either."

"I have been thinking about it. And I agree, as much as it pains me, I don't think these women were murdered on purpose."

"Not sure how you can murder someone by accident," said Forrest, grinning.

I smiled and nodded.

"What I mean is, I think at the very least we're looking at manslaughter. But yeah, I agree, they probably weren't murdered."

Beeves and Forrest nodded.

"Also," I added. "Going back to this being an international criminal organization. It's pretty ballsy branding your women like that, don't you think?"

Roberts nodded. He finished his latte and tossed his cup into the trash can. It landed next to mine.

"It certainly identifies these women as theirs," said Forrest.

"And it identifies them," I said. "If we knew who any others are."

"What else do we have that we can agree on?" asked Roberts.

We all ruminated for a while.

"These women all come from similar backgrounds," said Beeves.

"How so?" asked Roberts.

"Like Carrick said. They're all from working class families. That's smart because if these young women were from well-connected or rich families you can be sure more resources would be put into finding whoever did this to them," said Beeves.

"More than that," I said. "It looks like these women didn't have a lot of options on their horizon. I'd be surprised if the money they're earning isn't pretty decent."

"As much as I agree with you," said Roberts. "That's more speculation than fact at this stage. I think what Beeves said is more factual from the files we've read. Can we agree at least, that they're working class women?"

We all nodded to that.

"Not to point out the obvious," said Forrest. "But all these women so far. These Forgotten Five, if I can call them that..."

"I like that," said Roberts. "Let's go with that. The Forgotten Five."

"Well, they're all white. None of them are women of color."

"Absolutely," said Roberts. "But I wouldn't want to bet against there being women of color that are used either."

Forrest nodded.

"True, but that's the facts right now."

"It is," said Roberts. "Does it lead you anywhere?"

"Not much that hasn't been said already. But the world is still run primarily by old, fat white men and perhaps they prefer, by and large, young white women. If that theory is correct, then this international criminal organization or whatever it is, is probably overwhelmingly white in its upper ranks."

We all nodded. It seemed obvious but nobody had pointed it out, and Forrest was right.

"Can anyone think of anything else that we can agree on as far as these five victims go?"

"None have been found outside of Europe and the US," I said. "No women found in Asia or Africa for example."

"Which goes along with what Forrest was saying about them all being white."

I nodded.

"True, but that's not what I was specifically suggesting. There are white women in Asia and Africa. I'm just wondering why these five were found where they were. If this is an international criminal organization, then why the lack of international victims?"

"Perhaps they are not all international but rather limited to Europe and North America," suggested Beeves.

"Or they don't have these women working for them outside of Europe and North America," said Forrest.

"That's some good theory," said Roberts, "but it isn't a fact for certain at this point."

"I agree," I said. "The only things we know for sure are that all victims so far are white. All are under twenty-five years old. All have the kanji scars that brand them as comfort women or prostitutes. The victims have only been found in the US or Europe at this time. They all come from working class families and most seem to have had difficult childhoods..."

"But not all," said Roberts. "Again, let's just stick to the facts."

"Ok. They're all from working class families. All were left out in the open and scantily dressed so that they would be found but difficult to identify. Four out of the five were left with ten grand near them and I would speculate that Valadon would also have been left with ten grand if it wasn't used to bribe Gorky. They all had sex at the time of their death or slightly before and they all had drugs in their system. At least two and often three. Those drugs being ketamine, cocaine and cannabis."

I looked around at the three of them. They were nodding like bobbleheads.

"One thing to add," said Roberts. "They weren't intentionally murdered. It would seem, from what we know, that their deaths were accidental."

We all turned into nodding bobbleheads.

"What do we do with all of that?" I asked.

"Well, Anthony," said Roberts. "There's a homicide almost every day here in LA and we have more than one case to juggle. We'll keep this one open for a bit and make inquiries as we find things to inquire about. But honestly, what else is there to go on? Unless we can find another victim or find this laundry van which we've put an APB out on, I just don't know what else can be done except sit around here and think about it."

Roberts looked around slowly at each of us. None of us had anything to offer up. We were mute faces staring blankly back at him.

He wasn't wrong. I just wanted to overturn some pebble of some worth someplace and get some traction on this case. That wasn't happening. I'd spent a little over a week investigating this case and I hadn't found anything further to pursue. It was upsetting me. But Roberts wasn't wrong. He had other cases to deal with. I just hated losing a case. And this being my first, I couldn't deal with that. Not when it was some young women who didn't deserve to have their lives snuffed out so quickly and so recklessly.

It'd be one thing if we were trying to solve a gangbanger's murder by a rival gang. Those are tough to sell. And not to be unsympathetic to the loss of any life, but when you live by the sword there's a good chance you'll die by the sword.

Roberts patted me on the back.

"I know this is a tough one to let go of, Anthony, but unless there's some angle you can think of that we haven't pursued, I've gotta put it on the back burner."

I looked at him and nodded slowly. Then I shrugged.

"Yeah, I hear ya. I can't come up with anything either."

Roberts nodded sympathetically.

"If it helps, even with this loss, you're still LAPD's winningest detective," he said with a soft smile.

I nodded.

"That's not what this is about. These women deserve better."

"I know," he said.

We stood in silence for a few minutes.

"Take the next couple of days to collect your thoughts and send in your report and findings. I'll need you again soon."

"I'm not finished," I said. "I'm going to call Camus and see if I can't find out anything else about this bullshit."

"I can't authorize that on LAPD's dime," said Roberts.

"It's on my dime," I said.

Roberts nodded solemnly.

"Good luck, old pal. Keep me informed if it gets you anywhere. But please, be careful with these people. They aren't going to like their feathers ruffled and I'm not sure they're really your friends."

"I'm not looking to ruffle feathers, I'm looking to get a bead on justice."

"And you've historically done that by ruffling feathers, Anthony. Use a lot of honey this time."

And just like that, we had given up on this case. I knew it was inevitable. Roberts and them didn't have the luxury of time to sit and navel gaze about a specific case that wasn't going anywhere. And there wasn't anywhere to go with this case. He wasn't wrong to be putting it on the back burner as much as I hated that.

They started talking about another homicide they were working on. I said my farewells and left the station. I sat in my car for a while and thought about next steps. I was going to call Albert Camus and I was going to call Ainley. M had heard enough of my bitching about this case. Now it was time for Lloyd to be my sounding board.

Leave a Message

With difficult cases I sometimes like to walk the beaches close to where I live. Sometimes I drive for a while and find a quieter spot to sit in my car and watch the waves crash upon the shore. That's what I did after I left North Hollywood. I took the one oh one out west to San Buenaventura State Park. There's a lot of parking out by this state beach and plenty of picnic tables.

The beach itself is not heavily used. At least not around eleven in the morning on a Wednesday. There were only a handful of other cars in the parking lot. An early seventies Camaro, green in color, had an older man sitting in it eating a sandwich. His windows were open and he ignored me as I drove by. He was not a happy-looking man. By that I mean he had the lines of deep sadness and worry drawn over his face by a child given a chisel and wet clay.

A mid-two thousands white Malibu was parked several stalls away from the green Camaro and inside, a married couple in their mid-fifties were having a picnic. That was my interpretation of what was going on. I made that up by the sandwiches I saw them eating. I guess it was a sandwich kinda day.

I pulled past them and parked nose-in several stalls away from them. There were a few other vehicles, all empty, in the parking lot. I was facing towards the ocean. Likely about six or seven hundred feet away from the curling waves as they lapped at the sand.

It was a mostly cloudy day and I rolled down my windows. By that I mean I pushed a button and the windows rolled down auto-magically. The breeze was cool and refreshing. The air seemed a little cleaner out here. A little further away from the steady smog that lived over LA like a specter. The day was warm. Seventy-four degrees according to the announcer on KJAZZ.

I listened to KJAZZ for a while as I watched the aborted waves die upon the hard brown sand. The waves were small here. Not much good for bodysurfing and certainly not enough for a real surfer's enjoyment. I thought about luck, both the good kind and the bad. On this case I didn't have either.

But here I was, sitting at a park that literally meant 'good luck'. San Buenaventura, or more colloquially known as Ventura, was named after Saint Bonaventure. I don't know what Bonaventure stands for, but it's probably similar to the Spanish buenaventura. I needed a little help. Maybe Saint Bonaventure was the patron saint of hopeless causes.

I took out my phone and searched for Saint Bonaventure. Nope. He wasn't the patron saint of lost causes. I should have known that. The patron Saint of lost causes was Saint Jude, otherwise known as Jude the Apostle. He is not Judas Iscariot, though that man was certainly a lost cause for having sold out Jesus. If you believe these stories are factual rather than mythical.

Saint Jude, I learned, is also the patron saint of desperate situations and hospitals. I hadn't been to church in, I couldn't remember how long. I'd forgotten most of my prayers but I mumbled a few words in my mind to Saint Jude. At this stage I was desperate. I asked him if it wasn't too much trouble to pull himself away from sick children to help a gumshoe I'd be grateful.

No, I didn't say that. He should stay with the sick children. All I asked was for a little help if he could spare it.

Saint Bonaventure I learned was the patron saint for intestinal problems. I didn't have any of those so I thought about the good luck aspect of being at a park that was named good luck. I'd heard it said that rubbing the belly of a Buddha statue can bring good fortune. That seemed fair, but I didn't have a Buddha to rub. There was also the rabbit's foot. Though how a dismembered limb was supposed to bring good luck I didn't know. Felt more like it would be a curse.

While I was on this train looping around thoughtsville, I wondered if gumshoes actually had a patron saint. They don't, not that I could find. What I did find was that murderers even have a patron saint. Saint Julian who killed both his parents is the patron saint of murderers. So many questions. The most obvious being, how does a murderer become a saint?

The next thought led me to see how justice is sometimes hard to come by. Especially when the murderers have patron saints. There was hope though. Police officers had their own patron saint too. Saint Michael. Michael the archangel and archangels were high ranking angels. So there was that.

I got out of the car. I needed a walk to stop my head from getting trapped in the intricate folds of the world wide web. I didn't bother to take my socks and shoes off. The sand I quickly learned was quite compacted and none was coming into my shoes.

I headed north. When you've headed west as far as you can, the only place to go is north, south or east. East led me back to my problems. So did the south. North was new and so that's where I headed. I walked towards the Ventura Pier which didn't seem all that far away.

The breeze was light and I pulled out my phone after a while and searched my contact list for Camus. I dialed the number. I waited a long time. After the thirteenth ring it went to voicemail.

"Leave a message," said an AI voice that sounded like a human female but not fully accurate. Something about the intonation of the voice gave it away.

"This is the first man," I said, "looking for Albert Camus."

I hung up and walked the rest of the way to the pier. The Ventura Pier used to be the longest wooden pier in California. Now it's in the bottom half of the top ten of longest piers in California, and around number six longest wooden pier. It's a little over sixteen hundred feet or almost a third of a mile.

It's an historic landmark which was originally built in eighteen seventy-two. It wasn't very busy as I walked along it. The railings are angled so as to provide some support as you leaned against it. Why you'd want to do that I wasn't sure. Large parts of the railing had been used as targets for bombing sorties of the guano kind. Perhaps the railings are tilted to allow fishermen to lean their poles against it.

I kept to the straight and narrow and walked down the middle of the pier. I passed two sets of itinerant musicians or homeless people. Hard to tell which. They both had bicycles with baby carriers filled with stuff which I didn't study all that carefully. One couple was a female and male pair. They were old. He had a scraggly beard that was mostly gray but also stained with the yellow of nicotine. They both wore bandanas on their heads.

The other couple were both male. Looked like friends more than anything else. The one had a guitar in a soft case. They were younger. Maybe in their forties. They sat on the benches that were dotted along each side of the pier here and there.

Further up on the pier towards the bulbous end was an old, slim man leaning against a set of inner railings. The inner railings prevented you from falling into the ocean as there was a large hole in the pier at the end. For what purpose I didn't know. Maybe just to look down into the ocean from.

But that's not what he was doing. He was leaning against it and looking north. I couldn't see anything interesting that might have caught his eye. I looped around the end of the pier where a handful of fishermen were trying their luck to no avail. None of their buckets contained any fish. Maybe they should become fishers of men. Perhaps their luck would improve.

That got me wondering if fishermen had a patron saint? I didn't know, but by their lack of success at the pier I had my doubts. But then again, if murderers get patron saints why not fishermen? And why not gumshoes?

I stood at the end of the pier for a while and looked back the way I had come. I looked south but I couldn't see much. The views were fine but there wasn't much to see. I kept my hands in my pocket and stood and thought and stood some more.

I got no inspiration so I turned back and walked down the pier and towards my car. Walking back always seems to take longer than walking to the place you had just been to. Maybe that's because it's new. You're heading on an adventure. Walking back is just retracing your steps. Retracing my steps got me back to my car but it didn't get me any clarity.

I stood at my car door for a minute. I was lost. Not literally, figuratively. I fished out my phone and called Ainley. I made an appointment for next Monday. I got into my car and rubbed the worry beads on my komboloi that I had wrapped around my rearview mirror. That didn't take the worry away.

My stomach grumbled and I realized I hadn't eaten anything today except for the eclair that Roberts had offered up. I decided to head back homeward and stop by at Joe's Main Diner for some all day breakfast.

Four Roses

It was later that evening when I got the call back from Camus. I had been home for hours it seemed without much to do. I had started writing up my report for Roberts. That's what I usually did when I wound up a case. It was part of the contract I had with the LAPD. The end of every case required a report of my findings, what I did and how I came to my conclusions. Nothing onerous, and yet I still found writing these things hard. And they weren't all that long. Perhaps five or so pages. Sometimes more depending on how convoluted or involved the case was.

This Forgotten Five case wasn't all that convoluted or difficult. The problem wasn't so much finding the clues as finding any clues to look into. I sat at my laptop for an hour. In that hour I got down the first paragraph. But that first paragraph had been written and rewritten dozens of times.

I can write well enough, it's that this case was leaving me unsatisfied, and with an empty feeling in the pit of my stomach that weighed me down. I couldn't figure out why. They say a painting is worth a thousand words. I'd sooner have painted my way out of writing this report.

And that's what I did. After that hour trying to craft a single damn paragraph I gave up and went to my easel and started a new painting. It was more abstract. It was a visceral and raw attempt at dealing with my feelings and unsteadiness about this case. I called the painting 'Slaughter of the Unseen Sabine'. I made good progress with it and after a couple of hours of that, I was hungry and thirsty. The painting wasn't done, but I figured it would be something that Ercole Kon at The Bauhaus might be interested in. I figured I'd show it to him first before Declan Dawson here in LA at the Triangle Gallery.

That was another thing that was weighing heavily on my mind. I'd only sold four paintings this year and it was already almost November. One had sold at the Triangle Gallery and the other three had sold at The Bauhaus in New York. It was one of my worst years for sales in a long, long time. I hadn't sold this few paintings in probably a decade or more.

Times were tough, is what I had been told from both sides of the country as an explanation as to why my paintings hadn't sold. Next year would be better. Declan had even suggested lowering the prices of my paintings to two to three grand. I wasn't on board with that proposal. The idea is that an artist's work gets more valuable over time, not less. And it wouldn't be fair to those who had bought at five grand. I kiboshed that idea.

After I'd worked on the painting for a while which was heavily tilted towards the red color spectrum for obvious reasons, I went and sat down and watched some baseball I had pre-recorded. That helped me take my mind off the case but not off my money. I checked my accounts on my phone. I had enough money to last the rest of the year which was only around two month's worth of expenses.

This case would help. Once I got paid for this, that would give me another couple of months of living expenses. But I was tired of living hand to mouth. This year especially. My car was in pretty good shape mechanically, not that you could tell from the body. Within a couple of years I'd probably need a new one. There was no money for that. In fact, I'd been at five hundred bucks a day plus expenses for years now. Pretty much since I'd started consulting with the LAPD. That needed to change. I needed to have that uncomfortable conversation with Luca Abt, Chief of Detectives.

But you know how the city is with money. They love to hand out golden parachutes to the assholes at shitty hall but when it comes to paying the working man they're always claiming poverty.

But back to what I was doing. My hunger wouldn't quit. I'd downed a couple of beers with the baseball but that wouldn't satisfy the growl in my belly.

I went into the kitchen to see what I could make myself for dinner. I had a chicken breast in the fridge, eggs and a box of mixed salad greens, a tomato and some red onion. I also had bread crumbs and mozzarella and a can of pasta sauce. I figured that would make a solid attempt at chicken parm.

I beat an egg, beat the chicken and then dipped it into the eggs. Next I poured the breadcrumbs over both sides of the chicken and put it into a frying pan with some butter. I had already turned the oven on to pre-heat. While the chicken breast was frying I started on the salad. When the chicken was finished frying on both sides I took it out of the frying pan and put it into the fire. Much like my life.

I jest, but only a little. I was in a sour mood over the case. I put the chicken in a baking dish. I poured a little pasta sauce over it. I grated a good amount of mozza over the chicken and sprinkled some Italian seasoning over it along with some salt and pepper. The chicken went into the oven and I finished up the salad.

I was starving, so instead of waiting for the chicken I put the salad into the bowl and went out into the living room and ate the salad. I'd made an olive oil and balsamic dressing for it. The salad was good. Wasn't too long after I'd finished it that the oven bell rang. I was back on the couch by then.

I got up and got the chicken and put it on the plate. The cheese had melted nicely. Pirate had smelled the chicken cooking and came to see what the chef was going to prepare for him. He was in luck, there were no cans of cat food in the fridge which meant he got a fresh, room temperature can of food. I opened it up and put a dollop of it in his bowl. The smell had him meowing at me impatiently. I put it down. He started eating, I got a knife and fork and the plate of food and went into the living room again to finish watching the baseball.

I needed a good stiff drink. I put the food and cutlery down on the coffee table and went over to my liquor cabinet. A nice Irish whiskey would go down a treat. I opened up the cabinet and my smile turned upside down.

"Fuck," I said, under my breath.

All I had was half a bottle of bourbon. That's a bit of a lie. There was also about a quarter of a bottle of vodka, a bottle of gin about two-thirds empty, a bottle of vermouth two-thirds full and a small bottle of orange bitters that I didn't look at. There was also a mixing glass set because I'm a fan of stirring drinks rather than shaking them. I mean, really, who wants a bubbly or frothy martini other than that pompous Brit we all know so well?

But I didn't want a martini. I hardly ever drank a martini. A martini was not a good drink for a man. Have a proper drink not a prissy drink.

Drink a whiskey or a vodka over ice if you must, hell, even take a gin and tonic but a martini, no. Just no. It's overhyped to the extent it's become a trope of itself.

I guess it was bourbon for me. I took out the whiskey glass and the bourbon. It was a Four Roses bourbon and I poured out four fingers. The math just made sense to me.

I went back and sat down to my chicken parm. It was a pleasing dish. Probably something that M would like. I'd seen these vegan chicken breasts she'd cooked before. Something to try the next time I made dinner for her.

It was coming on seven and we were in the eighth inning. The Cardinals and the Cubs were tied at five a piece when my phone rang. I had finished my food, I was feeling satiated and the bourbon was treating me better than I had treated it. I recognized the number as the one I had called earlier today when I'd tried to get Camus on the horn.

Ekklesia

" Hello," I said.

"Is this Anthony Carrick?" came the reply.

"It is."

"Anthony, this is Albert Camus."

What I heard was the L Bear going Ka-moo. I almost chuckled. Stupid, I know, but the bourbon and the beers were tickling my insides.

"Thanks for getting back to me," I said.

"I think I know what this is about," he said. "It's about the Eighth House, isn't it?"

"Uh, nope."

"I should have been more clear. You're investigating the death of Suzanne Valadon."

"Yes, that's right," I said, trying to hide my surprise. "But there were no houses where she was found."

Though at this point in the game I really shouldn't have been surprised. Albert Camus, or whatever the fuck his real name is, knows a lot. He's obviously well connected.

"I know. She was found at the Calabasas dump."

"It's starting to sound like you're involved," I said, not sure if I was joking or serious.

There was silence on the other end.

"Why did you call it the Eighth House?" I asked.

"It's an old astrological term if you're into that sort of thing."

"I'm not, can you explain it?"

"The Eighth House, Anthony, in astrology, is the house that governs sex. Do you know what the French call the orgasm?"

I shrugged.

"The French word for orgasm," I said.

Camus chuckled on the other end.

"No, they call it 'le petit mort', or the little death. Orgasm then, is a sort of small death. With each orgasm we leave a little something of ourselves behind. A little death, if you will."

"That's interesting, Camus, but I'm not dealing with orgasms I'm dealing with le grande mort."

"It's la grande mort," said Camus. "Nouns are gendered in French. And big is female while small is male."

I wasn't interested in a French grammar lesson.

"I still don't understand what astrology's got to do with any of this."

"This group of people that are responsible for these women's deaths call this their Eighth House."

Now I was intrigued.

"I'm listening."

"Not much more to it than that," said Camus. "Once a quarter, or whenever they feel like it, they'll get together at the Eighth House."

"And they have an orgy then, right?"

"Right. It's more than that, though. It's a way of rewarding loyal servants," said Camus.

"I don't understand. Which servants?"

"As you probably figured out by now, probably by the time we finished our last conversation, the world is run by a loose affiliation, a coalition or a cabal, if you will, of men attempting to mold the world in their own image."

"Right," I said. "Like the Bilderberg Group."

"Uh, not quite. The Bilderberg Meeting is made up mostly of men and some women who are not part of the inner circle. Think of the Bilderberg Group as our frontline soldiers. They think they're calling the shots in the trenches but actually, those shots are being called from elsewhere."

"So who is actually in charge?" I asked.

"The Ekklesia," he said.

"And what's that?"

"The seventy-seven of us who are shepherding this ship of humanity in the direction of our choosing."

"That sounds an awful lot like hubris," I said.

"Perhaps," was the reply.

"No, really, Camus," I said. "I don't understand what the fuck you and your pals are up to but I don't like it. First, you're involved with a plumbing company that doesn't exist but that sends out plumbers to assassinate people. Now you're telling me that you buy or rent or kidnap women for orgies when you feel like it and toss these women aside when they no longer suit your needs. What kind of fuckery is this?"

There was a long silence on the other end. Sometimes my mouth runs off without the stewardship of my mind. I had to remind myself that I needed Camus more than he needed me. If I was going to get anywhere in this case, I needed his help.

"You there?"

"I am," he said. "Just waiting until you've finished your tantrum so that we can have a conversation like adults."

I bit my tongue.

"Please explain," I said.

Another long pause.

"That plumbing company was mine. However, like I said to you originally, I wasn't as hands on as I should have been with it and some of my people had gone rogue. I've now cleaned that up."

That's as I remembered our first conversation.

"Why is so much death following you around then?"

"Power corrupts and absolute power corrupts absolutely."

"Lord Acton," I said. I knew the quote well, my sergeant at the Academy drilled that into us. "The full quote goes something like this. Power tends to corrupt, and absolute power corrupts absolutely. Great men are almost always bad men. I'm trying to figure out if you're one of the good guys or one of the bad guys."

"In your vernacular, I'm one of the good guys. Not all of us are..."

"Us being the Ekklesia," I said.

I had downloaded a recording app previously so that I could record my conversations with Aibhilin. To have something to remember her by when she wasn't around. Now I figured I could use it to record my conversation with Camus. I put him on speaker so that I could search for my recording app. Speaker didn't work for some reason.

I had to keep my ear close to the phone so I could then search through my apps. I was looking for "WotsUp". I found it and opened it, but the damn thing wouldn't work.

"You can't record this phone call, Anthony," said Camus.

"Fuck," I said, under my breath. He had been talking earlier but I wasn't hearing him very well on account I was looking for my app and had to take my ear off the earpiece or internal speaker.

"Amongst us, Anthony, are differing opinions about how to best get towards our goal."

"And what is that goal?" I asked.

"Steering humanity towards a global, one world, peacefully led governing body."

"That sounds exactly like what the conspiracy theorists are suggesting."

"Well, they're not that far off."

"You're talking about setting up a New World Order," I said.

"Not quite, Anthony, the New World Order is a conspiracy theory developed by right wing nuts. What we're after is a cosmocracy, a one world, one government democracy."

"Why?" was about the only question I could come up with.

"Because humanity is sick, Anthony. We are all one people and yet we divide ourselves into tribes, along state and provincial lines and there is nothing more toxic than thoughtless patriotism. My namesake put it like this. I should like to be able to love my country and still love justice. I think that's impossible. Perhaps Oscar Wilde said it best when he said that patriotism is the virtue of the vicious.

"To answer your question, Anthony, patriotism does nothing more than divide people further. We believe that it is only through a single polity that humanity can best reach its potential."

"And this would still be democratic, of the people?" I asked.

"That's right. And as you can imagine there are great impediments to reaching this one united world of humanity. We have the Chinese and the Russians, amongst others, with their authoritarianism that has to be dismantled and we have to create a floor of economic prosperity for all of us, and that primarily begins with ensuring that everyone has a minimum standard of living that we're still far from.

"You only have to look to some of our best science fiction writers to see the benefit of a one world system. With everyone working under one flag and towards one common humanitarian goal of enlightenment and improvement, we can reach our full potential. In a nutshell, that's what we're trying to achieve. Having said that, there is a faction within our organization that would rather see the world burn and it is this faction that we are attempting to eradicate from our ranks."

"And these are the men involved with murdering these young women," I said, getting a little testy.

"Not quite, Anthony. Humans enjoy sex. It is a natural drive of ours to mate. The goal with the Eighth House was to manage that natural urge more efficiently."

"By kidnapping women to become sex slaves. I don't see it," I said.

"If you'd step back a minute from your volcanic emotions I'll try and explain it to you."

The Fairer Sex

I bet this is going to be good, I thought to myself as I waited on the other end for Camus to tell me about how forcing women into orgies is somehow what they wanted.

"First of all, these women aren't forced into anything," said Camus.

I thought of Aibhilin. She was starting to get interested in boys. That was starting to horrify me.

"I find that hard to believe," I said.

"I think I've found one of your blind spots, Anthony. Does Emily enjoy being intimate with you?"

I furrowed my brow. I had not told him about Emily. In fact, I had not told him much about my personal life.

"Who's Emily?" I asked, feigning ignorance.

"Emily is your girlfriend of a couple of years now, Anthony. She's also the Chief Medical Examiner for LA. She drives a red Tesla with license plate..."

"That's enough," I said. "I get where you're going."

"You don't. I'm not going anywhere, I'm not trying to threaten you, but you asked who Emily was. You and I both know who Emily is. So I'll ask it again. Does Emily enjoy being intimate with you?"

"Sure sounded like a threat," I said. I was still biting my tongue.

"No, no, no. I don't make threats, Anthony. I make promises and you have nothing to fear from me. In fact, I'm one of your biggest fans. Ever since that New York debacle you've helped me clean up house. Left a mess for the NYPD, but you've helped me clean up. And I appreciate that. This is why you and I can talk. Even with your temper, I'm happy to help you, Anthony, because, like you said, we're the good guys."

I didn't know what the fuck to believe coming out of this guy's mouth. But he's all I had. And if I had any hope of bringing any sort of conclusion to this case I needed to hang in there with him.

"Of course Emily enjoys being intimate with me otherwise she wouldn't be intimate."

"And what about porn stars, do you think they enjoy sex?"

"Perhaps, but I'm sure they wouldn't be doing half as much of it if they weren't getting paid."

"That's not important. Your weakness, Anthony, and the problem generally with society at large is that we don't allow women to fully express and embrace their sexuality, or enjoyment of sex. We want a princess on our hand and a porn star in the bedroom. That is to say, we want women to be pure as the driven snow outside of the home and yet we want them as nymphomaniacs in the bedroom. It's a bit schizophrenic. Why can't women just enjoy sex as much as men do? Or rather, why can't they be as horny as men?"

"The answer, Anthony, is that they can and they do. It's just that societal expectation doesn't allow them to fully embrace their enjoyment because men are all insecure about women's sexuality. And for you, Anthony, it is a big blindspot."

"I wouldn't say that," I said. "I'm for the legalization of prostitution."

"Yes, I know that. You'll do the right thing but sometimes you don't understand the right thing."

"I understand it very well. It would be safer for everyone, lower the disease and violence risk as well as lower associated crime."

"That's right, but when it comes down to the individual women, you'd rather not think of them banging away and craving more sex and more cock, would you?"

I didn't say anything. Probably because he was right.

"And that's alright. Like I said, you're one of the good guys, but that still doesn't mean you fully understand women's desire or ability to enjoy sex like men do. I know where that comes from."

"And where's that?"

"From your sister's disappearance when you were eight."

"She didn't disappear," I said. "She left."

"That's right. Why did she leave?"

"You know about my sister then you know why she left. It's one of the reasons why I always dreamed of killing my father."

I had told very few people that. And I didn't know why my tongue was being so loose with Camus. Maybe because he knew so much already, or perhaps it was because he had a way of riling me up.

"She was being sexually abused by your father. She left for the big city and went into prostitution. Not just common prostitution, rather she started to work for an escort agency."

I knew this. At least I had heard rumors. My father and mother arguing about her and my father calling her slut. That's rich, but as an eight year old it's hard to make sense of it all. I often wondered if my mother was aware of the abuse. She must have been. And yet, my earliest memories of her until I was about twelve or so, when we left, is that she was distant and discombobulated.

I later came to learn that my father had encouraged her to get medical help for problems she didn't have. But in those years when I was a child she was probably heavily sedated on benzos, prozac and other antidepressants and anti-anxiety meds.

"How is my sister?" I asked, trying to change the topic slightly.

"Your sister is well enough."

"Where is she?"

"Last I knew, she was in the Boston area."

"And is she still in the escort business?"

I wasn't sure she would be. She's eight years older than me which would put her in her early to mid-fifties.

"She is, but she'd started saving her money to retire. Though you'd be surprised how much interest there is in mature women," said Camus.

I didn't want to go down that rabbit hole. But I wouldn't mind much seeing my sister again.

"Do you have an address for her?" I asked.

"I do, but I won't give it to you," said Camus, rather bluntly I thought.

"Why not?"

"I don't know why she hasn't been in touch all these years," said Camus. "Maybe there's bad blood between her and your mother. Maybe she'd sooner forget about her past and you remind her of that."

And people tell me that I was a little rude and inconsiderate. Camus was at a whole other level.

"Could you at least get her a message from me?"

"That I can do."

"Tell her I'd like to see her and give her my details."

"I will."

I decided to change the subject.

"So, you're telling me that women enjoy sex just as much as men. I can buy that, otherwise humanity wouldn't be crawling over every goddamn inch of this planet like a parasite," I said. "But just because women enjoy sex doesn't mean they want to do it for money with just anyone."

"Well, you have a point there, Anthony. And most women are like that. But people with limited means and a certain disposition are quite capable of enjoying sex for money. These women that are part of the Eighth House are chosen specifically because they have a greater desire for sex and they're quite happy to do it for money. These are the women we seek out for employment. Have you ever been to a bachelorette party?"

"No."

"At a lot of these parties there are a few women who will give the stripper a blowjob or even sleep with him. Why? Because they enjoy sex more. You might say they are nymphomaniacs. Whatever reason, there are women out there willing to have sex for money and they like it too."

It wasn't a thought that I was comfortable with but I had to grant it to him that he was probably right, as much as it didn't quite fit perfectly within my world view.

And I wasn't naïve. I hadn't worked in vice, but most of the women I'd interviewed who were prostitutes had sad stories. But maybe that was because they didn't have much agency in their employment as prostitutes. Perhaps it was different for self-employed hookers.

"Sounds to me like you're trying to justify criminal activity."

"I'm not here to convince you of anything, Anthony. I'm just trying to tell you how it is. Some women will happily get paid to have sex with men. Now, they might not always like the specific man, but they always like the sex. These are the women that we investigate and hire."

"And how do you do that exactly?"

"We have many people employed under our various enterprises and organizations including psychologists, psychiatrists and sociologists amongst others. In essence we conduct a very robust undercover investigation on potential hires that can take months. Then when we are sure they'd be interested we approach them and offer them employment."

"And most of them take you up on your kind offer," I said, sarcastically.

"We haven't had a thoroughly vetted woman turn us down yet," said Camus.

"And I suppose this is like Hotel California. These women can never leave."

"They can leave. After they've fulfilled their contract."

"And how long is that?"

"Usually ten years, but it depends. We've only ever had three women choose to leave."

"And how many have you employed over the years?" I asked, not sure I wanted to find out the answer.

Cold Case Cupboard

"At this stage there must have been over three hundred," said Camus.

"And only three have left voluntarily," I said, sounding incredulous to myself even.

"That's right, Anthony. Our vetting process is very thorough and very complete. We allow these women to express themselves as they want and to enjoy sex without any moral baggage. It might be hard to believe but they like that."

I did find it hard to believe. But I'd been wrong before about matters and I could be wrong again.

"And I suppose they can turn down any man they choose," I said.

"Yes, they can. Women are not as focused on looks as men are, Anthony. And these women are happy to have sex with all sorts of men and women, as it so happens. Occasionally they decline the interests of a particular man who will then find someone else who is happy to be intimate with him. We haven't had to change our policy yet."

"What happens when they age out or get too old to be of interest to these men of yours?"

"Nobody ages out. Some of the older women mentor the younger ones and will take care of some of the day to day running of the compound. You'd also be surprised how much interest these older women get from men, some of them quite a bit younger."

"What do you mean when you talk about a compound?"

"These women live together and socialize together."

"Just like that with no chaperones or guards?" I asked.

"With both chaperones and guards who all happen to be homosexual so that they might focus on the task at hand. Listen, Anthony. I'm not going to give you anything that will help you find us. In fact, I'm running out of time. How can I help you?"

"You talk about all of this prostitution as if you're doing these women a favor. Yet, since the late seventies, five women have ended up murdered. Three by asphyxiation. I want the asshole or assholes who did that."

"Nobody's doing anyone a favor. It's a business relationship. Some people like being firefighters or hoteliers, others like to be escorts and to be desired by men."

"Firefighters are not the same as prostitutes."

Camus didn't say anything to that. So I tried again.

"How can I get the asshole or assholes who murdered those three women who died of asphyxiation? The last one being Grace Smith from my neck of the woods."

"You can't, Anthony, because he is no longer with us."

"You've kicked him out of the organization?"

"That's one way of looking at it. The point is, he will no longer harm any women that work for us."

"And so he goes unpunished."

"I didn't say that."

"He's been put down, killed, snuffed out. Is that what I'm hearing?" I asked.

Camus didn't say anything.

"Well?"

"Well, I thank you for once again helping me get rid of the detritus within my organization."

"So he's dead then, is he?"

Still no response. Then after a while.

"If there's nothing else, Anthony, I'll bid you good day."

"Hang on," I said, trying to think quickly on my feet. "I'd like to attend one of these Eighth House events to see for myself that these women are apparently happy with their chosen profession."

There was a long pause on the other end.

"Listen, Camus. You can't or won't give me the asshole who murdered those three women. Was it just him all three times?"

"Yes."

"Okay, so I have to take your word on it that it's been handled. Still, this case has been eating me up. Young women like that found tossed aside at garbage dumps like trash. It would really help me put this behind me if I can just see for myself."

Another long pause.

"Ok, Anthony. I'll see what I can do. These soirées only happen every three or four months. You'll need to be patient, though usually we have a soirée around Christmas or New Year's."

"Thank you."

"Anything else?"

"Just a couple small things. If these women are so happy with their work, why were all of them found with a cocktail of drugs in their system?"

"It seems that women who enjoy this sort of work also enjoy other risky activities like drugs. I don't know why that is but that's the way it seems."

"Do you provide the drugs?"

"Not me specifically, but we do provide them. We do this so as to ensure the quality of the drugs. We discourage their use and no one is required to take any drugs, and if they do they need to be responsible about it. Some of them have overdone it, as you know."

"And so they're just discarded then?"

"No, Anthony. They're taken to a quiet place to rest and hopefully recover. That usually happens. However, some of them take too much and we're unable to get them the help they need."

"I think you can do better than that, Camus, with their care."

"You're probably right, but this happens so infrequently that it doesn't make sense to have a staff of nurses and physicians on call for these events. There have only been five unfortunate deaths in the last fifty-five years. Not to discount the loss of those five women, but that's only one every decade or so."

I was doing the math in my head.

"This started back in sixty-five, this Eighth House business?"

"Exactly. Before my time, but as I understand it it was in place more informally in the early fifties not long after the Ekklesia were formed."

"Which was?"

"Sometime before that."

Camus wasn't going to give me exact dates.

"Did you know that these women were left with ten grand by their bodies?"

"I am aware of that."

"What's its purpose?"

"To help with burial costs. Why do you think the bodies are left in areas where they'll be found?"

"So that they will be found," I said.

"Exactly. We want the families to get closure."

"That money could also have been stolen by passersby," I said.

"We're careful about that."

"Why not an electronic transfer?"

"In the mid-seventies that wasn't a thing," said Camus.

"A wire transfer then."

"Much more complicated back then. Cash was left with the body and that worked, and so we continued with it."

"I don't think that's good enough."

"What do you think is good enough?"

"I think you should wire a million bucks into the surviving families' accounts. And that million bucks should have been based on the first death and increased with inflation since then."

"That sounds like you're trying to get us to plead guilty to their deaths when nobody forced these women to take drugs."

"I'm saying that most decent businesses would have an insurance policy that covers the death of the employee while on the job and these employees, if you like, died on the job."

"You make a good point. I'll think about it and take it to the Ekklesia. Anything else?"

"No, but I'd really appreciate it if you can help me get some closure. You know how I hate not to solve a case and this will be my first. If I can see these women at work apparently happy, I'll drop it."

I was lying through my teeth. But I needed any help to continue this investigation and getting into one of these parties could possibly be a huge help.

"I'll see what I can do. But I must warn you, Anthony, that if you are invited you're to tell no one, at least not until after the fact. Understood?"

"I understand."

"I know you're a decent, upstanding guy, but still, this needs to be said. Don't tell anyone, don't wear any wires and don't try to figure out who's who. No police either. If you do, life will become very hard for you."

That sounded like a threat.

"Do you understand?"

"I understand you're threatening me, Camus, and I don't like that."

"Listen, Anthony. I know you think we're pals. But we're not. I'm helping you because you helped me and I like you. But you're one of the common people. I am not threatening you, I am making you a promise. You will never work for the LAPD again and you'll never show any of your art in a decent gallery in the world if you fuck this up. Am I clear?"

"Clear as my conscience," I said.

"Ok then, I'll be in touch either way if I can get you an invite to an Eighth House event."

And with that he hung up. I looked at my phone for a long while. I thought about getting Roberts to get a warrant on my phone to figure out where the call had come from. But that would be insanity. I had already done that the first time and came up empty. Still, perhaps a second time would be lucky.

I called Roberts and told him I'd had a conversation with Camus. He asked what it was about. I filled him in on all the details except for the possible invitation to the Eighth House.

Roberts said it gave him some comfort knowing that these women's deaths were accidental and not intentional. It would be easier for him to put it in the cold case cupboard. I didn't feel quite as confident as he did. And I wasn't finished with this case yet either.

Almost Invited

Almost a month went by before I heard from Camus again. And those three to four weeks went by painfully slowly. I read once about how Einstein had explained relativity. He'd said that an hour spent with a beautiful woman could feel like a minute and a minute spent on a hot stove could feel like an hour. That's relativity. I felt like I'd spent the past month on a hot stove and it had felt like a year.

I had managed to finish up the two paintings I'd been working on. America: The Grave, I decided to send a photo off to Declan Dawson here in LA. He liked it and said he'd take it. The other painting, Slaughter of the Unseen Sabine, I sent a pic of to Ercole Kon in New York. He too, decided he liked it and would take it for The Bauhaus, his gallery. Now I just had to get the damn things to sell.

The week of Veterans Day had just passed and I'd spent it with Aibhilin. Today was the eighteenth of November. That's a Monday and I'd just dropped off Aibhilin back at Racquel and Artero's mansion. We'd had a fun time hanging out at the beach eating ice cream on the Monday just gone and then we'd taken the Griffith Park Trails to the Batcave at Bronson Canyon.

I was worried about that, but Aibhilin insisted. I was worried about the number of people clogging up the trail on Veterans Day, but my fears were misplaced. It was quieter than it had been on most of the other occasions we'd hiked the trail. Aibhilin likes it because of its colloquial term as the Batcave, which is well earned. It was, in fact, the location used as the mouth to the original Batman television series' cave. It's a fifty foot long tunnel that was part of a quarry in the early nineteen hundreds. It's been used by a lot of film and television since then. Batman as mentioned, as well as Invasion of the Body Snatchers amongst others.

I had received a letter in that day's mail. Well, not just a letter. There were a bunch of bills still that I hadn't opened yet. I had the money to pay my current living expenses but not a lot of room for much else. Besides, there was a letter from afar. From foreign lands.

I looked at the envelope. It was a white envelope with my mailing address on the front. It was addressed to "Anthony Carrick". I guess I was no mister to this grifter. Just an undignified untitled name on an envelope. It looked like it was typed. And I mean that literally. I gently rubbed my fingers over the letters of my address and felt that they had left their mark on the paper. A slight indentation. I had a suspicion that this had been typed on a manual typewriter. The font looked like a generic typewriter font.

I turned the envelope over. there was nothing else written anywhere on the envelope except for my name and address on the front. I was holding the envelope carefully along the edges with the tips of my fingers. I was going to have CID take a look at this for any prints if they could. Not that I'd expect to find any, but a man can dream.

I'd brought my mail up to my living room and placed it on the coffee table. I went into the kitchen and put on some kitchen gloves. I went over to my liquor cabinet. In a small carved wooden rectangular box that sat open on a short side I took out the letter opener. The letter opener was a gift from M. It looked like a miniature sword. The swashbuckling kind that you might have seen the musketeers use. It has a basket guard and tassel.

I took the letter opener back to the coffee table and looked at the envelope again. There were two stamps on it. Both were Swiss. I knew that because I searched online for the name of the country as it wasn't obvious just from looking at it.

Though the postal mark, which also appeared to be the killer of the stamps, had the city's name it was mailed from with the date and time which we'll get to later.

The stamps were identical to each other. They both had three curved bands of different colors. The bands were green, red and orange and from them jutted four hands. Two of the hands on each band were shaking hands with another. The other two hands of each band looked as if they were about to hold hands.

In the left corner was "helvetia" and next to that "100". At the bottom of the stamp was written "International Labor Organization" and the dates "1919-2019". There was also the ILO's logo.

The ILO is a United Nations agency with a mandate to promote social justice and decent working conditions by setting international labor standards. I took that almost verbatim from Wikipedia. Helvetia is what told me that the stamps were Swiss. Well, that and the postmark. Helvetia is the female personification of Switzerland and is named after the early Gaulish inhabitants of the area prior to the Roman conquest. Those Gauls were known as Helvetii. That got me thinking about Asterix and Obelix. They were Gauls, if memory serves, fighting the Romans. I read a few of those comics in my youth.

The postmark was dated the twelfth of November which was last Tuesday. Quick service. It was postmarked at Geneva. I looked carefully all over the envelope but there was nothing of note. Not an additional mark out of place. No return address on the front or the back. Nothing other than my name and address and the killed stamps. I took the letter opener and opened up the envelope. Inside was a single sheet of paper, folded in half.

I opened up the piece of paper. It didn't have a lot typed on it. It too looked like it had been typed using a manual typewriter. The same typewriter as used to type my address on the outside of the envelope. I inspected them closely. I figured the reason this had been typed rather than written electronically and printed off was to eliminate the microdots that printers put on all copies that you can't see. Those microdots provide the date and time and location of where that copy was printed.

Not the location specifically, but the serial number of the printer which can be tracked to find out where or to whom it was sold. That information, unless the printer was resold, will give you the location of the printer.

"Dear Anthony,

You will be invited to the next Eighth House meeting whenever that may be. Invitation and further details will be provided the day of.

Best,

Albert Camus"

There was no date written on the letter. There was also no handwritten signature. There was however a long rectangular stamp on the top of the letter and justified to the right. It was a dark brown stamp that simply said, in block letters, "FROM THE DESK OF CAMUS". Next to that tagline was what looked like a rough woodcut stamp of the real Camus' face. In fact, the whole tagline and portrait looked like it had been cut from one block and stamped with one long three inch stamp about two inches high at its highest.

Looking at the letter it dawned on me that Albert Camus and I shared the same initials. I was surprised at myself that I had not noticed that before. In fairness, I usually just called him by his last name. But here, in black and white was his name, Albert Camus. Anthony Carrick and Albert Camus. It was interesting but it didn't give me any insight into the case. Perhaps that was why Camus had an affinity or affection for me. Didn't matter, I'd use any angle I could to help get some traction on this case.

I looked at the letter again. I turned it over. There wasn't anything on the back. It was not a thin piece of paper and yet there was nothing that stood out about it. I imagined it was likely the sort of generic paper that you get at any office supply store that sells five hundred sheet reams.

I stood up and walked over to a bright window that was letting in a bunch of sun. I held it up to the light. There was no watermark. Nothing really of note. It was just white unaltered paper. Nothing much special about it. There were no handwritten marks. Camus had not signed it in ink. He had only typed his name. Hell, maybe he hadn't actually sent it from Geneva. Maybe he'd had one of his minions do it. I went back to the couch and sat down.

I read the contents again. At least I was going to be invited to an Eighth House event. He called it a meeting. That might have been clever, it might have been irrelevant. It certainly didn't give anyone any details about what this "meeting" could be about.

I placed the letter and the envelope on the table and sat back into the couch. I clasped my gloved hands behind my head and tilted it towards the ceiling and closed my eyes.

At least I'd be able to see how the cogs in the machine worked a little with this invitation. It also meant that I needed to make myself available from now until the end of the year at the drop of a hat. Or in this case, at the drop of an invitation that would be sent the day of the event.

That seemed smart. It gave me, or anyone for that matter, no time or very little time to prepare for the meeting. I shouldn't have expected anything less, and yet here I was still surprised by the thoroughness. What else was I expecting though, from an organization that had been having these orgies since the sixties that had led to the death of five women with no clues or arrests made in any of them? People and organizations that careful are well-funded and thoughtful.

I leaned back towards the coffee table and picked up the letter. I folded it and placed it back in the envelope. I left it on the coffee table as I got up and went back into the kitchen. I found a clean, clear, plastic freezer bag in one of the drawers and took it back out to the living room. I put the envelope inside and sealed the bag. I took my gloves off and placed them on the coffee table. My hands had started to get a little clammy in the gloves.

I took out my phone and dialed Roberts. He picked up quickly.

"Lonely hearts are waiting," I said.

"What the fuck, Anthony?" he said.

"You picked up quickly. I don't think I even heard it ring."

"Oh, yeah. Well, I just happened to be at my desk here and my phone was close by. You finished the report for me."

He was talking about my final report I submit after a case is closed. Or in this case, put into cold storage.

"No, not yet. I'll have it finished by the end of the week. I'm calling about some mail I got today."

"Yeah, what's that?"

"Camus sent me a letter inviting me to the next Eighth House meeting," I said.

"You've jumped ahead," said Roberts. "You've just mentioned something that makes no sense to me. An Eighth House?"

"Right, I didn't mention that on my previous update about the telephone call with Camus. I told him I wanted to see for myself that these women were not just sex slaves. He told me he'd look into inviting me to the next Eighth House event. The Eighth House is the euphemism they use for these sex parties or orgies. It comes from astrology. The Eighth House rules sex, apparently."

"I see. And he's invited you to one of these events? When?"

"I don't know. But I'm under strict orders not to tell you about it. Any whiff of police involvement and I'll never work in this town again. At least that was the gist of the threat."

"And here you are talking to me on the same phone that you used to speak with him. Am I right?"

I nodded.

"Fuck, yeah, you're right. But I can't just be buying burners willy nilly just to have a conversation with you."

"All I'm saying is that if this guy is as well-connected as you seem to think he's probably aware you're calling me."

"I'll tell him I was updating you on how my final report is coming for this case."

"Well, you'll need to tell him something."

"Listen, Dad, I didn't call to get a lecture. I called to tell you that I'd received this letter from him."

"And what does it say?"

"Just that I'm invited to the next Eighth House meeting. What I want is to drop it off with you and see if CID can't tell us if any prints can be found on it and maybe what kind of typewriter was used to type it out."

"It wasn't printed on a printer?" he asked.

"No," I said. "He's well-connected, right? He'd know all about microdots."

"Ok," said Roberts. "Bring it round so we can take a look at it. As for typewriters, that's old school. I'm not sure we do a lot of that kinda work anymore."

"Maybe Cardigan knows somebody who's interested in that still. Look, anything we can get off the letter is good. Though I have my doubts we'll get anything of note."

"Worth a try," said Roberts, agreeing with me. "When is this next 'meeting' as he calls it?"

"He said they have them every three to four months and usually something around Christmas."

"And have you told Emily about this yet?"

"No, but she'll understand."

"She'll understand you having sex at an orgy for work reasons," said Roberts, laughing out loud.

"I won't be having sex," I said.

"Really? You're trying to infiltrate a sex party to gather intel on an international criminal organization and you'll be like, no, I'm good thanks, I had sex earlier."

"I'll figure something out."

"You probably should, and the first thing you should do is talk to Emily about it."

"Christmas is a long way off."

"Christmas is just around the corner, Sid. Have you not been paying attention to anything?"

And he was right. We were about a month and a week away from Christmas. We hung up and I drove over to the station to drop off the letter.

Christmas in LA

The month before Christmas seems to go by very quickly. I had received the promising letter of an invitation to the Eighth House on the eighteenth of November. That was a Monday. Christmas was a Wednesday just over five weeks later. And in those five weeks I was amazed at the amount of Christmas songs and advertisements I was hearing. I felt like a kid experiencing his very first Christmas. Though I was more filled with trepidation than awe and wonder.

Christmas in LA is a lot different from Christmas in New York. It doesn't have the same spirit. It's warmer for one thing and downtown LA is probably not as well known as downtown Manhattan or Times Square where they put on a great Christmas display. We also don't have anything similar to the Rockefeller Center Christmas Tree display they put on each year. A tree almost eighty feet tall.

Descanso Gardens puts on a pretty neat light show called the Enchanted Forest of Light. Although not specifically Christmas themed, it is enchanting and the kids love it. Rodeo Drive puts on a display with the businesses getting involved. But that's for the shoppers mostly. The Getty dolls itself up for Christmas and offers mulled wine. Disneyland puts on a great Christmas theme in its park but that's out in Anaheim. Closer to home you can stroll down to Santa Monica for their Winterlit Celebration. Aibhilin likes it and she's got refined taste.

For Christmas trees specifically, you can check out Christmas Tree Lane in Long Beach. You'll manage to see around a couple of dozen lit Christmas trees with musicians on the weekend.

Why am I telling you all of this? Well, frankly, because I was bored and I had Aibhilin a couple of times during that month before Christmas and we went around and saw them all. They're all good, but LA just doesn't have the same sort of feeling or spirit about Christmas as New York does. That's a shame for Aibhilin but more of a blessing for me.

It's a shame for Aibhilin because she loves Christmas. When Racquel and I were still together we always tried to make Christmas special for her. Christmas really is for kids. The wonder is contagious.

It's a blessing for me and some of you will understand why. If you've ever grown up with an alcoholic parent, Christmas is a nightmare. It's one of the few events in the year when you're guaranteed that your alcoholic parent is going to tie one on. And if your alcoholic parent is also a mean drunk, well, you've got the recipe for a powder keg of a shit time. Some of you are with me. I hated Christmas as a child, until I was twelve and we left Stillwater for LA. Then Christmas got more fun. At least my mother tried to make it more fun. But by then I was over it and couldn't get behind it.

By the time I was in my teens, I'd never had a chance to enjoy Christmas, and by then you're so over Christmas anyway because it's just not cool. And for the first few years my mother and I spent a lot of that time looking over our shoulders.

LA is far away from Stillwater. But still, my father being a mean old drunk, you just never knew. But back then it was easier for folks to disappear. There were no cell phones. Hell, there wasn't an internet to speak of. At least not for the public. This was the early eighties after all.

So not only was this Christmas not my bag to begin with, but I was waiting for an invite to an orgy. Where Santa and his elves got into all sorts of manner of naughtiness. For almost five weeks I waited every day for a piece of mail. I checked my mailbox every day too. And nothing came for weeks and weeks. I was fully aware of Christmas and a part of me was even enjoying the season. The songs and the decorations did make things look festive. It might have also been helped by my enthusiasm for getting to peek behind the veil, if you will. I was anxious for any access to these women and hoping that I might find some clues to put the Forgotten Five behind me.

And so it was with those mixed feelings that I waited and waited. And as the days grew closer to Christmas Day itself I wondered if I'd been forgotten. I had assumed that the orgy wouldn't happen on Christmas Day. I had a couple of reasons for feeling that way. First of all, most of the men invited to these orgies were probably married. At least that's what I suspected. Single men aren't as easy to corral or manipulate. Married men helping an organization have more to lose. But I could be wrong.

The second reason I figured that it would likely not happen on Christmas Day was because that was supposed to represent Jesus' birthday. Having an orgy on Christmas just didn't seem like something most people would be up for.

Sunday, the twenty-second of December, came and went and with it my hope and optimism that the party wouldn't occur on Christmas Day. Christmas this year I was getting Aibhilin. I was supposed to pick her up mid-morning on Christmas Day. I didn't want to have to postpone that to the twenty-sixth. There was always the chance that the orgy could be held between Christmas and New Year's, but Camus had specifically mentioned an orgy around Christmas time. To me that meant up to and including the twenty-fifth, but not the twenty-sixth onward.

By the mid-morning, I've usually received my mail from the letter carrier. And I had checked at just after ten in the morning of the twenty-third. There were some bills and a letter from New York. The return address was for The Bauhaus. Ercole had told me he had sold my most recent painting. I was hoping this was a check for that. A cash infusion into my dying bank account was just what I needed round about now.

It was a check for five thousand dollars. That would get me through a couple of months if I was careful. I wanted to head out to celebrate my good fortune, but I was also scared as hell to leave the apartment. I had assumed the invitation would arrive by courier but I had been checking my mail everyday just to be sure.

It was Monday afternoon. I had poured myself a Redbreast single pot still Irish whiskey that had been aged for fifteen years. Redbreast had a bunch of other single pot still whiskeys aged from twelve years to twenty-one, but I have a helluva time paying more than a hundred bucks for whiskey. And this fifteen-year-old had set me back just around that much.

It was worth it though. I was sipping on three fingers, listening to old jazz crooners sing Christmas songs and eating a self-made club sandwich. The secret to my club sandwich is chutney. Mayonnaise on both slices of bread and chutney on the top slice on top of the mayonnaise. The normal fixings include turkey and freshly fried, crispy bacon, lettuce and tomatoes. You don't need mustard if you've got chutney. Try it, you'll like it.

Dean Martin was singing Baby, It's Cold Outside when the buzzer rang. Some social justice warriors had taken issue with the song suggesting that what was actually going on in the song was a date rape or forced sex. Sex isn't mentioned once. The guy just wants to hang out with his lover. You've gotta remember the times when the song was written. It was a more chivalrous time. Sure, men were perhaps more dogged in their pursuit of women, but has that really changed? I didn't get it. It was a good classic Christmas song.

I put the last morsel of sandwich in my mouth and wiped my face with a napkin. I got up and went to the intercom and pushed the button.

"Yeah," I said.

"Is this Mr. Anthony Carrick?"

"It is."

"I have a package for you, sir, that requires a signature."

"Come on up."

I buzzed him in. He sounded young and polite. That was nice. I figured this was my invitation to the orgy. Which meant it was happening tonight. It was just after two-thirty. I wasn't expecting a package. Maybe it wasn't a package. Maybe it was just an envelope with an invitation in it but they still wanted my signature. I'd find out.

I went back to the coffee table and picked up my dirty plate and napkin and took them into the kitchen. I had just come back out and taken a sip of my whiskey when there was a knock on the door.

I went to the door and opened it up. Standing before me was a young guy with a little bit of acne. He was probably past his teens, but not by much. I'd have been surprised if he was of legal age. In his hand he was holding a squarish box that looked like it could have fit a pair of shoes. The height was the shortest length.

He held out what looked like a small tablet.

"I just need your thumbprint in the square, sir," he said.

He was polite and friendly. He also wore braces.

"I'd prefer to sign for it if it's all the same."

He shook his head sadly, as if he were a puppy I'd just scorned.

"I'm sorry, sir. I need the thumbprint in order to release the package."

I didn't give it to him. I decided I'd try and be an asshole and see if that worked better.

"Do you have a card? I'd like to speak to your supervisor, because this is bullshit. I've never had to give a print to receive a goddamn package."

My tone was harsh. I was playing it up. The courier was unmoved.

"I understand, sir. I'm just following my orders."

He smiled and kept his friendliness. He was more polished than I gave him credit for. And more polished than I was at his age. He put his hand in his shirt pocket and pulled out a card and handed it to me. The card was a light green. The sort of color that might be called artichoke or asparagus green. That was the same color he was wearing. He was in green slacks, a green button down shirt with two pockets and a matching green cap. His shoes were brown to match his belt. His baseball cap had two stylized capital D's on it, leaning to the right as I looked at it as if to suggest motion. Just above his left breast pocket was his name embroidered. David, in cursive.

I took the card and looked at it. I turned it over. There was nothing on the backside.

"Just wait here," I said.

He smiled with a friendliness and warmth that seemed sincere but I wasn't buying it. I turned around and walked back into my living room to grab my phone which I had left on the coffee table.

The card just had the name of the business on it. Dionysus Deliveries in block letters. Below that was a slogan in Latin. Veni, Ecce Tradidi. I had no idea what that meant. Underneath that was a number. I dialed it and put the phone to my ear. It only rang once.

"Anthony, he's leaving. Give him the thumbprint or you'll be left out."

"Out of what?" I asked.

And the phone went dead.

"Hello... Hello?"

Nothing. It sounded like a recording. I turned around and my apartment door was open and David was nowhere to be seen. I walked to the door and looked out. David was almost at the end of the hallway. Fuck, I cursed under my breath.

"David!"

He turned around and looked at me. He was still smiling.

"Come on back," I said.

He started the return journey. When he got back to me he offered me the tablet.

"Just inside the square, sir," he said, never losing his politeness.

I placed my right thumb inside the square. Above it was my demographics. More accurately my name, telephone number and address. There was also a small photograph of me as well. Looked like my driver's license photo.

"Is this Dionysus Deliveries a real company?" I asked him, grasping at straws.

"Yes, sir," he said.

"Then why no address on the business card?"

He shrugged.

"Maybe to save on having to reprint the cards when we move."

"Where is the location?" I asked.

"We're online, sir. A quick internet search will tell you."

He took the tablet back and pushed the package towards me. I took it.

"Have a great day, sir," he said, grinning.

I wasn't sure if it was the grin of a young man with insight into the inside joke or if he was just friendly. I nodded at him and he left again the same way he had just come.

I watched him walk down the hall to the door to the stairs and then exit through that same door. He never once turned around to look back at me. I closed the door and went back inside and put the package on the coffee table. I went into the kitchen and got a small knife. The package was a classic brown delivery box that I had to cut away the tape on in order to get into it.

Inside was a sturdy, high quality white box that looked like a small suitcase, but not obviously so. There were no buckles on it. It looked like a fancy package you might receive from a tech company having spent several thousand dollars on a high tech purchase.

Live, Laugh, Love

On the front of the white box was a cliché. Live, laugh, love. It was in a large font. A non-serif font, but other than that I couldn't tell what kind. On the left of the cliché was a smiling santa face emoji about the same size as the font. I'd say they were about two inches tall on the white front of the box.

I turned the box over but all remaining sides of the box were just white. I couldn't tell if the box was paper or plastic. Whatever it was, it was quite sturdy. The lid was flush with the rest of the box and only the smallest of seams gave it away. I placed the box face up on the coffee table. The slogan was the right side up and on top in the middle of the box. At the very bottom of that same front side, closest to me, was another fingerprint scanner.

I looked at the box and tried to open it, but it wouldn't open. I looked at the fingerprint scanner again. It was a small, black, slightly indented strip about two inches long and one inch wide. The left half had scrolling white words that looked to be of the same font as the slogan. I watched it for a few seconds. "Place thumbprint inside the white square —>" was all that was written as it scrolled past over and over again. To the right of that arrow on the other half of the strip I could make out the corners of a white square. I put my thumbprint on it. The same thumbprint I had offered David from Dionysus Deliveries.

I heard a slight whirring sound and a click. Then the lid popped up a half inch and I was able to open the box. The lid stayed attached to the rest of the box on the far side. I looked inside and took everything out that was in it.

There was a card placed in the top right corner that I took out and put aside. Below that was a box that contained, from looking at the image on the box, a high tech type of watch band or smartwatch. I took that out and placed it next to the card. Lastly, taking up the whole other side of the box was another rectangular box that had an image of Santa's face on the front. It looked like it could be a mask. I took that out and placed it behind the other two items I had just taken out.

I grabbed my tumbler and took a sip of my whiskey while looking at the items I had retrieved. Everything was packed into the main box very carefully and with care and attention. I looked again into the box and these were the only items that were inside of it. I figured I'd start with the card. I'd read the instructions for a change. I picked up the card and looked at it.

It was a nice cream-colored, heavyweight cardstock. The card had embossed lettering on it and the outer edge was bordered with fancy gold leaf in an intricate pattern. The embossed lettering was also gold leaf. There wasn't a lot of writing on it. This was the sum of what was written on it.

"Put on the watch. It will only work for you. Do everything the watch tells you and nothing else. The watch will cease to work if it is not on your wrist by 303pm."

I turned the card over. That was it. There was nothing else on the card. I'd give the card to CID when I was done with this soirée. Maybe one of these items had a fingerprint on it that we could get somewhere with. I looked at my phone which I had also placed on the coffee table. The time was two fifty-one. I was impressed with the care and the logistics in planning this whole event. I opened the box with the image of the watch on it. I pulled out the watch which looked more like a two-inch wide bracelet with a black screen that was seamlessly imbedded within the wide strap.

The watch looked like one piece as best as I could tell. However, the circumference was wide enough for me to put my hand through it. The bracelet or watch was white and the watch face which was unlit at this time was black. The watch was now loose on my wrist but the face came to life. Writing appeared on the watch face and told me to place my thumbprint anywhere on the watch's screen. I did so and the watch tightened itself around my wrist. Secure, but not too tight that it was uncomfortable, but I couldn't fit a finger under it. I could possibly get a flat knife under the watch but that was about all. It was unnerving.

I picked up the empty box the watch had been in to see if it came with any instructions or anything else to let me know what it was and how to use it. But other than a picture of the watch on the front of the box there was nothing else on it. No writing at all. No trademarks or FCC symbols or any other symbols you might come to expect on a modern electronic device. There was literally nothing else on it. The watch vibrated and I looked at it.

It was giving me the ground rules. It told me not to try and take the watch off. That any attempt to do so would cause the watch to cease working and I'd lose my privilege to attend the event. It told me not to talk to anyone about tonight in any manner whatsoever. It told me that it could hear everything that was being said around me and that it was also monitoring my vitals.

The watch also said that it would not be intrusive with instructions and that when it needed to inform me of something it would vibrate to draw my attention to it. It asked me if I agreed to these terms and that if I did to say yes.

"Yes," I said, and I watched the waveform change as my voice spoke.

The watch acknowledged it had heard my agreeing to the terms. Then it told me to place the mask, the empty watch box and the card back into the box if any of those were still not in the box. I did so. Then it told me to close the lid and press my thumbprint on the box's strip to secure it. I did that and the box locked with a similar soft whirring sound.

The watch explained that I was to keep the box with me and showed me, by way of an icon, how to eject a handle from the near side of the box by pressing both thumbs against the narrow front side where two faint fingerprint icons were now showing. I had not noticed those before, or they were not there. I pushed both my thumbs onto those icons and then let go. A moment later a handle was ejected from that portion. It appeared to be a curved bridge that popped out from the box, long enough and deep enough for me to get a hand under it to carry the box.

The watch told me I'd be given instructions later on when to put the mask on. I was instructed to call a cab company of my choice and request a pickup at such a time that I would get dropped off at my destination by seven that evening. I was told to request a drop off at the north entrance of Echo Park by Park Avenue and Lemoyne Street.

I called the cab company and I was informed I'd be picked up from Vista Al Mar at six to give me enough time to get there by seven. I got up and went into my bedroom where I grabbed my laptop and brought it out into the living room. I wasn't as familiar with Echo Park as I used to be when I had still been on the job. I knew Echo Park was getting gentrified, but I couldn't remember a place discreet enough or big enough to have a house sex party at. There weren't really any mansions at Echo Park.

I zoomed in on a maps application in satellite mode and poked around a bit. There weren't any obvious choices for what was supposed to occur tonight that could happen in Echo Park. I started to think that Echo Park was not my final destination. I mean, that's what I'd do if I was bringing someone new to an orgy. You'd want to move them around a bit so that they lose their sense of direction. Yeah, I was pretty sure that Echo Park was not my final destination.

I picked up my phone and dialed Roberts. I was about to connect the call when I noticed the watch on my hand. I didn't want to get booted out of the party before I was even in. I decided to text him instead.

Me: Got package delivery for party tonight.

I waited for Roberts to acknowledge. It took him a few minutes.

Roberts: It's on?

Me: Yeah, got this watch. I've gotta wear a Santa mask for later and a card of instructions. High tech!

Roberts: When does it start?

Me: Gotta be at north Echo Park by 7

Roberts: Weird place for a sex party

Me: Probably not final destination

Roberts: Keep us posted when you get to your location. I'll have people standing by

Me: Can't do that. This watch hears everything, might have a camera on it too. I probably shouldn't even be sending this

Roberts: Roger that. Keep in touch if, when you can

Me: Will do

That was our total conversation. Camus had made it difficult to keep in touch with law enforcement. I certainly couldn't make any calls. Not with the watch listening to me. And texting was slow and awkward. Besides which, I was now starting to worry that Camus had access to my phone records. If so, or if or when he decided to look at them he'd see that I had texted Roberts. I could maybe sweet talk my way out of one exchange but not more than that. I needed to be very careful now.

I finished my whiskey and put my box next to the door so that I didn't forget to take it with me. By that time it was three fifteen and I had almost three hours to wait before the cab got here.

My watch vibrated. I looked down at it. I had received a warning. The screen pulsed red, the letters were off-white.

"Last warning, Anthony. No talking to law enforcement by ANY means! If you understand, say 'I do.'"

I cursed to myself. They could hear pretty much anything I did on my phone and they could probably see whatever I was doing on my phone. Not, see, see, but see the data that was being transmitted to my provider. I didn't think my phone had been compromised. I hadn't downloaded any apps recently and I hadn't received any weird texts with downloads or attachments recently either. No, I figured that Camus et al had tapped into my cell phone provider's network.

"I do," I said.

The phone vibrated again. I looked at it.

"One more squeak or letter to LEO and you're out."

It didn't ask me to acknowledge anything but I knew what it meant. I couldn't talk to Roberts or anyone attached to this case. Camus probably had access to their personal phones too. I was on my own. I knew that. But still, it was unnerving. I turned my thoughts to what I could do with the next couple or so hours.

I wasn't hungry and I wasn't thirsty. Still, the weather was nice for the end of December. My phone told me that it was a relatively warm sixty-five degrees outside and mostly sunny. The wind was light coming from the north. I decided to head out to the beach and walk around.

It takes around thirty to forty-five minutes to walk to the pier from where I live. Depending on the routes I take and how energetic I'm feeling. I was feeling contemplative and a walk was exactly what I needed. I gave Pirate some food just before I left. That was taking a risk as I'd fed him not long before that and his spring-loaded stomach had a tendency to throw it up if I fed him too close together. But I hadn't been thinking carefully about that as I had other things on my mind.

By the time I was down the hall, down the stairs and out the building my concerns over Pirate's puking olympics were out of mind. I was thinking about the sex orgy tonight. I wasn't worried about the sex part. I had promised M that I wouldn't be doing any of that. She asked if having sex could get me the clue I needed. I said I'd find another way. And I meant it.

No, I was worried about how this whole event was going to go. I was worried about how to figure out who was who at the zoo when I had a mask to wear and I imagined everyone else did too. What I wanted to do was to sit down with one of the women and see what information I could get out of them. But they'd likely be cagey and probably have been prepared to expect me. And with that, they'd probably been fed answers to all scenarios that could be thought up.

Didn't matter. I was still getting to the party and people often show you how they're doing more often with what is unsaid than what is said.

So I walked around letting my mind wander and flit from one topic to the next. I was as prepared as I could be. There was nothing else to be gained from worrying about a future I wasn't fully in control of. After about an hour just hanging around on a bench and watching the waves come and go, I had centered my breathing and I felt relatively calm and confident about tonight's investigation. Because for me, that's exactly what it was.

I got back home by a little after five and freshened up. I didn't know if the watch could answer questions but I asked if it was waterproof and it said it was. So I showered and changed. Put on deodorant and cologne and felt like a man heading out on a first date. A first date he hadn't had in ages. I was a little nervous. Call it hopeful optimism.

Masked Man

The cab was right on time at six. I grabbed my box with the cliché on it and after filling Pirate's bowl with dry food I headed out. Locking him inside safe and sound. Sometimes he tries to make a run for it if he sees me leaving. Today was one of those days.

"Going to see a woman about another dead woman," I said to him as I shut him in. "I'll be back before midnight. Scout's honor."

The cab driver asked me where to. I told him. He was chatty. I was sitting in the back with the box on my lap.

"My wife has one of them framed on a wall in the guest bathroom," he said.

I had no idea what he was talking about. I put him in his sixties or seventies. He had a couple days worth of stubble and his hair was unkempt. He wore gray slacks and a pale blue short sleeve button-down shirt. He reminded me of Dom Deluise but with hair.

"Not sure what you're talking about," I said.

"That writing on your box there. My wife has that saying printed up and framed. She really likes it. Live, laugh, love. She calls it our family motto. I'm a pretty funny guy. I'm always laughing at something and playing practical jokes. My wife thinks that I invented the dad joke. Kids think that too but they're long gone now..."

And so it went. The kids weren't dead, they'd flown the coop. He was a talker and I liked that. I didn't have to do any of the heavy lifting and it took my mind off my worries. An exclamation here, an easy question there, and that was pretty much the extent of my involvement in the conversation that was rather an oratory by the cabbie, Gerald.

By the time he got me to north Echo Park, my destination, I knew a lot about him. He had three sons and one daughter. All his kids had been given their names based on his favorite blues musicians. In order of age his son's were Muddy, Buddy and Wolf after Muddy Waters, Buddy Guy and

Howlin' Wolf. His daughter who was actually his oldest was named Billie after, yeah, you guessed it, Billie Holiday.

At school she went by Liz, her middle name, because of the teasing she got in elementary school for what the kids teased her as a boy's name. Now she likes it. I learned he had lost a child whose name was Etta after Etta James. She would be his second oldest but they lost her in the late seventies when she was three from measles. Now he gets his flu shot every year. But he said he wasn't against vaccines, in fact, he thought they were important. His kids had had them all. Still, Etta was a sick child from the start.

And on and on he went. I learned what all his kids are up to as adults now. Only one of his sons lives in California. His daughter got married and ended up in Oregon. He and his wife have been married over forty-six years but none of their parents are still alive.

He told me the story about how his parents came to America with nothing but the clothes on their backs and fifty dollars between them. In fact, it was quite a nice distraction. He never asked me about anything of real note. He once asked what I did and I told him I paint. Without asking what sort of painting he told me about a friend of his who had started out as a painter and soon owned his own painting business and retired really well off. He painted houses, Gerald told me, and that got me thinking about contract killers and the mafia.

He told me a couple of jokes and they were funny. I laughed more enthusiastically than they deserved. He was no John Candy. But he had a charm that was quite compelling.

I got to the north side of Echo Park around ten to seven where he dropped me off in the parking lot there. I offered to pay but he said the ride had been taken care of. I asked him who had paid for it. Said he didn't have that information, but dispatch would if I wanted to call them. I said I would and thanked him for his troubles. He headed off and I tried to discreetly take a photo of the back of his car with my watch hand, the watch being on my left hand, holding the box and placed behind my back. I shot the photo from the hip.

I looked around to see if there were any other Eighth House attendees close by carrying a box similar to mine. I looked at my watch again. I had nine minutes before I was supposed to be at this location at seven. I figured

I'd take a quick little stroll and see how much of this north part of Echo Park I could see. I started walking towards the lake, still in the parking lot. There was a walking path to my left so I decided to head towards that direction.

The watch vibrated after I'd only taken a dozen or so steps. I looked at it. It told me to please stay closer to Park Avenue and that my next ride was seven minutes away. I decided to ignore it and play dumb. I made it another dozen or so steps before I got a nasty shock on my wrist. The same wrist the watch was on. It had shocked me.

I stopped and looked at it. I was informed that the watch had enough power to knock me unconscious and that this was my last warning. I wondered what would happen after that. Would the watch no longer be effective? I was more interested in getting to the party. I took a few steps backwards towards Park Avenue. I stopped and took my time to look around. I took a bunch of photos, shooting from the hip again trying to capture almost one hundred and eighty degrees of the view towards the lake I was still facing.

I couldn't see anyone else with a box that looked similar to mine. There were a bunch of people out and about. Walkers, kids playing hacky sack which I hadn't seen in years, a few joggers and some others feeding birds. Some had backpacks and purses, but nobody had a white box similar to mine.

I walked back closer to Park Avenue and waited just off to the side of the entrance into the park's parking lot on the sidewalk. I was informed that my car was three minutes away. I was again informed when it was one minute away.

Shortly thereafter I noticed a black Cadillac Escalade driving towards me from the west on Park Avenue. The car's windows were all blacked out so much so that even seeing the driver was difficult. It was also difficult because what I did see of him was him wearing aviator black sunglasses and a black driver's peaked cap.

He pulled up and double parked just in front of me where there was a small space between two cars for me to get to the Caddy. The watch vibrated and told me to get into the back of the Escalade. I did that.

The Escalade was just as an Escalade is supposed to be in the back. Only this one had a wall between the driver and the back passengers. The sort of barrier you usually see in stretched limos. There was a window in the middle of this barrier which was closed and it was tinted black to the degree that I couldn't see out of it. I looked around. I couldn't see out of any of the windows. That was clever. It meant I couldn't figure out where I was going.

But it wasn't clever enough. I still had my phone with me which had a maps application. I decided I'd open that and have it active while I was being driven to the Eighth House. That way I'd be able to figure out where I had been driven that night and who owned the house. It was something. Something that might be helpful.

The interior of the Caddy was dimly lit to provide ambience. I also figured while I was being driven around that I could review my photos to see if I had captured anything of note, maybe do some internet research and make use of the time. I pulled out my phone but quickly realized I couldn't do anything with it. It wouldn't open up. I hadn't powered it off. But I tried powering it back on just to be sure, but the phone was just unresponsive. Almost as if I had no juice in my battery. And when I had left I knew I had over fifty percent.

I was impressed with this sorcery, but pissed off too. That meant I had no way of figuring out where I was going and no way to plant breadcrumbs. I couldn't see out and I couldn't use any tech. Camus had thought about pretty much everything. The watch vibrated and I looked down at it. It told me to put on my mask and that the car wouldn't start moving until I had done so.

I didn't know why that was important. Nobody could see me in here and I couldn't see out. Nevertheless, I opened up the box with my thumbprint and took out the box that contained the mask. I opened that up and took out the mask and put it on. It was a weird mask. The upper half covered my eyes and most of my nose with Santa's eyes and nose like a traditional half face mask. That would have been enough to disguise me but there was more. From the bottom of the mask was attached a white beard that covered the rest of my face and hung loosely from the mask but with ample room for me to eat or talk without covering my mouth.

I packed the lid of the box back into itself and put the mask box back in the shoe box. The watch vibrated again. I looked at it. I was informed that the remaining trip would be between an hour and an hour and a half. This was my last opportunity to use the washroom before I got to my destination. I was told to use the washroom at the park if I needed to. It asked me to respond with yes or no as to whether I needed the washroom. I said no.

The doors locked and the car pulled away from the curb.

Time Out

As the driver pulled away from the curb and headed towards the Eighth House wherever the hell that was, he spoke to me through an intercom system. His voice had been digitized and changed somewhat to make it sound deeper than it probably was. He asked me what sort of music I'd like to listen to. I told him jazz. He said he'd put on some jazz but otherwise would be unavailable via intercom to talk to.

Jazz piano started tinkling into the Caddy. It sounded like the urgent warning of Dave Brubek on Blue Rondo à la Turk. It's an iconic jazz song. A standard really, ever since it came out. I wondered if the driver had put on Time Out from which Blue Rondo à la Turk is the first track on the A side if we're talking vinyl. And of course I still had a dozen or so vinyl records, one of which was Time Out. A top ten jazz album if you're asking me.

I knew Time Out well. It was one of my favorite jazz albums. I brought the album to mind and tried holding it in my hand. I counted six, no seven songs. The album ends with Pick up Sticks. Seven jazz songs. Some can be long, but I didn't recall Time Out being an especially long free-form album. If I remembered correctly it wasn't much longer than forty to forty-five minutes. Probably closer to forty minutes.

I leaned back and closed my eyes. I had earlier shoved my face right up against the window to see if that made it easier for me to see out. Only marginally. I could barely make out movement. Shadows of cars going by but nothing that could help me identify locations or where I might be. But knowing this album was, let's call it, around forty minutes would help me figure out how long the ride would actually take.

Now, if only I had asked for specific albums. I would have asked for Kind of Blue which is probably closer to forty five minutes. Add Time Out to that and you're at around an hour and twenty to an hour and thirty minutes. I could make a more accurate determination once I was free to find out the exact length of time. After that I might have asked for A Love

Supreme. That album is only around thirty minutes but the first couple of songs are around seven minutes long each.

I cursed myself for not having thought of that earlier. Didn't matter. I knew the jazz classics pretty well, they were my favorites. If the driver didn't veer too far into the unknown I might be able to figure out what he was playing after Time Out. If that was the case then I could probably get a pretty reliable number as to how long I was in the Caddy for.

It wasn't much, but it was a little something. I mean an hour or an hour and a half travel time in LA, depending on traffic, can get you to a lot of destinations. Now, if Camus and friends were smart, and I believed they were helluva smart, then they'd have the driver do some back and forth driving to confuse me even more. And that's what I figured was going on. Twenty minutes into the ride and I'd already lost count of the turns we'd made and in which direction. I had lost count at around thirteen. I couldn't keep my mind still enough. I should have done more meditating. But there was no point berating myself now. I still had about half of Time Out to enjoy.

I didn't mind being driven around, but why I had to wear my mask was a question I didn't have a good answer to. I listened to Dave Brubek and his band. Dave was a jazz icon, just like Miles Davis, and just like Miles Davis, you need exceptional musicians to back you up. A jazz quartet's album sounds the way it does thanks to a lot of people, not just the frontman.

There's production that does a lot to tighten up the sound but before that there's the other musicians playing along. In Dave's case you had three other great musicians complementing Brubek's piano. Paul Desmond on alto sax, Eugene Wright on the bass, and keeping time on the drums was Joe Morello.

I listened to the rest of the album with closed eyes. Pick up Sticks came and went. I wondered what would be served up next. I wasn't disappointed. John Coltrane came on with his sax on A Love Supreme. I wasn't sure it was the album being played, but by the time part two, Resolution, came on, I knew it had to be. If I got through this whole album before reaching my destination I'd have been driving around for about an hour and ten minutes. A Love Supreme being around a half hour and Time Out being about forty minutes.

I did make it through the whole album. I was left briefly wondering what else would play. One of the problems with jazz albums is that the successful ones are often remastered at a later time with additional tracks or takes included. That hadn't been the case so far with Time Out and A Love Supreme and I wondered if it would be the case with the third album that had just started. Another classic. This was Moanin' by Art Blakey. I didn't hear the short warm up session that was included in later versions so I figured it must be the original cut. It started off quick and bright with the self-titled track.

Moanin' was an album that was also about forty minutes long. That would take me up to an hour and fifty minutes of driving time if I got to hear the whole thing, which I doubted I would. I was thinking these sorts of thoughts as the car slowed down. It had slowed down before, but this seemed different. I couldn't hear much so I squashed my face against the window again to see if I could make anything out.

I thought I might have seen the shadow of a metal gate or something of that sort moving. After several seconds the Caddy started off again slowly and about seventeen seconds after that it came to another stop. I was about halfway through the first track, the self-titled track on Moanin'. I did the quick math in my head. I had been driven around for about an hour and fifteen minutes give or take. That meant it would be eight fifteen or thereabouts if I could get the time on my phone, but of course my phone was still not working.

For all I knew we could have been driving around in circles and where I'd ended up might just be twenty minutes away from Echo Park where I was picked up from. Maybe once I was out of the car I could get a better bead on where I might be.

I felt my watch vibrate. It told me to get out of the car, and at the same time I was reading that I heard the doors unlock. I was instructed to take everything I had on me with me and to head to the main door where a gentleman would greet me and give me further instructions.

I opened the door and got out. It was dark outside and I looked at my phone. It still wasn't working. I had been dropped off right in front of the main door to a large house. I couldn't see it exceptionally well as it was dark and there were limited lights on outside but it was huge. A mansion. I had my cliché box in my one hand. The Caddy had not yet driven off. I could tell it was on a curved driveway, like a semi-circle. I looked back behind it, but it was blocking a lot of my view. There were a lot of trees in this front yard of this home and to my left was the gate where I had come in. It was tall. Hard to say how tall, but probably a good ten feet tall or more.

That could be helpful. There weren't likely a lot of homes with perimeter walls that high.

"Eyes front, Mr. Carrick. This way please," said a male voice just behind me who had now grabbed me by the crook of my arm and was trying to lead me away from the Caddy towards the house. I turned to look at him. He was not wearing a mask though he was probably wearing a disguise. He looked like Hugh Hefner, and his colleague keeping a careful eye on me from the large door at the front entrance of the house, he too, looked identical to his friend and like Hugh Hefner.

Ground Rules

As I was being strong-armed up the steps and into the front of the house I heard the main gate open. It was a quiet, muffled sound on account of how far away the main gate was. But it meant someone else was joining us. I craned my neck to get one last peek as I heard my Caddy drive away and the nose of another one starting to show as the gate opened up.

It was hard to tell from my glimpse, but it sure looked like another black Escalade. Maybe that's how everyone was getting driven here, in Escalades. It made sense. They were a common vehicle and didn't stick out around most cities like a sore thumb. As I was finishing those thoughts I was brought into the front hallway.

It was also dimly lit, but much brighter than it was outside. It was a large entranceway, as you'd expect from such a house, and the entranceway had been blocked off up ahead. It had been partitioned into three small rooms, or so it seemed to me, with an entrance into each that looked like an airport security metal detector.

I was transferred to another Hugh Hefner who invited me through the leftmost metal detector. I entered through it and it beeped. Probably on account of my wallet, keys and phone. Hugh Hefner the third followed me through the detector into what was a larger room than I was expecting.

There was a small metal dumb waiter on wheels in the room which had a small electronic device on it.

"Please empty your pockets onto the tray," said Hugh, pointing at the tray next to the squarish electronic device. I noticed he wore medical gloves like the other Hugh I'd seen.

I emptied my pockets onto it which included my phone, my keys and my wallet.

"I'll take your box from you as well," said Hugh, holding out his hand.

I passed it to him and he passed it through a small slit flap in the room. These rooms seem to have been put together much like a big top at the circus, only at a much smaller scale. What I meant by that, was that they were aluminum framed with a canvas or heavy vinyl shell. Yet I couldn't hear anyone in the middle room which would have been right next to me. Maybe there wasn't anyone there.

Hugh picked up my phone, wallet and keys and put them through the flap. A few moments later he put his hand through the flap again and when it came back into our room he was holding a small rubberized bracelet. The bracelet was white and had a number on it. That number was eleven. It also had on it, what looked like a small black chip or perhaps even digital screen, though it was just a dull black, not displaying anything at all, if it was a display.

"This bracelet is to be kept on until you're ready to leave. It is the only way to claim the contents I asked you to place on this table. When you're ready to leave, one of the hosts will help you retrieve them. If you are ever unsure about any of this you can ask the watch. Understood?" said Hugh.

"Yes," I replied.

He put the bracelet on my right wrist. It didn't do anything fancy like the watch strap had done. It was just what it looked like. A rubberized bracelet with maybe a small display or chip on it.

"I also need to take a drop of blood to ensure that you are not carrying any STDs. Place your index finger in here and keep it there until I tell you that you can remove it. You'll feel a quick sharp pain."

I put my finger into a small cylindrical sheath that was part of the electronic device that he had taken from the side of the device. My finger only fit into it up to the first knuckle. I felt a small, sharp pain and then some sort of throbbing or sucking. Yeah, it felt like my finger was getting sucked slightly, but not a wet suck. It was weird. A few seconds later I was told I could pull my finger out.

I did so and a small drop of blood started to bulge from the prick on my finger. Hugh gave me what looked like a small alcohol wipe which I used to wipe the blood away. It did more than that though. It made my finger tingle and left a slight gel on my finger that quickly dried or turned into a second skin. Whatever it did, the slight pain was gone and my finger stopped bleeding. I put the used wipe in a small, yellow biohazard box that

Hugh had put in front of the tray for me. I noticed he also took the sheath out of it's housing and dropped that into the biohazard box too.

"While we wait for your bloodwork, I'll go over some house rules," said Hugh, as he put away the attachment that had held the finger sheath.

"Sadism or masochism will not be tolerated. In fact, no violence towards any of the women, staff or other guests will be tolerated. Everything that happens here is to stay here. No talking about it. Anything you want to do with any of these women is at their discretion though most will be up for most activities. However, if one of these women tell you to stop, you stop right away. There are beverages and food that can be had freely. Treat this house as if it were your own. You are free to roam anywhere in the house except for the basement. Do you understand?"

I said yes.

"Failure to obey any of these rules will get you evicted and may end your relationship with us. Everything here tonight is being recorded but will not be shared with anyone outside the organization. Do you understand?"

"Who is us?" I asked.

"Do you understand?" was the only reply I got.

I nodded.

"You need to verbalize your understanding," said Hugh.

"Yes, I understand."

"Good," said Hugh. "Your blood is clean, you are free to enjoy yourself. If you have any questions you can ask your watch or you can ask any of the Hughs."

With that he opened up a flap behind him and bid me to go through it. I did. The light on the other side was a bit brighter, but everything was still quite dim, warm and romantic. I stepped through into the orgy.

Pearl Necklace

I had stepped through into an even larger entranceway. The one that sort of looked like the house in Gone With the Wind but with modern styling.

Frankly, my dear, I do give a damn, and that's why I'm here, I thought to myself. It was decorated for Christmas. Minimally, but lights, Christmas trees and other Christmas decorations were carefully placed here and there.

A young woman in some sort of lingerie with a sheer shawl over her shoulders came by. She looked me up and down. I looked her up and down and I liked what I saw. Her bosom was firm and perky and uncovered except for her sheer shawl she had over her top half.

"You're a handsome man, are you looking for me?" she said, smiling coyly.

I'd never been one for one-night stands, I'd had enough of them, but they were never as fulfilling as sex with a woman you connected with. But this young woman could have convinced me otherwise if I was a younger, single man.

"What's your name, sweetheart?" I asked her.

"Jezebel," she said.

"From the bible," I said.

"Only the naughty parts."

She winked at me.

"What would you like to do to me?" she asked. "I've been a naughty, naughty girl."

I grinned at her.

"I'd like to get a drink and talk for a bit first."

"Oh, ok," she said. "Follow me."

She took my hand and led me to the left where we entered a large lounge through large wooden doors that were open. The decor was minimalist with minimal pieces of art on the wall. Christmas decorations were tastefully placed about the place. It looked like a legitimate designer had given the place the once over. The pieces of art I had seen so far had all been abstract. I had seen no sculptures. The only items on the floor were pieces of furniture which were being well used. Other than the Christmas trees.

Jezebel led me to one of the Hughs who was serving at a mobile bar.

"What do you want?" she asked me.

"Irish whiskey, three fingers," I said.

She gave my order to Hugh. I looked around at the rest of the room. There were several men here with women on the different pieces of furniture. Each piece of furniture was covered with an opaque netting to provide some semblance of privacy. What that semblance was eluded me. I could see just as well through the netting as I could see Jezebel's breasts through her sheer shawl.

On a small love seat a man in a Santa mask and wearing a gray suit with his pants down to his ankles sat while a naked woman lay to his right with her head in his lap, sucking his cock.

On a larger L-shaped couch further away a man was having sex with a woman doggie style while she was giving a friend cunnilingus who was in turn giving fellatio to a second man. The orgy was in full swing, it appeared. A very Bacchanalian event. Not that I expected anything different.

Against a far wall, and not covered by any netting, a man stood with two naked women in front of him. They were taking turns sucking him off. I should mention at this time that not having been to an orgy before, this is as I had expected. The men, from the shape of their bodies and some of the telltale signs of the color of their hair on their heads, arms and legs from what I could see, were likely in their fifties or older.

All of them that I had so far seen were not fit. They had varying amounts of fat around their midsections and their hair was either artificially dyed or gray. If it was there at all. Other than the orgy going on, I felt like a barber at a bald man's convention.

The look of the men was contrary to the nubile, beautiful, tight bodies of the women. All of whom seemed to be in their late teens to early twenties.

Not that I could tell for certain. But their tight, milky-white skin - I had only seen white women so far - suggested they were young. Their faces, which I had not spent much time looking at, on account of their other beautiful attributes were all covered in what I felt was best described as Mardi Gras masks.

Looking around, it appeared that only the women were wearing different masks. They were all Mardis Gras type masks with feathers, sparkles and other colorful attributes that only covered the top half of their face. Roughly from their mid-foreheads down to around their noses. It gave them anonymity but allowed their mouths unimpeded access to drink, eat and suck.

The customers here, the four I had seen so far, all wore Santa masks just like me. The Hughs all wore Hefner faces. We too were anonymous, but unlike the women, we were interchangeable with each other except for our physiques.

The Hughs, or chaperones were supposedly gay. Yet none of the Hughs I had interacted with seemed obviously effeminate. I realize that not all homosexual men are effeminate, but I was in unchartered waters, finding myself at sixes and sevens. I felt a tap on my shoulder. I looked at it and it was Jezebel offering me my drink.

"Would you like that?" she asked me, as I took my drink from her.

"Like what?"

She looked over to the Santa against the wall who was now climaxing and shooting his wad all over the two women kneeling in front of him. I must have been looking in that direction.

"I can get a friend to help me suck your big cock," she said.

I grinned at her.

"You haven't seen it to tell," I said.

"I'd like to."

I could see the appeal to this Eighth House. It seemed to me that this was all catered towards men's fantasies. Jezebel, whether she was sincere or not, was playing the perfect nymphomaniac.

"Let's go sit for a minute and let me get to know you better before we get down to the sex."

"Ok," she said, grabbing my hand again, and as she did so she not so accidentally rubbed her hand against my crotch.

"Ooh," she said, "somebody likes me."

She licked her lips. I ignored her.

"Just a minute," I said.

I turned towards the bartender.

"What whiskey is this?" I asked.

He pulled out the bottle from under the mobile bar he was on the other side of and showed it to me. Like every other Hugh, he too was wearing medical gloves. I noticed the women weren't. It was Writers' Tears Double Oak. I liked the taste of it. It was spicy with a hint of vanilla. Very smooth. My hand was getting tugged. I followed Jezebel as she led me away.

We headed to the long end of this lounge where it turned at a right angle and continued on along what must have been the backside of the house. I counted another three men with two women each. Looked like they were reenacting porn scenes of various kinds. Well, the kinds I suppose you'd only find if you searched FFM on one of these porn sites the kids visit. So I'm told.

We found a daybed that was unoccupied somewhere in the middle of this section of the room. It was back against a wall and covered with a netting as well. I sat down and Jezebel sat down on top of my lap and started to gyrate. Her bosom was practically in my face.

"You like sex?" I asked her.

She nodded and moaned. Her distractions were working and I wasn't finding it helpful.

"Uh, I want to make you cum so bad," she said.

That's not what I wanted.

"Do me a favor and just sit next to me so that I don't spill my drink," I said.

"You could spill it all over my wet pussy," she said.

I picked her up and put her next to me. And by doing that I didn't even spill a drop of my Writers' Tears.

"Listen, mister," she said. "A little less conversation and a little more action."

She bit her lower lip and pouted.

"How long have you been doing this sort of work?"

She looked at me quizzically.

"Three years."

"And you like it?"

She nodded.

"What do you like about it?"

"Sex. I like sex and I get paid well. Are you going to let me make you orgasm or not?"

"Why so eager?"

"We get a bonus grand for each guy we make cum," she said.

I nodded. That explained it.

"And I like to make guys shoot their loads," she said. "Last time I made an extra three grand."

"You popped three corks," I said.

She giggled.

"Yeah, that's right. I like that. I'd like to pop your cork."

"You remember a girl called Suzanne Valadon?" I asked.

Jezebel put her finger to her mouth and thought for a bit. She cocked her head to the side and looked up at the ceiling. Even though much of the top half of her face was covered she was a beautiful woman and I wanted to sleep with her.

"That name sounds kinda familiar."

"She was found dead at the landfill in early fall," I said, trying to be helpful and keeping my mind off her breasts and body. I reached for my phone, thinking I'd show her a picture. Then I realized I didn't have my phone with me.

"Oh yeah. I remember her now. We don't use our real names. I knew her as Pearl. Pearl Necklace," she said, giggling. "Do you have a pearl necklace for me?"

This was clearly not going as well as I had hoped it would.

"What can you tell me about her?" I asked.

Jezebel leaned back and looked at me.

"You're that guy they told us was coming and was gonna be wasting our time. I'd sooner be making my bonuses."

"What guy is that?"

"Um, the private dick. They said you was coming to ask questions about that dead girl."

I nodded.

"Are you going to answer them?"

She shook her head.

"Not unless you let me ride your cock."

She looked at me while she sucked seductively on her index finger. I grinned at her.

"You could also fuck me up the ass if that's your thing. If you don't like that, I'd get a friend to help me suck you off."

I thought I might like all of it. But that's not why I was here.

"But then you'd have to share the bonus right?" I asked.

She shrugged.

"Better than nothing."

"I'll be honest, sweetheart," I said. "I'm not here for sex. I'm here to get some questions answered about Pearl."

Jezebel stood up.

"I don't mean to be rude, mister, but that's not why I'm here."

"What if I gave you a grand for talking to me?" I asked.

"First of all, that would only get you around five minutes."

"Why only five minutes?"

"Because that's about how long it'd take for me to make you cum, and secondly you don't have that kinda money."

"How would you know?"

A couple of Hughs were keeping an eye on us.

"I've seen the kinda clothes the guys that come here wear and they aren't much like yours. Besides, you don't have anything on you except your erection."

She wasn't wrong.

"So long, mister, you're missing out. We know how to take good care of our men."

"Hang on a minute," I said, grabbing her by the forearm. The Hughs started towards us. I let her go. "Would there be anyone who might talk to me?"

She looked down at me for a minute.

"You could try Lotta. She's upstairs in one of the bedrooms. She's tall. Around your height. Black hair. She might be up for a talk."

Jezebel walked away. A couple of other men had started entering the home and were walking around. A couple of women, and now Jezebel started towards them. I stared at the Hughs. They looked away.

I got up and started to walk the way I had not come from. The musky stench of sex was starting to permeate the air. To my right was a room. Looked like it had been made into a large bedroom. Couldn't tell you what it would have been. The doors had been taken off their frames and put someplace. Someplace where I couldn't see them.

I walked into the room. It held a few beds, a decorated Christmas tree and other Christmas decorations. As expected, there were three men in the room. One on each bed. One Santa was sodomizing a nubile young black woman. She appeared to be enjoying it, or she was good at pretending. Another bed had two women sitting on one man. One on his crotch, one on his face. I couldn't be bothered to look at what the third bed's occupants were up to.

I continued walking through the room, and beyond that I came through another doorway without a door which had brought me back to the place where Jezebel had originally found me. It was the large Gone with the Wind entranceway. I downed the rest of my whiskey. I really liked it. I made a note to look for Writers' Tears on my next visit to the liquor store. I placed the tumbler on a table by the banister that appeared to be just for that purpose. It held another couple of mostly empty glasses.

Another couple of men had entered through the portal of sin and into the entranceway where beautiful young women were gathering to welcome them, like sex-hungry valkyries welcoming warriors to Valhalla. None of the women gathered on this main level were as tall as me. I noticed all the women were wearing flat shoes. Ballet slippers or something like that.

I started up the stairs, climbing around a Santa who had his head tossed back in ecstasy as a woman was giving him head. Upstairs was quieter at this time. I guess the Santas were eager to find love on the main floor. Perhaps upstairs was for later when the place started to fill up more.

I poked my head into one room.

"Come to me, darling," said one woman, lying half naked on the bed. She started to crawl towards me on her hand and knees, still on the bed.

"Lotta?" I asked.

"I've got a lot of love to give," she said.

"What's your name?"

"Moana."

"Where's Lotta?"

"Two doors down," she said, not happily.

I poked my head into the next room just to be sure. I was met with a woman who called herself Steamy. She was also a blonde. Not the black-haired Lotta I was looking for. Like Moana said, Lotta was found in the second room from hers.

Lotta Love

Being a gentleman I knocked on the door frame. There was no door. Lotta was sitting at a dressing table that had three mirrors on it. The outside two mirrors were angled towards her. That gave her a good view of me. It also gave me a good view of her.

She was wearing a red chemise. I only knew it was a chemise because M had bought one recently and I asked her about it. Depending on mood, I was a fan of the chemise. It's a short satiny dress that comes down to barely cover the woman's ass. It's held up with two slim shoulder straps.

I like it because it doesn't let the body announce itself aggressively. With the open bosomed teddy that seemed popular amongst the other women I'd seen, the chemise is low key. Often worn by a woman with a stunning body who doesn't have to announce it to the world.

Lotta looked at me in the mirror. Her hair was tied up in what I could best describe as geisha-style. Her black, silky hair was tied up in a bun just above her neck and pinned in place with what looked like chopsticks.

"Hello, stranger," she said. "Is it me you're looking for?"

"I'm looking for a whole Lotta you," I said, thinking myself quite funny. It got a grin from her.

"I've gotta Lotta Love for you," she said.

"Is that your name, Lotta Love?" I asked.

She nodded. I grinned. Lotta undid her hair and it fell onto her neck and bounced off like black crashing waves against the sandy shores of her tanned skin. Her hair was wavy and bouncy and went to her mid-back. She was stunning. Even looking at her reflection bounced off the mirror and with her mask covering the top of her face I could tell she was a looker. Her lips were full and red. As succulent as cherries. I had nasty thoughts. I imagined those red, pouting cherries topped with my cream.

I felt like I had taken viagra a couple of hours before I arrived. I hoped M would be feeling frisky when I got back later tonight.

Lotta stood up from her dressing table bench and bent over to fiddle with something on her table. I didn't notice what she was fiddling with on account that the chemise had ridden half up her bum and I was looking at her smooth, naked, naughty bits.

My eyes had not yet caused me to sin and therefore there was no point in plucking them out. I did, however, enjoy the view for the few brief seconds that Lotta was playing with my fragile manhood.

There was a small Christmas tree in the corner of the room. It was lit and decorated in white. Smaller than the others I'd seen around the house. Six foot or so was a small tree. Lotta turned around and started towards me. She came towards me slowly, surely until she was inches from my face. Her nipples were hard as stones, ready to pierce the chemise. My manhood was straining to pierce my pants.

Lotta put her arms around my neck and kissed me. It was a sensual kiss. No tongue, not lingering but warm and sweet. I wanted more. She pulled away and her hands brushed down my back until they came to my waist where they slipped around and she gently grabbed my cock with her left hand. I leaned my hips back and her hands fell to her side.

"Is that big package for me?" she asked, licking her lips.

I wanted to say yes. I shouldn't have come to this event. I thought I could handle myself better. But these women were stunning and more than that, they were acting as if on cue to accommodate every man's fantasies.

"You're a beautiful woman," I said. "But I'm here to talk to you about Pearl Necklace, if you don't mind."

Lotta didn't say anything for a while. She put her finger to her lip. She had moved a couple of paces away from me. She looked me up and down.

"Who have you seen so far?" she asked.

"Here?"

She nodded.

"Just you, and, well, Jezebel found me when I arrived."

Lotta nodded again.

"Then you've heard about our bonuses," she said.

"Is that the only reason you do this? For the money?"

She shook her head.

"It's the only way I know how to be a woman. My father raped me starting when I was twelve and now sex is the only way I know how to make a man happy and to find love."

I looked at her with half a smirk on my face. I didn't think she was telling me the truth. It seemed way too honest and upfront of a thing to share with a stranger. There was also something about the way she said it. I saw Lotta's face slowly fold itself into a grin which became a smile and then a chuckle. She tossed her hair back and it felt like a punch to the gut. My knees went weak but I held it together.

"I'm j/k. My father was a hardworking man. He never abused me. A little distant but whoever had the perfect parents? Let me see what you look like and I'll decide if you're worth my time."

She stepped in and closed the gap between us. I smelled apples, vanilla and maybe a hint of cinnamon from her. Sugar and spice and all things nice. She reached for my Santa mask and slowly took it off. I could feel my groin leaking. I wasn't sure this was allowed. I looked towards the door and saw a Hugh across the way. He had to move around the perimeter of a square to get to me, but he gave no indication of doing so. The first floor had no ceiling but rather the rooms up here opened up to a hallway with railings that looked over the main entrance of the first floor.

Lotta tossed my Santa mask on the bed and kissed me again. This time more passionately. I was losing my resolve. I was this close to tearing off her chemise and taking her on the bed that was only an arm's distance away. She stopped kissing before I could pull away. She whispered in my ear.

"You want me, don't you, handsome?" she said.

I could have said yes, and it wouldn't have been a lie. No, would have been a lie. I said nothing. She pulled away again and as she did so her hand rubbed against my groin.

"Let's fuck and then we can talk about anything you want," she said.

Her tone was matter of fact. She said it like you might talk to a child about eating their dinner before they can have any dessert.

I thought about it for a minute. I wondered if I'd do it if I wasn't with M. I figured I probably would. Who was I kidding? I'd tested clean when I came in and I was pretty certain these women would be clean. A quick knocking of the boots to remove the crud. Sure, why not? But I was with M and I'd given her my word.

"Don't get all guilty. Most of the men. No, I'd say all the men that come here for our female skills are married. We're very discreet. We won't say anything and you'll likely never see us again."

She was leaning against the pillar of the bed. Her bosom was thrust towards me. She watched me watching her.

"I'd like to see you unmasked," I said.

I felt more naked without my Santa mask than I would have felt undressed. Lotta grabbed the bottom of her chemise and with one helluva sexy move she took it off. Her mask was still on. She had misunderstood me.

But, by God, she was stunning. She was lean but soft. Curvy without being round. Hairless save for her eyebrows and head of hair. She sauntered back over to me. I noticed her scar. The three kanji just like Valadon and the others.

Her body was smooth as créme caramel and the same color. Her bosom was perfect. Taut, firm and natural, the advantage of youth. She pushed her breasts into my chest and put her hands around my neck. We were eye to eye. I stared at her eyes. They reminded me of someone. I couldn't pinpoint.

"Let me melt all your troubles away," she whispered.

"I'd like to see you unmasked," I said, again.

"I'm naked," she said.

"But not unmasked."

She grinned and stepped away. She took off the mask and tossed it onto her crumpled chemise which lay on the floor at the foot of the bed. She looked Asian. Most likely not Japanese for her warm, brown skin suggested a warmer climate. If I'd have to guess I would have said Thai. But that's not why I was here. I swallowed hard.

Her beauty was undeniable. She was the everywoman to everyman's dreams and hopes. She was a ten in my books and I'd bet you a Benjamin she was a ten in yours. She was the sort of woman, looking at her naked, that would bring a man a lifetime of happiness. She was the unsullied Eve to every Adam. But there was something else about her that clogged my throat. And it took me a minute to realize it.

It was in her eyes. As I looked at them, I was looking back in time. Just her eyes, and only her eyes reminded me of So-yi. I swallowed the lump in my throat. Lotta must have noticed.

"What is it?" she asked, her hands still around my neck, her bosom warm and firm against my chest. My groin, well, I'm trying to leave my groin out of this.

"You remind me of someone I really liked," I said.

"Your wife," she said, laughing. "I sometimes get that, but not usually from men like you."

"What does that mean?"

"Usually Asian men will tell me that."

I nodded and then shook my head.

"I was on a job in New York a few years back and I worked with a New Jersey detective. Her name was So-yi Park. You remind me of her."

Lotta smiled.

"I'm also Korean," she said. And then preempting me. "My mother's Thai, my father's Korean."

I didn't say anything.

"Were the two of you lovers?" she asked.

I shook my head.

"I watched her die," I said. "Actually, I watched her get murdered."

Lotta stepped back. Her face was a mask of shock. Her hand went to her mouth.

"My God," she said.

"It wasn't him, but he wasn't around to help either," I said.

I reached out for her hand. She took it and came to me. She hugged me tight.

"I'm sorry," she said.

"Not your fault. It's just that when I look into your eyes I see her eyes."

She held me longer than I deserved. I still wanted to lie with her. After some time she pulled away. She kept her hands around my neck and looked searchingly into my eyes. I felt hot under the collar.

"You really aren't here for sex, are you?"

I shook my head.

"No, but you're the kind of woman who could change my mind. You're stunning."

"Let's do it. I'll help you forget So-yi for a few minutes."

She took my hand and started to lead me towards the bed.

"I can't," I said.

"Why not?"

"I promised."

"Your wife? I'm pretty sure every man here is married. It's just a one off. Your wife will never know."

"I'm not married, but I'll know."

She stopped and looked at me for a minute and then nodded.

"You're a sexy man. Unlike most of the men we get to serve around here. I'd really enjoy being with you."

I smiled.

"You are a beautiful woman. Under different circumstances I'd take you up on it."

She nodded.

"Can I put on my gown then."

I grinned.

"That's not a bad idea. It'll help keep me out of trouble."

She smiled and kissed me on the cheek and stroked the other cheek with her hand. She picked up a satin dressing gown that was on the bed and put it on. It was the same blood red as her chemise that lay crumpled on the floor. Her mask on top of it.

Love What You Do

Lotta went to the bed and climbed on top of it. It too was reds and pinks. The passionate theme of the night. A red-blooded night for a red-blooded gumshoe trying to staunch the flow of death and mayhem. Lotta slapped some pillows and propped them up against the headboard. She lay on the bed, leaning against the pillows. She slapped the bed next to her. I walked over to the other side and climbed aboard. We were looking out the door frame.

"Ask your questions, sailor," she said.

"What's your name?"

"What's your name?"

"Anthony Carrick," I said. "What's your name?"

She looked at me for a while and bit her lower lip. There are some women. Very few of them, but some, that just ooze sex appeal. Maybe it was the comfortable nature they had being in their own skin, maybe it was an innocence they had about their own beauty. Whatever it was, some women were sexy doing anything. Lotta was like that.

"We're not supposed to tell our real names for safety and privacy reasons."

I nodded.

"I understand. Maybe once we've gotten to know each other you'll tell me. I'm here about Suzanne Valadon."

"Who? Oh, you mean Pearl Necklace?"

I nodded.

"What can you tell me about her?"

Lotta looked up at the ceiling, oozing sex appeal.

"She was nice."

Lotta shrugged and looked at me.

"I don't know what you want," she said.

"Did she talk much about her family, her childhood, anything personal?"

Lotta thought about it for another minute.

"Not much. She didn't like to talk about her family much. She did say they were nice, but too controlling. She was from Utah. I forget where. I think she had a brother but I can't be sure. You see, she wasn't part of our main group. There are, as I understand it, three groups of ianfu here."

I interjected.

"Ianfu?" I asked, playing the mug.

"It's Japanese and basically means comfort women. That's what we are. We provide comfort to men. Look here."

She opened up the left side of her robe, wide. I could see her left half, all naked. Her bosom that slowly moved with her breath. Her nipple was still hard. She pointed to the scar down by her inguinal crease. She grabbed my hand.

"Feel it. It feels strange," she said.

She took my hand and rubbed my index finger over the slightly waxy, raised scar. I was looking down at the scar. It wasn't the only thing I was looking at. I had seen scars like this before. I hadn't seen other things quite as beautiful as she was.

She took my hand off her scar and placed it on her breast. It was warm and firm.

"These are real, even though they might not look like it. Are you sure you don't want to have a quickie? I'll give you all the time in the world to ask your questions."

I took my hand from her breast and covered her up with her gown.

"How about you let me melt you in my mouth?" she asked. "I really want to suck on your big cock."

"You haven't seen it."

"I've felt it," she said, "and it felt like more."

I grinned at her.

"It's hard to tell if you mean it or if you're play acting," I said.

She looked at me almost as if I'd slapped her face.

"Of course I mean it."

I didn't say anything for a while. She started to nod.

"I get it now," she said. "You've never experienced something like this, have you?"

I shook my head.

"No."

"Then maybe this is hard for you to understand, but we're chosen for this work because of our love of sex. Our love of cock. Even our love of pussy. I love fucking, Anthony. I love sucking cock and feeling a guy melt in my mouth. I love eating pussy and I would especially love to fuck you. I mean, sex is enjoyable with most of the men we see, but it's not often we get a younger, good-looking and well-built man like you. Let's say I like cake. Most men are plain old vanilla. Maybe a little too much baking powder or not enough sugar. Maybe a little dry and a little old. But it's still cake and I like it. But with you. You're like the ultimate Black Forest Cake."

She looked at me. I watched a man in a Santa's mask walk by with a couple of nubile women on his arm. They glanced into our room and continued on past. She was forthright and blunt. I wasn't sure if she was trying to shock me or if she was just being matter-of-fact.

"Does that make sense?"

"Sort of," I said.

From this angle I couldn't see Hugh. That was my preference. I didn't know how men could have sex out in the open like this with a bunch of Hughs watching them. I didn't think I could. But then I looked at Lotta again. Yeah, maybe I could. But that's not why I was here.

"Did Pearl like sex, like you're suggesting?" I asked.

Lotta nodded. She was grinning at me.

"You really haven't been to something like this before, have you?" She asked a second time. Not believing me the first time.

"No, but that shouldn't make me unusual," I said. "I imagine most men here had to have had their first at some point."

Lotta nodded.

"Sure, but that was a while back. Most of the men are familiar," she said. "Haven't had a newbie since last time. They're rare and most of the women are keen on them."

I didn't say anything.

"Jezebel must have been disappointed you didn't get with her," said Lotta.

I shrugged.

"She did ask, didn't she?"

I looked at Lotta and nodded.

"You're really into sex with older, out of shape men?" I asked.

"All of us. Yes, Anthony, as hard as that might be to understand."

Lotta stopped and looked at me.

"You never went to Catholic school did you?"

I shook my head. Too expensive and too far away for my parents even though my mother wanted to send me to one. There weren't any in Stillwater. Closest was Guthrie which was still over thirty miles away.

"Catholic school girls have this reputation, and I don't know if it's true, that they're fairly easy on account of the strictness of their upbringing."

"I take it you never went to Catholic school then either," I said, grinning.

Lotta chuckled. It was infectious.

"No, I guess I didn't. All I was trying to say, is that in spite of what you might have thought, many women enjoy sex."

"Yeah, but every night with different, strange men?"

"It's not every night. At most it's once a month, but usually about every three or four months."

"That's how often you have these events?" I asked, not finding the word 'orgy' palatable in my mouth.

Lotta nodded.

"We can also turn down anyone we want. These men are reminded to be clean and presentable before these events."

"I wasn't," I said.

"You're special. We were told you were coming. A gumshoe with a conscience. That's how they described you."

"Who's they?"

"Madam Virginia."

"Madam Virginia?"

"Yes, we usually just call her ma'am," said Lotta, smiling. "Like they call the female bosses in those British crime shows."

"What's Virginia's last name?" I asked.

"Don't know, and I probably wouldn't tell you if I did."

"Who is she then?"

Lotta looked around.

"She's here somewhere. Virginia is sort of like a traditional brothel madam. She takes care of us, sort of like a mentor."

"If she's here does she do the work too?"

Lotta looked me up and down.

"You mean does she have sex with some of the men here?"

I nodded.

"Well, yes, if she wanted to. But it's been some time since she's done that. She'd probably have a go with you, though."

I smiled at her. So you keep telling me, I thought.

"How do you become a madam?" I asked.

Lotta shrugged.

"I'm not one hundred percent sure but you have to have been with the company for some time and I think you're recruited."

"But there are older women here who are keen on..." I wasn't quite sure how to talk about these things. "Some older women are keen on..."

"Sex, Anthony. Yes, there is no mandatory retirement. I think tonight, Mona is our senior ianfu."

"How old is she?"

Lotta chuckled.

"Do you think women go around sharing their real ages here?"

I shrugged.

"How old would you guess her to be?"

"Probably in her sixties. You interested?" asked Lotta, grinning.

Not the Moana I had met earlier, I thought. She wasn't in her sixties.

"If I was interested it would be with you."

"Good answer, mister," she said, looking me up and down and biting her lower lip. She knew what she was doing.

"And Virginia. How old would she be?"

Lotta looked at me carefully.

"Maybe around your age. I think. How old are you?"

"Forty-seven," I said.

"You don't look it."

I smiled at her.

"Would Virginia be about that age?"

"Maybe. I thought she was about your age, but then I had you at around late thirties. So there's that. She could be around your age, maybe younger, maybe older."

"How would I know her to find her?"

"She's walking around in black, red and white lace. She looks exactly like a bordello madam from the late nineteenth century or early twentieth century. She's about five five or six. Attractive with dirty blonde hair. She also carries a riding whip."

I nodded. I hadn't seen anyone like that.

"So, how do you get involved in prostitution?"

"I prefer being called an ianfu or a comfort woman. That's really how I see my role. I bring comfort to hard-working men."

I grinned.

"I don't care what you call it, so long as you aren't pissing in my ear and telling me it's raining."

Lotta laughed. It was a compulsive, naked laugh that put a large grin on my face.

"You're funny, Anthony. I never heard that before. I got into this kind of work because I didn't find anything else that I fancied doing. Not that I expected to become a comfort woman. I just sort of fell into it."

"Tell me about that."

"I wasn't a great student and I wasn't a great athlete but what I found I was good at and what I liked was sex. In my last year of high school I had a threesome with a girlfriend and my boyfriend. I found out I could switch hit and I liked that too."

"I still don't get how you got into it. I don't see any recruitment ads next to Joe Camel."

"You don't see any Joe Camel anymore, either," she said.

"True. I get it that you like sex, but how does that get you from there to here? I like hot dogs but I don't know how to become a competitive eater."

"I don't know how that part is done. But Virginia found me at a party shortly after I had graduated and we started out by becoming friends and then she took me to other parties and introduced me to other girls and slowly and steadily started letting me know that I could make good money doing what I loved. And here I am."

"What's good money?"

"We get ten grand a month and all of our expenses are paid."

"They pay for your apartments, food and all of that?"

Lotta sort of tossed her head back and forth.

"Sort of. We get ten grand a month and we all live together in a large home. Probably a dozen of us live under one roof. That's our group here. We all live together."

"Where?"

"Can't tell and I won't tell."

I looked out the open doorway again. Hugh was now fully in view, discreetly watching over me.

Triangles and Other Angles

"But you know where you live, right?"

Lotta nodded.

"Do you think we're captive here?"

I didn't say anything. I looked at her.

"You really don't get it, Anthony, do you?"

She stared at me with a sweet smile.

"Help me understand it then," I said.

"We do this work freely. All of us. We can leave whenever we wish. We're not slaves or kept against our will. I can leave anytime I want. I just don't want to."

"Have there been women who have left?"

Lotta nodded.

"I've heard so, though I've never met anyone who has left since I got here."

"And when was that?"

"I was eighteen when I started doing this with The Collective."

"The Collective?"

"Yes, I work, well, we all work for The Wabi-Sabi Collective," said Lotta.

"What is that?"

"I guess it's the business I work for. I get paid by The Wabi-Sabi Collective."

"And who runs that? Who owns it?"

Lotta shrugged.

"I think it's probably Madam Virginia," she said.

"And the other two groups of ianfu. What are they called?"

"There's The Shibui Collective and The Kintsugi Collective."

"Sounds like Japanese names. Like ianfu. Are they?" I asked.

Lotta nodded.

"Wabi-sabi is a Japanese aesthetic that sort of brings to mind the beauty of the incomplete or the impermanent. Shibui is a Japanese idea or aesthetic about simple or subtle beauty and Kintsugi is the art of repairing the broken with gold and thereby making something that was broken even more beautiful."

I nodded. It was more enlightened than I was expecting.

"And The Shibui Collective and The Kintsugi Collective would be run by their respective madams, I'm assuming?"

Lotta nodded.

"Yeah, that's right. Madam Gloria runs The Shibui Collective and Madam May runs The Kintsugi Collective."

"Which collective was Suzanne with?"

"Pearl?"

I nodded.

"She was with Madam May and The Kintsugi Collective."

"Are there any Japanese men or women involved in the management of these collectives?"

Lotta shrugged.

"I don't know. The only men we see on a regular basis are the Hughs that protect us. We don't live with men otherwise and I've never seen Madam Virginia in discussions with a man or men. Seems that women run the show which is as it should be."

"Are you allowed to date?"

Lotta shook her head.

"No. But if we need sex we can get that organized. Most of us are highly sexed women and sometimes we need it more than once a month."

"And what happens then?"

"We get to choose from a menu," she said.

I was taken aback. I laughed.

"You choose from a menu?"

"It's not funny. At least I wasn't trying to be. Yeah, we choose from a menu. I guess sort of like actors or models would be chosen by a client. We get a book of men... or women. And they're fully naked shots of these men or women with their physical attributes included. So like, if you wanted a guy with a six-inch cock you can choose that. Or you want a woman with a thirty-four double D you can choose that."

"Take out sex à la carte," I said.

Lotta nodded.

"Do you have to pay for that or do these men and women provide the service for free?"

"The Collective pays for it. These are professionals offering their services, Anthony."

"So, probably porn stars, then?"

Lotta nodded.

"You said you've never known a woman to leave since you've been here and you've been here since you were eighteen. How old are you now?"

"I've been here six years."

"And you like it?"

"Yes. You seem to have a difficult time with that."

I did. Maybe it was my fucked-up upbringing. Maybe it was the relationship with my mother or daughter. I couldn't see them... Scratch that, I wouldn't want to see either of them in Lotta's position. And then I remembered my sister. This is probably what she's doing. And that thought twisted me up inside.

"Look, Anthony. I don't know how to best tell you this. But women have used sex as a tool ever since we figured out how it works. Sex sells. Advertising men know this. Why do you think there's always a sexy woman next to a car at an auto show?"

I hadn't been to an auto show in a while and I couldn't remember if they still did that.

"Women like sex, Anthony. Most women anyway, like most men. And it makes sense. If we didn't like sex how on Earth could humanity continue? But society has put women on pedestals to a degree whereby a woman isn't allowed to fully own her own sexuality. Nothing we're doing here is illegal."

"Isn't it?" I asked, buying myself some time to figure out if that was the case. At its most basic level this was an orgy in a private home. I didn't see any drugs and I didn't see anyone paying for sex and therefore the state had no reason to be concerned. At least it shouldn't be concerned. But there was something else going on because if there wasn't then why the hell had five women died who were doing this for a living.

"No, it isn't illegal. No money is changing hands. At least not for the sex. In fact, in the seventies, one of these events was busted by the police. Long story short, the judge had all charges dropped."

Lotta looked at me with a smile. All I thought about was that the judge must have been a client.

"Maybe the judge was bought and paid for," I said.

Lotta didn't say anything.

"Do the Hughs wear masks when they're at home with you?" I asked.

Lotta shook her head.

"No, but here they do to provide the Hughs with anonymity."

"But you could probably tell who they are, right? What about that Hugh?" I asked, thrusting my chin towards the Hugh who was diagonally across from us on the other side of this rectangular overlook of downstairs.

Lotta looked at the Hugh I was nodding at. He wasn't looking in our direction. He was looking over at our left to another room at something that must have caught his attention.

"That's probably Seb... or maybe Phil. They seem to carry themselves similarly."

"Do you know their last names?"

Lotta giggled.

"You're sure trying hard. They said you were thorough. None of us are allowed to share our last names with each other. And I'm not even sure Sebastian and Philip are their real names."

"You feel safe with them?"

Lotta nodded her head.

"They've never tried it on with you?"

Lotta giggled again.

"No, all the Hughs are gay, Anthony. I thought you knew that."

"I did, but that doesn't mean they might still not want some sexual release now and then."

"They can also choose sex à la carte. Just like us."

I nodded. I couldn't help but think that Lotta and the lot of them seemed to be into this of their own choosing. But then why are women ending up OD'd?

"What about drugs? Who supplies you with the drugs?"

"Lucy and Jane are provided by The Collective. That's all."

"What about coke or special k?" I asked.

Lotta shook her head. She looked at me closely for a while.

"You've done your homework. We're not allowed special k or coke or anything else for that matter other than Lucy and Jane like I told you. But I'm not gonna lie, some of the women here take coke and special k."

"Where do they get it from?"

Lotta shrugged.

"I'm not sure. I don't use any of that. It's probably one of the Hughs or they've got a connection themselves. But if they're busted with it, Anthony, they can get kicked out of The Collective."

"Has that happened?"

She shook her head.

"Not since I've been here. Though rumor has it that it has happened before out on the East coast."

"So there are more collectives other than the three you told me about?"

"Yes. There are collectives all over the place but I don't know much about any of the others except for the three here in LA."

I decided to change the subject. Sometimes that's a helpful angle to take in an interrogation. Not that I was interrogating Lotta like a suspect but changing direction and subject during an inquiry keeps the other person on their toes and often gets you better, if not more accurate, information.

"The Hughs wear masks for anonymity. I'm sure the johns wear them for the same reason. I was told not to take mine off. You've taken mine off but no one seems to mind. Why is that?"

"Because you're the gumshoe we were told about and I wanted to see what you look like."

"So you can take anyone's mask off if you want?"

Lotta shook her head.

"No. You've been granted special privileges. It came from the top."

"Who's at the top?"

"Someone higher up than Madam Virginia," said Lotta.

"And who's that?"

Lotta shrugged.

"I don't know. Whoever Madam Virginia works for never visits The Collective."

"What about you then? You took off your mask. Is that allowed?"

"If I want to. But hardly any of us do so. You're lucky," she said, smiling at me.

"What happens if a john takes off your mask or theirs?"

"They get kicked out and are never allowed back."

"Are they roughed up?"

"I don't know, Anthony. I don't think so. All johns wear the magic watch. Just like you. That controls them fairly effectively. I saw a john getting rough with one of us once. Before he could do anything serious he was on the floor incapacitated. Those watches are powerful. You be careful."

I smiled at her.

"So if I leave here I have to put my mask back on?"

Lotta shook her head.

"No. Like I said, you've got special privileges."

"The only privilege it sounds like is the ability to walk around here without a mask."

"And the privilege of turning all of us down and asking all the questions you want."

I nodded.

"I want to get down to the real reason I'm here..."

"Which is about Pearl," said Lotta, finishing my sentence.

I nodded.

"She was murdered," I said, lying.

"Not quite true."

"But two other women have been murdered who have the same brand as you."

Lotta nodded.

"And that doesn't worry you?"

"It does worry me, Anthony, but we've been reassured that something like that will never happen again."

"It's happened four times before," I said.

"Yes, but only two of those four were murdered."

"How do you know about all of that?"

"The Collective respects us and whoever is really running this show favors honesty above all else."

"I thought you said Madam Virginia runs the show."

"She does as far as I'm concerned. But I'm not that naïve, Anthony, I know that Madam Virginia couldn't arrange all of these events all by herself."

I nodded and watched as another set of triplets walked by. It was a man with two ianfu. There was something about his manner that reminded me of someone. I couldn't pinpoint it. They didn't even offer a passing glance.

"How long do these events go on until?"

"They're usually wrapped up by two."

"Do you know how the other two were murdered?"

Lotta nodded.

"Asphyxiation. Both Golden Showers and Pussy Galore died that way," said Lotta.

"You all have sex-related nicknames?" I asked.

Lotta nodded.

"Some of them aren't all that good. Madam Virginia used to be Candy Nytes."

"That's a good one."

"It is. But how about Tunnel Funnel?"

"Yeah, that's a bit of a groaner."

Lotta laughed.

"It is."

"What happened to the johns who murdered Golden Showers and Pussy Galore?"

"Well, from what I've been told these women weren't actually murdered. It was asphyxiaphilia."

"That's a big word."

"Just because I like sex doesn't mean I'm gormless."

I smiled at her.

"That's a word I do not know."

"It's mostly British and means stupid or lacking in intelligence. I can enjoy sex and words, Anthony. You might like to think of me as a multipotentialite or a polymath. You strike me as much the same."

"How so?"

"You were once one of LAPD's most decorated and most successful detectives. Some say that when you left you left an unblemished record of cases closed. And on top of that you're a gifted painter. At least that's what I hear."

I didn't say anything to that. I was here to get information and it appeared that they'd done a decent job on gathering intel on me. I wasn't surprised. Camus was not a man to be underestimated. But that he shared as much as he had with the ianfu was surprising.

"Have you seen any of my paintings?"

Lotta shook her head.

"Haven't had the chance yet. I only found out much about you a week or so ago. You're at the Triangle Gallery here, right?"

I nodded.

"I'll be sure to take a look."

Staying Unsatisfied

I thought I'd try a different tactic.

"You didn't know Pearl all that well, right?"

"That's right."

"So why do you think I was offered this Eighth House to attend?"

"Maybe The Kintsugi Collective is not working this week," said Lotta.

"That's charitable."

Lotta shrugged.

"I can't help you there. I was only told a few days ago that you were coming and to give you every courtesy."

"Including trying to fuck me," I said, a little more sharply than it meant to come out.

Lotta grinned.

"No, that's all on me, Anthony. You're a sexy man. But you know that, even if you pretend not to."

I could hear moaning and groaning coming from the room to my right. That would be your left if you were at the door frame looking in on us. I ignored it.

"Let's assume I believe you. That you do this freely and you like it and it pays well. Why the scarification? That looks to me more like ownership or slavery. Why allow that?"

"It's part of the deal. They put a topical anesthetic on it beforehand and you barely feel it. It's really quick. I don't know why they do it other than they've been doing it for decades. It's just the way it's always been done. But like I said, I'm free to leave at any time I want. I'll always have the scar but I could make up any story about that for any boyfriend I might get intimate with if I left. But I sorta like it."

"Who did it?"

"Madam Virginia. She does all of the girls at The Wabi-Sabi Collective."

I decided to take a different tack.

"Have you ever had a john get rough or inappropriate with you?"

Lotta nodded.

"Once. This was years ago. Probably in my first year here with The Collective. This guy wanted to fuck me up the ass and I wasn't into that. At least not with him. I told him no. Then he overpowered me and tried to force me into it. He didn't get very far. Moments after I had started yelling for him to stop he was writhing on the floor and the Hughs were taking him away. He was barred from ever coming back."

"I was wondering about that," I said. "It seems like it'd be pretty hard to get one of you to do anything you didn't want to. I mean, the Hughs are everywhere. Seems like there isn't a nook or cranny that isn't watched by a Hugh. There's no privacy. No doors on the doorframes. I can't see how a woman could get asphyxiated and nobody notices."

"The last woman who died from asphyxiaphilia was Pussy Galore on New Year's Day in two thousand. Back then, the men, or johns as you like to call them, didn't have these fancy watches that you guys wear now," she said, tapping my watch that was on my wrist but which I had forgotten about. "Back then there was also more privacy offered, especially for high value clients..."

"What makes a client high value?"

Lotta shrugged.

"I don't know. There isn't any of that hierarchy anymore. All johns are treated the same now. But Pussy was with one of these men in a private room with the door closed. She probably couldn't shout out and with the client not wearing a watch nothing was recorded."

"And now everything is recorded."

"They probably told you that the watch recorded everything. Visually and audibly."

I nodded.

"I'm sure that's not the only recording going on," I said, looking around for cameras but not noticing any that were obvious. Though I'm sure they wouldn't be obvious. Probably hidden somewhere. Maybe behind a painting or an unobtrusive jewelry box or some other clever place. I looked at Lotta. She just smiled at me.

"Do you know who this client was?"

Lotta shook her head.

"No, and from what I understand he's never been around since."

"When did the men start using these watches or items like it?"

"Two thousand and one. The spring so I've been told."

"That was developed quickly."

"They have a lot of amazing tech. You should see the phones we have. Android and Apple have nothing on it. But I don't think it was developed in one year. Probably something that had been in development for years behind the scenes."

"I notice you don't wear anything like that," I said.

Lotta shook her head.

"Only the clients."

"And they don't mind being recorded?"

"They have no choice. We're all being recorded. I've heard, and I believe it, that there are satellite cameras up there that can zoom on you specifically and track you indefinitely. It can even read the text on your phone messages."

"And how do they do that?"

"The technology is that good. But I guess they find you from your cell phone and track you that way."

That might be the case, I thought, but it sure wasn't something being offered up for the LAPD to use.

"Closer to home, what happens to the video that's taken at these events?" I asked.

Lotta shrugged. I watched her breathing raise and lower her bosom. Her nipples were still firm under her dressing gown. She caught me looking. She uncovered her right breast. It made me horny. I looked away. My eyes were slowly causing me to sin. I covered her up again.

"That's not helping," I said.

Lotta giggled.

"You want me. I can tell."

"I want justice for Pearl," I said.

"Pearl wasn't murdered."

"Maybe so, but who gave her the drugs and why did she feel the need to take them if this work is so great?"

"We've been told there's an investigation going on behind the scenes and if anyone is found to be dealing anything, they'll be fired."

"That's very reassuring," I said, sarcastically.

Lotta didn't say anything.

"Has anyone been fired yet?"

"No, but it's ongoing."

"Ongoing for over two months now."

"Maybe these things take time."

Another couple walked by. I figured there was a third floor to this house and it was starting to get busier. I wasn't sure there was much else I could find out from Lotta.

I believed she was happy doing this kind of work. It did pay well if she wasn't lying to me about that and I didn't have any reason to think she couldn't leave if she didn't want to.

Still, this whole mess wasn't bringing me any satisfaction. Pearl, rather, Suzanne might not have been murdered but someone gave her too much ketamine and cocaine. Why would she be taking a cocktail of drugs if this work was so great like Lotta said? I decided to ask her.

"Maybe you can answer one more question for me," I said.

"I'll answer any question for you, especially the question I want to hear you ask."

I decided not to encourage her. I was a man walking on thin ice with pickaxes for legs.

"If this gig of yours is as great as you say, why did Pearl have the need to numb herself with coke and special k?"

"Probably the same reason I take Mary Jane."

"And what reason is that?"

"It enhances sex, Anthony. Have you never taken any drugs?"

I decided to lie. I shook my head. Lotta looked at me for a long time and slowly grinned, nodding her head.

"If that's what you want to tell yourself. Cannabis, at least a little hit, helps enhance the sexual pleasure. Cocaine can do the same, but I find cocaine to be too intense. Marijuana's like that chill friend who always knows how to make you feel good. Coke is like that old frat buddy you're only happy to see occasionally but he comes in like a hurricane and fucks up your life, though it's fun while you're partying but the mess the next day is next level."

"And special k?"

"Special k with coke is too dangerous. I've never done it. I've done special k by itself but not together. But I've heard from some of the other women that it helps take the edge off the coke. But, as Pearl learned, it's dangerous. The combo can be lethal."

"And here we are. Some shadow group is doing an investigation and yet there have been five women die in the past few decades and all of them had at least two drugs in them if not three. The last woman, Pearl, OD'd just a couple of months ago."

"I don't know what to say. We've never had that problem with The Wabi-Sabi Collective. Maybe the other madams are not as concerned. Madam Virginia takes it very seriously. She once suspected that one of us was taking drugs other than Lucy and Jane and she went ballistic. She did her own investigation. She took it to her boss and we had an outside investigator come in and interview everyone. In fact, you remind me of him a bit."

"What was his name?"

"Philip Marlowe," she said, grinning.

"You're shitting me."

She shook her head.

"Nope. That's the name he gave."

"Clearly not his own."

"Probably not, but I never saw any government issued ID. We were the ones being investigated," she said.

"What did Marlowe find out?"

"No evidence of other drug use was found, but I think the thoroughness of the investigation scared us all straight. Like I said, we all really love our jobs and we're respected and cared for. Nobody wants to be kicked out and we've never had a problem since then of any of us doing anything other than Lucy or Jane. And most of us don't do Lucy, unless it's a small hit, before a house meeting."

"A house meeting?"

"Yeah, this is a house meeting. All Eighth Houses we call house meetings."

I nodded.

"And Pearl, like you said, was with which Collective?"

Lotta grinned.

"You're trying to see if I can keep my story straight, Anthony, because it's the truth. The great thing about this sort of work, at least with The Wabi-Sabi Collective is that I don't know much about what happens behind the scenes."

"Explain that for me," I said.

"I know the girls and the guys that live with us and Madam Virginia. I'm pretty sure that Madam Virginia doesn't run this show by herself, she probably has bosses she answers to, but I don't care and we aren't informed. All I know, I know because of my own senses. This organization, and I'm not naïve enough to believe this isn't run by some larger group, is layered to make it safer that way for everyone. I have no trouble telling you everything I know because what I know is limited. It's one of the things that brings me comfort."

"You like being in the dark?"

"I like knowing I'm cared for and that The Collective is run efficiently. Anyway, like I told you earlier, Pearl was with The Kintsugi Collective headed by Madam May. Not to speak ill of other Madams but perhaps Madam May is not as concerned about drug use amongst her ianfu. Though if she has any sense and likes her job she'll probably have smartened up by now after what happened to Pearl."

We sat next to each other on the bed for a while like two lovers who had just spent their coins of coitus. I started to swing my legs over the bed when Lotta reached her hand over towards me. I stopped.

"I've been good to you," she said. "Why don't you be good to me."

She was biting her lower lip. A different day in a different time and I might have obliged. I grinned at her and got off the bed.

"You'll forget about me as soon as I'm out of sight," I said.

"Never."

I walked around to her side of the bed.

"Now that we know each other are you going to give me your name?"

She looked at me under hooded lids. She was still trying to seduce me. She was sexy and she was stunning but it wasn't gonna happen with me.

"I'll whisper it into your ear as you ram your cock inside me," she said.

I grinned. I had lost my embarrassment about the way she talked a while ago.

"So long, darling," I said, as I turned to leave.

"Achara Lee," she said.

I turned around halfway to the door.

"Say again."

"Achara Lee," she said. "That's my real name. Don't overuse it."

"I like it," I said. "A beautiful name for a beautiful dame. Suits you."

She blew me a kiss and I turned and walked out. I was getting bored. I was about ready to leave. I didn't see any other reason to remain. This was just a den of temptation and I doubted I'd get anything more than I got from Lotta from any of the other girls.

Biff! Bam! Pow!

I believed Lotta that she enjoyed her work and wasn't here against her will. Looking past my own hangups it seemed reasonable that women should enjoy sex as much as men. How the hell would we have found our way to over seven billion living souls if it were otherwise?

Some men worked as porn stars and some women did too. Why would it be different for the women as compared to the men? Maybe this was a case of my old-school hangups getting in the way of seeing the world clearly.

I didn't like this case. Five women had died in the decades since the seventies and two of those deaths were suspicious. Sure, maybe I'll get around to accepting the egalitarianism of sex work. Still, women are more vulnerable if only because they are physically weaker on average. That meant they needed to be treated with a little more care. Especially if they were offering their body in service, and all five of these women hadn't been cared for as they should have. That's what irritated me.

I wanted some justice and I wasn't sure I was going to see it. Even assuming Suzanne died of an overdose at her own hands there were crimes that had been committed. At the very least I was pretty sure that it was against health and safety codes to dispose of a dead body inappropriately, and dumping a body at a dump was certainly inappropriate.

But more than that, I wanted the asshole who did that. I also wanted the asshole that procured and provided the drugs to her. And that asshole was also probably the person who murdered Gorky. I didn't have proof of any of that, but my gut told me it was likely the same person. That would give me some satisfaction. And if anyone was listening to my silent prayers, having the asshole who asphyxiated Pussy Galore would be the icing on the cake. If that person was still alive. You never know, sometimes you get a lucky break and nature provides you with a win.

If I could manage that minuscule amount of justice I'd consider this case won and closed. But I wasn't sure I was going to get that lucky. I decided to look for a washroom and to see if I couldn't find Madam Virginia before I left. I assumed I'd be given a ride back.

I found a washroom on the second floor I was on but there was a woman sitting on the toilet giving a guy head. I went upstairs to see if it was quieter there and if I could find a washroom. The washroom on the second floor, incidentally, was also doorless. Seemed they'd taken off all the doors to all of the rooms in this house. I guess it was safer that way. Less private but more safe.

The washroom was empty but the door was off the frame. I pointed Peter at the porcelain and did my business which made me feel surprisingly better. It was quieter up on this third level but by no means empty.

I wandered around. There were bedrooms and a games' room and an entertainment room up here. All the rooms held occupants in various stages of coitus. I passed the games' room which had a double wide opening on account that it likely held double doors. There was a guy in the room bladed with his back to the door who was having doggie style sex with a woman who was leaning her elbows on the arm of a couch. Another woman was lying on the couch with her legs up on the arm of the couch while the first woman who was taking it from behind was giving her friend oral sex.

That wasn't what caught my attention. It was the man's voice. I thought I recognized it. I stopped to listen for a minute. He was grunting and thrusting. His white shirt like a muleta waved in front of his thrusting buttocks.

"Yeah, you like that cock in your ass?" he asked.

The woman groaned something behind a mouthful of pussy. I knew the voice, but I couldn't believe it.

"Who wants a pussy creampie?" he asked.

That didn't get much of a response. My blood boiled and I rushed into the room.

"You mother fucker, Artero! This is the respect you show Racquel and my daughter. You snivelling cock-sucking poltroon!" I yelled.

He turned around to look at me. His eyes wide, his small little pink slug of a prick popping out of her ass.

"Anthony, Anthony... I can explai..."

He didn't get any other words out on account I hit him across that lying mouth which dropped him like a rancid bag of flour. I wasn't far behind. I'd forgotten about the special watch I was wearing.

I felt a tingle and a buzzing at first. But that was only for the briefest of moments. Immediately after that I felt like I'd been stuck with a cattle prod. I lost control over my limbs. I fell to the floor, vibrating in pain before I passed out.

Next thing I knew I was being hoisted up by two Hughs. One grabbing me under each arm. I was semi-cognizant of my surroundings. I tried talking but it felt like I was mumbling something incoherent after having drunk a bottle of whiskey and being punched in the mouth. My lips felt like tires.

Someone kicked me in the stomach as I was being dragged away. I think it was Artero. I thought I heard him tell me I was the asshole. He couldn't kick worth shit.

People were looking at me as I was being dragged down the stairs to the second level. Felt like I was looking at them through a kaleidoscope smeared with vaseline and although I could hear them, it sounded like I was listening to them over bells ringing in my ears after someone had stuffed my ears full of cotton wads.

On the main floor I started to feel just the tiniest bit better. People were gathering on either side of the Hughs as they dragged me like a beaten Christ towards Golgotha.

"Who the fuck thought it was a good idea to invite him?" I heard someone say. That someone sounded like Frank Burton. I looked up towards the voice. I still couldn't see clearly and he'd spoken through a Santa mask but he seemed to carry himself like the asshole I'd known him to be. More importantly I noticed the ring on his right ring finger as he pointed at me.

It was the LAPD Chief of Police ring. Looked like a championship ring with a ruby in the middle. The gemstone was chosen by the wearer. Frank liked rubies on account he was born in July. This he had told me once when we were still on good terms. He was also a Cancer, but that was neither here nor there. Around the top rim of the ring was the date he first became Chief of Police and his initials.

All of that I thought I glimpsed in the moment I was being dragged past and his voice caught my attention. I couldn't be sure. I wouldn't swear to it in a court of law. But in the court of vigilante justice it was all the evidence I needed.

They dragged me down another flight of stairs into a basement. Nobody was in the basement. Just like I'd been told, probably everyone else had been told that the basement was off limits. I was dragged to a corner of the basement into the furnace room which had a cement floor and sturdy metal pipes. They handcuffed me to one of these pipes. Just my left hand and took off my special watch they'd given me and the bracelet that I needed to claim my stuff. I didn't have the fight or strength to complain. I'd figure out claiming my phone, wallet and keys when I could think straight.

They turned on the single, uncovered lightbulb which had a noose as a pull switch for it and then they left. A couple of minutes later as I was starting to feel more like myself a single Hugh came back in and tossed a plastic bedpan in and a bottle of water.

"When will I get outta here," I said, through a voice that sounded like it came through a clogged sewer grate.

That got me nothing. Hugh didn't even look at me. He left and closed the door again. I heard it lock. I hadn't met a door to a furnace room that had locked before. I sat down against the cold cement with my legs splayed out in front of me and my right arm in my lap and my left arm on the cold cement handcuffed to a pipe. I felt like a real winner. All I needed now was a chicken dinner.

And that got me to thinking. I was hungry. I hadn't had dinner yet and I figured it must be coming up to midnight. Maybe? I hadn't looked at the watch or the time for a while. But I figured it must be at least past eleven. Could be close to the witching hour. I didn't imagine I'd be getting room service.

One Thousand and One Nights

Time dragged in that cold basement furnace room. At least the pipe I was handcuffed to was long and provided me with a little bit of a leash. It came out of the hot water tank and not far from it took an elbow turn up towards the ceiling. The pipe was warm or hot depending on whether it was being used or not. That offered a couple of problems.

The first one was that it was mostly too hot to hold most of the time. And when it was cool enough, or just warm enough to handle, I couldn't turn the pipe at the elbow joint where it looked to have been threaded into that elbow joint.

Not that I expected I could free myself easily. But a man's gotta try. I stood up and explored my reach. I could move up and down quite easily but my reach was basically just my wingspan from my hand handcuffed to the pipe to the tips of my fingers on my other free hand. I could touch the wall closest to me and with a stretch I could touch the main furnace duct but that was about all. Around the side of the hot water tank and up towards the ceiling was another pipe that had a lever on it. I could reach that too. I figured it was probably the water mains valve.

I could sit down on the concrete floor but not lean back against the wall. Not that I wanted to. The floor and the closest wall were cement and cold. I decided to stand and explore my surroundings. It was good of them to keep the light on for me. I looked around. The furnace room was clean and immaculate. Nothing was stored in here. That wasn't helpful because it meant I didn't have anything to think about or that could help me free myself.

I checked my pockets on just the off chance that I had something in there that could help. Maybe a small pocket knife. Though what I could do with a pocket knife in here was unknown to me at this point. Maybe cut off my hand and free myself? I jest. In any event I didn't have a pocket knife. I couldn't even find lint in my pockets.

The handcuff was securely on my left wrist. I couldn't slide my hand out. I tried but gave up after I started to scrape the skin off the lower fleshy part of my thumb.

I cursed. I couldn't see a way out of this, then I had an idea. I started to use my foot as a brace against the elbow of the pipe just where it had shortly come out of the water tank. I used the weight and strength of my whole body and leg to test the sturdiness of the pipe. I figured that might be its weakest point, close to where it joined the tank, on account that it looked like the tank was attached to the metal pipe through just a short plastic piece. I hadn't noticed that before and I didn't know if all hot water tanks were like that.

Didn't matter. It did, however, give me a chance to test the strength of that joint and I found it to be lacking. I figured that with enough effort and tries I could probably shear the pipe off the plastic joint, but it would take some effort.

At least it was a potential option to free myself. But I wasn't in a rush. I figured I'd give it time. I didn't want to free myself too quickly only to have to fight with a bunch of Hughs, a fight that I couldn't win against all of them. I decided to bide my time and listen for signs of when the house was emptying.

That was harder than it seemed on account that the furnace was kicking in about every fifteen minutes or so, from what I could figure. LA can get cool at night in the middle of winter and December the twenty-third was close to the middle of winter, but it hadn't been an especially chilly evening when I'd been picked up.

I guessed that it was probably between fifty and sixty degrees outside. Still, most of the debauchers inside were naked on account they were fucking around like rabbits. Naked people prefer the temperature on the warmer side compared to when they're wearing clothes.

Still, I had around fifteen minutes each time after the tank kicked off to have a listen for signs of life. I couldn't make out a lot, but I could make out some.

I could hear footsteps overhead on the floor above me periodically and, occasionally, I could hear a low rumble that sounded similar to far off thunder. That was from animated voices but I couldn't make out the words.

Sometimes I could hear grunting and what must have been sex talk coming from somewhere in the basement. I could only hear snippets like, "oh my god" or "fuck you're great". Things of that nature.

Time dragged in that basement. There was almost a rhythm to it. And that got me to thinking. Being biological, it seemed that humans were driven by rhythm and routine and the biological urge to fuck. There was a lot of that going on. We were, at our core, just naked apes with too much intelligence which was causing all sorts of havoc on the natural world.

But I wasn't here to wax philosophical about the nature of man, as sullied as it might be. Rather, I felt like Scheherazade enduring her one thousand and one nights. I wanted to try and find a way to escape. Worst case I figured that whoever owned this place would come back to a busted hot water tank. And so I bided my time.

If I escaped too early, I'd find Hugh and his chums still kicking around. I didn't fancy fighting my way out of this mansion and I wasn't sure I'd succeed in any event. I hadn't tested the mettle of any of the Hughs, but I figured that they surely had some tactical training if they were the security for the ianfu which it appeared they were.

That meant I needed patience. I didn't fancy escaping only to be attached someplace more securely that I couldn't escape from. Because as much as I fancied myself a decent journeyman of the sweet science, I knew my limits. And going up against two or three even relatively well-trained tacticians would likely be more meat than I could chew.

And so being locked in that furnace room and handcuffed to a pipe gave me lots of time to think about a lot of things. One of the things I thought about were the times I'd been stuffed into dark closets, basements, and yes, furnace rooms when I was small. That was the kind of asshole my father was.

If I'd done something pretty egregious, like say, stand up to my father on my mother's behalf, well then, after the beating I'd be given a "time out" to "think about what I'd done". And what I thought about during those one thousand and one nights was all the ways a young boy might kill his father. A favorite of course was with a gun. I also entertained stabbing him to death and finding a poison to sneak into his food.

Of course I didn't. You know that. But I thought about it a lot. I just didn't have the courage back then as a ten and eleven year old. It took awhile for my old man to turn me into the asshole I can sometimes be. Do I regret not killing him? Yeah, sometimes. But it's a big ask for a young boy to kill his father. But if I'm to be honest, some people don't deserve the life they've been given.

Nevertheless, those closets I spent hours and hours in, not in one sitting. To be fair to my father, I don't think he left me in a locked closet more than a couple of hours at the most. But after the first couple of turns in dark corners all by myself I came to enjoy it. It was one of the few times I could rely on peace and relative quiet. And when my father was raging as an alcoholic, which happened to be the times he put me in closets, well, that was especially the time you wanted peace and quiet.

I also got to thinking about the plumbers out of New York from a few years back. What they'd done to So-yi, well, I don't regret what happened to them. That's a classic example of vigilante justice that doesn't bother me in the least. What does bother me is what they did to So-yi.

And here's the problem with giving me too much time to think. It's easy to spiral into a dark pool of negativity. And that's what I did. I started to think about all the assholes I'd known in my years on the job. There'd been a lot. Most of whom I'd sorted out. Still, you can't help but end up stinking if you're the one unclogging the sewer.

But the time I spent all alone in that brightly lit furnace room was not all wasted. I managed to spend a good deal of it meditating. And I noticed something neat. Like a buoy on the ocean of my mind it was tumultuous at first but after a time the ocean of my mind became more like a slowly heaving and breathing ocean and I found some clarity with this case. I found some peace with it. I wasn't responsible for and nor could I be the cure for all ills.

Nevertheless, after the meditation, the mind sometimes goes back to old tracks and ruts and I wanted some justice out of this case that had taken up too much of my time following dead ends. And as I was thinking about that I noticed that the house had gone quiet for sometime. Not completely quiet. I still heard footsteps overhead here and there. I heard what sounded like a drill and maybe furniture being dragged over wooden floors. And maybe even some vacuuming. But I wasn't sure about that, that sound was far off and more like a mosquito that came within earshot but never close enough to swat.

There were also low voices rumbling now and then. They sounded mostly male if I was to be honest. I listened for a while. I figured they were putting the house back together for the occupant. If I was a guessing man, and in detection, your guesses or hunches are sometimes helpful, this house wasn't connected to Camus in any way. Probably an Airbnb or some other rental.

That seemed to take a while. Maybe a couple of hours. And still I waited in silence. I drank some water from the bottle but I didn't use the bedpan. After what seemed like a half hour of absolute silence, and it could have been anything from about fifteen minutes to an hour, I decided to wait another half hour to be absolutely certain I'd been left alone. That last half hour was excruciating.

I tried counting my way through it but only got as far as seven minutes in. Try it sometimes when you're bored. Counting sixty seconds thirty times, takes great discipline and fortitude. Something I was clearly lacking in my eagerness to get out and take a look around.

So I waited in absolute silence. Only the occasional tinkling of water in pipes and the creaking of wood now and then. I also noticed I was getting colder. The furnace hadn't kicked in for what seemed like a long time and I was getting cold. Silence grew, not so much like a cancer, but more like a fungus. And then I couldn't take it anymore. I reached for the main water valve and shut that off.

The pipe I was handcuffed to wasn't hot, yet another suggestion that I'd been left alone for a while. I grabbed it with both hands and gave a good kick where it came out from the hot water tank. The pipe didn't break free, but in the silence, not growing like a cancer, it made a racket. Clanging of metal that sounded not so much like bells but perhaps like some small train on a small track speeding up.

I stopped and listened for a few minutes. If there was anyone left inside then surely they'd come and see what all the racket was I was making. But I heard nothing. So I gave the pipe another go. Still didn't break it free from the tank.

Then I took a moment to think about what I was actually trying to do. Hot water, probably hot enough to scald would gush out of the opening at the bottom of the tank. And it could burn me if I wasn't careful. Thankfully there was a grated drain in the furnace room. Still, I wasn't sure how much of a stream the hot water would make when it came out so I kept that in mind when I braced my right foot on the elbow joint where the pipe attached to the bottom of the furnace.

I grabbed the pipe with both hands. Bent my knee and heaved into the pipe and the elbow joint with all my effort pushing with both hands and foot in the same direction. I heard a crack and the pipe broke free from the plastic hot water attachment. Hot water gushed out like a giant taking a hot piss. Some of it splashed on my lower calf, quickly soaking the pant leg and sock of my lower right leg. It burnt. It was fucking hot, so hot that even though the splash was brief and soaked through fabric I felt the burn.

I wanted to reach down and pull up my pant leg on that side and take off my sock, I couldn't. I needed to keep pushing hard on the pipe to keep it away from the opening. I looked like a man leaning into a hurricane with a giant pissing over my shoes. Well, my legs were behind the streaming hot water but the right leg was burnt. I figured I'd get a blister at the very least.

I managed to keep the rest of the gushing water from splashing on me but it came back towards me as a lake, seeking the drain. The leather of my shoes was starting to get uncomfortably hot. I stepped back even further away from the river of water seeking the drain and that helped take it from hot to tolerable.

For several minutes I stayed like that with the hot water tank emptying. Finally, the stream became a leak which turned into a dribble. I slid my left hand down the pipe and freed it. My calf was hurting but I had more pressing concerns.

I tried the door and noticed that some of the hot water had probably escaped the furnace room before me. I was jealous. The door was still locked. I thought about the best way to break free. Kicking the door towards the outside was probably not the best way on account that the door opened into the furnace room which meant it was braced against any direct assault towards the outside by the door frame.

I decided to kick at the handle from the side. That worked well. Only took a few good kicks and the handle came free and I could open the door from the hole left by the handle. I opened it and peered out.

Blue Moon

Nobody was out there. I waited under the doorframe and listened. No sounds that suggested humans were present. The house was pitch black and I didn't know my way around it. The light from the furnace room bled past me and spilled my long shadow out into the length of basement in front of me.

I went back in and picked up my bedpan and water bottle. I drank the rest of the water and started to feel like I could empty my bladder anytime soon. I kept the light on as I ventured out into the basement. I had been brought down here against my will and as such, I wasn't familiar with it.

I found a light switch at the base of the stairs that led up to the main level. I turned it on. Then I went back and turned off the furnace room light. I did it this way through much of the house until I got back up the main level.

I went to the main hallway where I had been tested and where they had taken my phone, wallet and keys. It was empty. I looked in the closet but that was empty too. There was a small table by the front doors with a drawer under the tabletop. Nothing was on top of the table and the draw was empty too. I started to believe that perhaps they'd stolen my stuff as a perverse sort of punishment.

These folks had been thorough. I wandered around the main floor, looking into all the rooms. The doors had been hung back onto their frames and the rooms looked like they had, except most of the bedrooms had different bedding on the beds. Everything looked like this house was ready to show. There was no sign of the sort of debauchery that had been taking place earlier in the previous evening and into the morning. The carpets had been shampooed and vacuumed and were still slightly damp. The wooden floors were gleaming. If I were a betting man I'd bet that a blue light wouldn't pick up any stains anywhere.

I searched all the rooms on the main level and the bedrooms. This was a large house. In one of the bedrooms the alarm clock told me it was six eighteen in the morning. The sun probably wasn't up yet. I pulled back the curtains to take a look. The room looked out onto what appeared to be a fairly large backyard, but it was dark. Almost pitch black. But the sky was not black. Across the eastern portion of it the color was lighter. I'd call it a dark royal blue.

I figured I had at least an hour or so before anyone might arrive. I wasn't sure who that would be. This house, as it presented, didn't seem lived in. At least not full time. I figured it was used for short term rentals. Not that it helped me. Just a sense I got by the cheap and cheery furnishings. Well, that's not quite true. The furnishings were cheap but not so much cheery, more like a modern, minimalist aesthetic. You might be willing to argue with me, but I never found minimalistic, modern design to be cheery. That's one of the last things you could say about it.

I took a whizz in one of the upstairs bathrooms. I searched high and low in the house for my belongings. Not only that, I searched for anything out of place. Anything that might offer a clue as to the case I was here on. Alas, nothing was found.

The kitchen was the last place I searched. But that was where I found my spectacles, testicles, wallet and watch. Not really. I found my wallet, keys and phone on the kitchen counter. But it had been years since I'd used the expression. Probably not since I'd been an altar boy. Both figuratively and literally.

I found a recycling bin and put in both the bedpan, still unused, and the empty water bottle. I went through the house again in my socks. I had left my shoes by the front door on account that the house was so clean I didn't want to sully it up. I still came up snake eyes.

I went back to the front door and left the house. Wearing my shoes. I had put them back on. I looked at my phone and opened up the maps app. I had service. Camus' black magic Faraday cage or whatever else he used to knock my phone offline was no longer present. I found myself in Beverly Hills on Tower Grove Drive.

I took note of where I was, leaving a place mark on my maps app and then I called a cab. I walked down the driveway to find the main gates locked. There was a small pedestrian gate next to the main gates that I could open from inside and let myself out. It closed and locked behind me. I could expect a twenty to thirty minute wait for the cab I was told.

I didn't have to wait more than five minutes for my ride, but it wasn't the cab company I saw. I was sitting on a large rock just to the side of the driveway entrance when a couple of black and whites rolled up followed by JR's unmarked. I stood up and went over to Roberts and Beast. I nodded at Beast. He nodded back.

"Fancy seeing you here. Is this who the cab company sent?" I asked.

Roberts grinned.

"I want to know how the hell you end up locked in a basement in a mansion in Beverly Hills?"

"How did you know?"

"We got an anonymous tip that we could find you in this house."

I looked back at the home.

"Not sure how you were going to get in other than scaling the gates," I said. "They're locked."

Roberts nodded.

"They gave us the codes for the main gate and the main door."

"Who was it?"

Roberts shrugged.

"Don't know. We tried tracing it. Turned out the phone call was untraceable."

I shook my head.

"Fuck," I spat under my breath.

"Yeah, we figured it's probably Camus and his buddies," said Roberts.

"Did he say as much?"

"No, it was a woman's voice. Sounded cute though."

I looked at Roberts for a while. I was tired and hungry. Roberts looked at Beast.

"Why don't you roll on in, I'll take Carrick home."

Beast nodded. But looked at me first.

"You look like crap," said Beast. "What were you doing in there?"

"Enjoying an orgy," I said.

Beast looked at me.

"No, seriously."

"Seriously, there was an orgy in there last night. You won't know it on account they've cleaned it, but that's what I was doing in there."

Roberts looked at Beast.

"I told you it was an orgy. Sid here was taking one for the team.

Beast grinned and nodded.

"I just wanted to hear him say it," he said, and walked off to the black and whites to talk with the guys in uniform. I craned my neck and watched him go. The sun was rising and bleeding all over the eastern sky. Maybe it was commiserating with me.

"Listen, you probably want to get a warrant. This case is difficult enough and if we find anything there, we'll want it by the book."

Roberts grinned.

"You trying to teach a grandfather to suck eggs? I've forgotten more about case management than you've learned, son," he said, grinning. "Beast has the warrant. Let me take you home. You look like shit."

"I feel like shit. I'm hungry and I've got blue balls the size of Neptune's moons."

Free At Last

We got into Robert's car and started off.

"So tell me everything. Did you really manage to keep it in your pants?" he asked, like we were seventeen again.

I looked over to him. I had closed my eyes. I was tired and crabby.

"Have you had breakfast?"

"I've had a coffee and a donut," he said.

"Ok. Let me get some shuteye. Take us to Joe's Main Diner and I'll tell you all about it over bacon and eggs. I just really need thirty minutes to reset. And yes, I kept it in my pants."

"Sure thing, Sid. Take thirty."

And with that, I closed my eyes and Roberts drove towards Joe's Main Diner. At least there, I could stumble home and grab the rest of my sleep. It takes around thirty minutes give or take a nickel on either side of that to get from Beverly Hills to Santa Monica.

The car lurched to a stop and I woke up. Johnny Rotten did that on purpose I figured, to wake me up. I opened my eyes. It felt like I had just closed them moments earlier.

"Really? You could have tapped me on the shoulder," I said, rubbing my eyes that felt like the sandman had poured all the sand from all of the oceans into them.

Roberts grinned at me.

"You were in such a deep sleep that I just couldn't bring myself to give you a gentle wakeup," he said.

"Dick," I said.

We got out of the car which was parked right in front of Joe's. The place was packed. Joe's usually is early in the morning.

Wendy noticed me at the front entrance and she came over right away, smiling and sunny as she usually is. She's an attractive redhead. Slim, average height with a sunny disposition. I'd put her in her late twenties. Unmarried, but I didn't know about a boyfriend.

"Sid and Johnny," she said. "My two favorite customers."

I was looking around.

"We can't be your favorites if we can't sit down and eat," I said.

"Don't pay him much attention. He's just crabby because he was up all night at an orgy," said Roberts, grinning.

Wendy looked at me.

"Don't pay him any attention, hun. It was strictly business and I wasn't partaking."

"That's unfortunate," she said.

"Not if I want to keep my girlfriend happy," I said.

"Table three will be leaving any minute," she said. "Just give me a minute to clear and clean and it's all yours."

We nodded and I leaned against the main entrance door. The one that didn't open.

"There, see. They're leaving now," said Wendy, as we watched an older couple get up from a table against the far wall. "I'll be right back."

Wendy went off towards the table and said something as she passed the couple leaving. They grinned and nodded, said something back, and then came past us as they left the restaurant. Wendy waved us in from the far corner. We went over and sat down.

"Coffee?" asked Wendy.

"As much as you can make as fast as you can make it," I said.

Roberts nodded and picked up his menu. I didn't.

"You know what you're gonna have?"

I nodded.

"The Farmer's Market, with home fries instead of hashbrowns."

Roberts looked at the menu.

"Two fried eggs, four pieces of bacon, hash browns, two sausages and two pancakes and toast. You're a hungry man."

"Not the pancakes, Wendy doubles up the bacon for me instead."

"Still that's a hungry man's breakfast."

"I'll get the Boy Howdy. No pancakes but has pretty much the same as yours but only half the amount. You recommend the home fries over hashbrowns?"

I shrugged.

"They're both good. I just feel like the home fries this time."

Roberts nodded.

"Then I'll join you with that."

Wendy was right over with a carafe of coffee and a small jug of cream. Sugar was already on the table as was steak sauce, ketchup, salt and pepper. We gave her our order and she went away.

"Alright, Sid, we're here. Tell me all about it," said Roberts.

So I started to tell him. I told him how I received the package. What was in it. The watch and the mask. Told him the watch was super high tech. I tried to explain what it could do as best I could. It seemed like a marvel of technology. Didn't look much different to any of the smart watches out there. Other than it was a single piece, or so it looked, and it self tightened.

It was also always watching and recording. Aware of everything all the time. I explained what the Santa mask looked like. I told him how I took a cab to Echo Park. How the watch wouldn't let me walk around there much. I was looking for others carrying a small white box slash case like mine. Mine had a happy Santa emoji on it along with the cliché live, love, laugh. I didn't get to see if any of the others did.

I explained how I got picked up by a black Caddy and how my phone stopped working once I got inside. I could barely see out the windows but figured I was driven around for about one and a quarter hours. I told him how I figured that out by the jazz albums that were played to entertain me.

I told him about Lotta and before that, Jezebel. I confessed to how stunning Lotta was and what she told me. I also told him that I was starting to believe that some women are happy doing sex work. That's when he said the following.

"Sometimes you're a bit of a puritan," said Roberts. "You never went to Catholic school. Neither did I, but I dated some Catholic schoolgirls back in the day. All I'm gonna say is that women can enjoy sex just as much as men. It just has to be on their terms."

I nodded. I kept eating my breakfast which Wendy had brought not long after I'd gotten to the part where I was telling Roberts about the Hughs and the house and how I was pricked for blood and robbed of all my possessions.

Roberts went on to say something about conflating the hookers we encountered on the street on the job with escorts who were pretty much doing the same thing as the hookers only for more money and less grief. "They're pretty much untouchable, Sid," he said.

He wasn't wrong. The street walker is a more vulnerable and sad sex worker and the ones that we mostly dealt with. In my experience they usually had horrible childhoods, mental health issues and most often drug addictions.

Like Roberts said, I had never met an "escort", at least not knowingly. Back in the day, Vice had tried to run an op called "Pillow Soft" where a bunch of their male investigators signed up onto one of these platforms where escorts will offer their services discretely. After charging a couple of these escorts the DA told us, not in so few words, but basically to fuck off. Wasn't worth his time and the judge wouldn't hear of it.

Some thought the judge was a patron of these services though there was no evidence of it. I wasn't involved nor did I give a shit. I mean, what men and women, or any combo of that, want to do behind closed doors when everyone is an adult and consenting is up to them. More than that, the state should stay the fuck out of the home unless someone is getting abused or hurt.

Then I filled Roberts in on what happened after I left Lotta. I told him I went to find a bathroom. On my way back I was taken by a voice and stopped to listen more carefully. I told him about Artero and how I ended up on my ass from the watch, being dragged down the stairs by two Hughs and bumping into who I was pretty sure was Chief Frank Burton. Roberts had tried to interrupt when I got to Artero. But I told him to hold on, that it got better.

"Jesus Christ, Anthony, are you telling me the fucking Chief of Police was at this orgy?"

"You've been listening," I said, as I finished up the last bit of food by wiping my plate with my last piece of toast on my fork.

"Are you sure it was him?"

"I'm feeling more and more certain the more I think about it. Could I swear to it in a court of law? Probably not, but between me and you I'm ninety percent certain that asshole was the asshole I saw. His voice gave him away, and his ring."

Roberts was shaking his head like a man worried. He had finished his plate before me on account he'd had a baby's portion and he wasn't doing much of the talking.

Wendy came by, refreshed our coffees and took our plates away, but before she did she asked me about still not smoking.

"Been over six months now," I said.

"Good for you," she said. "You inspired me to quit too."

I nodded.

"It'll be better for you," I said.

"What helped?" she asked.

"Vaping cannabis," I said.

She looked at me and cocked her head. Don't know why I told her, but hell, it was legal and I wasn't ashamed.

"For real?"

"Yeah, I've got a medical prescription," I said.

"Well, we should get together to share a sesh," she said. "I have a medical prescription too."

I smiled at her and she left.

"Share a sesh?" I asked Roberts.

He shrugged.

"I think she means she wants to get high with you," he said, grinning.

"That wouldn't do me any favors," I said.

I set up my coffee how I like it. Roberts did the same.

"The fucking Chief of Police, Sid."

I nodded.

"I know. I never liked that asshole. I always thought he was a bad seed but I never quite knew why. Now I know."

Roberts was shaking his head.

"I know, you told me and I downplayed it. I guess you were right."

"Yeah, well, back then it was a feeling. Now I know why."

"Still, Sid, he's obviously connected to Camus et al. He's probably untouchable."

"Fuck that, Rotten, nobody's untouchable. Not on my watch anyway."

"Jesus, Anthony, you're a private detective, you don't even have the badge behind you anymore and you're talking like you're going to go up against the Chief of Police."

I shrugged.

"I've got ninety-nine problems and the Chief is just one of them. I'm more concerned about getting justice for Suzanne, aka Pearl."

Roberts was getting exasperated.

"What justice, Anthony? She wasn't murdered. She was given access to drugs but from what you've told me, she took them herself, and likely, without being strong-armed."

I shrugged. Then I nodded.

"Yeah, you're right. Still, I want some justice from this case. I want the asshole that asphyxiated Grace Smith, aka Pussy Galore. And I want the asshole who put Suzanne's body at the dump who is also probably the guy that murdered Gorky."

"I don't know how we get the guy who shot Gorky. Might need to ask your friend, Camus for a favor. As for the Pussy Galore thing, I mean that's a couple of decades ago. Who knows if that asshole is even still alive."

"I plan to ask him. That's if he picks up my call and will even listen to me. He told me to behave at that Eighth House. I wasn't on my best behavior."

"Yeah, well, you probably didn't do anything I wouldn't have done. I mean, Artero, for fuck's sake. Your daughter spends half her time with that cocksucker."

"That wasn't what he was doing."

Roberts laughed.

"You know what I mean. Shit, Anthony, what are you going to do? Are you going to tell Racquel?"

"Fuck yeah. I don't want that asshole around my daughter. Who knows how flexible his morals are? She'll soon be coming into womanhood."

I didn't need to say anything else. Roberts understood what I was saying.

"When do you get Aibhilin next?" he asked.

"Tomorrow sometime before noon."

Roberts nodded. We didn't speak for some time. Wendy came by and asked if we needed anything else. Nothing but the bill. She brought that for us and Roberts paid.

"Listen, Sid, I know this case hasn't gone as you'd have liked. Hell, it's been a dog's breakfast from the beginning. But as your friend, I still don't think there's anything here to reopen it. I'm going to have to keep it a cold one."

I nodded. He wasn't wrong. I didn't have anything concrete.

"Just do me a favor. Do a thorough search of the house and try and figure out who owns it, why they rented it for this orgy and how they're connected, if they are?"

"That goes without saying. But don't hold your hopes up. You know how secretive this organization is that Camus either controls or is part of, and they've probably thought this through every angle."

I nodded.

"I'll follow up with Camus and then we can compare notes," I said.

"Well, might have to be until the new year. A lot shuts down between now and the second of January. And Merry Christmas. Wish Emily the same. What are the two of you doing for New Year's."

"Probably just something quiet," I said.

"Well, Jen and I would like to have you over for a celebration. The way this year's been, I think we deserve a blowout party to kick it to the curb."

"I'd like that. I'll confirm with M and get back to you. It's been one helluva year."

Roberts nodded.

"We'd like to have you over. Just a small group," he said.

And that's how we left it. I thanked Roberts for breakfast and I dragged myself the couple of blocks home and crawled into bed. I was too tired to care.

Merry Christmas

Christmas morning I hauled the tree out of storage along with the box of ornaments and placed them in the living room. I set up the tree but didn't add the ornaments. It's a fake one I pull out every year. Just six feet but it works well. M approves on account she believes it's better for the environment than having living trees chopped down in their youth just for a week's worth of holidaying.

I started using fake trees after Marcello Marchesi, the owner of Vista Al Mar, requested all residents do that on account of the fire hazard of real trees. This was after a neighbor on the second floor almost burned down the building by not keeping their Christmas tree hydrated. Aibhilin didn't care. And if she didn't, I don't.

Racquel called around eleven to let me know that they were just about to leave. I asked who "they" was. She told me it was her and Aibhilin. I asked after Artero but she said he had to go into work for half a day. On Christmas Day. I called bullshit on that, but didn't vocalize it. I asked her to wait when she got here. I had something to tell her. Usually she just drops Aibhilin off and leaves once I buzz her in.

Emily had stayed over last night. I had told her what had happened at the Eighth House. One of the things I love about her is her trust and almost lack of jealousy. She asked if I had been a good boy and I told her that I had. That was the end of her concerns about me keeping it in my pants. Besides which, I was such a horndog last night that, well, let's just say that neither of us got as much sleep as we both would have preferred.

After I had hung up the phone with Racquel, M came into the living room with fresh coffee and gave me a mug. She had one for herself too. She sat down next to me, curled her legs up under her on the couch and leaned her hand against her head. On the turntable I was playing Ella Wishes You A Swinging Christmas.

"Are you going to tell her?"

I knew what she was going to ask, but I was surprised she hadn't asked last night.

"Tell who what?" I asked, playing the country bumpkin.

"Tell Racquel what happened to her husband. I heard you wanted to speak with her when she gets here."

I nodded.

"Yeah, I'm gonna tell her. My daughter spends half her time with that asshole."

Emily looked away and took a sip of her coffee.

"Be gentle, Anthony, I know she pushes your buttons. But she's the mother of your child and this is going to be difficult for her to hear."

I had leaned towards the coffee table where my rolling tray was. A simple tricolored bamboo tray which contained a jar of cannabis, my vape, a packing tool and my grinder. I wanted to enjoy Christmas with my two favorite people in the world and Mary Jane had a way of keeping me mellow. I packed my vape and turned it on. I took a hit and offered it to M. We shared it back and forth.

"I'll do my best to be gentle. But you know how he pisses me off."

"Artero?"

"Yes. There was always something about him I didn't like. Not just because he was fucking my ex when we were still married."

"True, but it takes two to tango," said Emily.

I nodded and blew smoke rings.

"I'll do my best," I said. "This will help." I raised the vape that was in my hand and passed it over to M.

"It does give you space from your edginess," she said.

And she wasn't wrong. I wasn't half the prickly pear I could be when on the wings of that green angel.

We spent the rest of the time listening to Ella on my turntable. I'm not a hipster who thinks that LPs are the cat's meow when it comes to fidelity or warmth or tone or whatever the fuck else they think makes vinyl better. I have a turntable and play records because when I started buying music that was the best way. It was better than tape, that's one thing hipsters and I can agree on. You also got a much better view of the album art.

But is vinyl better than CDs or even the high bitrate streaming music that's available now? I didn't think so. It's definitely different, but I think it's a subjective opinion. I like vinyl, and when I want to own music that's how I buy it.

There was a time from the early nineties to the late two thousands where vinyl sales were a trickle. In two thousand for example, vinyl made up less than half a percent of all music sales. Now it's just under five percent from what I've read. It's made a comeback but I doubt it'll see its heyday when it was making up over fifty percent of all music sales like it was in the seventies.

By the time the door buzzer went off it was coming on noon and M and I had finished Ella and were well through A Dave Brubeck Christmas. I got up from the couch and went over to the wall and pushed the talk button on my end.

"Wait for me, honey, I'll be right down."

"Ok, Daddy," said Aibhilin.

I turned to M.

"I'll be right back," I said.

She nodded.

"Be gentle," she said, as I closed the door behind me.

I got downstairs and found Aibhilin in the waiting area of the apartment complex. I opened up the door and found her looking at the bulletin board where she was looking at a lost dog flyer. She looked up at me and came over quite enthusiastically and hugged me.

Aibhilin's at that awkward age where she's not quite a teen but sometimes behaves like one. This was not one of those occasions. She was happy to see me.

"Hey, baby doll, Santa visited last night and left you some presents under the Christmas tree even though we haven't decorated it yet."

"Daaaaad," she said, rolling her eyes at me. "Santa is not real."

"He's real if you believe he is," I said.

More eye roll.

"Is Emily here?"

"She sure is, she's waiting upstairs. Why don't you go on up. I just need to speak with your mother quickly."

"Ok, is it about Artero?" she asked.

"Why do you ask that?"

She shrugged.

"No reason," she said, and I unlocked the door to the apartments and Aibhilin headed on up. I walked through the unlocked main entrance to the apartments and found Racquel's shiny new Mercedes parked in a loading zone just outside. I walked up to the passenger side window. Racquel lowered it and leaned towards me, her shades tilted down so she could look at me disparagingly over them.

"Be gentle," I heard M's voice in my head.

Racquel was still an attractive woman. She had a great figure and she took care of herself. But it had been a long time since she'd done anything for me in the lust department.

"What is it, Anthony?" she asked.

I grinned at her, leaning my hands on the top of the car and lowering my head so I could look in through the window. The air was cool and there was a breeze. It couldn't have been more than fifty or so and the sky was threatening rain. I thought I felt a spot of wetness on my hand now and then but I could see no raindrops on the car's windshield.

"Well," I said. "I'll start with Merry Christmas."

"We use Happy Holidays now, Anthony, it's the politically correct way."

I chuckled.

"I use Merry Christmas because it's the holiday I celebrate. Besides, what the f..., hell, Christmas hasn't been a religious holiday since before you and I were kids."

"Ok, Merry Christmas, Anthony, how's Emily?"

"She's well, thank you."

There was a pause in the conversation. Racquel and I were trying to get along better nowadays on account of our daughter.

"What did you want to talk about?"

"I wanted to talk about Artero's face,"

Racquel frowned and leaned in towards me even further.

"What about Artero's face?" she asked.

"Did he tell you how he got that shiner?"

"He was mugged coming home from work on Monday. I've told him he shouldn't be working that late alone."

I smirked. I shouldn't have, but I couldn't help myself.

"Have you ever wondered why he works late, alone so often?"

"No, I haven't, Anthony, on account that our relationship is built on trust. Not like ours was when I was with you."

I wanted to tell her that it was difficult to have a relationship built on trust when your wife is fucking around behind your back when you're out on the street putting your life at risk. Instead, I said this.

"That's not true."

"What's not true? Artero doesn't work late more than a handful of times a month. He's a very important financier, Anthony. You know that."

I knew that Artero fancied himself as a man of importance. I also had my suspicions that he was fucking around with his secretary. I had no proof, but when I had spent some time investigating him things looked too cozy between him and his secretary.

"No, that's not what I meant. He wasn't mugged."

Racquel started flapping her hands around inside the car. They reminded me of trapped birds trying to escape a cage.

"And that's another thing," she said. "How did you know that Artero had been mugged?"

"Because he hadn't been mugged," I said. "I gave him that shiner."

There was a moment of silence. Racquel stared at me for a bit, then she looked out through the windshield. People walked by behind me. Then she looked back at me.

"You're lying," she said, but there wasn't a lot of fight in her voice. I smiled softly at her.

"What I'm going to tell you is not going to be easy for you to hear. But I'm going to tell you because I loved you once, more than that, you're the mother of our child and I don't want Artero around our daughter if I can help it."

I was trying to speak softly and carefully.

"I'm not leaving Artero, Anthony, he provides well for us," she said.

Her voice was soft. There was no prickle to it. It sounded like the gasp from a dying relationship. Racquel wasn't a fool. Hell, Aibhilin probably knew that things probably weren't all hunky dory between her mother and Artero. How could they be if he couldn't keep it in his pants?

"You're a smart woman, Racquel, and you've probably had your doubts about Artero working late. Here's what happened, just hear me out and then you can say whatever you want, please."

I looked at Racquel. She had placed her shades properly back on to cover her eyes. She was looking out the front windshield and her hands clenched around the steering wheel were causing her knuckles to go white. She didn't look at me. In the background the Mercedes purred like a kitten.

"A little background first," I said. "I'm working on a case with the LAPD. A young, attractive woman was found at the Calabasas dump a few months back. No leads. She died from an apparent overdose of a cocktail of drugs. From the investigation and autopsy we've determined that she had sex the night she died and she's a sex worker. A high class escort and I've been trying to figure out why she died and why she was left the way she was at a dump."

My voice was soft and calm. I was expecting Racquel's acerbic and sarcastic commentary but she just kept staring through the front windshield, her knuckles white as yogurt.

"I've since come to learn that this case is connected, loosely, to a case I had back in New York a couple of years ago. I've come to believe that there is a loose affiliation, or maybe it's not so loose, of men, and probably women, who are trying to move the world in the direction they want it to. These are very powerful people."

Still nothing from Racquel. But now it really was trying to rain. It was spitting. I noticed the odd small raindrop on the windshield and on my hands which were still on the roof of the car.

"Through that New York case I came to speak with someone deep within this organization. They call themselves the Ekklesia. To make a long story short, I spoke with someone who calls themselves Camus, like the French philosopher. He's been helpful in the past. He explained that they host these parties for powerful men that help their organization. These parties are euphemistically called the Eighth House on account that in astrology the eighth house governs sex and lust, et cetera."

I looked at Racquel. She was a statue.

"On Monday evening, just past, I was invited to one of these eighth houses. Basically, Racquel, it's an orgy. Young women, much like the one who was left at the landfill are in abundance to serve old, fat men, most of whom, scratch that, all of whom at least on that evening were white. The men wore Santa masks to provide anonymity and these sex workers, called ianfu, wear mardi gras-type masks. The women are there to serve the men sexually. I was there to try and find out what I could about my victim."

I leaned back and squatted on my heels and rested my hands on the lower ledge of the rolled down window on the passenger car to give my neck a break.

"I was just about to leave on account that I wasn't able to get much information that could help my case, and I wasn't there for the orgy, when I heard who I thought was Artero. I stopped for a moment to verify. Artero had his back to me as he was sodomizing a young woman who was leaning into a couch. He was saying some pretty nasty things that I won't repeat. I lost my shit and yelled at him. He turned around and tried to start apologizing but I clocked him across the face which tore his mask off so that I knew it was him. Shortly after that, I was carried away by a couple of bouncers."

The First No Well

I stood up and leaned into the car, resting my hands on the open window ledge of the door. I didn't say anything for a moment. I was looking at Racquel. A tear rolled down her right cheek.

"Would you like me to drive you home? I'll get a taxi back," I said.

Nothing for what felt like a full rotation of the Earth. Racquel still stared straight ahead.

"Jesus, Anthony, on Christmas Day! Why won't you let me have just the smallest happiness? You're always trying to fuck up my life."

And just like that, Racquel peeled away from the curb and I wobbled trying to keep my balance on account my hands were ripped away from the doorframe. A car screeched to my left, just behind Racquel as she sped away. It came this close to an accident. I rubbed my head. Bits of my hair were getting wet from the rain.

I watched after her for a few moments. I felt a little bit like a schmuck. I had loved Racquel once and even though she was a prickly pear it was only because her heart was a large marshmallow if she trusted you and exposed it to you.

Not to forget everything she did to me. The deception, the lying and all the fucking around. But she was the mother of my daughter and I felt sorry for her. We're all really just lonely ghosts riding the horror bus of life careening towards Armageddon. It was starting to rain with a little more effort. I walked back into the apartment building.

Upstairs in apartment three thirty-three, that's my apartment in case you didn't get it, Emily was making Aibhilin a hot chocolate in the kitchen and the talk was lively.

M looked at me searchingly. Having been a cop as long as I had, I had a whole cupboard full of poker faces and I had put one on before I entered the apartment.

"What are you ladies up to?" I asked, smiling at them.

"Oh, we were just talking about how Christmas is our favorite holiday," said Emily.

"Is that right?" I asked, looking at Aibhilin.

"That's right, Daddy," she said.

"Me too, baby doll," I said.

Aibhilin gave me a look like I was trying to rob her blind.

"What?" I asked.

"I don't think it's your favorite holiday, Daddy," she said.

"Oh yeah, how do you know?"

"I've heard things," she said, like a wise little Jedi.

"Well, how about this. It's my favorite holiday when I get to spend it with my two favorite people in the whole world."

That made Aibhilin smile. I don't lie to my daughter. At least not as a rule. Some things I won't tell her, even if pressed. But I won't lie to her. I mean, little white lies are different. Saying I love Christmas to make it special for her is a little white lie, but it's harmless. It's the important things, consequential things I won't lie to her about.

"Do you want a hot chocolate, love?" M asked.

"Sure, it looks delicious," I said. "Especially with that whipped cream on top."

"It's vegan, Daddy, and underneath Emily put vegan marshmallows in. It's yummy."

"Then make mine a pappa bear size," I said, and I kissed Aibhilin on her forehead. "I'm very happy to have you for Christmas this year."

That wasn't the case last year, when Racquel and I couldn't see eye to eye.

"Me too," said Aibhilin, licking at the whipped cream topping.

"Hey, once I've got my hot chocolate, let's go decorate the Christmas tree and bring out the presents."

Aibhilin nodded and M said that was a good idea. M made my hot chocolate and we all took them out into the living room. We put them on the coffee table and Aibhilin opened up the box of decorations and asked for my help in putting up the lights. We like to put the lights on first and then the rest of the decorations after. The angel is placed on top at the very end. I let Aibhilin do that.

We took breaks now and then to drink our hot chocolate and to step back and take a look at our handiwork. We had listened to A Charlie Brown Christmas already and I swapped that for A Christmas Together with John Denver and the Muppets. I put that on the turntable. Both were still favorites with Aibhilin. Chit-chat was friendly and fluffy until we got to about the halfway mark in decorating the tree when I put my foot in my mouth.

"How was Christmas Eve and this past week at your Mom's?"

It was a reasonable, non-offensive question, at least I thought, but Aibhilin took it and turned it into a hand grenade that she casually tossed back.

"It was fine," she said.

That meant it wasn't fine.

"Tell your Dad what your Mom and your stepdad got you," said Emily.

"I got a new iPhone," she said.

I looked at M and frowned. That seemed like an expensive gift to get a twelve year old. Mind you, M had encouraged me to get the most expensive item which was on Aibhilin's list for us. An Apple Watch. I wasn't on board at first, but M has a way of getting me to see things. Another problem was the shit income I'd made this year. Lack of paintings selling didn't help either.

"That's nice," I said. "Do you love it?"

Aibhilin nodded.

"It's the SE," said Emily to me.

I looked at her and shrugged. I'm not a technophobe. I like tech well enough and for a guy my age I can figure my way around it. I have a natural ability with it, I guess, but I don't keep up with the latest and greatest.

"It's the cheapest one," Emily mouthed at me. "Four hundred bucks."

I nodded.

"Do you want to show it to me?" I asked.

"It's in my bag. Maybe after we've finished decorating."

"Sure," I said.

And so we continued to decorate the tree. Aibhilin would make a great designer if she wanted to pursue that. She's got an artistic eye for design and aesthetics.

I had a feeling she wanted to talk. Wanted to get something off her chest. I didn't press. That usually doesn't help. I give her space and she comes to me when she's ready. She was singing along with Miss Piggy in Christmas is Coming.

"Did it go well?" mouthed Emily to me, who was slightly behind Aibhilin.

I shook my head just before Aibhilin turned to me. She was holding a little drummer boy hanging decoration that she had made in elementary school years ago. In fact, a good handful of the decorations on our tree were made by Aibhilin for school projects.

"I don't think Artero loves Mommy anymore," she said, as she went to place her decoration.

"What makes you think that, baby doll?" I asked.

Aibhilin shrugged and put another decoration on the tree.

"They seem to fight. I hear them sometimes after I've gone to bed. Sometimes Artero is home late. He works late sometimes and sometimes Mommy doesn't like that."

"How do you know that?" I asked.

"She asks him if Vivienne was working late."

"Who's Vivienne?" I asked, knowing full well who that was. It was Artero's secretary and he was probably fucking her.

"She's the lady that works with Artero."

"His secretary or his boss?"

"His secretary."

"Well, maybe he needs his secretary to help him when he's working late," I offered.

"It's not like that. The way Mommy asks him about it, I think there's something going on between the two of them."

"What something?"

I got an eye roll and an exasperated "Daaaad!"

"What?" I said, playing the naïve father.

"They're having an affair," said an exasperated Aibhilin.

"How do you know that?" I asked.

"Because I'm a detective's daughter," she said.

I had to hand it to the kid, she was as sharp as a tack. But then my daughter often surprised me with her wisdom and insights.

"I think you should let Mommy and Artero figure it out, sweetheart."

I could tell immediately that I had said the wrong thing. Aibhilin's eyes started to water.

"I have to live there," she said, as she started to sob. I brought her into my embrace.

"I'm sorry, sweetheart. What can I do?"

I kissed her on the forehead.

"I want to live with you," she said, gasping for the words.

"I'll need to talk to your mother about that, but I'd love to have you live with me."

She slowly started to calm down.

"I'm also scared, Daddy," she said.

"What are you scared of, baby doll?" I asked, stroking her hair.

M had gone and fetched a box of tissues. She handed one to Aibhilin and Aibhilin took it and left my hug.

"Artero came home with a black eye yesterday. He said he was mugged, but maybe it was Vivienne's husband."

Vivienne was young and unmarried. I knew that from having investigated Artero. I told Aibhilin that.

"How do you know that?"

"I just do," I said.

This was where I slowly found myself sinking into quicksand. I didn't want to lie to her.

"How do you know, Daddy?"

I could see M just behind Aibhilin shaking her head and mouthing the word "no" to me.

"I just do, sweetheart. You don't need to worry about that. You and Mommy are safe."

"This is not fair," she said. "Everybody treats me like a baby. Like I don't know what's going on. This affects my life too, you know."

Her eyes were welling up with tears again. One thing I had wished I had growing up, other than a decent father, was honest parents. It was something I swore I'd offer my daughter. Radical transparency and honesty I had called it. Aibhilin read my mind.

"What about all that radical transparency and honesty you promised we'd share when I lied to you about having kissed Gavin."

She wasn't wrong. I nodded at her. M was shaking her head at me and mouthing the word "no" several times.

"You're right sweetheart, I did say that. But sometimes I don't tell you things because I don't want you getting worried or upset."

"I'm already upset, Daddy, and I'm scared and I don't know what's going on. Please tell me what's going on. I can tell you know."

I looked over at M who was still shaking her head at me. Aibhilin looked over at her too and M stopped shaking her head.

"You know too, don't you?" Aibhilin asked Emily.

"Ok, baby doll, I'll tell you what I know. It's not pleasant and I don't think you'll like it."

Aibhilin looked over at me.

"I'm ready. I'd prefer the truth, Daddy, than sugar-coated lies."

I sighed.

"Years ago when your mother and I first separated I did some investigation on Artero."

"Why would you do that?"

"Because your Mother was cheating on me with him behind my back and I didn't trust him."

Aibhilin frowned.

"What's wrong, baby doll?"

"You and Mommy both told me that you were splitting up because you didn't get along anymore."

"Well, that wasn't a lie, sweetheart. When I found out that Mommy and Artero were together I was very upset and it broke the trust in our relationship and we started fighting a lot. We didn't get along after that and I didn't want to unnecessarily upset you then. You were only four after all."

Aibhilin didn't say anything.

"I've kept an eye on Artero ever since then and that's how I know that Vivienne is not married."

"Is he having an affair with her?"

"I don't know for certain, baby doll, but I believe he is. I've seen them pretty cozy before in a way that would lead me to believe that they are."

I sighed again. This was not the sort of conversation I wanted to have with my daughter on Christmas Day. Aibhilin looked at me.

"There's more, isn't there?"

She looked at me for a long time. I didn't say anything.

"There is, isn't there, Daddy?"

Her lower lip started to quiver. I nodded slowly.

"Yes, sweetheart, I'm afraid there is more and it's worse.

Explaining Sex Work

" Do you really want to know?" I asked, Aibhilin, as M was shaking her head slowly at me. "I'm not sure this is a conversation we should be having on Christmas Day. Maybe tomorrow would be better?"

"You said honesty, Daddy, and now I'm very upset. Putting it off until tomorrow is not going to make it any better."

My daughter was leaning into womanhood and I was trying to keep her in childhood. Clearly, I was losing.

"I know how Artero got that shiner, sweetheart, because I gave it to him," I said.

Aibhilin looked at me with big eyes. She didn't know what to believe. She blinked a few times.

"Why? Why would you hit him?" she asked.

"Well, baby doll, sometimes I forget to use my words when I get angry."

I wasn't sure Aibhilin believed me. She blinked slowly, then she turned to look at Emily. Emily nodded her head.

"I don't understand, Daddy. I've never seen you angry. You've never even raised your voice at me."

I rubbed my eyes. This conversation wasn't going to get any easier.

"You've never met your Pops," I said. "You've met Popsie, but not Pops. Pops was a difficult man. He was a mean father to me when I was young and I promised myself that I'd never hurt my kids like Pops hurt me."

I smiled sweetly at Aibhilin. I was trying to thread the needle between honesty and fear. The eye of that needle was tighter than a hangman's noose.

Aibhilin reached around and gave me a hug. She nestled into my chest. This was the best place in the world to be. She looked up at me.

"Did he hurt you with words or with his hands?" she asked.

She looked up at me like a young doe, innocent of the monsters in the forest.

"Both," I said. "But it's what made me swear to never lay a finger on any of my kids and never raise my voice if I could help it. It's also the reason I swore never to lie to you."

"Is that why I never met Pops?" she asked.

I nodded.

"I didn't want you to meet him. You are my angel and he was a mean man. But he died a few years before you were born, in any event."

Aibhilin was putting on another decoration. A Christmas Together was now finished. I got up to change the vinyl.

"Any requests, baby doll?"

Aibhilin shook her head.

"You choose, Daddy."

I didn't have a ton of Christmas vinyl. I had the two kid's albums and I once had A Chipmunk Christmas which I had long since donated since it had come to claw on my nerves like a grinch after it was the only thing for a few years that Aibhilin had wanted to listen to at Christmas time.

I looked through my boxes of records. There are only three of them, and I found something that might soothe us all. I put it on. It was A Jolly Christmas From Frank Sinatra. I went and sat back down as Old Blue Eyes started singing Jingle Bells.

The Christmas tree was almost fully decorated. Only a small handful of decorations were left.

"How did you get so upset at Artero that you hit him?" she asked.

I was deep in it at this point and figured I should probably get it over with. I rubbed my face and took a deep breath.

"I'm working on a case. Well, it's actually been a case I've been working on for a few months. I told you that we had found a young lady who had been left at the landfill."

Aibhilin nodded. I don't usually talk to Aibhilin about my cases, but sometimes she asks and I won't lie to her. She doesn't get any gory details but I give it to her straight. Maybe in ten, fifteen years her psychiatrist will tell me I was negligent about this. But I believe kids are resilient and they can handle the truth so long as you keep it appropriate.

"Well, I've been trying to find out what happened to her to end up there in the first place. She wasn't hurt, but it seems she took too many drugs and her heart couldn't handle it."

Emily wasn't looking at me. I was a shipwrecked man floating on a splintered boat of honesty in an ocean of shark-infested human immorality.

"Why did they leave her there?" Aibhilin asked, now engrossed in my story and not putting up any more decorations. M took one and added it to the tree.

"Well, from what I can tell, she was working for some people who were doing some naughty things and they didn't want to get caught."

"What naughty things were they doing?"

I was a Sasquatch walking over a deep, dark lake covered with paper thin ice.

"Do you know how babies are made?"

"Yes, Daddy, I know all about sex."

I was seesawing between shock and thankfulness. Thankful that I didn't have to talk about the birds and the bees to my daughter, again, but shocked because I didn't want to think about my daughter as a sexual being. To me she was still my baby doll. Literally and figuratively. I looked over at M. She was grinning at me. It wasn't helpful. I imagined myself a worm stuck on the hook dangled in front of a shark.

"Okay. Well, when you're older and married, you'll come to understand that sex can be enjoyable between people who love each other and are committed to each other."

Aibhilin was still hanging onto every word. That didn't make it easier. I paused. She had no questions. I carried on and all before me was a horizon full of landmines with the sun blinding me.

"Some people, well, they want to have sex without loving someone or marrying them," I said, "and some women will offer that for money."

Aibhilin rolled her eyes.

"Daaaad! I know about prostitutes," she said.

I obviously had not been keeping up.

"How do you know about prostitutes?"

"Artero told me about them." Aibhilin must have seen my temperature rise. "Mommy, Artero and I were driving home from dinner one night and

I saw a couple of women who were standing on the side of the road and they didn't have a lot of clothes on. One of the women went and spoke to someone in a car. I asked Mommy and Artero why those women weren't wearing a lot of clothes and that's when Artero told me that they were prostitutes and offering sex for money."

I rubbed my head. This was worse than the dentist. I nodded. I guess my baby doll was no longer as innocent as I had hoped.

"Okay. This is a little awkward for me, but I'm glad you understand sex and prostitutes. I'm going to go a little faster now and you stop me if you have more questions, okay?"

"Okay, Daddy."

"So, some women who work as prostitutes, though I think nowadays the correct term is sex worker. Anyway, some sex workers offer sex for money in more discreet settings. Women no longer have to hang around on street corners and look for clients, they can now do it from their homes and using the internet.

"There are also businesses that offer these services by women and this business will rent a house someplace and bring clients there where the women are. On Monday evening I went to such a place."

Aibhilin looked from me to Emily.

"That's true, Avy," said Emily. "Your father told me about it. He was trying to find out more information about that young woman who was left at the dump."

"So you knew?" she asked Emily.

Emily nodded. Aibhilin turned to look back at me.

"You went to a house to pay for sex, ewww, I don't want to know," she said.

I shook my head vigorously.

"No, I didn't. I went to the house to interview other women who were sex workers, and I was there to ask them about their friend who was left at the dump. Nothing more."

"And did they help?" asked Aibhilin.

"A little. At least I got some clarity that she wasn't murdered, she just took too many drugs."

Aibhilin looked back at Emily. I started to wonder if they were conspiring against me.

"Your father has a hard time understanding that women would offer those sorts of services for money."

"To make a long story short, just as I was leaving after having spoken with a couple of these sex workers, I saw Artero having sex with one of the women. I lost my temper and I became upset because he was dishonoring you and your mother. I hit him in the face and that's how he got the black eye."

I didn't know how Aibhilin would take it. Would she burst into tears thinking me a monster for using violence or would she be shocked? I didn't know.

"I understand, Daddy," she said.

"What do you understand, sweetheart?"

"Artero was being disrespectful to Mommy. That wasn't very nice of him, but I'm madder because he lied to us."

Aibhilin looked into the box of decorations, took out the last couple and hung them up on the tree. Then she came back and picked up the angel that was the last item in the box.

"Let me get you the step stool," I said, getting up and going into the kitchen to retrieve it.

I brought it back out and opened it up in front of the tree. I helped my daughter onto it so she could put the angel on the top of the tree. Aibhilin got down from the step stool and hugged me.

"Thank you for telling me the truth, Daddy."

I hugged her back.

"I'm sorry it's not a happy truth."

Aibhilin pulled back.

"I think I should call Mommy and let her know."

"That's not a good idea, sweetheart, I already told her when I came down stairs when you arrived and she didn't take it well. She's very upset. I think we should let Mommy and Artero have the day to work it out. Why don't you call her tomorrow instead?"

Aibhilin looked up at me and nodded.

"I have to go to the washroom," she said.

"And show us your fancy new phone when you get back," I replied.

I looked over at Emily who was grinning at me again.

"What?"

"It was fun to watch you squirm," she said, with a big smile on her face.

"Yeah, well thanks for your help."

Sun Over The Yardarm

M leaned over and hugged me.

"I love you. Especially your idealization of women," she said.

"What do you mean?"

"You're like a man who was born seventy years too late. You're chivalrous, you're attractive to us, you enjoy sex and yet you still somehow try to keep us on a pedestal."

"Probably comes from seeing how my mother was treated and how I, as a young boy, thought she should have been treated."

M nodded.

"I love you for it. But women are autonomous beings and enjoy sex as much as men. And honestly, Anthony, women have been selling sex for millenia."

I didn't say anything to that. What was there to say? M wasn't wrong.

"Quickly, how did it go with Racquel downstairs?"

"Not well. She was like a statue when I was telling her how Artero got his shiner."

In a corner of the apartment I heard the water run in the pipes. Aibhilin was finishing up in the washroom.

"Her hands were choking the steering wheel and she just stared straight through the windshield. A tear rolled down her cheek. When I was finished telling her she cursed me and told me that I was always trying to ruin her happiness. Then she veered out into traffic almost causing an accident and sped off."

M nodded slowly.

"You know you're not responsible for her happiness. Or rather, it wasn't you who ruined it."

"I know. Still, I feel bad for her. At least I hope she'll do the right thing."

"Leave him?"

"Yeah, obviously."

"Well, you probably didn't tell her anything she didn't know or wasn't suspicious of. She's going to have to face it now."

Aibhilin came into the living room again, carrying a shiny red phone. She showed it around, as happy as if it were a puppy. We oohed and aahed. After she had shown her new toy around I went into my bedroom and retrieved our gifts for her. We set them under the tree and let her have at them.

The most expensive gift. Well, the only gift really, except for a new pair of pajamas and a couple of items of clothing and a stocking full of knick knacks was the Apple Watch. She loved it.

Early afternoon found Aibhilin heading to her bedroom to play with her new watch, phone and tablet which she had brought with her. That was an Apple product too. Aibhilin was a big fan.

She asked M to call her when she was going to start Christmas dinner. This wasn't the first Christmas dinner we were sharing. It was the second one. We'd likely be having the same meal. M had introduced me, and Aibhilin, to this product called Tofurky. The word is a portmanteau of tofu and turkey. It's vegan and made of soy and wheat, stuffed with a rice based stuffing and looks like a smooth brown or tan ham.

I'm not selling it very well, but I gotta tell ya, with a good gravy, roasted potatoes and veg, it's tasty and goes down easy without leaving you in what I like to call the turkey stupor.

M and I were cuddling on the couch listening to the Lena Horne Stormy Weather album when she turned to me. By the way she did it and the pause that led up to it, I knew we were going to have a serious conversation.

"You know that Aibhilin would be more than welcome to live with us," she said.

I nodded, looking straight ahead at the black television. M squeezed my arm.

"I really want us to live together, my love, and Aibhilin is like the daughter I never knew I wanted because I had never wanted children of my own."

I nodded again. Silence slipped into the room and stretched it out like taffy.

"Don't you want to marry me?" she asked.

I turned to her and smiled.

"I do, but this year has not been a good year for me. I made less than fifty grand. I can't provide for you and Aibhilin on that pittance. At least not the way I'd like to."

M smiled at me.

"Your net worth is not your real worth, my love. At least not to me."

"Well, I'm struggling with it," I said.

"You know there are a lot of women who have a bigger income than their husbands and they make it work. Take Oprah for example, or Julia Roberts, or Kate Moss."

I nodded.

"My love, if I wanted a man who made as much or more than me, I'd be severely limited in finding suitors."

I didn't say anything.

"Does the idea of a prenup bother you?"

"No," I said. "Your grandfather and your father have built a successful business and that needs to be protected."

"There you go. I didn't build the business, I got lucky being born into the right family."

I looked at her.

"Still, you work hard in keeping it a continuing success."

"Then what is it?"

"I guess it's my own idea of relationships between men and women. Perhaps it's cultural or sociological. I don't know. Maybe I'm old fashioned, but I've always felt like a man should be able to provide for his family."

"But you provide in so many ways. You're not destitute. You treat me with respect and love. You're chivalrous and kind. You can cook," she said, laughing, "and I want to spend the rest of my life with you."

"I know."

"I don't understand, my love. Just because I got lucky and you didn't, at least not yet, does that mean we can never get married?"

"No, that's not what I'm saying. You just need to be patient with me. I've gotta get used to the idea. I never imagined in my wildest dreams that

I'd fall in love with a stunningly beautiful woman who just happens to be a billionaire."

"Okay, I'll leave you with this. Couldn't it be considered a little sexist that you won't marry me because I'm wealthier than you? Doesn't it seem a little off that you expect to marry a woman that is poorer than you? I mean, if that's the case then basically you're not as into equal rights and feminism as I thought you were."

Her tone was not biting.

"That's unfair," I said.

"Exactly, because it's not who you are. No man has ever treated me with as much dignity and respect as you have. For an old-timey gumshoe, you're the most egalitarian man I've known and I love you for it and, dammit, Anthony, I want to spend the rest of my life with you and to be able to proudly call you my husband."

There was a little voice behind us.

"I think you should marry her, Daddy," said Aibhilin. She came over and hugged Emily from behind the couch. "I love her."

Well, there you go.

"In time," I said. "But more importantly, you shouldn't be listening in on private conversations."

"I know, Daddy. I only heard the last bit. And anyway, if it was really private you should have had it in your bedroom behind closed doors."

See what I mean. She was straddling that fine line between childhood and teenville or womanhood. But she wasn't wrong. Though I had another problem. I didn't want to get ganged up on if we all moved in together. I'd be outnumbered.

Aibhilin wanted to watch some television. So that's what we did after Lena Horne bid us farewell. I put away the vinyl and turned on the television. We watched it for about an hour and then M and Aibhilin went into the kitchen to cook.

It was just after four. I figured the sun was over the yardarm. Well over. In the traditional, nautical use of that the sun usually passed the yardarm around eleven in the morning. I had some catching up to do and some next steps to figure out.

Mi Hogar

There are almost two weeks between Christmas and the first Monday after New Year's Day. That's where I was. It was Monday the sixth of January and I wanted to start the new year fresh by closing the case. If only for my own sanity.

I'd spent the quiet times between Santa and champagne thinking about things. And there were a lot of things to think about. I'd given a lot of thought about moving in with M and I figured I'd do it. I had just signed another lease for the year at Vista Al Mar. The apartments that didn't have an ocean view in spite of their name.

That way I had a year to figure out if M would keep me or kick me out. Or maybe I'd find it wasn't to my liking. I'd spent almost ten years living on my own. I wasn't sure I could get used to domestic life. But I was willing to give it a try.

I'd also given a lot of thought to my experience at the Eighth House. It was time to put that case to bed. Suzanne Valadon hadn't been murdered and Camus had said he'd clean up the ianfu as far as drug use goes. But there was a murder, and that was Gorky. I wanted the person responsible and I also wanted assurance that no more assholes were going to be choking women out during sex. Ideally, I'd like that asshole on a platter too. And the person to give that to me would be Camus. He'd be the first call I'd be making this morning.

I also wanted to speak to Johnny Rotten. I wanted to know if he'd found anything out about the house that had been rented for the orgy. His silence didn't tell me anything. After all, we'd just been through the Christmas and New Year break. But now it was time to get back to business.

But first things first. And the firstest of the first things is always breakfast and coffee. M had brought me some groceries. Vegan sausages, vegan bacon and vegan eggs. The scrambling kind. I preferred the real fried kind but I'd seen my doc late last year and he was concerned about two things. My high blood pressure and my high cholesterol. I was concerned about one thing. And that one thing, just like Racquel had said, was why everyone was trying to ruin my happiness.

I jest. Doc gave me two options. Valsartan or veganism, atorvastatin or apples. Well, he didn't quite say it like that but he did tell me it was diet or drugs. I looked at the side effects of the drugs and the choice was clear. M also provided a lot of research that said that both blood pressure and cholesterol could be brought down with a vegan diet. I'd give diet a try first.

The vegan eggs come in a bottle. You pour some into a frying pan. I was now using olive oil in place of butter. It makes a difference, but you get used to it. I fried up the eggs and then I fried up the bacon. I made toast and I made coffee. No butter on the toast, just a little margarine.

The bacon made it onto the toast first and then the tomatoes followed by a little salt and pepper and lastly the scrambled eggs. The thing with frying the fake bacon is that it's a lot quicker than the real stuff. I learned that the hard way. The first time I cooked it, and I like my bacon crispy, I turned it into a stiff cracker. But I'd since learned my lesson.

I took everything into the living room and put on the TV. Nothing much was on. I turned it off and put on jazz radio. It was raining outside. Just a drizzle, but it was cool, at least for LA. I knew that because I went out onto the balcony, which is off the kitchen for some reason. I never understood that. Should be off the living room or main bedroom. The balcony, like much of the apartment, faces the street.

I ate while listening to Diana Krall. That was followed by Etta James and then Édith Piaf who I hadn't heard in a long time. Piaf had a difficult and tortured life. Just listening to her sing you can probably figure that out. Piaf was followed by a clean plate that I took into the kitchen and cleaned up. I came back out, turned down the radio and made some calls.

The first was to Camus. I was expecting an automated voicemail like it had been the other times I'd called. After a long bout of ringing a voice answered. It was female. Sounded anywhere from mid-twenties to mid-fifties. A good telephone voice. The kind of voice that was sexy and sultry and might, on another day, be found on the other end of a sex line. And I got all of that from one word.

"Hello?"

"Hi there, who am I speaking with?"

"Simone de Beauvoir," said the sultry voice.

"And which company is this?"

"I'll let him know you called."

And the line went dead. I looked at my phone, then I put it back to my ear to make sure the line really was disconnected. It was. I'd always heard that the French were rude. Not that I'd been to France to find out, but Simone de Beauvoir had just hung up on me. So there's that.

Still, with all the sultriness and sexiness behind the voice, there was no French accent. I wondered who I had spoken with. I tried calling again. I let the phone ring over fifteen times. That's when I stopped counting and waited several seconds more. No pickup and no voicemail. I gave it another go. This time I waited three minutes for someone to pick up. That's a long time listening to a ringing tone. No answer, no voicemail.

I gave up then. She said she'd give him the message. At this point I was sure she knew who was calling even if I hadn't announced myself. I wasn't familiar with Simone de Beauvoir other than I knew of the name somewhere from the recesses of my muddled mind. I did an internet search.

She was a feminist French philosopher though she didn't consider herself a philosopher. She had a long and open relationship with Sartre, another French philosopher. I guess that being French, smoking Gauloises while sitting in cafes, and drinking le vin rouge makes you a philosopher. I jest, of course. Still, why did Camus and his ilk choose to use French philosopher pseudonyms? That was a puzzle for another day.

There was someone I knew who always looked forward to my call. My old friend and confidant, Johnny Rotten. That was the next number I dialed.

"Sid," he said. "Long time no hear."

He was kidding. We had spoken on New Year's Day when I had called to thank him and Jen for hosting the New Year's party that we'd gone to.

"I wanted to thank you for the New Year's party," I said, barely stifling a laugh.

"Just because I only do one once a decade doesn't mean I appreciate your facetiousness," he said.

"I joke, old friend. I just tried calling Camus again."

"Oh yeah, and you left a voicemail as per usual?"

"Nope, this time I got a live female voice."

"Huh."

"Yeah. She called herself Simone de Beauvoir."

"Is that supposed to mean anything other than it sounds French?"

"If you'd taken a liberal arts degree instead of that BS in Criminal Justice you took, you'd know who she was," I jibed.

"Yeah, like you knew."

"This is not about me. Anyway, she's another French philosopher who swung both ways but was in a long term open relationship with Sartre."

"Now Sartre I know. He won the Nobel Prize in Literature, if I recall."

"You recall correctly."

"I'll put a point in the win column. But how is this relevant?"

"It's not," I said. "But it's something to keep in the back of the mind. Perhaps it'll become a clue one day to uncover who Camus really is. Why has he chosen a French philosopher's name, and why did that woman, whoever she is, answer the phone and use another French philosopher's name?"

"Maybe de Beauvoir has decided to have an open relationship with Camus now," said JR.

I laughed. It made as much sense as anything else.

"Listen, the reason for my call was to check in on what you might have found about that Eighth House. Anything of note?"

"Well, we flooded the place with blue light and Fluorescein but we couldn't find a trace of any blood or bodily fluids. That house was pristine. Looked like it hadn't been lived in, except for your feet impressions on the newly cleaned carpet."

"No evidence of anything to indicate what had happened the night before?"

"Nothing, Sid. Honestly, these guys are pros. If I hadn't known you were at that orgy and you asked me to investigate that house, well, I wouldn't have believed you that anything had been going on in there. We looked in every cupboard and every nook and cranny. Nothing."

"What about the owner or who rents it and why?"

"The owner is a widow, Lois Creighton. She lives in Palm Springs now in a senior residence. One of those independent kinds where you have your own kitchen and bathroom and take care of your own apartment but there is help if you need it. A nurse is available et cetera, et cetera."

"Not what I was expecting," I said.

"She's seventy-nine. Lived in that house for over forty years..."

"Forty years ago it was an expensive house."

"Right. Her husband had an import, export business. Dealt in products and goods from the Commonwealth with a focus on the United Kingdom. He died a few years ago and with the recommendation of her kids, she moved to this place in Palm Springs and lets a management company take care of the Beverly Hills property."

"That's a lot of information you gathered."

"Nah, wasn't me. You know how good Forrest is. I sent him to see her. She might have been a little lonely too. Didn't get the impression she gets a lot of visits from her kids, and Forrest could even get a nun talking loquaciously about sex."

I laughed.

"Long story short, Sid, the owner is hands off."

"And the management company?"

"That's Lares Management. Lares, incidentally, are guardian deities of the Roman religion. Just something I learned that might be neither here nor there."

"What did they have to say?"

"They rent out high end homes, usually short term up to a year. Lois' Beverly Hills home was rented for the week from the twentieth of December to the twenty-seventh. They say they only rent that property on a per week basis minimum."

"And who rented it?"

"Nicole Ray. She paid with a credit card in her name and showed a valid driver's license with that name."

"Did you get a copy of that driver's license?"

"No, because Lares Management doesn't keep copies of them. They only view them to validate the renter. They deal with high end, short term rentals, and their clients prefer discretion."

"Of course they do."

"Sid, what did you expect? You've dealt with Camus for what, a year now?"

"Over two."

"There you go, and we can't identify him. We took down the transaction number for the credit card which was done with a high end card. We followed up with the credit card company which required us getting a warrant and the card is registered to a company. The company's name is Joro LLC."

"What do they do?"

"Can't tell. I think they might be an umbrella company or something. The boys and I have spent too much time on this already. Joro LLC is an anonymous LLC registered in New Mexico. The address is a New Mexico address that turns out to be a post office box number in a small Mexican restaurant that apparently provides that service as a small side hustle. That particular address hasn't received any mail since they rented the address according to Matías Botello the proprietor of Mi Hogar. Mi Hogar being his restaurant."

"What about who set up the account at Mi Hogar?"

"Nicole Ray. Paid by cash for five years."

"How much is that?"

"Five grand, including a multi-year discount."

"Matías sure is a hustler," I said.

"I don't know what to tell you. I mean, we probably should have expected they'd take such lengths."

"How much was Creighton's rental?"

"That's twenty-five grand."

"A month?"

Roberts laughed.

"You're a funny guy. You realize this is LA we're living in. That's twenty-five grand a week."

I whistled.

"It's a nice house in a nice neighborhood. What can I say?"

"Didn't know enough people had that kind of money."

"Depending on time of year and type of year, Lares is able to rent out Creighton's place sixty to seventy-five percent of the time. Not everyone lives on a city salary or an artist's pittance."

Roberts wasn't wrong about that.

"What about this Nicole Ray?" I asked. "What do we have on her?"

"Nothing, Anthony, because there are twenty-three Nicole Ray's in California alone and I just don't have the manpower to go through that many Nicoles for a cold case. And you know what we'll find anyway, right?"

"Yeah, none of them will be our Nicole Ray."

"Right, most likely it'll be a pseudonym."

"Did you get any description from Matías or Lares Management?"

"Lares said that Nicole looked to be in her thirties, slim with heavy makeup and jet black hair. Between five five and five eight. Matías described Nicole as early thirties around five six, slim, blonde who wore sunglasses and wore average makeup."

"Average makeup?"

"That's what he said when Forrest interviewed him and asked about the makeup being heavy or average. Both described her hair as being down to her shoulder blades and wavy."

"Probably the same Nicole wearing a slight disguise. What about the height though?"

"Well, I'd probably put that down to the height of the men who Forrest interviewed. Forrest put Allen Cole from Lares at about five ten and Matías at about five six. I'd give more weight to Matías' description of her height in that case. Both men said she was white. Does that help?"

I shook my head.

"No, not really. There must have been at least a dozen or so women at the Eighth House when I was there. Most of them were between five four and five eight and most of them were white. In any event I didn't get their names. Not their real names anyway. Sounds like this Nicole is average enough that she's forgettable."

"Except both men said she was attractive."

"Attractive women in California and New Mexico, they're what, like a dime a dozen," I said, only half sarcastically.

"You know what would make me happy enough to put this case to bed?"

"Yeah, I do."

"What?"

"You've told me plenty of times, Sid. You want Gorky's killer and the asshole who can't stop strangling the women, if it's one and the same."

"Yeah."

"I can't give that to you, Anthony. I wish I could. You know that. But some cases we just can't get a break on, and I think this is one of them. Maybe Camus will hear you out."

"Yeah, maybe."

There was a pause on the other end.

"Speaking of unpleasant outcomes," said Roberts, "have you heard from Racquel recently?"

"Yeah, I guess I didn't tell you, but Aibhilin is now living with me for the next few weeks. Racquel dropped her off while she gets her life back on track."

"Huh, I'm a little surprised by that to be honest."

"About what?"

"I wasn't sure Racquel would leave him."

"Why not?"

"Really, you're going to make me say it?"

"I don't know what you're talking about."

"She was fucking around on you, Anthony, while you were on the job."

"Yeah, we already know that."

"Well, I just figure she shouldn't be surprised that those chickens came home to roost. What's good for the goose and all that."

"Maybe she's taking a page out of my book. I ended my marriage when I found out she was fucking around. Maybe she figures that's the best approach. And I agree. It is."

"No doubt."

"But it gets worse."

"How so?"

"M has offered, and Racquel accepted, M's guest house. My ex and my current squeeze living together. Jesus, JR, is that not the icing on the cake?"

I heard a chuckle on the other end.

"What's so funny?"

"Your ex and your current girlfriend together. That is funny, Sid. Really, it is. Still, good on Emily for offering that up."

"Yeah, I love her for it, but c'mon, it better not turn into something long term."

"Maybe they're maneuvering for a threesome."

"Ugh, God, no, that doesn't do it for me," I said.

Roberts laughed.

"Listen, I've gotta go. Let's get together for a beer soon."

"Sure thing."

I hung up the phone and moments later a sleepy Aibhilin came into the living room, rubbing her eyes. It was ten thirty.

"Are you hungry, baby doll? I can make you some toast and eggs and bacon, all vegan of course."

Aibhilin and M had become as tight as thieves and because of that, Aibhilin had recently informed me she had become vegan.

Gray Walls of Sky

It seemed like my daughter and my girlfriend continued to gang up on me. We'd spent much of the week at M's. It made sense, Racquel was there and M thought it would be a good idea to let Aibhilin have easy access to her mother. And it did, despite my reservations. I was the one who found all of this awkward.

Emily had asked me if it was alright. I said it was, even though it made me a little uncomfortable. I told her that too. She said she'd be happy to get Racquel a new place if I was really finding it too difficult. But the more I thought about it the more I realized that my awkwardness was a small price to pay for the kindness that Emily was showing Racquel, but also for the limited upset to Aibhilin's life.

I knew she wouldn't say it directly, but Aibhilin was taking her mother's separation from Artero well, all things considered. And I figured a big reason for that was because Racquel was easy for Aibhilin to access. Aibhilin also gave me constant updates, and it seemed that Artero was trying on a daily basis to win Racquel back, so much so, that Racquel had stopped answering his phone calls. I was begrudgingly proud of her for that. He had also wanted to see Aibhilin. That was only going to happen over my dead body. Racquel wouldn't allow it and Aibhilin wasn't interested either. Put that in the win column.

Emily had also put Racquel in touch with one of her friends who happened to be one of the best divorce lawyers in the city. This lawyer had had several successful high profile divorce cases won for her clients. What I only recently found out was that Emily was paying for the lawyer. I wasn't happy about this, but she said that Racquel had promised to pay her back depending on what sort of a win she got.

I bit my tongue. I loved M and she was a good person, but paying for Racquel's lawyer wasn't something I was able to get around, until we had an argument about it. An argument that M won by dangling my daughter in front of me. And she wasn't wrong. Without a good lawyer for Racquel, Racquel would probably end up with little and the case would drag on and on upsetting and prolonging the pain that Aibhilin, in particular, would have to go through.

You can win any argument with me if you can convince me my daughter would suffer in the alternative scenario. That's what M did, and that's how she won.

And that's where we were today. Today being a Wednesday and the fifteenth of January. I had seen more of Racquel in the past couple of weeks than I had the previous year. But she kept mostly to herself and didn't stay longer than necessary in the main house where Aibhilin, Emily and I were.

M and I were sitting in the main living room, overlooking a cement-colored sky that drizzled rain across the backyard. The rain fell softly onto the slate gray water of the pool creating what looked to me like erupting goosebumps on the water's surface.

We were drinking coffee, M and I. Aibhilin was in the guest house with Racquel. It's a two bedroom guest house and Aibhilin had stayed overnight with her mother at the guest house. M and I were complaining about the rain never coming when it was needed, like in the summer or fall when most of the fires were, when my phone rang. I usually don't answer numbers I don't recognize, but it had been over a week without a phone call from Camus.

I was getting spammed by fake calls from the IRS, tech support and other scams of the day, but right now, I felt lucky.

"Hello," I said.

"Anthony, this is Albert."

"Hello, Albert," I said, pronouncing the name like an anglophone. And that got me thinking about Fat Albert. That thought got me to thinking about men in power and their rapacious ways. I wondered if Camus was such a man. I wondered if he was even white. He sounded white, but he was probably using voice modulation software or some other sort of trickery even if his voice sounded normal.

I had tried downloading an app to record my voice calls, but for some reason that probably Camus knew, I couldn't record telephone conversations with him. The app just became unresponsive.

"You did exactly what I told you not to do," said Camus, his tone smooth as plain yogurt and just as bland.

"I wanted to talk to you about that," I said. "You never told me the Chief of Police was going to be there and more importantly that my ex-wife's current husband would be there. I lost my temper, Albert. My daughter lives in that fucking man's house."

I could feel myself getting hot under the collar.

"Your temper gets you in trouble, Anthony, and I warned you about that."

His voice was as monotonous as the gray wall of sky I could see through the large windows. It could have been painted it was so bland.

"You know how I am, and yet you didn't give me the courtesy of telling me that my ex-wife's current husband would be at the house banging other women."

"I am an important man, Anthony. And I say that factually and without pride. As such, most of the minutia within the organizations I run are of no concern to me. In other words, I pay no attention, for example, as to who attends these events. However, I understand some good came of it."

I looked out at the guest house which was at the far end of the garden on the opposite side of the pool. It was angled towards us, not quite at ninety degrees. More like forty-five or thereabouts.

"I hear Racquel has left Artero. That's a silver lining. You never liked him, and obviously for good reasons."

"It doesn't bother you that this Eighth House of yours ruins lives. Ruins marriages?"

"Anthony, lives are ruined everyday. Marriages are torn apart just as often. Sometimes over nothing more than the way someone holds their toothbrush or drinks their tea. So no, it does not bother me that marriages are ruined. They were destined for that without my intervention. There is a big storm gathering in the west that will soon rock our shores."

"I don't know what you're talking about."

"This is some insider information that very few people are aware of at this stage. There is a coronavirus pandemic coming ashore. In just a few days the first case will be found in this country. Within a couple of weeks, the WHO will declare this to be a public health emergency of international concern. And that's underplaying it. This pandemic is going to be the worst since the Spanish Flu. Keep your loved ones safe."

"I don't understand how this is relevant to the Eighth House."

"It's not, Anthony, I'm offering you insider information. This pandemic will kill over a million people within the first year. Governments around the world will bungle the management of it. The American government will be especially incompetent in handling it. This is why the Ekklesia is here, Anthony. To lead humanity to a great awakening. I'd tell Emily to sell her stocks and go to cash. In late February the stock market is going to panic and we'll likely see around a thirty percent decline by mid March. Which will only be the first decline. If Emily asks, tell her not to think about getting back in until at least spring of next year."

Sometimes Camus spoke about things that seemed conspiratorial to me.

"Back to the subject at hand. Did you find the visit to the Eighth House helpful?"

"Depends on what you consider helpful. Lotta or Achara or whatever the hell her real name is was quite helpful, but not in the way I was hoping."

"You were hoping for some twisted conspiracy. But as I told you, Anthony, these women are chosen specifically because we know this is a calling for them."

"That's a little rich," I said. "Prostitution is hardly a calling."

"For a reasonably enlightened man, Anthony, you sure do have a lot of blind spots."

I didn't say anything.

"For instance. We call it sex work and it's probably one of the oldest occupations. If I were you, I'd talk to Dr. Ainley about it, as your hang ups are your blind spots and your Achilles heel."

Nothing surprised me anymore about what Camus knew.

"You do believe, if only begrudgingly, that these women are not there under duress, don't you?"

I had to give him that much.

"Yes, I have to admit that much."

"Then what's still stuck in your craw? Tell me your fondest wishes as if I were your fairy godfather."

"I want the asshole who kept on strangling those women and I want the asshole who murdered Gorky. There were real crimes committed here, Camus, and if you believe in even the smallest sliver of justice then you'll help."

"Our lives are just brief candles snuffed out by uncaring gods, Anthony, but I'll see what I can do."

"You've also gotta get Frank Burton off your payroll."

"Who is that?"

"I thought our relationship was built on trust and honesty?" I asked.

"Honesty, yes. Trust is something that takes time. What makes you think we have Chief Burton on our payroll?"

"Because I saw him at the goddamn orgy."

"I see."

"Well?"

"Well, as I've said before, I help you out sometimes because it suits me. I'm not willing to discuss who our friends are."

"He's nobody's friend. He only looks out for himself. And I'm going to bring that asshole down if it takes me my whole life and that might put you in the crosshairs."

"I'm not worried about that, Anthony. But I would be worried about you overextending yourself."

"Is that a threat?"

In truth, I was getting tired of putting out fires that just kept erupting over and over again.

"As I've said before, I don't offer threats, I offer advice. Let me be clear, Anthony, if I wanted you dead I could wave my arms theatrically and my wish would become another's command. But let's keep things cordial betwixt you and I. If Burton is the misanthrope you suggest he is, then I'd suggest that replacing him would only put another misanthrope in his place."

"Burton is a special kind of asshole," I said.

"As much as I always enjoy our chats, I must be off. Is there anything else I can help you with while I take away your humble supplication and think upon it?"

"No."

And that was how the call ended. Camus hung up. I held the phone to my ear for a few moments. Then I said, hello. There was no response so I looked at my phone and the phone app indicated the call had ended.

Thirty Pieces

M looked at me as I put my phone back down on the coffee table in front of us.

"Everything okay with Camus?" she asked.

I looked at her and twisted my mouth into the corner of my face. Then I sighed.

"There's something about him that just rubs me up the wrong way. He's almost smug and fastuous. I don't like him."

"Maybe it's not him, maybe it's what he represents. You've often had difficulty with men in power," she said. "And that's very understandable."

I wasn't looking for a psychoanalysis of myself. I nodded absentmindedly.

"What did he say when you asked him for help?"

"He said he'd think about it."

"And would that give you some peace with putting this case to bed then?"

I looked over at her and nodded.

"Yeah. I've got to admit that perhaps there are women out there who enjoy working in the sex trade. Maybe I've just idealized the perfect idea of a woman and placed her on a pedestal."

"That's true. But women are entitled to enjoy sex as much as men."

"That's not what I said."

I was getting a bit testy. I didn't mean to, but I was mad. Mad at myself for not being more enlightened. I was also tired of having to rely on the discretion of one man on getting the justice I felt the case deserved. But perhaps what pissed me off the most was the fact that so much was out of my control. And I don't mean just this case. I had never really believed in global conspiracies but perhaps there was a loose cabal of men, and maybe women, who really had an agenda that they were slowly fulfilling in leading

469

the sheeple into the valley of what these shepherds thought was good for us. But who the fuck were they to decide?

I went to pick up my mug of coffee from the coffee table only to notice that it was empty. I put it back down.

"There's more in the kitchen, darling," said M.

I looked at her and smiled.

"He had something else to say. Sounds weird but I'll tell you anyway. He said there's a pandemic coming. The US will have its first identifiable case in the next few days. It'll make the Spanish Flu look like a mild cold in comparison. I'm embellishing, but he said there'll be over one million dead within the year."

I shrugged.

"Huh, that's interesting. Being in the medical field we get a lot of information about medical diseases, epidemics and so on. There were some rumblings from eastern China about a new contagion that I read about somewhere last week or the week before. Didn't have much details and it was hard to get a lot of facts about it.

"But if that's true, Anthony, it's something to be very concerned about. Did he say where it was coming from?"

I shook my head.

"Did he say what kind of disease or illness it was?"

"Uh, I think he said something about it being a virus, a coronavirus, I think."

M was nodding.

"A novel coronavirus," she repeated.

"He didn't say anything about novel."

"Just means that it's new."

M's brow furrowed.

"Everything alright?"

"No, not really. These coronaviruses can be quite deadly. MERS and SARS, which were both coronaviruses, had fatality rates of around thirty-five percent and ten percent respectively."

"Hmm, that doesn't sound very good."

"We're going to have to be fastidious about our personal hygiene, especially hand washing and also avoiding crowds of people. Let your mother know too."

"Okay," I said, "but we haven't even had the first case here."

"Anthony, these things can spread like wildfire before we even know it. If we're going to be identifying our first case here in the next couple of days then it's likely this virus has already been here for a week or two, at least."

I nodded.

"There's something else he said. He told me to tell you to go to cash. He said the stock market will crash at the end of next month."

M looked at me steadily.

"Really? He said that?"

"Yes. If he's right about this pandemic then why shouldn't the market lose it? Might be worth the lost gains just to go to cash for a month or two."

M said nothing as she thought about it, nodding her head slowly. Then she looked at me.

"You don't have any money in the market do you?"

"Never had enough to bother with. Just got my thirty pieces of gold."

I had been buying gold coins since my early twenties. Whenever I had squirreled enough money away I'd buy a coin. Usually American Eagles and usually I was able to save enough to buy one gold coin a year. Some years none, occasional years two or three.

In ninety-nine I had started to invest in the stock market. We know what happened to that over the next few years. I didn't get in at the top but I was dollar cost averaging my way there. I also didn't get out at the bottom because watching the value of my holdings lose thirty percent had me out shortly thereafter.

It wasn't a lot of money. A few grand, but it burned me and I've never been in stocks since. I like something tangible. Something that has been around for millenia. Something that has shown it can keep its value, and for me, that's been gold.

"You make it sound like you're Judas," said M, giggling.

I chuckled too.

"Well, a richer version perhaps. He only had silver. I'm talking gold, baby. Actually, it's just how many I've been able to buy over time. As you know, I buy a coin whenever I've saved enough. So far that's been thirty pieces. Some of those I'll give to Aibhilin to help her out with college."

"I know we've had this conversation before, but stocks are generally the better investment for gains."

"I know. I just feel safer in gold. You know what happened to me in ninety-nine into the next couple of years."

M nodded.

"You should tell your parents and brother," I said.

M nodded. I got up and took my mug and M's to the kitchen. I filled them with coffee, non-dairy creamer and sugar and brought them back through. The sky was still a bland wall of gray and the heavens pelted the earth with tears. I came back and sat down.

"Do you think this Camus is legitimate?" asked M.

I looked out at the rain. It was bothering me today. Maybe it was the unrelenting steadiness of the downfall, the gray sky that gave the land a dour look. Maybe it was just me. I sighed.

"Yeah, I have to begrudgingly admit that he hasn't lied to me yet. Except for a small lie of omission when I asked him why he didn't tell me the Chief of Police was at the orgy. He pretended not to know who Frank Burton was. But other than that he's been spot on. So yeah, if I had money in stocks I'd probably sell and go to cash."

M nodded her head slowly.

"I think I'll call my broker," she said.

"The downside is small. If the market is bent on going up you can always get back in come March or April."

M nodded.

"I'm going to call Mom and Dad and Evan and let them know."

"Do you think they'll believe you? I mean it sounds weird, don't you think? Anthony heard from an anonymous source that the market is going to crash at the end of next month," I said. "Might be hard to take seriously."

"They trust me and I trust you. That'll be good enough. In any event, if we lose out on ten even fifteen percent which seems unlikely in a couple of months, that's not the worst that could happen if the market does crash."

I nodded.

"I need to call Roberts and let him know what I've learned from Camus."

And that's what I did while M called her parents. Roberts was happy to hear from me but less enthused about my conversation with Camus. He wasn't convinced that Camus would follow through with any of my requests and he was probably right. There was nothing we could do. He urged me not to get my hopes up.

I told him I was about ready to close the books on this case. That made him happy. I could tell he was fatigued from hearing from me on this case for all these months. I couldn't blame him. I also told him about the pandemic and the stock market crash. He thought that was pretty random but in any event it didn't apply to him. He, like me, didn't have any money in the stock market.

The rest of the day was spent watching a wall of rain and pottering around the house until dinner. Dinner was swell. All four of us sat down for dinner at the main house on account that M invited Racquel to join us. Maybe I was getting that threesome like Johnny Rotten had suggested.

Conversation was awkward, facile and vapid but nobody yelled at anyone else. I was still waiting for even the smallest amount of gratitude from Racquel on account I saved her from a life with a womanizer. But that gratitude would probably never come. Neither did the threesome, which was just as well. It wasn't something I was into. Not with my ex.

Justice Wakes

The week rolled on into another week like tumbleweeds drifting past an old lonely man's window. Problem was, there were no tumbleweeds. The rain had been steady for a week with just short breaks as the heavens took a breath before continuing their tantrum. It was unusual to have a steady week of rain. Not unheard of, but unusual.

Aibhilin loved hanging out at M's place. It was big, it was quiet and her mother was in the guest house. I could see we were practically living there now. There was also a school that Aibhilin wanted to go to that was closer to M's. Only thing was, there was no way in hell I could pay for it. And neither could her mother until she had resolved her divorce with Artero.

In any event it was going to be a hard sell from my perspective. I wasn't interested in having Aibhilin move schools despite what she might want. There were still good public schools in LA and I didn't want to contribute to the further dysfunctioning of my country as the rich continued to isolate themselves from the hoi polloi. I couldn't see a good outcome from that.

Here's a classic example. We'd spent the past week at M's place up in Hidden Hills, a gated community. I liked being closer to the scents and sounds of Santa Monica. The throngs and thrumming of the people. Up here, and God knows I love M, but it was almost sterile.

These were the thoughts I was thinking on Thursday the twenty-third of January. The rain had parted as if commanded by Moses and the sun started to dry up the ground. Three days ago, the first case of the novel coronavirus had been identified in Seattle.

M had forgotten to call her broker again. That earlier call he had convinced her to just hold tight. But now that the virus was here she was more adamant. She had called him again on Tuesday, the day after we had heard of the first case. It hadn't made a big splash in the papers but I had noticed it. M's broker had tried to convince her again, that the market was stronger than ever and that she'd be losing out on some good gains. She went to cash in any event. As you can imagine, that was a fair bit of money for most of us, but not for a billionaire. Well over ninety-five percent of M's wealth was in Stratham Surgical Services. Still, she had to sell a little over one hundred million dollars worth of stock. A small fortune by anyone's standards. And would take a few days in order not to move the market. At least that's what M told me.

I got a call around nine a.m. from a number I didn't recognize. I took a chance anyway on account I was still holding out hope I'd be hearing from Camus.

"Hello," I said.

"Anthony, it's Albert."

"Nice to hear from you, Albert," I said, this time pronouncing it like the French would. At least as best I could.

"You haven't heard what I have to say."

"Doesn't matter. You were right about the virus and M's gone to cash."

"Good, that's good to hear. A big crash is coming and it's going to come quickly. I'd recommend she doesn't look to get back in until at least the spring of next year and probably the fall before it settles to a new low. Don't let her be fooled by the bear market rally that will happen over this spring and into the summer."

"Sure thing."

"But that's not why I'm calling."

"Okay."

"I thought about our conversation. You'll get your killer and you'll get justice for the young women who were strangled. Now, this was accidental you realize. That man was just a bit of a deviant."

I wanted to say that I figured most of the men at the Eighth House were deviants, but I didn't.

"I understand they weren't murdered. Was it just one guy responsible for the two asphyxiations?" I asked.

"Yes."

"Both of them. The one from Moscow and the one here in LA?"

"Yes. Many of these men, as you can imagine, are men of power and persuasion. They are able to move around."

"I understand. What's his name?"

"I won't tell you that now. But tomorrow you will have your justice. I will tell you this. A well-known business man will be found dead tomorrow by apparent heart attack. This is your perpetrator and it won't be a natural heart attack but the coroner will determine it as such."

"And where will this happen?"

"Here in LA."

"And the guy who killed Gorky?"

"You'll figure that one out easily."

The line went dead. Camus kept doing that to me. It was rude and ignorant. But he must figure he's a more important man than me. M was making breakfast in the kitchen. She was putting muffins in the oven. I was sitting at the kitchen counter.

"What did Camus have to say?" she asked, leaning on the other side of the counter and cleaning up.

The muffins were carrot and fiber. I wasn't sure what that meant, but they smelled good. Sweet cinnamon tickled my nose.

"He said I'll get my justice."

M stopped what she was doing and looked up at me. She had scooped excess flour into her hand and held it as if it might be mercury.

"That's great news," she said. "Very good news. Who is he, or them?"

I shrugged.

"I'm not sure. I guess I'll find out. He said a well-known businessman will die tomorrow of an apparent heart attack. Camus said it won't be a heart attack and that it's the man who asphyxiated both women."

"Both women?" asked M getting back to work and wiping the flour into the composting bin.

"Yes, the first woman who was asphyxiated was in Moscow in eighty-eight, the other woman was the first victim that went unsolved here in LA. Her name was Grace. She too, was left at the Calabasas landfill on New Year's day in two thousand."

"That's good news, right?"

"It is."

"What about the person who killed the security guard who worked at the landfill."

"He said I'll get him too."

"Did he say who that was?"

I shook my head.

"No, but he said I'll know it when I see it, whatever the hell that means."

M finished washing up and then topped up my coffee. I was getting hungry. The sweet, damp scent of the muffins was not helping.

"This is all good, isn't it, darling?"

I nodded. This case had worn me down to a nub. I was happy to be over it. Justice, of a kind I suppose, would be served and women would still continue doing sex work and men would still pay for that work and the earth would still spin on its axis.

"It is good news," I said. "I'll take it as a win. Honestly, M, I'm just glad to close the book on this case."

"I know you are. It's dragged on. I wonder how you'll know who killed that security guard? What was his name again?"

"Arshile Gorky," I said.

"Oh yes, like the Armenian painter."

I nodded.

"I guess you'll find out tomorrow somehow."

"That's the thing. He didn't say when I'd know. I'm also assuming it'll be tomorrow but he didn't actually say that. He only said the asphyxiator will be found dead tomorrow. I hope I don't have to wait too long."

"I'll help by keeping my eyes peeled too," offered M.

It was kind of her. But my pal Roberts, being Captain of Homicide would likely be on top of all murders in LA, but I didn't have the heart to tell her that.

"Thank you, my love," is what I said instead. "Listen, I've gotta call Roberts and let him know what's going on. If tomorrow both of those assholes are found dead that would be an anomaly."

"How so?"

"There are around two hundred and sixty murders in LA each year, not quite one a day, but roughly one every business day. Sometimes they cluster with multiple in one day, many days there aren't any."

"That should make it easier to figure out who the killer of Gorky might be then, right? You only have to sift through none to a handful of murders each day."

I nodded.

"God, I can't believe we're talking about that as if it's a good thing. Three hundred murders a year is really an outrage."

"I know. It's not that many just as a number, but I get your point. It's too many all the same."

I picked up my phone from the counter but then put it down again.

"Did your folks go to cash? Evan too?"

M nodded and then she smiled.

"Yeah, they went to cash the day after I told them. Beat me to it."

"Good news. I guess in the next month or two we'll find out if Camus is right. I wouldn't bet against him. He also said not to get back in until at least next spring if not next fall."

"Well, losing out on two or three months of gains, if he's proven wrong, is not the end of the world."

I picked up the phone again and dialed Johnny Rotten. That's his contact information in my phone.

"Mr. Vicious," he said, answering the phone.

"Mr. Rotten."

"That's Captain Rotten to you," he said, behind a smile. "What can I do for you?"

"Wanted to let you know that I heard from Camus. He said I'll get both assholes."

"The killer of Gorky and the asphyxiator of women?"

I laughed.

"That's exactly what I said to M."

"What's that?"

"I called him an asphyxiator even though I don't think that's an actual noun."

"Should be," said Roberts.

"Agreed."

"Did he name these perps?"

"No. He said we'd know the asphyxiator as a well-known businessman who will be reported as dead by heart attack tomorrow. Obviously, it won't be a heart attack, but Camus said that's what the coroner will call it."

"And the Gorky killer?"

"Don't know. He just said I'd know it when I saw it."

"Tomorrow?"

"No, he didn't actually say when. He just said I'd know it easily and then hung up on me."

"Huh. Alright, I'll keep my eyes open and call you if anything like that falls my way. Hey, when are we going to get together for beers?"

"How about when we've found both these assholes. We'll celebrate."

"Until then. Anything else?"

"Nope, you tired of my velvet tones already?"

"No sir, I'd spend good money every day on hearing your velvet tones cuss and curse."

He was being facetious if that wasn't apparent.

"Just rolling up to a homicide. Gang-related."

"That's probably not the successful businessman," I said, trying to be helpful.

"Some of these gangsters fancy themselves as businessmen. This is low level stuff though."

"Alright," I said. "Stay safe."

"Later gator," he said.

"So long, bang a gong."

And we hung up. Who the hell knows why I said that? Sometimes I'm juvenile even when I don't feel like it. I sat and stared at the oven. The light was on and I could see those muffins rising like slowly erupting volcanoes in their baking tins. M noticed.

"Just about another five minutes," she said.

I nodded.

"I'm hungry."

"How many do you think you can handle?" she asked.

"All of them."

I grinned at her.

"I meant right now for breakfast?"

"I'll take two."

"Aibhilin and Racquel are coming. Maybe they smelled them," said M.

I craned my neck around so I could see out into the backyard. They were walking towards us. I wasn't feeling particularly social and I was still waiting for some sort of acknowledgement from Racquel that I had done her a solid. M told me not to expect it. I did the right thing and that should be reward enough.

She wasn't wrong, but I felt like Racquel owed me on account of the misery she had put me through. Years ago, but still, it would be nice to get even the smallest compliment.

Double Indemnity

I don't get up very early as a rule. In the summer I'm up between seven and eight because of the sun. In the winter it's usually somewhere between eight and nine. That's a holdout from my days as an art student. I was a night owl then, painting into the early morning hours when the world is dead and the imagination is free.

The ten years on the job didn't help that. At least the first three years when I was on the beat. The rotating shifts didn't help me. Now I'm a self employed gumshoe and I like the nights for painting. Some habits die hard, others have to be strangled like the little shits they are. I'm talking about quitting smoking.

Why am I telling you all this? Because this is what I was thinking when my phone woke me up buzzing on the bedside table at just after five in the morning. I had done this to myself. On purpose. Usually I set up DND, or do not disturb from around midnight to eight a.m. But since someone was going to be murdered today I figured I needed to be available.

I reached for my phone and looked at it. It vibrated in my hand. It read Johnny Rotten. That meant he might have found one of the men who needed dying. That started to slap the sleep from my somnolence. I answered it with a whisper on account that M was still sleeping next to me.

"Got one of them?" I said.

"Good morning to you, too," said a chipper Roberts.

"Yeah, whatever. Do you know what time it is?"

"Time to rise and shine, sunshine. We've got our guy who killed Gorky."

"Good news. Where are you?"

"Calabasas landfill. Same place where Suzanne Valadon was found."

"No shit, that's pretty bold."

"Well, Camus told you you'd know it when you saw it."

"I'll be right there."

"See you then."

I rolled over to the side of the bed and sat there for a moment rubbing my eyes.

"What you doing?" asked M, still half asleep.

"They've found a murderer, I'm going to meet Roberts. You go back to sleep."

"Okay. Have fun," said M, clearly still half asleep and not really listening to me.

I got up, went into the bathroom and cleaned myself up. Five minutes later I was out of the bathroom, changed my clothes and headed back up to the landfill. Five in the morning is cold at the end of January. It only took me around ten minutes and I was being waved through by a rookie cop guarding the entrance to the landfill.

I parked my car pretty close to where it had been parked before. The last time I was here looking at Suzanne Valadon. I got out, turned the collar up on my jacket and put on my hat. The fedora served two purposes. It kept my messy hair under control and it kept my head warm.

Roberts was in the middle of the crime scene. Two large lights on tripods were running from a generator in a van. The lights were bright and bathed the scene in cold bright white that washed away any reality. Forrest and Beeves were with him. I walked up to them and nodded all around. Cardigan was there dressed in his scene suit as I like to call it. Roberts grinned at me.

"Drinks tonight," he said. "On me."

I turned my mouth upside down and nodded at him.

"They giving out bonuses now based on each body you find?"

Roberts shook his head.

"No, but we got both our perps as you wanted. That deserves a couple of whiskies."

"Both?"

"Yeah, I had Beast grab a paper on his way here, just in case. I figured, maybe they'd give us both gifts on the same day. I wasn't wrong."

"Interesting, let's stick with what's in front of us first," I said.

I looked down at the body. It looked like the man that Gorky described who bribed him and drove the white laundry van up here. He was in his late thirties. At least that's how old he looked.

He was naked except for black boxers. Tucked into his boxers was what looked like the butt of a Glock. He had pale skin with tattoos on his upper arms. One of them I recognized as a marine tattoo. The tattoo was well done. It was probably several years old but it had held up well. It was a replica of the emblem in full color.

For those not in the know, the emblem is known as the EGA. That stands for eagle, globe and anchor. You've got a golden eagle perched at the north pole with wings wide and a banner held in its mouth that reads "SEMPER FIDELIS". That's Latin for "always faithful".

The anchor looks like it's either behind the globe or pierced through the globe. I think it's behind. The head of the anchor is at around two o'clock and the crown of the anchor points to around eight o'clock.

All of this is set on a red circular background with a blue ring around that. Around the blue ring at the top is "United States" and at the bottom is "Marine Corps".

He had a black beard, black eyebrows, blue eyes and black curly hair. Everything was too black. Probably overused men's hair dye. He had no marks on him other than a mishmash of tattoos on both upper arms. Skulls, the words "Liberty" in an old English font on one arm and "Freedom" in the same font on another. There was a heart pierced with a sword on his left shoulder. The EGA being on his right. I also noticed a yin and yang tattoo and a seated Buddha as well. His upper arms were busy with tattoos.

But those were the only marks he had. Didn't notice any scars. His nose looked like it might have been broken at one point and his ears were a little flowery from wrestling. His chest was modestly hairy and he was slim but muscled. I could see his eye color on account that his eyes were open. You get used to that.

I looked at Roberts.

"Who's this guy?"

"Winslow Homer, thirty-five, from Winslow, Arizona..."

"Seriously? Winslow from Winslow?"

Roberts grinned.

"True story. He was discharged dishonorably from the Marines ten years ago. He was involved in the rape and murder of an Afghani woman in Afghanistan. Did seven years in a military prison before being released on good behavior."

"That's not a good sentence for murder," I said.

"Wasn't charged with murder but rather manslaughter. Evidence issues apparently."

I nodded.

"That the gun used to murder Gorky?" I asked, pointing at the bulge in his boxers.

"Well, it's certainly not because he's happy to see you," said Roberts.

The four of us chuckled at that.

"Appears to be the same type and calibre, but forensics will tell us for sure," said Forrest.

"How'd he die?"

Roberts shrugged.

"Hard to say. No obvious signs of injury. Maybe he was poisoned or asphyxiated, but that's unlikely."

I nodded. I didn't see petechial hemorrhaging and there were no marks around his throat. I looked around at the rest of the scene. Didn't look like anything to be found. I asked anyway.

"Found anything of note, Mike?"

Cardigan shook his head.

"No. Not that I was hoping too. JR said these guys are pros. Left him pretty much like they'd left Valadon. Nothing left behind that could incriminate anyone."

"What about video at the entrance?" I asked.

Roberts shook his head.

"They're in the midst of replacing the video recording system on account of what happened with Gorky."

"He's dead, what's that got to do with it?"

"That's the other thing. They haven't rehired yet. And nobody was working last night's shift. As for the video recording system they're replacing that to make it impossible for the security guard to delete it. That, and both cameras were broken a couple of weeks ago. Probably kids with BB guns or catapults."

I nodded. That was something Camus and gang were probably aware of and why they chose this spot again.

A van drove up behind us. We all looked at it. It was the ME's.

"Let's give the reapers some space," said Roberts.

Sometimes that's what we called the ME's people, the reapers. Sometimes GR, but usually just reapers after the grim reaper. It's more of that gallows humor.

We all walked back down towards our vehicles, nodding at the ME's people as we crossed paths. It was just past five forty and the sky was still dark as coal. We all gathered down around Roberts' unmarked.

"You got that paper?" I asked.

Roberts nodded and thrust his head out towards Beeves. Beeves went round to the passenger side and pulled out a copy of this morning's LA Times. He brought it around to us and handed it to me. The paper was folded in half horizontally and then half again vertically, only showing me the top right quarter of the front page.

What that rectangle showed was a column about the CEO of WhiteWash, a PR firm that was notoriously known to provide spin and PR for top officials and business leaders found to be up to no good. They were good at what they did, but they were greatly disliked by the general public. They were quite a secretive organization but their client list had leaked before.

The LA Times obituary, if you could call it that, was quite flattering. Calling him a "Captain of industry", a "pillar of the community" and a "generous philanthropist". I had briefly misread that as being "philanderer". Being a generous philanderer was probably a more apt description.

It went on to suggest he had suffered a heart attack late last night. He was also missed by his wife, five children and six grandchildren. His name was Thomas Gainsborough and he was sixty-five. I handed the paper back to Beeves.

"Good riddance," I spat. "Pity he didn't suffer."

Roberts shrugged.

"We sure it was him?" I asked.

"Well, we'll see," said Roberts. "The day is young, but he's a well-known, well-connected businessman, especially well-connected in government. I doubt we'll get another well-known LA businessman dying today from a heart attack. So yeah, I'm pretty sure this is him, but we'll see what else, if anything falls from the tree the rest of the day."

I stood around with Roberts as the reapers took away the body and the crime scene investigators finished up their investigation. There was nothing to find. Just like at Suzanne Valadon's crime scene which was almost the exact same spot.

"Imagine getting away with murder," I said. "Having immunity like that."

I wasn't really talking to anyone, but Roberts heard me.

"You must be new to this," he said.

I looked at him and a grin slowly appeared on his face. I laughed lightly.

"I know," I said. "Happens all the time. Doesn't mean I have to like it."

Roberts nodded, leaning on the hood of the car. Then he turned to me.

"I do have some good news for you."

"Yeah, what's that?"

"Chris and Anissa Valadon, Suzanne's folks, called me yesterday."

"Okay," I said, not knowing where any of this was going.

"They came into some money."

"Good for them. They deserve it."

"You're not listening. They got a wire transfer into their bank account for four and a quarter million dollars."

I started to nod, then my nod turned my head into a frown. I started to put what he was saying together.

"Camus?"

Roberts shrugged.

"I think so. There was a note that came along with the wire transfer that said 'Sorry for your loss. In memoriam Suzanne Valadon.'"

"I'm glad to hear that."

"It gets better. Grace Cossington Smith's parents also received the same amount. Exactly the same, to the penny. Well, there weren't any pennies involved but the Smiths also received exactly four and a quarter million dollars. Same note with it. 'Sorry for your loss. In memoriam Grace Cossington Smith.'"

"Four point two five million exactly?"

Roberts nodded.

"I'm waiting to hear from Interpol about the other two women, see if they also got the same. I did some research. Remember how you told him that the families should receive at least one million based on nineteen seventy-seven rates?"

I nodded.

"Well, four point two five million is pretty much what one million in seventy-seven would be worth today. Looks like Camus came through like Santa Claus."

Monster Waves

I was fiddling with my kombolói. Dr. Ainley was sitting across from me. I was in his office. I had decided that in order to put this case away I needed to see him. Get some things off my chest. I had a coffee on a coaster to my left, on the coffee table that he had between the two comfy chairs we were sitting on and the couch on the other side of the table.

The coaster was of a colorful outline of the main Hawaii island. There was a pineapple tree in the top right corner and a surfer in the bottom left corner. A slogan was written across the top and bottom of the coaster. "Come for the pineapple" the top portion said. "Stay for the surf," said the bottom portion.

Along the wall, Lloyd had put up an old wooden surfboard that had been restored but still looked distressed. Lloyd had told me that legend had it that Duke Kahanamoku had used a surfboard just like that one, only much larger.

I didn't know my dukes from my earls, but Lloyd explained that he was only one of the greatest Hawaiian surfers ever to live. No, scratch that, said Lloyd, Duke was one of the best water athletes America had produced. Surfing, I learned from Lloyd, was invented by the Hawaiians, or more generally the Polynesians.

"I'm sure you're not here to learn about surfing," said Lloyd.

"No," I said.

"What would you like to talk about?"

"Men getting away with killing women," I said.

Ainley nodded slowly.

"That's a good opener."

I nodded slowly.

"Let me tell you how I came to be at an orgy almost two months ago," I said.

It was Monday the twenty-fourth of February and M had suggested I talk to Lloyd about the case. She could tell it was still gnawing at me a little. I had heard from Camus since then and I hadn't liked what he had said.

I had heard from Roberts too. He had heard back from Interpol and the other two women, or rather the parents of those women, the German and the Russian had also received four and a quarter million dollars. I heard that from Roberts. I confronted Camus about it and he had confirmed it. That wasn't what I had disliked about our conversation. It was something else he had said.

"If that's the beginning, it's probably a good place to start," said Ainley.

"It's not the beginning, but the beginning is a good place to start," I said. I reached down and took a sip of my coffee. "In October of last year a woman by the name of Suzanne Valadon was found dead at the Calabasas landfill."

Ainley nodded.

"I recall us discussing this the last time you were here. Never heard if you, meaning the LAPD, solved that or not," he said.

"In a roundabout way. But this whole thing is tangentially tied to a case I had in New York a few years back. You remember that case? I think we spoke about it."

"Briefly. That was where a detective who was helping you was murdered, correct?"

"Yeah. That case gave me a look inside a world I'd sooner have forgotten."

"In what way?"

"I was shown a device, or rather, the blueprints of a device that looked much like that old Nokia thirty-three ten cell phone. You remember those from around two thousand?"

Ainley nodded.

"I had one."

"Yeah, well these blueprints showed something like that. Only this wasn't so much a cellphone as it was a comprehensive computer device of some sort. What it could apparently do was quite astounding. It could act as a sort of taser within a few feet. You could point it at someone and get all information on them from all sorts of government and civilian databases. It projected a holographic screen. It controlled the electricity in the environment you were in. It was an exceptional device.

"One of the witnesses I interviewed had seen it in action personally. But that was the only device that was seen. The two people who had inside information about it were murdered. The journalist who interviewed the young man who had stolen this device from the business he worked at. To make a long story short, I couldn't find out who was the top dog at this organization responsible for all these killings."

"Including that detective?"

"Right. But then I got a call from a man who called himself Albert Camus."

Ainley was nodding his head.

"You've mentioned him."

"Yeah, well, he's like a piece of dog shit that I just can't scrape from the sole of my shoe. He seems to be popping up in everything I do lately."

"You told me that he seemed to be a very well-connected businessman."

I nodded. I took another sip of coffee. I looked at the coffee table book. "The World's Monster Waves" was the title. There was a massive curling wave on the cover with a tiny man on a surfboard about two thirds of the way down. If the man was, let's say six feet, that wave must have been about thirty feet tall. It was impressive.

"That's John Whittle surfing at Dungeons in South Africa in oh three. An unusually big wave that season measured thirty-three feet. Usually you can count on many eighteen to twenty foot waves. That year brought out the beast from the deep."

I grinned.

"You ever surfed a wave that high?"

Ainley shook his head.

"No. I had a twenty-four footer one time, but I was much younger and more foolish then and it was probably only a twenty footer. Exhilarating."

I nodded. Doing something in water that was described as exhilarating was not something I fancied.

"Anyway, back to Camus."

"Right, so I first heard about him back in New York. He called me."

"Out of the blue."

"I don't remember exactly why. I had tried calling some numbers related to a business there, a plumbing business, but I didn't get the sense it was a real business. I guess he had some rogue employees and these rogue employees had murdered those two kids, the journalist and the employee."

"They were kids?"

"Well, relatively speaking. Early to mid twenties."

"Were these rogue employees responsible for shooting you and murdering that detective?"

I nodded. I didn't like thinking about it. The cannabis had helped me get through most nights, but it still wasn't a period in my life I liked to think about.

"What happened to them?"

"The rogue employees?"

Ainley nodded.

"They got justice delivered to them."

"Do you know how?"

I looked at Ainley and I didn't like where this was going.

"That's not what I want to talk about."

"I understand, please carry on."

"Well, that was the first time I met Camus. Then this woman showed up at the landfill."

"Had she been murdered?"

"I assumed so. But as it turned out she wasn't murdered. She had OD'd on a combination of ketamine, cannabis and cocaine. She was naked except for a red satin dress. I think they call it a chemise.

"An autopsy determined she had OD'd. She was beautiful. Really lovely. Creamy white, unblemished skin. Hairless except for her head. She had also engaged in intercourse. She had semen in her throat, anus and vagina."

"You hadn't mentioned that last we spoke. You had just found the body, if I recall."

"Right. She was unmarked, and I mean no moles or freckles that I could see. The semen was from three different donors. But there was one mark on her that bothered me. She had a scar or rather a welt from a brand that looked like three different Chinese characters. They were all horizontal and deep in her inguinal crease. She'd have to be naked for you to see it."

"Did you find out what they meant?"

I nodded. I sipped more coffee and I fingered my kombolói.

"They meant ianfu, which translated means comfort women. It's Japanese kanji, the adopted Chinese characters used in Japanese. Basically she was branded as a prostitute. In the meantime, we find out that she was not the first ianfu to be found at the landfill. On New Year's day in two thousand another woman was found almost identically placed. She also had semen but from one donor. Some in her vagina and some in her anus. She had been asphyxiated. I figured that was murder.

"But that's not the first time a woman, or ianfu, or high end prostitute was found dead like this. The first woman we know of was found just outside the Black Forest near Baden-Baden in Germany. That was back in seventy-seven. The second was found in a park in Moscow. That was in eighty-eight. A third had been found in a wooded area just outside St. Petersburg, Russia."

"And you were certain they were all connected somehow?"

"Yeah. They had all recently had sex. They all had one or a combination of the three drugs, ketamine, cocaine and cannabis in their systems. All women had this same ianfu tattoo and all were unsolved."

"How did you know that Camus was involved?"

"I didn't but I had a suspicion. These crime scenes were immaculate. No footsteps of any value were left. Nothing really. Even the tire tracks were difficult to trace. We got no hits on the semen either so these weren't known rapists. All of this got me thinking that these women were highly paid prostitutes. Vice knew nothing helpful.

"We came up empty every turn we took. Eventually I reached out to Camus to see if he knew anything. He did, and he told me none of these women had been murdered. The asphyxiation was accidental. Sexual kink gone wrong. He invited me to one of these orgies they hold for important and powerful men that are in the pocket of this group that Camus runs, or is deeply involved with, called the Ekklesia."

"What's the Ekklesia?"

"Apparently it's the group of seventy-seven men who are behind the scenes trying to run the world or develop a new world order. What people generally believe to be the Bilderberg Group. But apparently the Bilderberg Group is just a front for the real puppeteers. So I'm led to believe."

Ainley was frowning at me.

"That sounds very conspiratorial to me," he said. "Hard to believe actually."

"I know. That's exactly what I thought too. But the things that this Camus knows and can do are extraordinary. On top of the phone weapon I was telling you about earlier. I'm starting to wonder if there isn't a shadow group paving and plotting the path for our future."

Ainley nodded.

"I know of the conspiracy theories, I just don't believe them."

"I find them hard to believe too, but I'm just telling you what's been told to me. The original Ekklesia, by the way, were the ruling leaders of Ancient Greece."

Ainley nodded. I sipped more coffee. My mug was getting low.

"Long story short, Camus knew about these women and he told me that they host these orgies where women, the ianfu, serve the sexual needs of these co-opted men. They call these events an Eighth House. I was invited to one on account that I was skeptical, that a, these women were willing participants and b, that they were not murdered."

"And what did you learn?"

"I learned that my ex-wife's husband was there, as was the LAPD Chief of Police. I also learned that I was wrong about women and sex. Some women are happy to be paid to provide sex."

"That was surprising to you?"

"Well, yes. I still sort of struggle with it."

"I think that's understandable."

"How so?"

"The way you've spoken about your childhood and your mother specifically. I think you've put her on a pedestal and that has colored how you see women and your relationships with them. You have historically been a ladies' man and I think that's because you love women and yet when you get physically intimate with them it grates against this virginal, almost idolization of them as pure and innocent."

I wasn't really here to be analyzed.

"And women, just like men, can be sexual creatures with sexual appetites as well."

I still didn't say anything.

"Are you sure it was the Chief of Police and your ex's husband you saw?" asked Ainley, changing lanes.

NWO

" Yeah, I'm sure it was the Chief of Police. I saw his ring and I heard him speak. He asked why the fuck I was there. But he really wasn't asking it of anyone specifically."

"You're talking about the current chief? Frank Burton?"

I nodded.

"And you think he's in their pocket?"

I shrugged.

"Probably. Why else was he there? My ex's husband was there too. I always thought he was up to no good. He's into some sort of financing or financial services. More than that, Camus told me as much. He told me these men were helpful to his group. Plus, I imagine Camus and friends have a lot of kompromat on them too."

Ainley didn't say anything for a while.

"Why is it called the Eighth House?"

"Has something to do with the eighth house in astrology overseeing sex and sexuality or something like that."

Ainley nodded.

"Clever."

"Well, they have these men close and in the fold. Most of them are probably married. These men can only be seen as easily compromised at this point."

"Perhaps this Ekklesia or whatever this group really is that Camus belongs to..."

"Or runs," I added.

Ainley nodded.

"Or runs. Perhaps it's best not to be poking that hornet's nest."

"You know I'll probably not be able to do that. Men of power abusing their position, that's right in the sweet spot of things that piss me off."

"You're not wrong. Perhaps that's why Camus has chosen you. Perhaps he wants some fun."

"Murder is not fun," I said.

"But you said none of these women were murdered."

"Yes, but that doesn't mean an organization like that isn't capable of murder. Look what they tried to do to me. And they murdered So-yi," I said.

My fiddling of the beads had increased.

"You haven't used her name before," said Ainley.

I looked up at him but didn't say anything.

"What was her full name?"

"So-yi Park," I said. "I had to fucking speak with her family at the funeral. They didn't say it, but I could see they were probably upset I hadn't prevented her death."

"Is that it, or are you reading things that aren't there based on your own guilt."

"Does it matter?"

"I think so, because for us to get through to the other side of this guilt we have to understand it and know where it comes from."

I didn't say anything.

"Back to Camus," said Ainley after a while. "I really think you should be careful there. I wouldn't put a bull's eye on him and make it your life's work to find out who he is. I don't think that will end well. Not if he's as powerful as you seem to think."

I didn't say anything.

"Maybe he wants to be your Moriarty?"

"Sherlock Holmes was featured in four novels and fifty-six short stories. Moriarty was only in two of them and primarily used by Doyle in order to kill off his golden goose, that being Holmes. Are you suggesting Camus is here to kill me?"

I was being sarcastic. Ainley didn't catch that.

"Fair enough. I wasn't trying to be literal about it. Rather, I was just suggesting that Camus might be your Moriarty. Not that he literally will kill you. But if he is as powerful as you've said, he could end up, well, he could end up hurting you."

"He'd need an army," I spat.

"Which he could probably afford."

I didn't say anything. I picked up my mug of coffee and drank the last little bit. It was cold and gross.

"Just be careful, Anthony, that's all I'm asking. The way you've described him makes me concerned. He's obviously a very powerful and well-connected man. He knows a lot about you and yet you know very little about him."

"You know all five of these ianfu women that we've found, all of them except for Suzanne, who was the latest we found, were left with ten grand. Ten grand US."

"This money was found on their person?" asked Ainley.

I nodded.

"Yeah, usually tied to a wrist or ankle in a small purse of some sort."

"And what do you think that symbolizes?"

"I don't think it symbolizes anything. I think he's feeling guilty and this is a blood money apology."

"Doesn't seem like much, except for maybe the first one back in the late seventies."

I nodded.

"Exactly, I told him as much. I said they should be left with at least a million dollars, inflated to current value from the first woman found in seventy-seven."

"How did he take it?"

"He takes everything well. I get the feeling that he thinks he's humoring me. Just recently I was told by Roberts that all five families have now received four and a quarter million dollars which just so happens to be about the amount that a million dollars in seventy-seven would be in today's currency."

"That's a small bit of good news, isn't it? At least the families will have some money to help them through the pain in their lives. I'm sure some of the marriages might not survive or they've lost their jobs due to the overwhelming grief. That was a good thing you did."

"Except it doesn't bring back their loved ones, does it?"

"No, it doesn't."

"None of it is traceable. We've tried. Even the phone number I reach him at is untraceable. It bounces around a bunch of networks and telecommunication providers across the globe before ending at dead ends."

"As I've said, I'd try not to worry about Camus too much. I really urge you not to make Camus your life's work."

"I'm not. I did tell him though, that I was gunning for Burton."

"The chief?"

I nodded.

"Why?"

"Because he's corrupt and it explains why half the assholes on the job are bent. He's the reason I was fired."

Ainley nodded.

"Just tread carefully, Anthony."

I ignored him.

"You see what's going on in the markets today?"

Ainley nodded.

"Yeah, it's a continuation of the downtrend from last Friday."

"It's more than that. This is the market crash that Camus warned me about related to the coming pandemic."

"Hasn't actually been declared a pandemic at this stage," said Ainley.

"Well, it's coming. I'd go to cash if I was you. Camus suggested I tell M that and she's glad to have done it. I still think there's time."

"I went to cash on the third of February, the first trading day after the WHO declared this coronavirus a global emergency."

I nodded.

"You know what really troubles me about what Camus said?"

Ainley shook his head.

"It's what Camus told me will come from this pandemic."

"What's that?"

"Great control of the citizenry."

"How will that happen?"

"This pandemic is going to be used as an excuse to unhinge the world off of the dollar and to move global currencies to digital currencies on the blockchain."

"I've heard about that. Isn't that what bitcoin is?" asked Ainley.

I nodded. "That's what I said to Camus, but it's not going to be bitcoin. I had the sense that bitcoin troubles him because he or the other puppeteers can't control it. But they're taking that idea and they're going to put the world onto a digital currency. Easily trackable, traceable and controllable. He had a pithy quote about it that I don't remember. But just imagine the power they'll have. The power to control you because they control your money. No longer is cash an option.

"Just think about it. Everywhere you go is tracked. Every time you buy something, they know what you bought. They can approve or deny transactions at their whim. To me, that's the scariest thing Camus had to say."

"Permit me to issue and control the money of a nation, and I care not who makes its laws," said Ainley.

I nodded.

"Yeah, that was what he said. Who originally said it?"

"It's been placed at Rothschild's feet, but there's no evidence he said it. Nobody really knows who said it."

"Well, doesn't matter," I said. "It still has the essence of truth to it."

"It does, and what you've said is disconcerting. But I don't see how they can get rid of cash. Even in this country, not everyone has a smartphone which I assume you'll need."

Ainley looked at his phone which had started chiming. I say that, because that's what the alarm sounded like. He reached over to his desk and turned it off.

"I'm sure some government officials would love to get rid of cash. If I'm being kind, maybe not to control the population, but rather to make accounting and manipulation easier. But I just don't see how it can be pulled off. As I said, something like twenty percent or so of Americans either don't own a cellphone or just own a dumb cellphone and not a smartphone."

"The conspiracist in me sees it as a wet dream for those who want to be in charge. The optimist in me hopes you're right."

"I'm sorry our time has come to an end. I don't feel as if we've made as much headway today as I would have liked."

"It's fine, doc," I said, standing up to leave. "I'll be back."

About the Author

Jason Blacker was born in Cape Town but spent most of his first 18 years in Johannesburg. When not grinding his fingers down to stubs at the keyboard he enjoys drinking tea, calisthenics and running. Currently he lives in Canada. Under his own name he writes hard boiled as well as cozy mysteries, action adventure, thrillers, literary fiction and anything else that tickles his muse. Jason Blacker also writes poetry and daily haikus at his haiku blog. You can find his haikus and other poetry at his website **www.haiqueue.com**. For FREE books and to stay up to date and learn about new releases be sure to visit **www.jasonblacker.com** where you can find more information about his writing and upcoming projects. If you enjoy space opera in the tradition of Star Trek then take a look at Jason Blacker's pen name "Sylynt Storme". It is under the name Sylynt Storme where you can find both sci-fi and vampire fiction written by Jason Blacker. "Star Sails" is the space opera series and "The Misgivings of the Vampire Lucius Lafayette" is his vampire series.

Read more at JasonBlacker.com.